pushkin press

KÄSEBIER
TAKES
Berlin

GABRIELE TERGIT (1894–1982), born Elise Hirschmann, was a
German novelist and reporter. She began writing newspaper articles
in the early 1920s under the psuedonym Tergit and eventually became
a court reporter for the *Berliner Tageblatt*. She rose to fame in 1931
with the success of her first novel, *Käsebier Takes Berlin*. In 1933 she
narrowly evaded arrest by the Nazis, fleeing first to Czechoslovakia
and then to Palestine before settling in London with her husband
and son. There, she worked on her colossal novel of generations of
German-Jewish life, *The Effingers* (1951) – forthcoming from Pushkin
Press – and acted as secretary of the PEN Centre for German-
language writers abroad.

SOPHIE DUVERNOY is a translator, writer, and scholar focused on
art and literature in the Weimar Republic. She was the 2015 recipient
of the Gutekunst Prize for young translators and is pursuing a PhD
in German literature at Yale University. Her work has appeared in
publications such as the *Los Angeles Review of Books*, *No Man's Land*,
The Offing, and *Lit Hub*.

GABRIELE TERGIT

KÄSEBIER *TAKES* Berlin

Translated from the German
by Sophie Duvernoy

pushkin press

Pushkin Press
71–75 Shelton Street
London WC2H 9JQ

Copyright © 2016 Schöffling & Co

English translation and introduction © 2019 Sophie Duvernoy

Käsebier Takes Berlin was first published as *Käsebier Erobert den Kurfürstendamm* by Rowohlt in in 1931

This translation was first published in the United States in 2019 by *The New York Review of Books*

First published by Pushkin Press in 2020

The translation of this work was supported by a grant from the Goethe-Institut.

9 8 7 6 5 4 3 2 1

ISBN 13: 978-1-78227-603-6

Offset by Tetragon, London
Printed and bound by CPI Group (UK) Ltd, Croydon, CRO 4YY

www.pushkinpress.com

CONTENTS

TRANSLATOR'S INTRODUCTION

KÄSEBIER Takes Berlin is a book about the power of the press. Not journalists or reporters, but the medium itself. Today, we might call it a tale of a story gone viral. In a week with no newsworthy stories, a journalist at a Berlin newspaper writes a short, throwaway article on an unknown popular singer, Georg Käsebier. But when the story is picked up by a famous poet and a young writer on the make, this nobody, whose name translates to "Cheese-Beer," becomes Berlin's new star, the everyman they've been looking for. Writers, photographers, movie makers, and bankers flock to Käsebier, hoping to convert his fame into reichsmarks. Berlin becomes a Käsebier economy. Yet fashion moves on quickly in the overheated capitalism of 1930s Berlin, and when Käsebier falls, many others fall too.

Though this novel is ostensibly about him, Käsebier is almost incidental to the story. The real protagonists of the book are the well-meaning journalists who unwittingly set off this fiasco. The writers at the *Berliner Rundschau* are a scrappy bunch of sleuths, critics, and know-it-alls dissecting and reporting on the world around them (though they can never publish the "really good stuff," as they like to complain). When the Käsebier boom engulfs their own newspaper, they can only watch helplessly as they fall victim to their own creation.

Gabriele Tergit wrote *Käsebier* in 1931, but its depictions of fake news, sudden stardom, and bitter culture wars between left and right feel unnervingly contemporary. As she wrote, the Weimar Republic's fragile parliamentary democracy was tumbling into dictatorship and Nazi terror. In only two years, she would have to leave the country, and would never live there again.

Tergit was born Elise Hirschmann, in Berlin, in 1894, into a family of successful Jewish industrialists. Ignoring protests from her bourgeois parents, Hirschmann became a journalist, writing under the pen name Gabriele Tergit. Today she is remembered as one of the few female writers of the New Objectivity movement, whose aim was to depict contemporary culture and society with cool dispassion. Within the writings of New Objectivity *Käsebier* stands out because it is a novel about the news, turning its eye on those who write about and reflect on events as they happen. Tergit's voice is brisk, acerbic, and witty as she tells the story of a metropolis in upheaval. This translation of *Käsebier* brings this story, and Tergit's trenchant brilliance and humor, to English readers for the first time.

In 1931, Tergit was at the height of her career, working as a journalist for the influential liberal newspaper *Berliner Tageblatt*. With her trademark round glasses, dark bob, and serious gaze, Tergit was a fixture of the Berlin literary scene, and could often be found at the Romanisches Café, the Café Adler, and the regulars' table at Capri on Anhalter Strasse, just around the corner from *Tageblatt* headquarters. Tergit had spent most of her career as a court reporter, covering abortion trials, thefts, murders, bankruptcies, and political violence. Her interests ranged widely, though, and she wrote articles on women in the Weimar Republic, humorous essays on everyday life, and pieces for Carl von Ossietzky's left-wing weekly *Die Weltbühne*. The publisher Rowohlt had just agreed to publish her first novel, *Käsebier erobert den Kurfürstendamm*, which would go on to be a hit. A year earlier, the *Tageblatt* had asked readers which public personalities the newspaper should profile. Alongside notables such as the poet Gottfried Benn and the cultural critic Oswald Spengler, they chose Tergit—the only woman featured.

It had taken willpower and hard work for such an unassuming woman to establish herself in the cutthroat newspaper world. Tergit published her first article at the age of nineteen, on women in the workforce. When she went to collect her pay, the editor exclaimed,

"If I'd known you were so young, I wouldn't have run the piece."
Tergit joined the staff of the *Tageblatt* in 1925 after cutting her teeth
at the *Berliner Börsen-Courier*. Modest and sharp, she eschewed literary bravado for careful reporting and had a skeptical stance toward
ideology, both right and left.

By early 1930, the economic depression and political instability
was taking a toll on her career and family. Tergit's salary at the *Tageblatt* had been reduced, and her husband, the architect Heinz Reifenberg, could only find occasional remodeling work. Her coverage
of the Feme murders, assassinations committed by far-right paramilitary groups, had brought her the undesirable attention of the
National Socialists. At five a.m. on March 4, 1933—the day before
the federal election that brought Hitler to power—SA officers knocked
at her door. Reifenberg told the maid not to open it, a choice that
likely saved Tergit's life. She quickly phoned a colleague with Nazi
affiliations who pulled strings on her behalf to make the SA leave.
She fled the following day to Czechoslovakia, while her husband and
son remained behind in Berlin.

Tergit and her family spent the rest of their lives in exile, settling
in London after several years in Palestine. She continued to write and
publish as a freelancer, but never again found the audience of her
prewar years. During and after the war she worked on *Effingers*, a
novel in the spirit of Thomas Mann's *Buddenbrooks*, portraying three
generations of a Jewish family in fin de siècle Germany. Tergit considered it her magnum opus, though the book found little acclaim
when it was published in 1951. In 1957, she became the secretary of
the PEN Center for German Writers Abroad. Between the 1950s and
the 1970s, she also wrote several successful books on the cultural
history of flowers. This led her to comment sarcastically to a friend,
"It seems that flowers are more popular than Jews." To Tergit's great
disappointment, her third and final novel, *So war's eben*, a social
drama that begins in 1898 and ends in 1960s New York, never found
a publisher.

Forgotten in her native country, Tergit was rediscovered in the
1970s, when Germans began to show interest in works written by

exiled authors. In 1977, *Käsebier* was republished and newly fêted by the press. At eighty-three, she reached her highest point of literary fame; her life's work was celebrated at the Berliner Festwochen, a major annual cultural and literary festival, where she read from *Käsebier* to a captivated audience. Tergit died in London, at the age of eighty-eight, on July 25, 1982.

Käsebier Takes Berlin gives a view of the heady final years of the Weimar Republic from the inside of the newsroom. In 1930, Berlin had the greatest newspaper density of any European city: forty daily newspapers with a combined circulation of over three million copies. (The city itself had around four million inhabitants.) Competition was fierce, and newspapers engaged in bitter feuds, journalists raced one another to break stories, and publishers sold multiple daily editions and dozens of special-interest supplements to attract readers. The sheer volume and diversity of Berlin's newspapers was overwhelming, yet many Berliners felt they could not afford to lag behind the never-ending stream of news. As Kurt Tucholsky writes in his satirical "Newspaper Reader's Prayer," "Dear Lord, please hear my prayer! Behold this stack, layer on layer! Dear Lord, I can't take any more; here I have just one week's score! And I have to read it all..."

Tergit's *Berliner Tageblatt* was among the most important newspapers in the German capital and the country as a whole; as the flagship daily of Mosse, one of the big three Berlin publishers, it was the sixth-most-popular newspaper in Germany in 1930, with around 140,000 subscribers. During the Weimar years, the *Tageblatt* was also a significant voice of liberalism. Its editor in chief was Theodor Wolff, one of the "great men" of German journalism and a founder of the German Democratic Party, a left-of-center party committed to republican democracy. The GDP was largely made up of working professionals, and it was the party that most represented the interests of German Jews. The *Tageblatt* advocated for these politics and provided a strong voice in support of Germany's fledgling democracy.

Tergit reported for the Berlin page of the *Tageblatt* along with two colleagues, Walther Kiaulehn and Rudolf Olden, with whom she formed a close-knit trio. The three friends embody the breadth and openneness of the intellectual scene of Berlin in the 1920s: Kiaulehn, who had worked as an electrician before joining the *Tageblatt,* came from a Prussian working-class family and held socialist sympathies; Olden had come to Berlin from Vienna, where he had already enjoyed a distinguished career working alongside Joseph Roth, Alfred Polgar, and Egon Erwin Kisch.

Tergit's novel centers on the newsroom of the center-left *Berliner Rundschau,* a lightly fictionalized version of Tergit's *Tageblatt.* Like the *Tageblatt* of the early 1920s, the *Rundschau* has a vibrant newsroom with a lively exchange of ideas, perspectives, and barbs. Both newspapers espouse progressive free-market positions, and have reporters who largely believe in the value of social democracy. But like the *Tageblatt,* which would face severe political and financial pressures in the late 1920s, the *Rundschau* ends up a splashy, slimmed-down version of itself—losing its credibility and public voice.

Kiaulehn and Olden, meanwhile, provided Tergit with inspiration for two of the book's main characters: the cheery, sarcastic reporter Emil Gohlisch, and the verbose, intellectual editor in chief, Georg Miermann. Though Miermann was a composite figure, a paradigmatic example of the genteel, bourgeois intellectual, Olden spent weeks carrying a galley of *Käsebier* around under his arm, convinced he was its embattled protagonist. Like Miermann, Olden was a liberal editor with Jewish roots; unlike his fictional counterpart, who is steamrolled by political opportunists, Olden was outspoken, publishing strongly worded attacks against the German Right, including a 1932 book on conspiracy theories entitled *Prophets in a German Crisis,* and the damning 1935 biography *Hitler the Pawn.* Olden considered it his mission to be both an artist and a truth-seeker. He imbued every piece he wrote or edited with sharpness and clarity. In her autobiography, Tergit uses the same words to describe Olden's editing that she had used decades earlier for the fictional Miermann: "He cut, reorganized, added punctuation, straightened out thoughts, lifted ideas out of the confusion of dim intuition and brought them into the clarity of enlightening prose, and only then did our articles become a good Kiaulehn, a good Tergit."

When Tergit began writing *Käsebier,* the paper had undergone major changes. The newspaper had been significantly restructured by Hans Lachmann-Mosse, the son-in-law of the original founder, Rudolf Mosse. Lachmann-Mosse had taken over the reins of the Mosse empire in 1920, but lacked not only his father-in-law's liberal convictions, but his business acumen as well. In the 1920s Lachmann-Mosse had undertaken a series of speculative investments, including a real estate development on a parcel of land long held by the family, which failed spectacularly (a central plot point in *Käsebier*).

By the late 1920s, staff salaries were low, as was morale. Theodor Wolff and Martin Carbe, the general director of the publishing company, frequently clashed with Lachmann-Mosse, who wanted to increase profits by taking direct control over the *Tageblatt*. By 1930, the Mosse empire was in peril. To save himself from ruin, Lachmann-Mosse drew money from employee pension funds and cut newspaper staff. Carbe resigned in protest and was replaced by Karl Vetter, a business-minded opportunist who reorganized the paper, added more illustrated supplements and lifestyle sections, and orchestrated large-scale advertising stunts. The *Tageblatt* became increasingly commercial, more entertainment than news.

In the federal election of September 14, 1930, the National Socialists increased their seats in parliament from 12 to 107. At first, many journalists doubted the Nazis would gain broader acceptance. The recognition of their error came too late, however, and soon the German liberal press lost its ability to intervene in the deteriorating political situation. After a string of failed cabinets, the German Democratic Party was dissolved, and a power vacuum emerged at the top of German government. Consensus on leadership was so difficult to achieve that by 1931 even newspapers critical of the Nazis had tempered their message, urging patience and cooperation with far-right politicians whom just two years earlier they had considered deeply repugnant.

The liberal press argued that Hitler should be included in the government, in the hope that this might temper his party's extremism. At the same time, journalists became increasingly fearful of repercussions for criticizing the Nazis or the army in print. What a few short years before had been a diverse and vibrant newspaper landscape was collapsing from within. On top of these internal problems, the ultranationalist Alfred Hugenberg had taken advantage of the economic instability caused by the Great Depression to buy up flagging newspapers across the country, including one of Berlin's most popular dailies, the *Berliner Lokal-Anzeiger,* and built a powerful far-right media giant. Hugenberg's company became the largest media corporation in Germany, one entirely at the service of the Right.

In this environment, the bustling world described by Tergit in her novel—the newsroom chatter, publishers' gossip, animated meetings at the Romanisches Café—ground to a halt. At the *Tageblatt,* Theodor Wolff was reduced to one lead article a week and was asked by Lachmann-Mosse to desist from criticizing the cabinet led by Chancellor Heinrich Brüning. Tergit's beloved editor, Olden, was dismissed in 1931, along with many longtime staff writers. Ultimately the war would separate Tergit from her colleagues too, both physically and ideologically: Tergit and Olden, both Jewish, and both politically undesirable, were forced into exile, where they continued to publish material against the Nazi regime. Kiaulehn remained, meanwhile, and while he initially received a professional ban from the Nazis, he later became a propaganda writer for the Nazis and an occasional announcer for the *Deutsche Wochenschau,* the newsreel of the Third Reich.

Along with the decline of the liberal press came a rise in anti-Semitism. The decline of the *Berliner Tageblatt*—tarred as a *Judenblatt,* or "Jewish paper"—was symptomatic of a broader cultural shift in which a liberal, cosmopolitan culture became displaced by a racist nationalist ideology. German Jews like Tergit, and her character Miermann, had made a home for themselves in modern Germany by adopting both German cosmopolitanism and a patriotism for the best of German culture. In *Käsebier,* Tergit shows the gradual exclusion of Jews from public life less through acts of overt anti-Semitism than through an increasing devaluation of high culture, or *Bildung*, of which Jews were a prominent and visible part.

Late in the novel, Miermann wonders whether his family's efforts to assimilate had been worthwhile. After walking past two Galician Jews with long beards and flowing caftans, he turns to ask his wife, "Have we become that much more beautiful, you with your blonde hair and blue eyes, and I with my books on romanticism and classicism?" An inextricable part of Miermann's—and Tergit's—German-Jewish identity is his love of Schiller, the liberal Romantic; Heinrich Heine, exiled Jewish poet and father of the feuilleton; and Anatole France, socialist progressive and defender of Zola in the Dreyfus Affair. Tergit believed that liberal thinkers were the spiritual fathers of the Weimar Republic, and remained the conscience of a nation that in the 1930s had lost the measure of things. Quotations from Schiller and Heine intersperse the novel as pointed references to a more civilized, open-minded time.

Tergit's Jewish characters might not seem noticeably so to present-day readers, since they are neither portrayed differently nor perceive themselves as different from the German characters. Tergit felt it was not only clear who was Jewish, but worried her portrayals verged on the anti-Semitic. Käte Herzfeld and Reinhold Kaliski, for example, are both Jewish parvenu socialites who turn their social skill into financial success. When *Käsebier* was reprinted in 1977, Tergit tried to cut the subplot around Kaliski and change Käte's last name to Brügger or Becker, fearing readers would find these characters unappealing. Her editors convinced her to leave the book untouched, however, leaving us with a picture of the social world of the 1920s in its original color.

The language of *Käsebier* is as colorful and varied as the world it portrays. Tergit's book is not self-consciously experimental, but, as a product of New Objectivity, it easily moves between realism and modernism through its inclusion of fragmentary street scenes, headlines, snippets of songs, advertising slogans, and newspaper articles, as well as extended reflections on architecture, housing, work, and fashion. With each of these comes another register of language and particular vocabulary. Translating the novel meant following Tergit's shifts from literary language to the most colloquial: a short conversation peppered with slang will be followed by a genteel description of an upscale apartment; the negotiation of a business contract will be interspersed with bawdy humor.

And, like all natives of the capital, Tergit has a love for Berlinerisch, the German spoken by the city's inhabitants. Berlinerisch is sometimes crude and often cheeky, like the novel itself. It mixes cosmopolitan sophistication with earthy humor, and includes words from French, Flemish, Hebrew, Yiddish, and Rotwelsch, an argot used by beggars and thieves. Berlinerisch is well known for its creative insults and its characteristic sound, in which hard sounds become soft—"*gut*" becomes "*jut*" (pronounced: yoot)—and soft, hard—"*Ich*" becomes "*Icke*." This translation attempts to convey the zip of Berlinerisch by using a combination of Anglo-American language of the era, everyday slang, and dropped consonants in colloquial speech. I deliberately chose this method over a distinct English dialect (for example, the slang of 1920s New York or London), which could distract from the novel's geographic focus on Berlin. My goal has been to give an immersive sense of the world Tergit portrayed and try to relay the spark of Berlinerisch with a light hand.

Contemporary references have occasionally been glossed when they proved too obscure, but sometimes a gloss cannot re-create the same immediacy and urgency. For example, when Käte Herzfeld is asked how her love life is going, she responds somewhat cryptically, "Vertically excellent, so not taking bids on the horizontal"—yet her literal words are, "Vertically excellent, so horizontally crossed-out letter." "Crossed-out letter," or "*gestrichen Brief*," refers to "-B," financial shorthand for an exchange rate that has been cancelled because there are only offers but no demand. In a scant six words, Käte makes a sly but self-aware dig at the sexual mores and all-pervasive capitalism of the era. The phrase is gloriously precise and utterly peculiar; it shows Tergit's journalistic knowledge of the floor of the stock exchange.

"Not taking bids" gets us only halfway there, but it is an attempt to uphold the spirit of the phrase, if not its specificity.

An important term that has no precise English equivalent is Käsebier's métier: *Volkssänger*. While the literal translation is "folk singer," a German "folk song" can include anything from a beer-hall *schlager* to a hiking song to a military melody or a show-tune. Käsebier conquers the hearts of Berliners because his songs, far from embodying the high ideals of Weimar cosmopolitanism and *Bildung*, are shallow and nostalgic throwbacks to the song traditions of Wilhelmine Germany, but even simpler, for the unsentimental, industrial present. But while his greatest hits—including "Boy, Isn't Love Swell?" and "How Can He Sleep with That Thin Wall?"—elicit an easy attraction for Berliners, they are finally too superficial to last in the chaos of the early 1930s. They offer no solutions, just memories. Käsebier's artistry is genuine, but it, too, gets swept away by events, and Käsebier ends his career in a shabby bar two hours outside Berlin.

Despite its ebullience and sprightly repartee, *Käsebier* is ultimately tragic. People lose their homes, their savings, and sometimes their lives. But along the way, the book also revels in the vitality and creativity of the people who made Weimar Berlin into a modern (and modernist) city. None of this was enough to ensure the survival of the liberal republic, of course, something Tergit knew when she was writing the novel. While she understood that this open, cosmopolitan Germany was still an unfulfilled vision rather than a reality, she saw in its spirit the best her country had to offer. It is this spirit that Tergit's writing upholds—that of Minerva atop the crumbling newspaper headquarters.

BIBLIOGRAPHY

Michael Brenner, *The Renaissance of Jewish Culture in Weimar Germany* (New Haven/London: Yale University Press, 1996)

Ursula Büttner, *Weimar: Die überforderte Republik* (Stuttgart: Klett-Cotta, 2008)

Modris Eksteins, *The Limits of Reason* (London: Oxford University Press, 1975)

Ernst Feder, Cécile Lowenthal-Hensel, and Arnold Paucker (eds.) *Heute sprach ich mit ...: Tagebücher eines Berliner Publizisten, 1926–1932* (Stuttgart: Deutsche Verlags-Anstalt, 1971)

Peter Fritzsche, *Reading Berlin 1900* (London/Cambridge, MA: Harvard University Press, 1996)

Bernhard Fulda, *Press and Politics in the Weimar Republic* (Oxford: Oxford University Press, 2009)

Peter Gay, *Weimar Culture: The Outsider as Insider* (New York: Norton, 2001)

Diethart Kerbs and Henrick Stahr (eds.), *Berlin 1932: das letzte Jahr der ersten deutschen Republik* (Berlin: Edition Hentrich, 1992)

Siegfried Kracauer and Tom Levin (trans. and ed.), *The Mass Ornament* (Cambridge: Harvard University Press, 1995)

Wolf Lepenies, *The Seduction of Culture in German History* (Princeton: Princeton University Press, 2006)

Peter de Mendelssohn, *Zeitungsstadt Berlin* (Berlin: Ullstein, 1959)

Georg Mosse, *German Jews Beyond Judaism* (Cincinnati: Hebrew Union College Press, 1985)

Juliane Sucker, *"Sehnsucht nach dem Kurfürstendamm"* (Würzburg: Königshausen & Neumann, 2015)

Gabriele Tergit, *Etwas seltenes überhaupt* (Frankfurt a.M.: Ullstein, 1983)

Gabriele Tergit and Jens Brüning (ed.), *Frauen und andere Ereignisse* (Berlin: Das Neue Berlin, 2001)

Hans Wagener, *Gabriele Tergit: gestohlene Jahre* (Osnabrück: Universitätsverlag Osnabrück, 2013)

ACKNOWLEDGMENTS

Books are never solitary endeavors; neither are translations. I owe a great deal of thanks to those who helped me make Tergit's world come alive on the page in English. Thanks go to my editor, Edwin Frank, who took a chance on a translator who had yet to cut her teeth. I am grateful for the support of Shelley Frisch and Tess Lewis, who have been kind champions of my work and advisors in times of need. Thanks to the Goethe-Institut and the committee of the Gutekunst Prize, who helped me start my work as a literary translator and have continued to provide support since. A big thank-you to the friends who helped me work out problems and listened to my translational musings: Becky Fradkin, Abby Fradkin, Lois Beckett—your spirit helped me translate many a boozy dinner party conversation. Thanks also to Michael Swellander for his insights on Heine. Matthew Ward kindly helped me figure out some of the curiosities of Tergit's German and smooth out my English. I am incredibly grateful to Michael Lesley for his voice, ears, and eyes, his creativity, energy, support, and perfectionism—thank you for throwing yourself into this with me, and making *Käsebier* as good as possible.

The biggest thanks go to my parents, Petra and Christian Duvernoy, who have been my editors, critics, and living encyclopedias for so many years. For *Käsebier*, my mother spent hours helping track down the meanings of period terms, deciphering Berlinerisch, and puzzling through countless odd phrases with great patience. My father, as always, pushed me to refine, check, and reflect on my own writing, and made sure my English sounded as close to Tergit's German as possible.

I would like to dedicate this book to my grandparents, Hans and Christa Zehetmayer, and Wolf and Eva Duvernoy. They were witnesses to this time, and their stories are always with me. Though their lives, which would lead them to East Germany and Detroit, Michigan, respectively, could not have taken more different paths, they taught me about the complexities and realities of German history. This book is for them.

KÄSEBIER

✦ TAKES ✦

Berlin

I

Nothing but slush

BERLIN'S Kommandantenstrasse—half still the old newspaper district, half turning into the garment district—begins at Leipziger Strasse with a pleasant view over the trees of the Dönhoffplatz, now leafless, and disappears in the neighborhood of factories and workers on Alte Jakobstrasse.

Oh, Dönhoffplatz! On the right, the Tietz department store: Sale, Sale, Sale! Stiller's Shoes: "Now Even Cheaper!" Umbrellas! They're all there: Wigdor and Sachs and Resi. A blind man with newspapers squats in front of Aschinger's distillery, waiting to snap a little something up. There's the best store for artificial flowers. Boutonnières for suits in the spring, corsages for balls in the winter. Singers from Stettin! Invariably, a tall skinny one and a little fat one. Pastry shops, perfumes, suitcases, and woolens. So far, so good. The trouble begins on the first floor. Sales are slipping. Everything's direct. Factory to retailer to consumer. If possible, straight from the factory to the consumer. That's most of Donhöffplatz.

But over on the quiet side, almost by Kommandantenstrasse and its tiny, nameless shops, were the editorial offices of the *Berliner Rundschau*. The wide, long old house was four stories high, its corners topped with two large Greek amphoras. In the middle were two oversize plaster statues of Mercury and Minerva; between them stood a Roman shield. This house didn't seem to have much business with Mercury these days. Half a floor was empty. It was unclear whether Miermann had joined the newspaper's editorial staff because he had been seduced by Minerva, with her historical stone tablets, or because there were rose garlands hanging below the windows; either was

3

possible. What was clear, however, was that he had not been enticed by the baroque helmets with ostrich feathers that crowned the windows above, as he disliked military uniforms. A large golden date in the gable proclaimed that this exceedingly genteel house had been built in the year 1868.

Downstairs was a small café frequented mainly by journalists, which reeked of cigarette smoke and was badly ventilated through a small shaft that let out to the courtyard. The garbage bins sat directly underneath the shaft. The courtyard was so narrow that the sun barely reached the second floor. It was always dark in the café; only a few iridescent tulip lamps and dim electric bulbs lit the place. There were red marble tables, and small wooden chairs with cane backs and no armrests. But the owner was proud of having an intellectual clientele. He came from Vienna and thought highly of journalists. He knew each and every guest, and—more importantly—his articles.

At the top of the thoroughly worn-out stairs of the house was a glass box emblazoned with the word RECEPTION. In it sat a very young man. Beyond lay the editorial offices.

Emil Gohlisch, thirty years old, tall, pale, and blond, with extremely red hands, stood by the telephone. The editor, Miermann, some twenty years older than Gohlisch, sat at a desk. He had the breadth of an epic writer and the bleakness of a comedian. His collar permanently flaked with dandruff, and he never thought to wash his hands. He was an aesthete, but not when it came to himself. He somehow managed to pair a green tie with a purple suit, yet could tell just by touch whether a porcelain figure was from the 1730s or the 1780s. His parents had sent him away to apprentice as a salesman, which he couldn't stand; his training was only useful insofar as it had expanded his horizons. Since he had never gone to grammar school, he couldn't go to university. That was how he came to an art dealership, but he wasn't particularly useful there either. He began to write. His family was glad that things hadn't turned out even worse. Later, when he had made a name for himself—though he was still burdened with debt from earlier days—they even mustered up some pride. His two brothers were rather dull, a doctor and a lawyer who had married money and championed Progress. They never said anything out of keeping, never uttered a phrase that wouldn't have been said by anyone else in their generation. Gohlisch hung up the phone.

Miermann looked at the clock. "If my watch is still accurate," he said, "tomorrow's Thursday. I don't have anything for Thursday's page."

"Someone should write about the new cafés sometime."

"What use is *sometime*? Try today! *Hic Rhodus, hic salta!* Here's Rhodes, here scatter your salt!"

"Let's see if there's anything."

Miermann pulled a yellow folder with manuscripts out of a desk drawer. "There's a good article on slush, but it's still freezing. None of these people can write. No one can write a decent story. They don't have any new ideas."

"Someone should write about the bathroom situation in the Berlin schools sometime."

"What am I supposed to run as the lead story tomorrow?"

Miehlke came in. He was the typesetter. Miehlke's face was completely bare—no hair to be found anywhere on his face or head.

"G'day, gents. The page's gotta be out by four thirty, it's three now. Get to it. I've set the long article on the new construction work. If I take that one, the page'll be full."

"That's far too long," said Miermann shyly. He was bashful because Miehlke was the man who had once told the journalist Heye—Heye, who wrote the famous front-page editorials—"If you don't cut this, Heye, I'll cut twenty lines myself. You won't believe how fast I can do that, and no one'll notice." And when Stefanus Heye smiled, Mielke added, "Maybe you think that one of your readers will notice? Eh, readers don't notice nothin', I tell ya. You gents always think something depends on it. Let me tell ya, nothin' depends on it."

"I don't care," Miehlke now said. "The paper can't wait for you and cutting's better than printing on the margins."

Miehlke left.

"So, what shall we do?" asked Miermann.

"Well, I'm going to order coffee," said Gohlisch.

Old Schröder came in. National desk. He still sported a full beard, a green loden suit with horn buttons, and a wide black bow tie. "Things looked bad in the Reichstag today. I think the government's collapsing, the Right's on the rise. Just wait and see, they'll pass all the taxes that they yelled at the Left over, no one but party members will get work, there will be pogroms, death sentences, and civil war. I know it. We'll see something, all right; five battleships, subsidies to the German nationalists, we may as well pack up and go home."

"I think they also put their trousers on one leg at a time," said Miermann. "I know for a fact that the nationalists are just as corrupt as everyone else."

"But Miermann! You have to admit that—"

"I never admit anything."

"Sales taxes, just you wait, nothing but sales and excise taxes until our eyes bulge."

"Maybe excise taxes are a good idea?"

"Miermann!" Schröder cried indignantly, "Be serious!"

"You ask too much of a man. I'm always supposed to get worked up: against sales taxes, for sales taxes, against excise taxes, for excise taxes. I'm not going to get worked up again until five o'clock tomorrow unless a beautiful girl walks into the room!"

"I should have been a political columnist. That old judge, now there was a man who knew every position, who had studied the whole state. Now we have a parliamentary system without a parliamentary commentator."

Gohlisch got up. "Why bother? Breaking scandals sells more. Connections and a cushy little job. You've got a bee in your bonnet with your political commentator and your old judge. Put the headline in Borgis three bold. Here's the coffee. Are you paying, Miermann, or is it my turn? I'll pay."

"What's happening with the page?" said Miermann.

Schröder left. Gohlisch said, "Listen, Miermann, let me tell you a pretty little story. Just recently, there was a man who went from door to door, introducing himself to the Swiss presidents of big companies. He was their compatriot, a representative of Faber, asked them to purchase their supply of Faber pencils from him. So they helped out their countryman, he went to Faber, bought leftovers, and sold crap for good money. One day, the boss asked for a pencil. He sharpened it, thought, *hm*, when the tip kept breaking off. Eventually, the affair came to light. The countryman was thrown out.

"You won't believe," Gohlisch said, "the things I learned on this trip. In Niedernestritz, the city council wanted to build a new town hall. Someone convinced the old servant he'd get a hundred marks, and the old dodderer, a slightly drunk figure who looks like a character out of Spitzweg,[1] went over one night and built a pretty little fire in the basement. He didn't skimp on gasoline or kindling, so the town hall burned and burned, the firefighters were only called in the morning—the servant hadn't noticed, after all—he implored them not to use too much water, and the building burned merrily to the ground. But now the servant was only going to be paid fifty marks for his troubles. Naturally, he was very upset, and went to the insurance company to tell them that he'd set the fire and was prepared to go to jail, but he'd never suffered such an injustice as with these fifty marks. The insurance company had already noticed that they were dealing with arson, with a nice, well-made fire. But they hadn't been able to sell any insurance in Niedernestritz or the surrounding area for the past fifteen years. They were quite pleased with the fire, since once people noticed how nice the new city hall the insurance company was building looked, they all got insured; it was practically raining insurance applications. The insurer was delighted; so was the city council, and everyone was happy."

"That's a nice story. Maybe the insurance company also paid the city council a little something, how about that?"

"That happened in Niedernestritz, but of course you can't write about that. You can never write about the really good stuff."

"Good story, but what are we going to do about the page?"

"I have an idea. An acquaintance recently told me about a popular cabaret: supposed to be a great singer there in Hasenheide, got to check it out."

"I've only got bad manuscripts; Szögyengy Andor's written about 'The Last Horse-Cart Driver' again..."

"What pests, these professional Hungarians!" said Gohlisch.

"There's been an article on weekend outings lying around since September, good article, but since I've gotten it there's been nothing but bad weather, so I can't use that. You can't run an article on weekends when it's so cold. You just can't."

Miehlke came in again. "Well, what'm I supposed to do, gents, the page has to be out by four thirty. I'll take the construction and cut it myself if you gents won't deliver. Like I said, nothing depends on it."

Miermann sat there, resigned. "All right, we'll take the construction piece, but we'll have to cut half of it. Gohlisch, you always leave me hanging. When will we run the article on the singer?"

"Next Wednesday, for sure. Upon my soul!"

"Well, that's something! When you say Wednesday in eight days, I can be certain that you mean Wednesday in eight months."

"I can't work on command, it has to come to me. I'm not a fountain pen. I'm a steadfast servant of thought."

"If it thaws next Wednesday, we'll run the slush article; otherwise, yours."

"Done."

"But I need to be able to rely on you. That page is getting worse by the week. You writers are out of good ideas, and we aren't getting any submissions. There's no talent."

"That's true," said Gohlisch, "but only because the untalented writers are popular and cheaper. A big shot publisher recently said that the worse newspapers are, the more they sell. What's talent good for? No talent plus a dash of sadism sells a lot more. A rape is more popular than a sentence by Goethe, although Goethe's still acceptable. Briand sat at the desk of the *Petit Journal* for over a decade and told people stories. That's how his newspaper got started. He never wrote a line himself. He was paid a handsome salary, and that's how Briand was made. But publishers haven't got a clue about the business of writing."

And with that, they vanished into the composing room.

2

Once again, nothing comes of the slush story

IT WAS even colder the following Wednesday.

"Have we ever had a winter like this?" asked Gohlisch. "If we still had one of my articles lying around on frost and ice or frozen lakes in the Mark, it would surely thaw. Here's the article. I'm going to order coffee now. Cake? No cake?"

"Cake," said Miermann.

"My dear Miermann," exclaimed Herzband the writer, who went by Lieven, as he burst into the room with outstretched hands, his cloak aflutter. "What do you have to say about that most exquisite piece Otto Meissner wrote about me?"

"I can say I read the lovely piece that you wrote about Otto Meissner," said Miermann.

"I can't ignore that your answer was meant to cut me to the quick. I admit that I'm vain to an almost ungodly degree. But can't friends praise friends? I ask you: *shouldn't* friends praise friends? Please, I ask you: isn't it one's duty to forge camaraderie in resistance to this world, inartistic as it is, bereft of gods? We few, creative, intellectual thinkers? The writer should praise his comrade, since only the like-minded can recognize one another! Have you already read my book, dearest Miermann, *Dr. Buchwald Seeks His Path*? Not yet? A political novel of the highest caliber! Nothing less, I assure you, dear editor, nothing less is offered than the solution to foreign affairs. I'll send it to you. The writer must be a traveling salesman for his own books, the writer must manage his own reputation since his fame furthers that of the nation. The writer's vanity is justified, and nothing can harm his stature more than if he looks upon the intellectual trade with scorn!

9

Think: my books have been translated into every culturally significant language, even Irish. Recently, I had a four-hour-long conversation with Bratianu on a trip to Bucharest. 'I've just read,' he said, 'a very beautiful novel by a German writer named Lieven.' I stood up and bowed. 'I am that very man.' What a moment! What an experience! What joy! Bratianu read a German novel; Bratianu loved this novel; Bratianu loved this novel's author; I am that author! So, dear Miermann, so as not to take up any more of your precious time, I ask you to run a notice regarding an event of European import: the great French lawyer and poet Paul Regnier has asked me to write a play with him on the trial of the Soviet saboteurs. I have accepted his request. We will begin our work shortly. This is the first sign of Franco-German cooperation on a European theme. In a few words, I have sketched the importance of this event. Here they are. An international item. Please place it in the evening paper straight away."

Gohlisch had, in the meantime, been looking out the window.

What a strange store over there, he thought. For years it had been a clothing store, but now it's disappeared, like all the clothing stores. Recently, at Hausvogteiplatz, an old lady said to me, "Isn't it awful, now D. Lewin's gone too. I've been buying my coats at Manheimer's for forty years. I just came in to the city from Karlshorst to buy myself a coat. V. Manheimer's gone. I think to myself, I'll go to D. Lewin. Lewin's gone as well." It was almost like the revolution, people spoke to each other on the street for no reason. Then the store became a wine shop. Germans drink German wine, but eventually they also began to sell Bordeaux and all kinds of schnapps. Six bottles of wine for five marks; even that was too much for people. Beer's cheaper. Then came a store for kitchen furnishings. All sorts of kitchen furnishings. Eschebach's Kitchen Units, three smooth cupboards next to one another, bottomless glass drawers; next to them, tasteful antique cupboards in carved wood or colored glass. Furniture stores don't work. A person needs rent, gas, electricity, heating, and food—lots of food—fresh food three times a day, but he can walk around in the same coat for years and get his kitchen cupboards at the flea market. The kitchen store vanished as well, thought Gohlisch, and a restaurant sprang up, but there are too many restaurants in the neighborhood. Good wine restaurants; Aschinger's, free bread, forty-five pfennigs for a sausage, peas with bacon for seventy-five pfennigs; then there's the old Münze, a beer restaurant, excellent; a kosher restaurant, separate meat and veg; lots of bakeries. Far too many restaurants in the neighborhood. New ones can't compete. The restaurant disappeared and the storefront stood empty again until another restaurant took its place. Young plucky things who stuck a pickled herring in the window.

"You're not interested in literature," Lieven said venomously, addressing the back of Gohlisch's head. Gohlisch was still looking out the window.

"Oh, certainly, but only good literature," said Gohlisch. "Karl May, or *Buried in the Desert*, or things like that. By the way, there's nothing doing with the slush," he added in Miermann's direction.

Miermann understood, and said to Lieven, "Excuse us, we have to put together a newspaper. Unfortunately, we're just honest workers. Not free spirits, but servants to the publisher. Obedient slaves to the public. I'm very interested in your book. No doubt I'll read it."

Lieven bowed, put on his big, floppy hat, his cloak flying. "I bestow my greetings upon the men of the world," he said.

"He's really gone soft in the head," said Gohlisch. "You only hear things like this about that man: 'Mr. Adolf Lieven will write a drama that takes place among artists.' No scenes, no title, no plot. Just 'artists.' Then they begin sending out press releases. 'Mr. Adolf Lieven announces that his book, *The Lame Vulture,* will be translated into new Siberian.' Mr. Adolf Lieven was received by the president of Argentina during his South American research trip. We don't get news like that from Gerhard Hauptmann. But what will we do about Thursday's page? Thank God, coffee. Say, girl, don't catch a cold without your coat. Are you paying, Miermann, or is it my turn?"

"I'm paying this time," said Miermann. "The slush isn't going to work. The streets are disgustingly clean. But the slush has to come one day, otherwise, where'll we get our spring from? I also have an article on marriage statistics."

"That'll fill a box, but you can't lead with it."

"I just received a lead article, a pleasant piece from Szögyengy Andor on the different ways that Berliners spend their Sundays."

"These professional Hungarians again! Why don't you take a look at my article on the singer, I don't think it came out very well, it didn't really come together—I'm not feeling that great anyways, I'm going to order a schnapps. D'you want one too?"

"Does a man stand on one leg?" said Miermann.

Gohlisch went to the phone and ordered two glasses of grappa.

Suddenly, there was a loud noise in the hall. The door flew open, and a scent wafted in; first the scent, then a very large woman. She wore a very thick, loose fur coat made of light brown bearskin, a thin, bright yellow dress underneath, out of which peeked a pair of long, shapely, pink-tinged legs. A yellow, brown, and red scarf fluttered around her neck. She wore a bright red beret perched atop many very blonde curls. The beret was set far back on her head, crooked and to the right. She was heavily made up, which only accentuated her gaudy appearance. She was young, and had a wily face. With a great din, she suddenly stood in the small room that was already packed with two desks. An engraving of the Forum Romanum hung on the wall above Miermann's desk. Gohlisch had tacked up a watercolor of a sailboat he had painted over his desk. She looked around for a second, then ran toward Miermann, who had jumped up. She put her arms around his shoulders, kissed him, and cried, "God, Miermann, my darling, I haven't seen you in ages, what's wrong with us? Here!" She pressed a manuscript into his hand. "Print it, sugar lips, print it! Don't you remember?"

"Of course, dear," said Miermann. "The Academy Ball, four thirty, second closet, fourth corridor."

She was out again in a flash. Gohlisch yelled, "I'm an honest republican from the clan of the Verrinas," and banged his fist on the table.[2] "Are you acquainted with that Kurfürstendamm slut?"

"No clue," said Miermann. "I only know who she is."

In that moment, a big blond man came in: Öchsli the theater critic. "What the hell was that?" he cried. "All of a sudden a gal came sweeping down the hallway, called out, 'Sweet Öchsli, haven't seen you for ages, d'you still remember?' But I don't remember anything."

"That happened to me too. She's not a friend, but I know who she is. That was Aja Müller. She has one car, two poodles, and two relationships: one with the playwright Altmann and another with the son of a director at the D-Bank."

"Must be quite nice sleeping with her," Gohlisch replied, and continued writing.

"The things she writes are quite nice too," said Miermann. "Snobby, but not too snobby given the topic. Parties and balls. I'll give it straight to the setter, since I don't have a lead. Maybe you can rework the thing on Käsebier."

"I'll see. By the way, the place was completely packed. Not a seat in the house, even at six thirty. A pair of acrobats performed, a lot better than in the big vaudeville shows. Käsebier is excellent. It's worth it. He sings with a partner, also very good, by the way, traditional songs from the Rhine, unbelievably kitschy. One was especially good, the story of a tenement, 'How Can He Sleep with That Thin Wall?,' quite excellent. And then he plays the pimp." Gohlisch picked up a scarf and took a few steps, soft and fresh. "Passage Friedrichstrasse, under the lindens green." He raised his chin, thrust out his lower lip, and raised his open hand to his face, jerking it once, twice, to indicate business. "I'm pretty sure that there's room for a thousand people in there. It's quite a thing with the acrobats; a man walking on a tightrope is already enough for me. But apparently that isn't enough. He also has to play the fiddle while he's doing it. It's a very strange thing: music as an accompaniment to a display of human agility. Plus an excellent clown; he wanted to sit on a chair but it was all wobbly, and he couldn't get it to stand straight. He took out a big cigar box and with a great deal of difficulty broke it into little pieces, deadly serious. Finally, he ended up with a piece small enough to shove under the leg of the chair, but it kept slipping away. All of our male gravity, gone up in smoke. The tricky business of preventing a chair from wobbling that still wobbles. I'm going to get some breakfast."

"You lack ambition," Miermann said.

"Ambition? For lead articles?" asked Gohlisch. "No, I don't have any. I don't try; I want to be asked."

"You're being asked."

"No, I'm not. I know only smooth talkers make it around here."

Miermann laughed. Gohlisch went to breakfast at a Hungarian place on Kommandantenstrasse. The place was decorated in white, red, and green, like a Hungarian country tavern. Ears of corn hung from individual booths, and the whole place was garlanded with corncobs. The booths were brightly painted and looked like rustic canopy beds, with four wooden pillars holding up the roof. Dr. Krone was sitting in one of them.

"Greetings, sir," said Gohlisch—then a conspiratorial figure who published unsavory exposés in various newspapers and magazines under the byline 'Augur' came creeping in. He carried twelve newspapers under his arm, kept his head down and his eyes up. Gloomily, without a word, he shook everyone's hand. The three gentlemen ordered a bottle of Tokay.

"What have you got, sir?" Gohlisch asked Dr. Krone, who hadn't opened his mouth.

"I'm completely depressed. What's going on with health insurance is unbearable. Ninety percent of the population has health insurance and the ones who don't will only see professors. The professorial title is pure gold. I don't see any way of moving forward. I don't have the time and the money to do research. Before the war, you could buy yourself a monkey; now I can't afford a monkey, and the same goes for rabbits. On the other hand, it's unbearable to sit in my consultation room and wait for patients."

"Well, why do you live in the west anyway?" said Gohlisch. "If you moved to Brunnenstrasse, you'd have plenty of work."

"I'd just be doing slapdash stuff. A hundred patients a day, ten minutes per patient, I'd have sixteen hours of work. The only way to make things easy for yourself is to stop examining patients thoroughly. My only consolation about all the undiagnosed carcinomas is that there's nothing to be done. I had another great case recently. I wanted to prescribe a hay fever treatment for a patient, now, during winter:

would their insurance approve it? It's a preventative treatment and costs eighty-five marks. What did the insurer say? Impossible, costs too much. So what am I to do? Become a charlatan or starve? You know, there are doctors who get lots of traffic."

"I recently went to see Dr. Ahlheim," Gohlisch said. "First, I wait in a room with five other patients. Nurses keep coming in: 'One moment, please.' I wait. One comes, yells, 'Mrs. Meyer to room one for an X-ray, please.' Another one, 'Mrs. Schulze to room two, undress, please.' A third one, 'Mrs. Kühne to the reception, please.' 'Mrs. Marheinke to radiotherapy, please.' 'The gentleman to the next room, please.' Fine, so I go into the next room. I wait, along comes another nurse, 'Sir, please undress in room five.' I tell her I've sprained my thumb, I don't have to get undressed. 'Very well,' the nurse says, 'then please wait.' I sit there for a while. In the meantime, the rigmarole continues. A nurse enters. 'Next room,' she says. By now I've been funneled into the third room. I wait. Next door, things carry on. 'Mrs. Niedergesäss under the electric arc, please, Mrs. Weltrein to electrotherapy.' 'Sir, please undress in room seven.' I explain that I've sprained my thumb, I don't need to get undressed. 'Very well,' the nurse says, 'then please wait.' Finally, the well-known, popular doctor comes in. I tell him I've probably sprained my thumb. 'Yes,' he says. 'You're right, you've sprained your thumb. Diathermia. Come back twice a week for diathermia. If it's not better in four weeks' time, we'll talk.' Well, I hadn't lost my mind yet. I went to a young doctor whom nobody had recommended to me, he twisted my thumb back into shape, case closed."

"That's how it is," Dr. Krone said. "You have to cram in the patients, things can't go on like this with health insurance. They've socialized the profession without nationalizing it. The insurers decide on the prices, but we're not paid by the state."

"It's the same everywhere," said Augur. "Service doesn't matter anymore because no one values it; we only talk about it. Instead of an economy run by and for the officers and the student corps, we now have hundreds of interest groups: nationalists, socialists, Catholics, salary groups, pension groups. Without a backroom connection you're lost. But they're all the spawn of capitalism. What can you expect of a capitalist economy in which there are only exploiters and exploited?"

"Well," said Gohlisch, "I think the terror of communism would be even worse."

"Last time that scoundrel Nagel, that slave-driver, got twenty marks out of me," Augur cried.

"I'm going to order three more grappas," said Gohlisch. "By the way, that's a disgrace, Augur."

"I can't find out anything," the conspirator said. "I run around all day putting a five-line story together, and then they haggle over the price. They furnished new rooms at city hall. First off, they're incredibly fancy, second, they were privately contracted. How's that possible?"

"I've been running around looking for a lead for ten days, I can't find anything out," Gohlisch said.

Dr. Krone bade them farewell.

"I feel sorry for Krone," Gohlisch said. "He can do a lot. Specialists know what he's worth."

"Sure, but he doesn't know how to exercise his authority," said Augur. "An acquaintance of mine went to him recently, he examined him endlessly and finally said, 'I'm still not quite sure what seems to be the problem. Come back the day after tomorrow.' You simply can't do that."

"That's rich coming from you, a man of the times! You don't understand the sense of honesty that allows a man to admit that he hasn't found the answer yet? You want him to tell you, 'Go to bed straight away, you've got pleurisy, keep yourself warm,' when he hasn't found anything? You also share that primitive persuasion: 'When I go to the doctor, he'd better prescribe something.' People who have medical and legal stock phrases at the ready are good for hysterical women. But it makes me sad that you can't appreciate someone *not* trying to pull the wool over your eyes for a change."

"Come on, Gohlisch," said Augur, "I appreciate it, I'm just giving you one solution to the puzzle of why Krone lacks for work. Success is a question of suggestion, not work."

"Miermann would say: 'That one sentence explains fascism completely, you're all cowards and slaves in search of authority.'"

They paid.

"Be well, Augur. Heil and Sieg and catch a fat one."

3

It thaws. The slush article is published, and the article on the singer is typeset

ON WEDNESDAY morning, Gohlisch rewrote the article on the singer.

The head of local news asked, "Will you allow Mr. Meise to make a phone call?"

Gohlisch responded, "I'd rather not, but if I don't have a choice. Let me order myself a coffee and a grappa first."

Mr. Meise was a crime reporter.

"Mr. Meise," said the editor, an old grumbling bear of fifty, who wrote quiet novellas in private, "Mr. Meise, we really must find out how Professor Möller's doing. His obituary is the lead article, and it's already gone to the typesetter. A man who redefined the natural sciences, so to speak—we can't lag behind the big papers or quote them under any circumstances. WTB doesn't know anything yet."[3]

"I'll make inquiries right away," said Meise.

"Be especially careful not to be tactless, please."

Hm, thought Gohlisch, Käsebier is out of luck, I'll never get on with the article if things keep going like this.

"Did you put the phone here?" he asked.

"Yes, of course," Meise said. It rang. "What, a car accident? On Pankstrasse? How many dead? —None? We're not interested if there are no dead."

Meise hung up, the phone rang again. "Tractor hit a streetcar? —How many dead? —None? Any severely injured? —Three? Fine, that'll do, which hospital? —Name and address please? Müller, Freisinger Strasse? —Thank you, Mr. Müller, many thanks, Mr. Müller, you can collect your money at the register when the article has run."

He hung up. "Well, I better conduct my inquiries on Möller very carefully." Gohlisch was curious to know what Meise considered careful. Meise picked up the receiver and dialed a number.

"Is this Möller? This is Meise, *Berliner Rundschau*. What? Oh, the missus herself, please forgive me for asking, but I wanted to inquire whether your dear husband is still alive?"

After a while, Meise put down the receiver.

"Well?" asked Gohlisch.

"Mrs. Möller appears to have hung up," said Meise.

"I can imagine," said Gohlisch. "You call *that* tactful?"

"So nothing's certain yet," said Meise, reassured, and left.

Gohlisch wrote. Miehlke, the typesetter, knocked.

"What's with the Käsebier story, Mr. Miermann wants to know, otherwise he'll take the slush story, the barometer just sank."

"Tell him that I'll bring it to him by three thirty. I just want to have breakfast."

With that, he put on his coat and went down to the café. Augur was sitting there.

"One breakfast with coffee," said Gohlisch.

"Did you know," said Augur, "Karl Lambeck has come to Berlin for his play at the Deutsches Theater. I bumped into him yesterday on Rankestrasse. I'd never seen him before, he didn't open his mouth, but he looked great, even better than in the pictures. Aja Müller was there, that ass Lieven, and a few others."

"So," said Gohlisch, who didn't much care, "why did Knorr get the gig to furnish city hall?"

"No idea," said Augur.

"How's your daughter, by the way?" said Gohlisch.

"She has a mild case of apicitis."

"I'd send her off to Switzerland."

"The doctor says she's in no condition to travel right now, maybe later. But it's not that bad."

"Shall we have another grappa?" said Gohlisch. "I'd ask a different doctor, maybe you can send her to Switzerland after all," and ordered two grappas. "The grappa is good here," said Gohlisch, "it's made of pure grapes. —Oh, look, it's already three forty-five. What a thaw! It was barbarically cold today. Let Miermann use the slush story. Another coffee."

"Yes," said Augur. "Do you know I'm the one who wrote the article on Black Friday?"

"Congratulations," said Gohlisch.

"What do you think I got for that information?"

"Well, you should have gotten a few thousand marks. It's stupid, that silly gossip rag became famous all of a sudden."

"I should have, but what I actually asked for was five hundred marks. You know what they gave me?"

"Hmm, one-fifty."

"Thirty."

"I'd sue."

"What can you do, they're my best clients."

"All the same, that's no good. We may be fountain pens, but a big publisher can't just take you for a ride."

"If I complained, I'd get four hundred marks and lose my best client. It may be a gossip magazine, but it's independent. No one else would dare to publish the dangerous stuff I get from the ministries. It's not worth thinking about."

"You need a steady gig."

"And to be dependent?"

"You're more dependent when you're independent. —It's four thirty now, let Miermann use the slush story. —You know, here's the thing: some people have a reputation and nobody notices they're no good; some people do good work but by the time anyone notices, they're no good anymore either. I'm a lazy bum, but nobody's figured out how to make hard work look good to a genius like me. Well, Heil and Sieg and catch a fat one!"

With that, Gohlisch went to Otto's wine bar. When he came back to the office at six, the slush story was typeset.

Miermann's wife was there: Emma, a slight older lady who always wore the same dark-blue dress. She was the same age as Miermann, who had taken so long to find a stable position and make a name for himself with a few thoughtful, well-written, little-read books. When Gohlisch came, she said goodbye with a friendly smile.

"I hope I haven't scared you off," said Gohlisch.

"God forbid, I'm happy to leave the young ones to themselves," she said, giving her husband a benign look.

Gohlisch brought in the article about the cabaret in Hasenheide—and Käsebier.

"Let's typeset it for next Thursday right now."

"Otto Lambeck's in Berlin. Augur saw him on Rankestrasse. He's here for his play at the Deutsches Theater," said Gohlisch.

"Your piece is a mess!" said Miermann. "There are as many commas as periods. If you say 'as well,' you need another 'as' somewhere. This sentence ends with *and*. Lord, Lord, forgive him, he knows not what he does. What do you mean by *partout*?"

"Thoroughly."

"It means 'everywhere.' I don't want to kiss Aja Müller *partout*, that means 'everywhere,' *not* 'thoroughly.' Gohlisch, Gohlisch! Keep learning. Keep improving. Do you find it pleasing to say 'anyway' all the time? No. You're my problem child. Go read Fontane. And read Heine and everything—everything—by Anatole France. He's brazen, but read him. I'll bring you something tomorrow."

Miermann worked on Gohlisch's "Singer" for two hours. Finally he sent it to the composing room.

4

The article on the singer is published

WEEKS passed. Miermann and Kohler were sitting in the office on a Wednesday afternoon.

It was Kohler's birthday, and a few people had remembered. Miermann had thought of it too. "What shall I give her?" he had asked Gohlisch.

"A book," Gohlisch had answered. "What else could you give Miss Kohler?"

"No, that's exactly why I'll give her perfume."

"Grand, how grand," she said to Miermann when he handed her the perfume.

"How are you, anyway?" he asked.

"Not too bad, thanks."

"Still because of Meyer?"

"Yes. I'd like to travel with him. He wants to, but he doesn't."

"But that won't do! You can't let him notice; if he does, you're done for. He'll never marry you if you make it that easy for him."

The young woman thought, It's 1929. In 1929, it's ridiculous not to have a boyfriend, especially when you're thirty. He's a bohemian from 1890. Still has notions of "dishonor." Out loud, she said, "Shall we order coffee and cake to celebrate? The beginning of spring, I mean."

The phone rang. "I've got to go," said Miermann. "I'm looking for a room, I posted an ad today. I've gotten an offer in the neighborhood. I'm going there later."

"It's tricky with the rooms around here. You won't find something you can count on. They're all disgusting. And the hotels are impossible," said Miss Kohler.

"You think so?"

"Is she quite young?"

"No, well over thirty."

"All the same, cafés and cars kill all love, it's ghastly."

"I'll take a look at the room," Miermann said as Gohlisch came in. "What will we run as the lead tomorrow?" he asked.

"I don't know either," said Gohlisch. "Is this the right kind of weather for thinking about the papers? You could write about old gardens, or Heine's balcony, or the first spring flowers, or love in Potsdam. But what's in the papers? Poland's demands on Germany. Notes on the budget of the Ministry of Transportation. Lord Asquith is dead, and there's a Negro singer in Berlin. That's how it is."

Miermann dug around in his folder. "Three articles by Aja Müller. 'Crowning the Queen of Fashion.' 'How Do I Clean My Nails?' 'An Afternoon with a Screen Actress.' That won't do. That's something for the society papers, but not for us; we still want to be taken seriously. I'll send it all back to her. Gohlisch, you know we still have the article on Käsebier in the overmatter, let's use it. We'd almost forgotten about it. Miehlke would say it doesn't matter."

"And nothing does," said Gohlisch, but he still went into the composing room. Miehlke couldn't find the set type anymore.

"It's gone," said Miehlke. "I can't find it. You'll have to come back round quarter to five."

Miehlke was the best typesetter in Berlin. No one understood why he hadn't moved on to the *Berliner Tageszeitung* long ago. But he was sixty-five years old, and at that age one doesn't like change. Miehlke searched the room, growing angry. Gohlisch stood in the corner, meek and unobtrusive. In the meantime, iron forms filled with type came out of the composing room. Cut-up bits of manuscript lay under each line of type. An elegant young man of about thirty, a bon vivant in a gray linen smock who always asked editorial for free tickets to the movies, removed the type sorts from the galleys and placed them on the table at record speed. Metal sorts lay on the table, which he picked up and reassembled into new galleys. It was a wonder that "Olympics Without Football" didn't get mixed up with

"Romanian Parliament Dissolves," or "Disturbances at the Halsmann Trial" with "The New Romanticism." But they didn't get mixed up; they were assembled. One man laid the type-filled galleys on the printing press, placed pieces of paper over the galleys, pulled the lever, and there was the article. He hung up the long galley proofs on hooks; one was labeled National Desk, another Foreign Affairs, one was Heye, another Miermann. Hooks for the culture, sports, and local sections were on the other side.

New manuscripts came out of the newsroom. Miehlke cut up the manuscripts as if in a sped-up film. He wrote "8-pt., ⅛." on them in red, "65, 66, 67," and cut the page at every number. Then the cut-up pages went into the composing room.

Galleys filled with type for unpublished articles lay under the table. Miehlke searched. It was almost five o'clock.

"I'm outta time," said Miehlke. "It's almost time to go to press, the pages've gotta go out." Gohlisch started searching too.

"Get outta here," said Miehlke. "You're in the way."

Gohlisch was feverishly trying to spot his article in reversed type. The big clock said 5 p.m.—five more minutes, otherwise it would be too late. He found it! Miehlke grumbled.

The printer put through the page. Gohlisch carried off the big galley, which proclaimed MONTMARTRE IN BERLIN, with the headline in Renata three.

Gohlisch went to Miermann. "I think the headline looks bad in Renata," he said.

"Quick, quick, take something else and set it twelve point."

Gohlisch deliberated. Koenig Bold, ugh, he couldn't stand Koenig Bold, everyone was using Koenig bold these days. Over the article, he wrote, "Cheltenham italic, Versalia bold, twelve point."

"Hey, that's something special, we don't see type like that every day."

"Mr. Miehlke, please—Cheltenham italic for the headline, set twelve point, Versalia bold."

Briese the typesetter came over and said admiringly, "That'll look good."

The article stood there, broken up by the names and numbers of the typesetters. Polte, machine 30, Schwarz, machine 32, Numratzki, machine 36, Hoppe, machine 25. Those are the setters, thought Gohlisch. They make between six and seven hundred marks a month, as much as I do, a compositor makes five hundred marks, and Miermann, our Miermann, gets eight hundred. He's been here too long. If you stay that long, no one appreciates you.

The article came back. The headline had been changed.

"Looks good," said Gohlisch.

"Very nice," said the head of the culture section.

The head of the printing room came and looked at the headline. "Very good," he said. "Cheltenham isn't used often enough, more Versalia bold would be better too."

"There's not enough variation in the typefaces," said Gohlisch.

Then the editors swarmed into the composing room in time for the printing.

Schröder stood there, ranting that there was too little room. New elections, metal workers' lockout, the German embassy and the Cavell Film company, the Wyszaticki trial, the committee debate on draft service. Administrative reform. Higher education. Statistics on Berlin. The warmest day in February. Massive fire in Charlottenburg. Streetcar collision with tractor. Where to put it? Where to put it? One is as important as the other. The new elections can't go, and every other paper has the German embassy and Cavell Film too. So cut thirty lines on "Higher Education"! Cut "Social Debates in the Reichstag" to sixty lines! Stick "Unrest at Yesterday's Boxing Matches" on page four! Arts section too long! Cut twenty-five lines on the world premiere in Vienna! And the fourteen-year-old who just had a child!

"Gohlisch, proofread it quickly, otherwise you won't make it."

Gohlisch read. Damn it, he thought, they typeset *earth* for *soul*. Typos, typos! You could never rely on the proofreaders.

Blumenfeld, the sports editor, called out, "For the 'One Thousand Guineas' race they typeset 'On Those and Guineas.'"

"Gohlisch, cut twenty lines, quick."

"I can't cut anymore, the article is completely pared down, what can I still cut?"

"Cut, cut," Miehlke shouted. "You always think it matters, it doesn't matter. Otherwise I'll cut. Can't print on the margins."

"You're right there, Miehlke."

Gohlisch cut. An old man came with pincers and cut away the excess. The page was done. Miermann ordered a printing. Gohlisch held the wet page in his hand; it smelled vile. The page looked good, possibly even very good. One-eighth ads. At the top, MONTMARTRE IN BERLIN. The headline in Cheltenham Italic, set twelve point, Versalia Bold; next to it, BERLIN STATISTICS as main headline. Below, a second headline: BIRTH, MARRIAGE, AND DEATH. And beneath, a third: BERLIN FACES DIRE FATE WITHOUT IMMIGRATION.

"Those three headlines are wonderfully complementary," said Miermann. "Bernhard bold twelve point for 'Berlin Statistics,' true objectivity, 'Birth, Marriage, and Death' is almost cosmic in Schwabacher Tertia, and bold Koenig Korpus for the swan song: 'Berlin Faces Dire Fate without Immigration.' No one pays any mind to the stuff in eight-point font."

Gohlisch continued to examine the page. One short piece: "The Warmest Day in February" and an article with the headline "Child Born from Own Father." Bernhard bold twelve point again. "Maybe," he said to Miermann, "Renata would have been even better."

The next day, the "Montmartre in Berlin" article appeared in the *Berliner Rundschau*. That same evening, Gohlisch received a letter from Georg Käsebier.

"Dear sir, I am indebted to you for your praise. I am sending you a passe-partout for all my shows, my wife thanks you as well. In expressing my highest regards and deepest thanks, I remain your Käsebier, who will never forget you."

5

A long chapter, at the end of which Käsebier is written up in the Berliner Tageszeitung

THE OFFICE of Dr. Waldschmidt, the publisher, was entirely paneled in wood. The desk stood in the middle; light came in from the left. A portrait of the founder of the house, painted by Anton von Werner, hung above the desk. Across from it stood a round sofa set made of black carved wood. Dr. Waldschmidt was on the telephone when a knock on the door came.

"Mr. Otto Lambeck," the valet announced.

"Send him in."

"Welcome, dear Lambeck, welcome," Dr. Waldschmidt said. He leapt to his feet and shook Lambeck's hand. "Please, just a moment, take a seat, I'm on the phone." Otto Lambeck sat down.

"The Chamber of Commerce is in session today, I hadn't thought of that. And the paper manufacturers' meeting is also at noon. A man can't get to work with all these meetings. By the way, Honig from the German wood paper manufacturers' council wrote me a very anxious letter about our tariff policies. —You may say newspapers are child's play and farming's the real issue. But I can tell you that if I have a son, I won't let him go into the newspaper business. Long ago, I could have lived off the odd news section alone. But in these times, with expenses eating me up; you call this a government? —Very well, goodbye.

"My dear Mr. Lambeck, you've caught me at the busiest time of the day. What can I do? I barely have time for myself. I'm thrilled to see you. How's business? You look good. Fresh, flourishing."

There was a knock. A folder was brought in, full of letters to sign.

"Put it there. So you're looking to make some money? Yes?" The phone rang. "You see. Excuse me a moment." He shrugged at Lambeck

27

and picked up the receiver. "Get me Privy Councilor Trölein. —You see, dear Mr. Lambeck, it's like this all day long. —Yes, hello, dear councilor, we can't make it. We've been out every evening since January, except on the days we have visitors ourselves. Sometimes we have three to four invitations a day. On Sunday, when the new exhibit at the Academy opened, we went first to the opening, then to dinner at Consul Weissmann's, then to a reception at the Lettes' that evening. We're barely human anymore. I come home, put on my tuxedo, and drive off again. It's been this way since October, but I can't go to two events in one night so late in the season, besides, my wife won't be back yet. —Cannes, yes, Cannes, she writes that the Englishmen are very stiff and barely any Germans. She brought far too many clothes. Well, you know our women. It's been two weeks that I've wanted to visit her, but right now I simply can't get away. There's been discussion as to whether we should proceed with paper orders collectively. If that doesn't work out, we'll be at each other's throats. I can tell you that with this drop in advertisements, newspapers can pack up and go home. I bumped into my friend Klauske recently. He's a manufacturer of Turkish hypericum oil, has a small business on the Rhine, muddles along with ten employees, and it pays off. That or the flypaper factory in Gera pays ten percent. Everyone's thought of radio, but what about flypaper? Now there's a product! We should start a sports paper or a tabloid. But it's not that easy to shift your operations. Well, we'll see each other at the meeting for the National Council of Economic Advisors. What do you think of Cochius, by the way? I worked for the better part of the year to get him on board, and the day I finally get him through, the *Berliner Rundschau* publishes an article opposing the board. You shouldn't get caught with your pants down like that! Unbelievable. Well, bye now! —All right, Mr. Lambeck, I'm yours."

"It's lively here, Mr. Waldschmidt," said Lambeck. "I feel—"

The phone rang. "You see how it is. Please. Just a moment. —Get me the privy councilor, please. —Good day, councilor. You're traveling south? —Yes, it's been a bit much, and markets are going down steadily, although I do think it's justified. The boom was dangerous.

Manufacturing is abysmal. The whole world's gone in for manufacturing now; they've shaken themselves free of old Europe. Industry is certainly no godsend for man, but now we're stuck with it. And we have no sales. —You're right. Too many people, far too many people! When people talk about luxury in Berlin, I feel sick. The handful of restaurants on the Kurfürstendamm is just the tip of the iceberg. Who's moving in behind Alexanderplatz? We won't be able to change that. Circumstances are more powerful than we are. —Yes, yes. —We're all being squeezed. Please give my best to your wife. —In Cannes as well. —Yes, too expensive and too British. —She says it's no fun at all? —Mine too. Actually, I wanted to go there for two weeks. But there's no sleeping car to be had. —Train to Basel? —Oh, no. I don't like having a whole day free to think. I'll find a sleeping car yet. Rest up! —Going to Karlsbad this summer—I must! —Yes, yes—these blowouts are nonsense! Give my best to your wife."

He hung up. "That's how it always is, Mr. Lambeck, this is how I spend my short days; a big operation, the National Council of Economic Advisors, and there's something fishy going on at city hall but my dear reporters can't crack it. On top of that, social commitments, gossip, and politics. Well, over to you, Mr. Lambeck. You're feeling good about the opening? Berlin's better than Vienna. You wanted Vienna first, right? Vienna's dead and tradition isn't worth the paper it's written on. Berlin is far better, and the *actors*! Come on; Bergner and Dorsch, Goethe and Schiller; you can't tell who's greater. I'd give up both for Sorma, but I'm still part of the old guard. And now to you, Mr. Lambeck."

"This city," Lambeck slowly began, "is doubtlessly enchanting." He fell silent again. "You have a very good man on your staff. I met him yesterday."

Dr. Waldschmidt was slightly taken aback. "Who?"

"Doctor Lohse, such a good, well-meaning man."

"You know, what about writing about this enchanting city? Even Goethe didn't mind trying his hand at newsworthy topics from time to time."

Lambeck considered it. The offer enticed him. He would enjoy not saving up his observations, for once, but bringing them to his publisher straightaway in nice, neat prose.

"Naturally, we would permit ourselves to offer you a special fee." Lambeck mulled it over.

"I'd have to discuss it with Mulert," said Dr. Waldschmidt. "But I'm sure he'd be very enthusiastic." Both men fell silent.

Lambeck said, "Please allow me to give thorough consideration to your offer. I'm not yet sure whether the short prose form will suit me." He fell silent again. The phone rang. A young girl brought in a signature folder with papers. Lambeck took his leave. God, what a dullard Lambeck is, Waldschmidt thought.

Otto Lambeck walked away. He was very tall, very thin, and very gray. He spoke little, preferably with workers and children. The new job tempted him. But where to begin? He walked slowly through the bustling city on a glorious day in early spring.

The lower part of Friedrichstrasse is a curious neighborhood. Films, films, lousy stores, cheap silk lingerie with even cheaper lace, seven-fifty for an outfit, blouses, and garish silk dresses. Across the way, at the corner to Schützenstrasse, was the good tailor. Maybe it would be smart to bring one's things there. They wear blue, they put together nice window displays. Newspaper hawkers stand by Leipziger Strasse, primroses on offer, a little girl says, "Look, Mama, dresses are getting longer again." It's one o'clock. The women have lovely, slender legs. The women of Berlin have grown beautiful; they are industrious and swift. They discuss shoes, hats, and coats. "Blue or beige," says one next to him. They have light, bright spring cares. On the corner of Leipziger Strasse the bourgeoisie mixes with a shadier class. Two corner cafés: a gathering spot for the darkest underworld; a rendezvous spot for genteel townswomen. People sniff around for opportunities. They hock loot. The newcomer sits and drinks a cheap cup of coffee. Ladies rest after shopping. Lambeck loved Gendarmenmarkt. He went through Mohrenstrasse and turned into the garment district. He ended up by the wool and silk shops, where people were weaving and stitching. "Dear God, in these times." Courtyards full of type-writers, ink, and books beginning with God and ending with a deficit. About money in ages past. On the right, a Catholic church and an old chestnut tree, recognizable even without its buds; otherwise a tree is a tree in Berlin, except for the lindens in June, which can be recognized by their smell. Generals whose names are held aloft by angels of peace. Because of the great artist? The victory? The era? The arsenal. Heads of dying warriors. Schlüter.[4] What a German fate! His equestrian monument—the greatest of its time—was unknown to the rest of the world, and he was treated shamefully and died penniless in exile. His widow, lacking a pension or any means, was rebuffed when she entreated the king. In that same era, an era that glorified the artist, Bernini was ennobled, heaped with honors and riches; a great man, a rich man who left behind millions. Mansard was made a count by Louis XIV. "From mighty Frederick's throne she went forth, inglorious, spurned."[5] Who wrote that again? "Come along, Cohn!" Fontane said, because Köckeritz and Itzenplitz hadn't turned up.[6] Artists in Germany! What a topic! There: Otto Gebühr, von Rauch, Helmholtz, Treitschke, Mommsen, and the two Humboldts = Germany. "Victi," said the nationalists, "will always stand; sound to the core, a healthy land," Heinrich Heine rhymed.[7] Universities and libraries. Youth in the budding garden, enamored of discussion, beginning with a search for links between Goethe's color theory, Egyptian architecture, and Marxism, and culminating in a thesis on the Gothic letter *E*. One sported white-blonde hair with a middle part, braids over her ears, and a white peasant blouse. She got on her bike; next to her stood young people in hemp shirts. Two gentlemen walked ahead of him. "The Lunapark is opening on the first," one of them said. I'll write about the Lunapark, Otto Lambeck thought, and walked slowly over the street to Ewest's wine bar on Behrenstrasse. He sat down in a beautifully shaped room paneled with dark wood. The walls, on which large paintings hung, were covered with red velvet. On the left, the old emperor, on the right, Emperor Frederick. Old Holstein ate here, Otto Lambeck thought; it's a museum that's preserved the atmosphere of another time. It was a different world. We were devout and proud, servants who worshipped uniforms. We respected authority. The Congress of the Three Emperors at

Sosnowiec.[8] It was a good idea to take the job, and I can just write from life. I don't know if I can give an interpretation. But where to begin?

Meise had prepared his expense report for investigating a murder. One murder investigated = 9 marks. Car to corpse = 3 marks. Car back from corpse = 3 marks. Several glasses of schnapps, due to nausea upon viewing corpse = 3 marks.

The boss received the bill. He pushed his glasses down and peered over them.

"I can't sign this," he said.

Gohlisch came in. Young Gross, a new reporter, said that a terrible romantic tragedy had taken place. The corpse in the lake, which had been sought for days, had been thrown into the water by her jealous husband.

"Well," said Gohlisch. "Copulation is a highly overrated business, but I predict it will continue to have a bright future."

"I'll go to the counter with my bill," said Meise.

"I'm curious as to whether they'll reimburse you for that," said Gohlisch, going over to Miermann's desk, where Miss Kohler was also sitting. Miermann was about to put on his coat.

"I have to go," he said.

Gohlisch contemplated Miermann with a fatherly mien. Dear Lord, he thought, he isn't just going to throw himself into an adventure, is he? What will become of that? He's not ready for it. He used to sit here all the time, now he's always prowling around. I want to write an epic about Miermann, I want to be his biographer, the biographer of a humanist and a square who acts as if nothing human were unknown to him. What will happen to this clever man who blossomed around 1900? Girls will laugh at him. Girls think feelings are silly.

"Kids, you're making me fret," he said to Miss Kohler. "Miermann is throwing himself into affairs that don't become him, and you're hung up on that stupid Meyer, that crooked-mouthed, bleary-eyed nancy."

"I'm not hung up in the slightest. Don't throw in the towel with the bathwater. He loves me too."

"Perhaps. Does he write you?"

"No. But he doesn't write anybody."

"Then I'd chuck out the baby too. But I'm more worried about Miermann."

"Why? Isn't it nice that he's waiting for a phone call and has a bright, light spring dream?"

"Oh, I don't know."

"Come on, just let it be."

Miermann was sitting in the room he had acquired through great effort. A desk with carvings and twirling columns. Red wool curtains hung in front of the doors; red cloth with velvet trim covered the windows. A bed in the corner; a chaise longue covered with a velvet blanket with a Turkish pattern; a sideboard with German Renaissance-style carvings and a small bookshelf, black oak, with green glass and pink sea lilies. Miermann sat on the chaise longue and waited. It had taken him just eight days to get the room. He lifted the blanket on the chaise longue; underneath were old boxes with a mattress on top. The landlady smiled.

"Yes, of course, sir," she said. "No one else lives here."

And now he wanted to go and meet Käte. That evening, he would take her to the theater, to dinner, and then ...! If she could, she'd said. She was getting divorced. One had to see. The whole affair had been going on for three weeks now. And still no kiss. Miermann walked slowly back to the office. Käte was from the year 1919. She was a *garçonne*. She had married a pedant when she was young. She was generous, prone to extravagance. He was a bureaucrat and pestered her more than was necessary. She was the opposite of a Prussian. She considered order, parsimony, self-control, and obedience the root of all evil. She flirted in protest, spent money in protest. She overvalued everything she couldn't have: nice clothes, entertainment, and education. Her marriage was without erotic delights. And so, when she met Miermann, she was seeking intellectual formation and professional advancement; she wanted her ambitions satisfied, her femininity acknowledged; and, of course, she was seeking social status. She was seeking.

She was a gymnastics teacher with a large, willowy figure. She had red hair, the piglet-like complexion of redheads, and an exceedingly intelligent face with a large nose.

Miermann had never met a completely independent woman of this type. She moved fast, got to know everybody, attended lectures, worked intently, and was incredibly intelligent, amusing, and witty, though completely unartistic. She found everything in this world phony: marriage, family, the state, the economy. She saw the downsides; she was against contentment. She was against most things. Happiness? Happiness was something that people convinced themselves of. She was a ferment. She was an armchair revolutionary. She liked communism, but would have felt very unhappy in a farmer's jacket.

Needless to say, Miermann was enchanted by this new animated spirit. He felt understood. And beyond being delighted by his new companion, there was the significant matter of epidermal love. He longed to be conjoined with her as he had never longed before.

But that evening, the beautiful Käte Herzfeld had gone to the theater with another man. The play was tiresome. Her gymnastics lessons weren't catching on. She was out of sorts. The man in the tuxedo with whom she went was an old acquaintance. He had once loved her sister, who was older than Käte by six years. Even then, he had been a gentleman. Twelve-year-old Käte was sometimes allowed to say hello or ask him for something. Once, he had tied the bow of her sailor's blouse on her breast, not without letting her notice that he'd felt it.

He was pleasant and took her out; he had good manners and a stream of money that flowed to him without having to struggle for it. He sent her flowers, an Easter egg, a Christmas present with poetry. He knew the world, had been as far as Africa, Asia, and America, the Excelsior on the Lido, the Savoy in London, and the Crillon in Paris. He didn't live there anymore. He far preferred the white, classicist Hôtel des Bains to the Excelsior's romantic, chintzy, faux-Moorish castle. In Paris, he took rooms in a small hotel on the Left Bank where the French nobility loved to stay. In Berlin, he stayed in a rented apartment on Matthäikirchstrasse with his mother. If you asked him why he didn't move into a house, a house truly furnished to his taste, he would reply that what he needed, a truly representative house from the eighteenth century, even one from as late as 1830, was simply no longer to be found in Berlin. And everything else was trash.

Fritz Oppenheimer called up Miss Käte Herzfeld roughly every six months. He then took her out, replete with every extravagance that delights a woman. She was out of sorts. He didn't notice.

"What can I do for you?" he asked.

"Shall we dine somewhere?"

"In the Bristol, or would you prefer Lutherstrasse?"

"Lutherstrasse's fine."

The maître d'hôtel at Lutherstrasse knew him. He was an elegant gentleman with white sideburns. Taken just as he was, from another era, the fact that he did not wear pumps was a grave error in style. The maître d'hôtel knew Mr. Oppenheimer. He called him Attorney Oppenheimer, though that was fifteen years ago and Oppenheimer had served on just one bench, a long time ago. Oppenheimer always ordered the right thing. He always knew what should be eaten where, and, more importantly, what one should drink where.

"Dear child," he said, "shall we order a bottle of Haut Sauterne?" He found her delightful. She noticed that he found her delightful.

"You're a cute little bug, great dress, super. Werderscher? —No? —Oh, does one shop on Kurfürstendamm these days? Funny—you want to work there? —What, —every day?"

"Yes, fancy that."

"With such a pretty little red head? Funny. And so nicely filled-out, such a tasty morsel! Funny. Please keep sitting like that, no, like that, half in profile, excellent! I'd definitely have married you if the thought had ever crossed my mind."

"Why are you discussing marriage with everyone lately?"

"I feel like it."

"Where shall we go now?"

"To the Königin?"

"Yes, fine."

In the car, he took her hand and stroked it tenderly.

"Does that feel good? Yes? That too? Yes? Are you excited? Yes?"

Oppenheimer's a real scream, Käte thought.

The car stopped in front of the Königin. Käte smoothed down her clothes. A new life had begun. She had finally escaped the cage she'd been in for ten years. At the Königin, they met the painter Zimbella Kastro, a lady from Paris; that is to say, a woman from Alsace, which is almost Germany.

"How're you doing?" asked Käte.

"Oh," Kastro said. "I was supposed to have a show, I'd already assembled the paintings. But there was no one around to frame my paintings, so I wrote to my friend in Finland. And he came, but he's so disappointed in me."

"How long has it been since you last saw him?"

"Twenty years."

"And he came from Finland just to frame your paintings?"

"Why not. Is it very far?"

"I think so. Are you staying here for a while?"

"No, I'm going to Dalmatia in a few days with my child, to paint."

"Oh, you have a child?"

"Yes, I see you're surprised by the news. I am, too. But I bore one. Although when I went to pick it up from the nursery, my infallible maternal instinct had me grab the wrong one."

"I'll ring you soon."

Then they ran into Margot Weissman, the consul's wife, who danced by.

"Hello Margot, how nice to see you. I've been meaning to ring you for ages, I've felt awfully guilty about it."

"Oh yes, me too, my dear. Are you rid of him yet?"

"Not quite."

"Be careful."

"It's going very smoothly."

"Talk soon."

"Yes, definitely. Give me a call sometime!"

"Now there's a terrible snob," said Käte, but Oppenheimer was uncomprehending.

"She's a nice lady, though," he said. "She has some beautiful Frankenthal, by the way. We recently got into quite a scuffle over a kakemono."

There were many dancers on the ballroom floor who would have been better served doing something else. But there were two girls, in white and gold, who were so beautiful that it was worth sitting here for their sake alone. The ballroom was warm and cozy, invitingly divided into alcoves and booths. Many ridiculous women and men shook each other's hands and said, "Good evening, how are you?"... and "I'll give you a call sometime,"... or, "How nice to see you, I've been meaning to call you for ages, I've felt terribly guilty about it." The day had long since turned to deep night. Ads for clubs catering to out-of-town husbands blinked along Kurfürstendamm. Blonde flesh behind the bar. A sweet face and young men who sought rapture and ended up with a hangover. A gentleman from the country was passionately caught up with a girl. Käte would have liked to tell his wife that she shouldn't take it to heart, even if it was grounds for divorce. These kinds of situations were common here and had no air of sin about them.

They walked out, retrieved their jackets from the coat check, got into a car, and were driven to a petit-bourgeois house. Somewhere on Steinmetzstrasse, or maybe Zossener. A figure opened the door with a cheeky grin. There were many wardrobes in the hallway. There was a damp, acrid scent, like a waiting room or a housing office. Neither Oppenheimer nor Käte would ever have set foot in an apartment like this. But Oppenheimer didn't find it particularly unpleasant.

"Nice and petit-bourgeois, isn't it?"

The figure opened the door once more and asked, "Would you care for something to drink?"

"No, thank you."

Things felt awkward. But as Käte often said, "The ultimate things between a man and a woman are, for the woman, only a matter of attitude, an affair to be undertaken with grace and dignity."

Oppenheimer was annoyed with himself. But he had been ac-quainted with countless women from his sixteenth year onward, always had money in his pockets, and had never been stingy with it. He drove Käte back to her two furnished rooms.

Käte hadn't spent the evening with Miermann. He called her the next day, at noon.

"How are you?"

"Fine, thanks," said Käte.

"Really?"

"Yes, of course. I have five new students, and I had an amusing evening."

"Where were you yesterday? I tried to reach you but you weren't around."

"At the theater: *The Wife.*"

"How did you like it?"

"A real piece of garbage. As if it mattered whether the husband had a girlfriend or not."

"But the acting was good?"

"Sometimes. But Mosheim is too maudlin and wears the most awful clothes."

"I didn't notice. I thought she looked lovely."

"Oh no, she's far too sentimental."

"I don't think so, she's quite soulful."

"Well, perhaps she has a bit too much soul! Either way, I can't stand her."

"Perhaps you're right, but overall, quite a delightful evening."

"Not for me. How are you?"

"I'm in trouble."

"I'm so sorry, darling, is it work?"

"Not on the phone."

"No one can guess what we're talking about. All this caution has made you overly suspicious."

"When will I see you?"

"I'm going to the academy ball tonight."

"I can't do evenings. Can't we squeeze it in earlier? Between three and four would be best."

"Fine, where?"

"Not in the newspaper district."

"Let's say Hilbrich's."

"No, too many ladies!"

"Leon?"

"Still too close to the papers. Dönhoffplatz is off limits."

"Hausvogteiplatz."

"I don't feel so good about that either. There's a small café on Mauerstrasse, right by Leipziger."

"Fine, that works. At three then."

Käte wanted a well-situated apartment around Kurfürstendamm for her gymnastics school. She would have to pay the previous tenant to vacate the apartment, then renovate and furnish it; or she'd have to rent furnished rooms. She didn't get a moment's rest all day. It was no great hardship to drive to Mauerstrasse at noon for a rendezvous. Miermann was very respectful, but boring. How long should she keep waiting? They had good conversations, but he hadn't gotten much farther than a caress every now and then.

Käte rang Margot that afternoon to discuss the ball.

"I think we're going back to being proper again," Margot said. "Not quite so naked. What's with the main line?"

"Nothing."

"He isn't interested?"

"He is."

"But?"

"I don't know whether he's that maladroit. Recently, he told me he wanted to put me on a pedestal."

"If I even hear the word pedestal!"

"Yes, it made me sick too."

"And the supporting cast?"

"Going quite briskly, thanks. I was out with O. yesterday."

"O.?"

"Matthäikirchstrasse."

"Oh, that one."

"Yes, he's still dating a model. She's probably faithful these days, but tiresome. He snatched her away from a guards officer twenty-five years ago. The whole affair was quite improbable; it all happened before 1913."

"So I'll see you tonight. Why don't you enjoy your freedom for a bit, then get married. Marriage is best, believe me. Why make such a fuss over silly gymnastics?"

"I don't want to get married. I couldn't bear it, even with the man of my dreams! So, what about the outfit? I was going to wear long pants and a sort of vest."

"That's good for you. You can emphasize your figure, I have to pay attention to my skin—I'll look for something with a décolleté."

"So tonight at the academy, ten o'clock."

"Ten o'clock is a bit early."

"Everything will be taken later. Don't you want something new?"

"Yes, but only if we've been introduced."

"I'm looking for adventure. Come by my place at ten."

They arrived and waited by the coat check for a quarter of an hour. It was drafty and cold. Inside, the fray was thickening.

"Oh, you're here," said a dancer from Käte's past. "How's it going?"

"Vertically excellent, so not taking bids on the horizontal."

"I'm reorganizing the Vienna Ballet."

"Congratulations."

"But I might stay here for a while?" he asked purposefully.

"No, my dear, it's been over for seven years."

"Look over there, see that girl in blue? She's living with Krause now."

"Is she divorced?"

"Oh, nonsense. Her husband lives with Korb from the Linke-Theater."

"Do people know that?"

"Of course, the whole world! It's quite official. They live together."

"What, all four of them?"

"Yes."

A man came over to the table.

"Charming, charming," he gestured to her naked back, "may I give you a kiss?"

She stood up and disappeared over the stairs in a sea of masks. Winkler the banker came by and kissed her hand, between her fingers.

"You still have your sweet girl's face, but you must be a great beast by now."

"I'm afraid not," she said. "My greatest mistake."

"A dance?"

"Yes."

His hands moved down her body and were satisfied.

"Listen, why should we stay here? Let's get a car, drive into the wintery night."

"No, I'm staying here."

"You're a fool," he said, stamping his foot. "You know I can't stand women who play hard to get." He was furious. She couldn't afford to lose him; neither his counsel nor his credit. Moreover, she didn't want to lose him because she liked him; he was a good friend. She smiled.

"It's unbelievable that you're still living in those furnished rooms, with your income," she said. "I'm hoping to get a beautiful apartment for myself soon. You should come by then."

"Yes," he said, already distracted.

"Strange," she said a few hours later, "I only ever have relationships with men I don't love."

"What!" he cried, feigning outrage. "You don't love me?"

"Most certainly not."

"Well, that's just swell. I love you passionately, profoundly, eternally," he cried, laughing. It would have been ironic even several minutes ago. But now that he had learned that she was taking this lightly, that there were no consequence for him, he began to love her and take her seriously. And he embraced her. As she was covered with caresses, she asked herself if this second-rate love might not be far preferable to a first-rate one. But as he stood in front of the mirror, turned, and proudly asked her whether his torso wasn't well built, she thought with a sigh that torso and well built were simply too much, and was anxious to get home.

Once again, Otto Lambeck had had an idea for a great drama. Why does it always have to be petty woes, orphanages, paragraph 218,[9] while the *dernier cri* is history, sex, and more sex? he thought. I want to put a hero on stage who'll make men marvel and young girls swoon.

He strolled over Kurfürstendamm on a clear March evening. The asphalt shimmered. The street lamps cast a haze of light over the spring trees. The longing of the many couples lounging on benches drifted from the Tiergarten. Ladies in fresh pale suits sat in front of cafés, wearing little hats on their little heads, drinking iced coffee and iced chocolate with straws. They were superbly manicured and massaged and creamed and rouged and whitened. Lambeck took in the air scented with freedom, brashness, and benzene. One-legged men sat on the stone terrace of a large hotel. The pavilion, bar, parlor, and roof garden where Lene Nimptsch had lived and Dörr's nursery had been. *Trials and Tribulations*.[10] Moving advertisements, a church, a waving constable. Cars, cars, cafés for watching the world go by and quiet cafés for love. The Kapitol lit up in pink, purple, and red. Cinemas, cafés, restaurants, palaces, marble, Gloria and the Königin, champagne, fine clothes, the Charleston and jazz, grub joints with bright salads and artichokes, flips and cobblers, red, green, and yellow lights, snake and crocodile, ermine and sable, silk and lace, varnished booths where beauty is forged from steam, a fatted hand, and crackling electric current for the furry creatures with their pink legs, reddened mouths, purses and eyes searching for men under the trees, which have shriveled up from a winter of longing for March. An American restaurant: bright, friendly, the image of an optimistic continent. You can drink something here with a straw, milk and coffee, for instance—they call it *frappé*. And his series? Where would he find inspiration?

"Good evening," said a young man he didn't know. "You don't

seem to recognize me. I had the honor of being introduced to you in the newsroom recently. My name is Frächter." Lambeck was angry; couldn't he have run into anyone else on this soft spring evening other than this dandified armchair radical? But Lambeck, who was a man easily inclined to overestimate people and their accomplishments, didn't think, Here's a journalist of the lowest rank. He thought, generously, Perhaps it's unfair of me to dislike him.

The young man walked beside Otto Lambeck. Lambeck hardly thought him pushy after a few minutes, although everyone else would have considered this an affront: this stranger had spoken to the great poet and was now walking beside him. Indeed, the humble man even asked, "Will you drink a cup of coffee with me, Mr. Frächter?"

Frächter and Lambeck sat down on the western side of Kurfürstendamm.

"In the office, I was told that you plan to write a series of articles on Berlin, and that this extraordinary essay on Lunapark was the first one."

"Yes, Dr. Waldschmidt asked, and I didn't want to turn him down."

And one thousand marks for one article doesn't hurt, Frächter thought.

"It's not that easy to write about Berlin. The best people have already ripped their hair out trying. It may only be possible in the movies."

"Film, for me, remains an instrument I am unable to use. Even on stage, it's not exactly easy to see how quickly individuals can take on the appearance of idiosyncratic actors. But photography, devoid of the human voice, human reality... —I think that film can do a great deal, and I can't speak highly enough of Chaplin's propaganda for the simple, suffering man. But I'm still afraid."

"You shouldn't be afraid. Think of everything film can express that the spoken or written word can't. By the way, there's an excellent book that was just published."

Dusk had passed. The lights had finally gained their right to shine.

"As I said, I'm currently writing about Berlin. I would have never dreamed that it would be so difficult to find material on my own."

"Did you happen to read a recent article on a singer, written by a young journalist, Gohlisch, I think?"

"No, where was it published?"

"In the *Berliner Rundschau*. About eight days ago, very well written."

"I would greatly appreciate it if you could send it to me."

Frächter was over the moon. This was his ticket to fame and riches. He had gotten in touch with Otto Lambeck; on top of that, he'd had coffee with him; on top of that, he'd given him a tip! He'd interview him, he'd publish "Walking with Otto Lambeck," he'd talk about him on the radio and get two hundred marks for sure. He was flying high again. He was thrilled with himself.

Otto Lambeck stood up.

"It's been a true pleasure," the polite man said.

Frächter bowed. "Do allow me to send you the article."

He sent it. On the next evening, Lambeck went to see the singer with Miss Kohler, whom he had known for quite some time. Lambeck loved public transportation.

Miss Kohler said, "Cars are litters, I always think of Heine: 'She stares out grandly at the common masses walking as her carriage passes.'[11] The only meaningful paths are the ones we traverse on foot. The people of Berlin are wonderful. You have to take the Aboag or the subway to really get to know them."[12]

"Yes," said Lambeck.

Kohler thought, with all due respect, that Lambeck didn't make it easy. They stepped off at Hasenheide. A light mist hung over the bushes. It was feeding time at the zoo in the first joint. For one cup of coffee, or even a soda, you got bears of all sorts. Hundreds of people sat under the massive roof of the theater, eight to a table. A liter of water for coffee cost one mark. The pot stood on the table. Enormous cases of beer and sandwiches, as well as fruit. Families. Colorful voile was the order of the day. The wine section was on a raised platform. A young couple drank no more and no less than an entire bottle of Malaga together. At one table, a couple had two bottles of Haut Sauterne standing before them. The young folks were doing it in style. It was a Saturday night, just before the first of the month, and spring was on its way.

A play was being acted out on stage according to the "just in time" principle. A couple fights. The father-in-law appears just in time. But the father, rather than the son-in-law, turns out to be having an affair. Just then, a soubrette enters. A baby is put in the arms of the wrong father. The audience howled. The show had been sold out for days. There were no ambiguities. The whole thing was incredibly ham-fisted. But it made them happy. Half an hour from Potsdamer Platz: Anno Domini 1900. Rococo salons and trumeaux prevailed.

A virginal pair, white, green, and silver. A Grecian dove balancing act. A dozen doves. The vestal girl placed the doves on her little head and shoulders, let them flap about. The boy formed a bridge. Doves crawled over his stomach and back, through his legs, and returned to his head. He seemed immune to tickling. The crowd listened to "My Faithful Little Dove." By then the man in the tuxedo had already come out and sat himself down on a chair whose one leg was stuck in a bottle.

"Wow, that's really something," said a specialist in bodily dexterity, perhaps a carpenter or roofer.

"Ridiculous," said Miss Kohler. "It denies all humanity and, because of that, it's unbearably sad. Dexterity for dexterity's sake, as a way of filling your days, is embarrassing—it's not for fun, *recréation,* which implies rebirth, renewal. We slide back into the Middle Ages when we take someone else's mortal peril for an amusing diversion. It's the same as burning people at the stake in the village square."

"You usually have a sense for symbolism. This is about grabbing the right rope, an action that is doubtlessly instructive. Let's wait for the main act."

The gentleman on the slackline wasn't bad either. He picked up a handkerchief with his teeth, carried a table, and rode a unicycle. This was honest work. Standing on a wire and picking up a handkerchief with one's teeth had nothing to do with death. Gravity was no longer victorious, it no longer bent the human body, that most sublime of instruments, into a crooked shape. Instead, man knew, and laughed at destiny. So far, nothing more had come of it than him lifting a round pine table high over his head with one foot on the wire, but something still could! It could!

Then at last came the main act: it was Käsebier, Käsebier himself, and he sang! First, something new. "If You Wanna Come with Me, Come with; and If You Don't, Go Your Way Alone."

Then, "Boy, Isn't Love Swell?" And finally: "How Can He Sleep with That Thin Wall?" Oh, what a fellow, how he suffered, standing there, crying, "Oh God, oh God, oh God, oh God, oh God—I'm sad." There he stood, wrinkles drooping, a faithful hound with hanging ears. And then: "Oh God, oh God, oh God, oh God, oh God— life's grand." Kicking his legs, corners of the mouth turned up, blissful eyelids, ears perked up. Käsebier was no Adonis, no Harry Liedtke, no Menjou.[13] He didn't make the girls swoon; he most certainly did not embody any erotic ideal. He was short, blond, fat, and flabby, with a snout, almost a mug. In the background: the Fortress of Ehrenbreitstein, a vine-covered roof, and a moon veiled in mist; next to him, Hedy, who could have been Claire Waldoff's younger sister.[14] The banks of the Rhine. A love song: "We had our first kiss..." It didn't go much farther. The audience believed him, felt heavenly longing, even if their spouses' hands were groping for their effects. Dr. Kohler would have liked Lambeck to do the same. Lambeck would have scorned it. So she hid her primitive feelings. Then Käsebier almost punctured the dream of the Rhine and the moon with a wavering tone; he came back with a little toy apron and a hoop, and sang all of our childrens' songs: "Fox, You Stole the Goose," "Little Hans," "Little Mary Sat on a Stone," "A Dwarf Stands in the Woods," "All the Birds." He bawled, "I do-hon't know what it mea-hea-heans," fresh, bold, out of tune. Too fat and too blond, a snout, almost a mug, he comforted fathers, mothers, and children, blood of the blood of this city. To ensure his place as the darling of the people, he sang an encore: "I'm dancing the Charleston and he's dancing the Charleston and she's dancing the Charleston—what about you?" What's the Charleston got to do with anything, five minutes away from Reichenberger Strasse, where they string up wires for wild grapes on the balconies after they get home from work and father has to be cooked for, patched, and washed? In unison, they sang, "I'm gettin' stamped and he's gettin' stamped and she's gettin' stamped—what about you?"[15]—"I need dough and he needs dough and she needs dough—what about you?"

"That's reason, this divine ratio," Dr. Kohler said to Lambeck. "He doesn't shriek about his pains for his coffee or bread and butter for an evening's entertainment. Instead, he sings. That's the answer. A chorus instead of a cheap thrill."

"Although we've long searched in vain," said Lambeck, "we've finally found irony, gallows humor, and the bliss of company."

6

A star is born

LAMBECK'S play opened eight days later. It was almost too late, as
March had already begun. Dr. Kohler found it terribly dull, a failure,
a total flop. How should she react? Gentility prevailed. She called
up Otto Lambeck.

"It was very nice," she said.

"You can go ahead and say it was a total flop. They're saying I'm
exhausted, finished, done. That I've always been a bit overrated
anyways. A reporter at a big-time newspaper called me senile, completely senile. 'After all that,' Ixo said, 'it's best we stick to the plot,'
and then he stuck to the plot. I won't even repeat what Öchsli wrote.
I don't want to discuss it anymore. I'm working on a new play now.
It's about an inheritance."

How awful, a play about an inheritance, Dr. Kohler thought.

"Oh," she said.

"Yes," he said. "I found the story in a sixteenth-century French
chronicle."

"Oh," she said. Why does this man, who has an unparalleled
knowledge of contemporary life, always pick such silly topics? He
uses sixteenth-century chronicles instead of police reports. Tragic,
she thought.

"Have you written about Käsebier yet?"

"Yes, I've begun."

He's like an ant, she thought once she'd hung up. His work may
get trampled, but he'll start right up again.

Otto Lambeck wrote about Käsebier. He described what he'd

seen and heard, and called him "underrated," a word that Gohlisch had already used.

The article appeared in the morning edition of the *Berliner Tageszeitung*.

That evening, Blumenthal the agent phoned up the cabaret director at the Primus Palace.

"Have you read Lambeck's article in the *Berliner Tageszeitung*? Listen, what a find! Don't you want to pin him down now?"

"Get out of here! Just cause a poet likes it."

"I'll have you know I've got a good nose. Right now, you can get that man for fifty marks a night. In three months, you'll have to pay three hundred."

"Get out of here," said the director.

At eleven o'clock on the following day, Lambeck's phone rang.

"This is Dr. Zwörger calling from the studio. Am I speaking to the master himself?"

"Yes," said Lambeck.

"My good sir, you wrote an article on Käsebier for the *Berlin Tageszeitung*. All of Berlin is abuzz. He's your find. I'm calling with a request. Would you be willing to interview Käsebier on the radio?"

"What do you want me to do?" Lambeck asked.

"Interview Käsebier."

"But I'm not a journalist, I have a terrible voice, and my reactions are rather slow. I'm not at all suited to such a task."

"Let me put it differently. Would you be willing to have a discussion with Käsebier the singer on the radio?"

"No, I won't do that either. But Doctor, please don't take this as my general attitude toward radio. I am an adherent of this extraordinary—I might even say world-changing—invention."

"Would you be inclined to hold a small lecture on him, about twenty minutes long?"

"Yes, I could do that."

"Perhaps Friday, in four days."

"That seems a bit too soon. I need to prepare. But I'd happily do it for next Friday."

"Let me see if we can add it in on Friday. One moment, please—good, Friday it is."

On Friday, March 10, Otto Lambeck talked about Käsebier on the radio. He called him "underrated," as he had already done in his essay, and as Gohlisch had.

After that, there was no stopping it. Fritz Grönemann wrote a long article in the *Weltschau* and likened the singer to the finest Parisian traditions. Otto Magnus wrote a short article for *Excelsior*, the magazine for modern living. Countess Bloomsiek wrote about him in the elegant right-wing newspaper, which was no different from the elegant left-wing newspaper. Here was a fundamentally German talent, she wrote, a sort of court minstrel and popular poet rolled into one, an extraordinary union of natural musicality and popular humor.

The *Rote Stern* wrote that this man was doubtlessly talented, but that his lyrics attested to the foolish glorification of a declining class, a fact that made it impossible for class-conscious workers to seek out such pleasure palaces.

"He has a profane tongue. His close connection to the people of Berlin (and not to the proletariat as a class!) is due only to his charisma."

"He portrays characters from the street and the underworld with such exceptional remove that indecency and double entendres no longer seem like subjective expressions, but attain objective form through art; thus, they are robbed of their moral danger," the *Zentrumszeitung* opined.

The exceedingly brilliant critic of the *Flamme* wrote, "Käsebier is talented, but he falls short of genius. He lacks the transcendental touch that the metaphysical realm bestows upon the talented artist, and which anoints him as genius." He continued, "Although Mr. Ixo has deemed him a brother to Guilbert, this is far from correct. Käsebier is a natural talent, but he readily slips into banalities when his subject exceeds the everyday—a slick banality that I personally value less than a raw cry wrenched from the breast of struggling youth."

The *Völkische Aufgang* wrote, "Once again, a talent is praised to high heavens by the Jewish tabloids. The lackeys in the pay of Mr. Moses Isaak Waldschmidt are raving about things they don't understand. Repugnant foreign Jews, plagued with hundreds of oversophisticated thoughts, abuse the German language to praise a socialist who is debasing our people's greatest treasure, the folk song, and misusing it for his own vain ambitions."

The illustrated magazines in Cologne and Munich ran articles on him featuring five to seven pictures.

7

Frächter publishes a book on Käsebier

TWO DAYS later, word had spread that Käsebier was to appear at the Wintergarten. But the rumor was premature.

Frächter offered the middling regional papers a series of articles on Käsebier. Leipzig, Breslau, Cologne, Dortmund, and Tilsit accepted. Ten pfennigs per line.

Frächter frequented the Romanisches Café in the evenings. Willy Frächter was very tall and had blond pomaded hair that was somewhat long at the nape. He was from Gotha.

The Romanisches Café is across from the Gedächtniskirche, and consists of a swimmer's and non-swimmer's section. The swimmers sit to the left of the revolving door, the non-swimmers to the right.[16] The Romanisches Café is filthy. First, it is as smoky as befits an intellectual haven despite its large windows; second, it is dirty because of the habits of its guests, who constantly throw the remains of their smokes to the ground; and third, because of the enormous number of guests. This café is a home for many. Hungarians, Poles, Yugoslavs, Russians, Chechens, Slovakians, Ruthenians, Danes, Bohemians, Austrians, Balts, Latvians, Lithuanians, Serbians, Romanians, as well as the great flock of Jews from the east whose minds were opened in Berlin—they all come here to meet their fellow countrymen. That's the way it is in Berlin: the censuses may be interested in Americans, but most immigrants come to Berlin from the East, along with the occasional Dutchman or Dane. No one makes much of it, but Berlin is one hundred kilometers away from the Polish border. Berlin is a suburb of the northeast, just as Vienna is one of the southeast. Berlin is not a fashionable capital, like Paris or Rome or London, where the

British, the Americans, the Spaniards and the French "go sightseeing" in the spring, or take a summer "trip." One comes to Berlin from the East to find work, make music, film, and paint, act on stage, write, direct, sculpt; sell cars, paintings, property, land, carpets, antiques; open stores, shoe stores, clothing stores, perfume stores; starve and study. Everyone sits in the Romanisches Café, first in the non-swimmer's section, then in the swimmer's section. They all talk and curse.

Willy Frächter was sitting in the swimmer's section with Heinrich Wurm, and was telling Wurm how successful his series on Käsebier had been. Heinrich Wurm said that he was currently writing about various construction projects in Berlin. A swimming pool, for example. He'd also heard that the houses on Spandauerstrasse, Stralauerstrasse, and Jüdenstrasse would be torn down.

"All of them?" Frächter asked.

"Of course, what else are they going to do with those dumps? They're going to build huge office buildings, nine stories high, made only of glass and this new stuff called Pathetix. Then they'll put up a hotel with a thousand rooms that all look the same and cost seven marks a night, right where the Kaiser-Wilhelm-Gedächtniskirche is. Two architects developed the project, Grützekopf and Hobel. I've already sold the story to the *Allgemeine Zeitung*."

"Sure," said Frächter. "The regional papers don't pay as well, but there are a lot more to choose from. I never want to be on staff at a Berlin newspaper."

"Oh, come on, Frächter."

"Well, it might be a different story if I could get a spot at the *Berliner Tageszeitung*. But really, do you think those moronic editors could appreciate someone with a gift for politics? I've been living quite well off my short stories," he continued. "I write two per month and can live where I want. I've gone from Ireland to Greece, even to the Soviet Union, and it's always worked out. I've never had to write more than two, but I wanted to live in Berlin for a while. You have to take advantage of capitalism while it's still hot; I'm already in it up to my neck. I had dinner with Lambeck recently, and he also told me that one should have lived in Berlin at some point."

He waited for Wurm to look impressed. Wurm did indeed, but replied, "By the way, do you know that WTB and TU[17] decided to report on Käsebier today? He's going to appear at the Wintergarten. A second Yvette Guilbert."

"I actually discovered him."

"How so?"

"I brought him to Lambeck's attention."

"Damn, why didn't you write about that?"

"It's very difficult to get something like that out if you're not a cabaret critic. But now I'm going to publish a book on him."

"With whom?"

"I haven't nailed down a contract yet, but I think it'll work out."

Lieven swooped down on the table.

"Have you already gone to see Käsebier? He's simply magical. Nothing less than a natural genius. Only these idiots in Berlin, our most dimwitted critics, could overlook the greatest actor of our time."

"I discovered him," Frächter said.

Lieven jumped up and grasped both of Frächter's hands. "Please allow me to congratulate you. I envy you. I wish I had done so myself. What are journalists good for if not to discover and profile the great men and women of their time? Why take up the pen if not to pave the path for genius?"

Frächter got up.

"Excuse me for a moment," he said, and went to the telephone. He squeezed himself into the booth and called up Mohnkopp, a young publisher. "Listen, Mohnkopp, we've got to publish a book, *Käsebier.* I've heard rumors that he's coming to the Wintergarten."

"What a great idea. Where would be good to talk it over?"

"Meet me at Schwannecke tonight."

Frächter was at Schwannecke that evening. He'd come this far in just three weeks. A meeting at Schwannecke already![18] Yesterday, he'd still been at the Romanisches Café; yesterday, the bare floor had been covered in tobacco, cigarette, and cigar butts; marble tables, milky coffee, and two eggs in a glass; today, there was parquet with carpet, cozy booths, wine, a roast, and sauce béarnaise. Frächter arrived at eleven o'clock. Käte was sitting in the booth next to him with a lawyer. She was wearing a black evening dress with a rose. She looked good.

He waited. People came and went. The most famous guests were in the back room, celebrating a premiere. People came and went. Large men, small men, large women, small women, women with black hair, blonde hair, brown hair; Englishwomen, pale blonde and tall; Italian women, small, raven-haired, and colorful; a Japanese woman with slanted eyes and yellow skin; a blonde Prussian; a flabby French-woman; a slender, thin, tragic screen actor; a slim, blond, melancholy painter; a fat, short filmmaker; an ugly theater director. All of them ended up speaking Austrian, even the Japanese woman.

Mohnkopp arrived. Frächter ordered generously and was quickly in media res. The book was to be no longer than five folios, and would contain illustrations. Each copy would cost one and a half marks. And the advance? Frächter demanded a flat fee plus royalties.

"Nah, can't do double," said Mohnkopp.

"So let's say an advance plus royalties."

Mohnkopp negotiated. He only wanted to give Frächter royalties, ten pfennigs per book.

"No. And I want two thousand marks in advance."

"Who's going to write it?" asked Mohnkopp.

"I'll ask celebrities to contribute short articles: poets, an actress, critics, journalists, sports figures, an industrial magnate, a government official. Let me take care of it. I'll sign on as editor. And what's more, there'll be a long article: 'Käsebier on Käsebier.' But I can't do it for less than two thousand marks up front. I guarantee it'll be a smash hit. That's why I want royalties."

They continued to bargain. Käte came over to their table.

"Have you already gone to see Käsebier?" Frächter asked.

"No," said Käte. "I've been putting it off every night. But I'll go tomorrow for sure. I hear it's so full-up you can't get in without an inside connection. Is he really that good?"

"Fantastic," said Frächter.

"Goodbye, darling," said Käte. "I'll ring you sometime."

"You see," said Frächter. "You see."

"My friend!" he called out to Augur, who was sneaking through the restaurant looking gloomy with his collar turned up, hatless, the latest newspapers tucked under his arm. "Have you been to Hasenheide yet?"

"Yes, it's worth going if you can take something like that seriously, it's worth it. Tempers are rising. The socialists want to approve the battleship."

"Yes, dreadful."

"I'll give you a call sometime."

"You see," said Frächter, "You see."

"You're something, all right," Mohnkopp laughed. "Fine, let's say a thousand marks and five percent."

"Done."

Frächter got on the phone the next day. First, he called up Käsebier and commissioned twenty pages on Käsebier, in addition to ten photographs, which would include Käsebier solo, Käsebier and wife, Käsebier at home.

"What do you like to do, Mr. Käsebier?"

"What'm I supposed to say?"

"Well, do you have birds?"

"Nope. Might have some bees in my bonnet, though."

"Any other zoological interests—I mean, dogs or cats?"

"Nope, just my wife."

"Any agricultural interests?"

"Nope."

"Do you have a summer house?"

"Nope."

"Do you play any sports?"

"Sure, I ride a bike."

"Fantastic. Let's get a picture of you on your bike."

"But I don't ride it all that often."

"Doesn't matter. Let's get a picture of you in a bicycle jersey."

"Well, the fellas are gonna love teasing me."

"No one's going to be teasing you once you're at the Wintergarten.

And six photos in costume. And don't write fewer than twenty pages for your biography. On a typewriter, single-sided. Six photos in costume, Mr. Käsebier!"

Frächter called up Gohlisch. "Dear Mr. Gohlisch, you simply must write five manuscript pages on Käsebier for me. Mohnkopp is publishing a book on Käsebier."

"And what're you doing?"

"I'm helping him with it."

"Well, aren't you hardworking."

"So you'll write something for us? I've got some first-rate folks on board. Not to mention Lambeck."

"Fine, I'll send you an article."

"How delightful, Mr. Gohlisch. You're the best local reporter in Berlin right now. I've read some first-rate stuff by you recently."

By evening, Frächter had put the book together.

8

The Paris correspondent of the Allgemeines Blatt *comes to Berlin*

"Well hello, pussycat."

"Marie Pantke speaking. Who's this?"

"What's with the fancy talk, Miss? Oskar Meyer here."

"Wow, Meyer. Since when?"

"This afternoon."

"Well, isn't that great news."

"How're you doing?"

"God, lousy. Too much work. Typical typist's life, work and more work."

"And the men?"

"No dice."

"Well then! Why don't we give it a shot?"

"It ain't gonna happen, mister."

"Let's forget about that and go out today anyway."

"I can't today."

"Why not? Tomorrow, then."

"Where?"

"Hasenheide."

"Gee, you came all the way from Paris just to take me out to Hasenheide, are you nuts?"

"Not at all, it's all the rage."

"You're kidding, Hasenheide? Listen, pal, I only go dancing at Mayakovsky's, I don't go south of Meinekestrasse."

"Fine, but let's eat at Stöckler's beforehand."

"Sure, I'm all for good eats."

"I'll pick you up around eight."

"It's a date."

"It's a date, darling."

"Hello, hello, Weissmann's."

"Is the lady of the house available? Meyer-Paris speaking."

"One moment, please."

"Margot Weissmann speaking."

"Oskar Meyer speaking."

"Oh, good day, Mr. Meyer, when did you get back?"

"Since this afternoon, my dear, and you're my very first call."

"I doubt that!"

"I beg your pardon, I'm thrilled to finally be speaking with a Berliner; my mother tongue, the sweet sounds of home."

"Well, shall we make a date right away? When can I have you over?"

"Let's talk about that another time. I'm planning an ambush. I want to meet you at nine o'clock, so guess where we're going."

"Käsebier!"

"Right on the money. So it's a good tip. Is there anything left to write about?"

"It doesn't matter what you write about it, only how you do it. Lambeck may have discovered him, but his article was a bit ponderous, as usual. So there's still lots of room for humor. Meyer-ish humor, of course. But nine is too late. I think we have to be there at eight if we don't know the right people."

"I have Käsebier's friend's card."

"All the same. Eight is better. Where are you?"

"In Halensee. Joachim-Friedrich-Strasse, as always."

"Come to Kurfürstendamm at half past seven and have a quick supper with me. My husband won't be coming with us, unfortunately, he has too much work right now. We'll easily make it there by eight with our car."

At half past seven, Meyer-Paris stood in front of Margot's house. They've slashed its belly open, he thought, God, these crazy architects are awful. The house, Wilhelmine baroque, had once featured a wooden door with windows on the upper half. The door had been enlarged up to the second floor, and was now made only of glass. It must be dreadful to walk up that steep staircase with the whole world watching, Meyer thought. He was relieved when he rang the bell on the first floor. There was a small vestibule on the right, just before the foyer. The foyer was made of red marble, and had fluted oak columns. Gilded Corinthian capitals over the doorway, painted bas-reliefs on top of them. Girls with hairstyles from the Gay Nineties wore pink, blue, and yellow chiffon, dancing a roundelay in a spring garden. A marble fountain stood in the middle of the room. It's as if I'm at my grandparents' house, but everything's from 1912, Meyer thought. He was led into the drawing room. Chippendale furniture, commodes, chairs, the walls hung with pink silk. Many sofas. Bulging cushions, Meyer thought, and was afraid to sit down. No matter how slender or small you were, it was always difficult to extract yourself from that much stuffing, and he mustn't dare topple into the lady of the house. He chose to stand. He studied Margot's portrait, which hung above the commode. Tasteful, he thought, which was indeed the intended effect. Blonde Margot in pale gray silk, looking quite unlike herself, painted from head to décolleté.

She waddled toward him in a friendly manner. "So, my dear, finally back, how are you? I'm just thrilled to see you! I have so much to tell you. Käte is in Berlin, have you heard? Well, if I tell you who she's carrying on with, you'll split your sides. But let's get going before it gets too late."

She drove. "Which way?"

"Ufer to Hallesches Tor, I think."

"Lovely, good." Oh God, I almost married that man, she thought. Might need to think about whether to go for the massage or not. I ran into Lotte Hoffmann recently; she looked so tired, so poorly dressed, so ugly, all because she's working so hard. But my life isn't all roses either. He's always exhausted at night, and it's not much fun for me, and he isn't very understanding. He thinks the dress from Hammer is too expensive, not to mention a new dressing room, although I can hardly get ready in front of my old mirror anymore.

"Well, Oskar, what is it?"

"I'm glad that you're looking so well, young lady."

"I always like to hear that, especially since I'm not that young anymore."

"You're fishing."

"Oh, you say that, but I often despair, Ossy, I'm . . . well, you know, we took dance lessons together thirty-two years ago."

"Thirty-four, Margot, to be exact."

"You wretch. Fine, thirty-four. Adolf is turning fifty soon. Who knows how long till I lose my charm. That's why I had the little one. I'd hoped it would make getting older easier. But it doesn't help much."

"But Margot, you're beautiful, rich, and elegant. You have a nice husband and a pretty kid. Are you just worried about lovers?"

"You underestimate love."

"And you overestimate it."

"Perhaps."

"Just don't say us two. Better you seek adventure within good bourgeois circles than with bohemians. Besides, you have no courage, my dear. With whom have you shared a pillow, if I might ask?"

"That's outrageous. One doesn't discuss such matters," she said, slightly piqued. She didn't know whether it was more desirable these days to have experienced a lot, or a little.

They had arrived. The car was stowed away. Another six cars were waiting. She wore a black dress under an incredibly thick muskrat fur. The dress made her look even thinner than she already was. She looked very dressed-up, though going to Hasenheide required a cheaper outfit.

Two dark figures stood outside. "Tickets here."

Meyer and Margot ignored them.

"Four marks apiece, you won't find any others, sir."

"Sold out." Some gentlemen were engaged in a shouting match with the cashier, while women in black rabbit fur waited impatiently.

"What nonsense!" one woman cried. "Just let us in."

The young man standing by the red rope at the entrance shrugged his shoulders and said, "Police."

"It's full-up," said an old man standing next to him.

"I'm not going anywhere, won't even consider it, you can stick a few more seats in there!" a fat man yelled.

"You're right, a few more seats. This is ridiculous," said a tall, thin man.

"You'd best leave it," said his wife. "It's not their fault there are no seats."

"Well, sure, but this madhouse is ridiculous."

"Come on, let's go."

"I'm not leaving, won't even think of it."

"I'm out of here," a very short man yelped at a high pitch across the room, as if he wanted to spite the world.

"I told you, we should have gotten here at seven," said Margot.

"This will be the first time I haven't gotten in somewhere," said Meyer. "Where's Mr. Gohlisch's table?" he asked the bouncer.

"I don't know, but I can't let you in, sir."

"'Scuse me, that gentleman is Mr. Käsebier's best friend. He's been saving two seats for me for an hour. I'll just take a quick peek."

The bouncer let him through. It was dark inside, and a girl was singing, "Wilted leaves, wilted leaves."

He looked for two chairs. It was very crowded, six to a table. The whole square hall was full. He found two seats on the upstairs balcony. Not great, but seats all the same. He politely reserved them, and bolted downstairs.

"Found my friends. There are two free seats on the upstairs balcony."

"I'll have to ask the manager first."

"Mr. Schwoller, the gentleman has two seats, can he still get tickets?"

"They're up to the left on the balcony, a friend reserved them for me. I'm happy to show them to you."

"Well, fine, you can still get tickets. If anyone makes a fuss, say they were reserved."

"Understood," said Meyer, pressed something into his hand, and went to the cashier.

Then the ruckus started.

"Why's that guy getting tickets?"

"Well, isn't this outrageous."

"Guess we're not fancy enough for Käsebier's parlor, huh?"

"I'm gonna complain."

"Where's the manager?"

"Well, this is a hoot."

"Says 'sold out' on the door, and now he's getting some. Unbelievable."

"They were reserved!" Meyer shouted.

"Yeah, right!"

"You little sneak, you!"

"Excuse me?"

"Who're you, anyway?"

"None of your business."

"I'm gonna complain."

Meyer had the tickets. "Gentlemen, I told you that they were reserved three days ago."

"In that case, everyone could've come."

"This is the last time I'm going to this joint."

Meyer quietly said to Margot, "Hurry up at the coat check, or we'll be lynched."

There was a blockade at the coat check. Honest men, average, upright citizens stood there like Caryatids. With raised arms, they carried their winter coats, their wives' coats, their hats, their wives' hats, their umbrellas, and their wives' galoshes. Some were holding the belongings of three or four people. A lone, full-bosomed coat check attendant moved slowly behind the counter. But it didn't matter. Even if she had moved quickly, the flood of garments would never have abated.

"Hopefully we won't have to spend the night here," Meyer joked, steeling himself for a long wait.

Margot was freezing. The coat check was in the corridor, and an icy wind blew in from the street.

"They call this spring," Meyer said.

Everyone waited patiently until Meyer got the ball rolling. "Would you come over here, young lady!"

"You're completely right."

"She's always over on that side, ignoring us."

"What a state, I'm telling you!"

"Don't forget about the left side, miss, the heart's on the left."

"My arms are getting stiff."

Margot and Oskar entered the hall at nine thirty. There were acrobats on stage. The girl had the body of a snake. She splayed her legs until her feet popped out in the most unlikely places. She bent over backwards, and her head hit her feet in a horseshoe. Her breasts were immovable.

Meyer was delighted. "I've got to say, I could still fall in love with a thing like that."

Margot was insulted. Why would he say something like that to her?

But Berlin has no climate for love.

You don't say something like that when a beautiful woman is next to you, Margot thought. It's tactless. Berlin men are impossible. Berlin has no flair, no grace, no charm. And then the bicyclists came on. Meyer noticed an acquaintance at the next table. He went over to him.

"May I introduce Mr. Gödovecz?"

"Are you here on business?" Gödovecz asked.

"I'll know around midnight. What about you?"

"Me? Yes. You know, I had a whole page just on Käsebier in the *Breslauer Illustrierte* this past Sunday. 'Käsebier Sings a Song,' in seven panels. I had loads of Käsebier in the Berlin papers last week."

"So business is good?"

"Yes, I'm not so talented, you know, but the others are really untalented. That's all that matters in the end. Mostly, the world is full of idiots."

"Waiter, another beer. Do you want something, Margot?"

"A sherry cobbler."

"A cobbler in the Hasenheide! Ah, sweets, I can't take you out to Hasenheide. You've got to order a beer, a sausage, or coffee here."

"Fine, coffee."

"You don't look very happy to be here."

"No, I think it's dreadful. Just look at the audience."

"Of course it is. Berliners don't know how to dress," said Gödovecz.

"And you only have to add, 'and the Berliners can't cook, either.' Then we'll be having the right conversation. But the Berlin woman is the chicest in the world today, and no European stomach can handle the food in Budapest. Paprika plus pepper—no thanks."

"Well, say what you like, but the general opinion is…"

And now Tubby Tub the clown had begun, the wonderful clown with the cigar box.

Meyer discovered Krienke, the press photographer, over in the corner.

"D'you know that Richard Thame is downstairs?" Krienke asked.

"You're kidding. Then this is the right place. Margot, do you know who Richard Thame is? Can't guess? What rhymes with fame, do you know? Find a rhyme for fame! Thame. Do you know how Thame found his way to his profession? One day, as he was strolling down Leipziger Strasse, he wondered which ran deeper, the Spree or his debts. Then he thought, *Thame, Thame, fame*, and he'd found it. He creates fame, but a highly exclusive, lasting kind of fame. Fame conferred by Dr. Richard Thame doesn't explode or expire. If Dr. Richard Thame finds someone worthy of fame, you can bet that there's a good reason for it."

"Well, now," said Margot, with the highest respect.

"You may say 'well, now,' but how does Dr. Richard Thame generate fame? By only photographing the right subjects. He's built a reputation until everyone says, if Dr. Richard Thame has taken a picture of him, well, there must be something to it. Take our friend Krienke. He photographs every Tom, Dick, and Harry, all the filler for the international press. If England has a new king, he's there; he's there for the Prince of Wales in Scottish, the Prince of Wales in French, the Prince of Wales as a Bantu, the Chancellor of the Reich, the Chancellors of the Reich, the French Prime Minister, the Boxing Champion of the World, the World Boxing Champion, the Boxing World Champion, some professor who's found a cure for cancer,

Stalin, Chicherin, etc. But our Dr. Richard Thame only photographs people he knows will live on forever—by means of a phone call to our dear Lord himself. The director of the Adda-Adda factories, for example, in the first cabin of the biggest Hapag steamer, or the Indian Countess of Kapurthala in conversation with the First Lord Lollipop, just so. If he's endorsed this member of the hoi polloi, then, Krienke, we can found a corporation on Käsebier's head. We'll get high returns. Whoever Thame photographs—or, rather, whoever is a subject of his portraiture—will live in eternal fame! Well, Krienke, not us two."

And then the show was over. Meyer drove home with Margot.

"Shall we go somewhere else?"

"Oh, we'd better not, I'd get back home so late otherwise."

"Fine," said Meyer, so quickly as to be insulting. He was thinking of Käsebier.

He helped park the car on Kurfürstendamm.

"Do you want to come up for a moment? My husband may still be up."

"Let's leave it," he said. "I still want to write tonight."

"As you wish."

"Thank you for the evening."

Her husband was still awake upstairs.

"Did you have fun?" he asked sleepily.

"Oh, a disgustingly pretentious fellow."

"I can't stand him either."

And then she was mad at her husband, who promptly fell asleep.

Meyer slowly wandered down Kurfürstendamm. Oddly enough, it seemed to him that it had gotten quite warm. It was raining. Three steps away from Margot's house, right at the intersection to Schlüterstrasse, at the newspaper kiosk, he ran into Miss Kohler. They both started. Meyer wanted to walk right past her. She came up to him.

"You're back?" she said.

"Yes, since today," he said. "But I have no time, I've always got things to do, it's terrible, obligations to my publisher, that scoundrel. No time at all."

"Even now, at midnight?"

"No, I still want to write."

"Can't we sit down for a moment, at least?"

"Oh, no," said Meyer. "I've got so much to do, it's awful, and it's so late already."

"But Mr. Meyer!"

"Well, fine, let's go in for a moment."

There was a small café on the corner. Only two couples were still sitting there, as well as a very, very old gentleman who'd stacked all the newspapers next to him.

Meyer said suddenly, "How lovely to be sitting next to you. What can I get you, an ice cream soda perhaps?"

"I don't care."

"One ice cream soda," he said to the waiter.

"What a beautiful round forehead you have, what a beautiful bridge to your nose, and your small smart mouth, dancing with irony!"

The waiter brought the order. Meyer picked up the spoon, heaped it with ice cream, and brought it to Miss Kohler's mouth, feeding her. He beamed, overjoyed. How he loves me! she thought. How I love her! he thought.

"I wish I were a sculptor, just so I could sculpt this hand." He picked up her hand and caressed it. "Can you imagine just how often I've tried? I know this little hand by heart. I've tried it with plasticine."

Is it possible to be this happy? she thought.

"Why," she said out loud, "did you leave like that?"

"If you knew how I—oh, I thought of you so much under the trees of Paris. I dreamed of you constantly. I always dream of you." He took her hand.

Is it possible to make someone suffer this much? she thought.

"I couldn't. But one day, I must show you my photographs of Paris." He took her head into both hands, and whispered in her ear, clipped, curt, and with shame: "And since the finest has slipped away, the body will feast instead." Then he kissed her forehead and carefully lowered his hands. "Check," he cried. They got up and left. It was raining.

"It's raining," he said. "It's always raining when we meet."

Her bus stop was close by. She steered them toward it.

"I'll bring you home."

"Oh, don't worry about it."

"Well, I'd prefer that, I still have something to do," he said, "and besides, my mother is expecting me. I promised that I'd be there to say goodnight at least."

"It's no problem for me to get home on the bus."

"We'll see each other soon," he said, "very soon."

The bus had already come. She got in and waved. She suddenly understood what it meant to be beside yourself. She wouldn't be able to work for the next eight days. She'd only think of him and her dream. A simple room with two beds in a country inn. She lay in the bed by the window while he washed himself over the washing basin. He was bare-chested and in his underwear. She watched him, noticed all of his ugliness, his underwear, his little socks, his back, which hadn't seen a day of exercise, and loved him. He came over to her bed, sat down beside her, and kissed her. Then she'd woken up. Despite this farewell, she loved him. What else mattered? She got out at Joachimsthaler Strasse, where she unexpectedly met a good friend, Dr. Wendland, and gave her a hug.

"My dear, I'm over the moon, let's go do something, I have to do something. Come along, let's drink a bottle of wine."

"Uh oh," her friend said. "Meyer?"

"Yes."

"He wrote you?"

"No."

"He's here?"

"I met him. Come!"

They went to a little wine bar. Her friend, a wine connoisseur, picked the wine. Rhenish wine, a half bottle. Miss Kohler ordered chicken mayonnaise. Her friend didn't want to eat.

"Chicken mayonnaise this late!"

"And why shouldn't I eat chicken mayonnaise today? I'm going to give a beggar three marks as well. Oh, I'm thrilled. One day it'll happen, just wait! He loves me!"

"Of course he loves you, but unfortunately, he's mad. Can you give me a good reason why you're sitting here with me instead of him?"

"No."

"So there's none."

"He has work to do, he said."

"He said that, huh? Nonsense."

"It's very difficult with the two of us. Great love is always difficult."

"Oh, baloney! He's mad. You're not difficult. You just choose your objects of affection poorly. But I won't say anything else. I'm just furious at him because he's broken you down, but maybe it'll all work out."

"Cheers! It has to work out. Otherwise I'll go mad. I can't tell you how much I love him. Do you know the saying, 'A hair on your head is dearer to me than life itself'? That's how I feel. And what about you?"

"I'll be glad if I can take another vacation this summer."

"And your personal life?"

"Sworn off."

"Nothing at all?"

"No."

"But why? Such a shame..."

"You know why."

"Yes, but, well, that was ten years ago. Do you still see each other?"

"Sometimes we pass each other on the street, but we don't say hello. He hasn't gotten married either, by the way. Looks like he won't."

"But there's more than just the one fellow out there, even if you loved him and maybe he loved you. Isn't it wrong of you to get so caught up and swept away by love for one person? Especially since he's entirely unsuitable as an object of affection?"

"*You're* telling *me* this?"

"Yes, I'm saying it because I don't quite believe you. You want to keep a clear head for your work, so you've built up an ideal in your heart on which to focus your desires. That's an easy way out, plus you're more productive. You're right, of course! When we're happily in love, not only is hair on his head worth more than life itself—worse, it's worth more than our productivity. The truth is, you can keep falling in love. You can even love several people at once, in different ways. But have trouble admitting all that to ourselves. All the same, life is rich."

"I agree. But do men belong in it?"

"I suppose so."

"I don't want a relationship, and these days, no man's going to stick around for any time without one. Sure, it'll go on for a while, but friendship is a rare bird when there's no prospect of ending up in bed together."

"And why don't you want a relationship? It could come to you. Without your frantically searching for it, you could just be ready. I couldn't do without one."

"Have you ever thought through what it means? The dependence, the fear, and what if the maid notices? A friend of mine who's changed her lifestyle was recently told by her maid, 'I'm always washing your silk underwear, you can do that yourself.' No, I couldn't bear it. If a man loves me in that fashion, there's no reason not to get married. And I could only marry the one man with whom it's not possible. Do I have to be afraid of the doorman's wife when I get home late? No thanks."

"God, I'm not trying to convince you of anything. I just think it's a shame. I think it's a shame for me, too."

"Oh, nonsense, we put too much stock in it these days. When we arrived at university, we were so excited and ambitious and wanted to prove ourselves and were terribly proud. And what happened a mere fifteen years later? The Girl came along. We wanted to create a new kind of woman. Remember how we burned with excitement, knowing that at last, everything was ours, that we now could learn it all, that great big man's world full of mathematics and chemistry and wonderful historical revelations? And now the result is that little sixteen-year-olds are sitting in my office hours and I'm just happy if they're not sick. Their heads are just there for their hairdos. I think that female academics have fallen behind quite a bit."

"Like all academics, and all intellectuals, and everything intellectual."

"There's poverty, and otherwise there's just a big old march to bed. We've been let down. No, don't deny it—we've all been let down, all of us who longed for the education, knowledge, and skills of men. We learned how life can open up when the search for truth becomes your guiding star. The next generation is a disappointment. Every day I see it in my office hours. I don't miss anything, I feel fulfilled, but the generation after us forgot everything. It's rotten."

"But there's a new, young generation that's already pretty promising. They're as engaged as the boys, sporty, not clothes horses."

"Take a look over there, businessmen are busy coaxing trade secrets out of shopkeepers and clerks with the help of a bottle of wine. Their right paw has the pencil, and the left one is busy stroking. There are two kinds of women: those who see the pencil and give the business world the runaround, and those who fall for the wine. That one's falling for the wine."

"How wonderful! By the way, we could go to Grunewald together on Sunday."

"We could indeed."

"How lovely that you're free, we'll go on a great walk, it's so beautiful outside now. You know, I'm very happy that we're not just chatting en passant for once."

"I agree, a real woman-to-woman talk is one of the best things in all the world. And how men fear it!"

"Really, men are such sorry animals. They don't have this discussing and confiding and explaining, this endless glorious chatter, our only solace and means of revenge."

"And a source of happiness too."

"Have a good night, then!"

And then it was half past one, and Miss Kohler had to catch a taxi.

Meyer felt dreadful after he'd said farewell, and couldn't see straight anymore. He wanted to take the tram toward Halensee, but it didn't come. He waited. A young girl was waiting next to him. She paced to and fro. Meyer gazed at her. She looked at him. She was young. Clearly from a good family.

"Shall we hail a taxi?" he asked. She nodded. He waved. A taxi stopped.

"Where do you live?"

"On Hubertusbaderstrasse."

He gave the taxi driver the address. They got in. He took her hand, and kissed it between her fingers. Then he felt for her ankle, moved up her leg, paused. Looked at her face, which was aroused, kissed it blindly, caressing her. Her fur coat was closed. He opened it.

"Can I come over?" he said just before Halensee bridge, his hand already quite far. She was silent. "You sweet thing." They got out. He entered a dark Berlin hallway. They went up the stairs in the dark, not daring to turn on the light. She unlocked the door to the apartment.

"To the left," she said. That was it. He turned on the bedside lamp in the white room. The girl came over to him. He saw her glow. It was over quickly.

"How do I get out?" he asked.

"Let me give you the key. I'll have a new one made fast."

They avoided addressing one another. He kissed her, although she didn't want to be kissed, tenderly even, as she stood there without memory or demands. He closed the door quietly and glided down the stairs in the dark, listening for noise. Unlocked the door. Stood outside. Tried to read the house number. Couldn't make it out, pocketed the key.

The girl, now truly exhausted, thought, That was nice after Paul, who doesn't want me, humiliated me so dreadfully. I almost forgot to turn on my alarm, have to be at the office by eight tomorrow.

And then it was half past one, and Meyer had to get a taxi.

On the following day, Meyer-Paris published an article in the *Allgemeine Zeitung*. "Käsebier, a Singer from Berlin." That Saturday, a page of Gödowecz's illustrations appeared in the *Berliner Bildschau*.

The following day, the *Grossberliner Woche* ran a whole article on Käsebier with photos by Dr. Richard Thame. Three photos of Käsebier, three more of "Käsebier and His Milieu." You could see the bicyclists and Tubby Tub the clown and the acrobats photographed from below. Then, six more pictures, "Käsebier's audience." One could only marvel at how many people Dr. Richard Thame knew. Even Margot was there. Mrs. Margot Weissman, the wife of Weissman, the industrial magnate, with Meyer-Paris. Then came a large table: the banker Reinhardt Hersheimer, Count Dinkelsbühl, the polo and golf player, Countess Dinkelsbühl, Countess Mercy, Mr. von Trappen from the foreign ministry and Mrs. Clothilde Meyer-Lewin. The industrial magnate Menke and his wife were quite a picture! One photo entitled "Colleagues from the Opera." Conductor Mäusebach, the alto Senta Sieger, the tenor Otto Glübart. Two pictures of "the crowd." One table with three young couples, one table with an old couple, their daughter and her fiancée, and an elderly aunt they'd brought along.

9

A girl wanders through the city

THAT SAME day, Meyer-Paris called up Miss Kohler and asked if she would accompany him to Käsebier that evening. This request left Miss Kohler so breathless she could only manage a timid "Yes." She dressed at great length that evening and met Meyer, who had come straight from the newsroom, at Hasenheide. At particularly exciting or beautiful moments, Meyer would squeeze her hand, and when a dancer danced the Marcelle, he uttered the word "Paris" in a melancholy tone.

"Do you know it? Yes?"

"Yes," she said. "A bit."

"I'm sure it would be wonderful with you."

Then, Indian fakirs drew scarves through fire unscathed.

"I like Käsebier an awful lot," she said.

"Well, now. I almost think he's a bit overrated."

It felt like a true spring night as they walked home.

"It's so warm out today," said Meyer-Paris.

Miss Kohler sniffed the evening breeze. "Spring really is in the air."

"Yes, spring finally has arrived. It's raining. It's always raining when we meet."

She nodded, enchanted. They got into a taxi by the church. She leaned against him.

"You sweet, clever girl," he said. In front of her house, he waited for a moment, watching her. She looked at him expectantly. He pulled her towards him, threw himself on her and kissed her on the mouth with a desire that was new to her, that she had never experienced before, an unbridled, untamed kiss devoid of all niceties. He released her, said, "I have your phone number," and walked away.

"Shall I order coffee?" Gohlisch asked.

"Yes, go ahead," said Miermann.

"I'll pay."

"Fine," said Miermann.

"Summer's coming."

"Yes."

"I'm moving into my summer house tomorrow. Aren't you going away for a bit?"

"I've got no spending money as long as the German people isn't giving me an allowance."

"But aren't you getting any money from the *Daredevils*?"

"Money? Don't you know that there's a nationwide plot—a league, if you will—to not read my books? Don't you know that? I've always earned my money ten marks at a time. Later in life, I earned fifty or a hundred. The only time I earned three hundred at once was when I brokered a property!"

"That's how businessmen make it," said Gohlisch.

"How can you say that?" said Miss Kohler, who had just walked in. "What about the headaches and the losses and the thousands of futile attempts for every twenty deals that go through? Everyone always thinks the grass is greener."

"But Miermann, you're a famous man," said Gohlisch.

"I could have been twenty years ago. Recently, you asked me why I treat good old Mahlke so badly. Good old Mahlke spent twenty years preventing me from becoming Miermann. For twenty years— twenty years!—that idiot was my editor at the *Allgemeine Zeitung*. For twenty years that ass cut my punchlines and added his Mahlke nonsense to my good Miermanns. I buried my punchlines in the middle of my articles for ten years, because I thought, He won't notice them in the middle, he only cuts at the end. But come on, how can an article turn out well if you're always writing sentences at the end that could get cut? I don't even greet him anymore. And if someone asks me, I say, 'Mahlke? An old sack. For twenty years, he stopped me from making a name for myself.'"

"Well, I'd agree that murder seems justified in this case. But murderers are rarely inventive. Recently, a worker near Berlin murdered his landlord. The landlord stood over his bed at six in the morning every day and said, 'Wake up!' every morning, without fail. He finally throttled him."

"Really, Gohlisch, you say the most terrible things sometimes."

"Well, aren't I right? Every morning, can you imagine that, six o'clock every morning? You should sooner be allowed to murder an editor who cuts your punchlines."

"A new job hazard: murdering editors who cut punchlines," Miermann said. "It's quite all right. If an engineer comes up with an improvement for a machine and the company in question alters the model so much that his invention doesn't work anymore, he can sue for damages. Can I sue Mahlke for damages for cutting my punchlines? Imagine a lawsuit: Michelangelo versus Bernini, St. Peter's dome!"

Gohlisch and Miss Kohler laughed.

"What're you laughing at, young'uns? Do you consider art so elevated that you think it can't be protected by the law? Or so base that you think a few centimeters on a building or cutting punchlines on finely filed prose makes no difference?"

"Why'd you never punch Mahlke in the kisser?" asked Gohlisch.

"You've heard it, Gohlisch is even for murder in cases like these!" said Kohler.

"Gohlisch may enjoy resorting to rough-and-tumble methods such as murder or knocking people's teeth in, but I'm now wondering whether Michelangelo could have sued Bernini for the nave in front of the dome, since it made the dome less effective. Would he have sued for specific performance or for damages? From what I know of Michelangelo, he'd have sued for specific performance, if he hadn't already died. But a journalist can't sue for damages. When I was young, I wanted to turn Catholic and join a baroque monastery. I would have made a wonderful priest with my aristocratic features. I would have held great, long sermons on Augustine, Nicholas of Cusa, and Hugo von Hoffmansthal. I would have preached about the need to shun films and radio and cars, which are the devil's work, and no one could have prevented these beautiful words from escaping my mouth. But I had to go and become a journalist instead, and was stuck with limping Mahlke as my boss instead of the pope, or Saint Peter himself. What could I have done, Gohlisch, my son, Kohler, my daughter? Could I have threatened Mahlke with excommunication and menaced him with heavenly justice, in which his nose would have been pinched off his face again and again, with pincers, for all eternity—the punishment for editors on this earth who cut their journalists' punchlines? At most, I could have threatened him with Löwenstein the lawyer, who would have demanded a retainer and wouldn't have been able to find any law that could force Mahlke to let my Miermanns be real Miermanns. The journalist suffers greatly, my children. On top of that, Mahlke called me a fool, because I fought for every word. I could have sued him for insulting me, or told him that Faust had his most profound thoughts because of a word, the word *logos*. Is it Power? Is it Sense? Is it Deed? But Mahlke would have thought that Faust was a busybody."

"How nice, we've finally gotten to Faust," Miss Kohler said.

"A dear friend recently told me that I should go to a psychoanalyst to work through Mahlke, that it wouldn't do to walk around full of half-repressed hang-ups. She said that today, a modern individual should go to a psychoanalyst if they're mad at someone. They can talk about their first words as a toddler and be cured of their rage."

"Come on, Miermann!"

"Yes; hate, anger, and love will all vanish one day. Each person will have their psychoanalyst at their side. The legal system will largely be dismantled. Emotions will disappear. Yes, with the help of psychoanalysis, even wars will no longer be waged. Those who have been psychoanalyzed the longest and best will form the court of cassation. And the courts of all countries will form the League of Nations. Yes! And now, let's descend to the fleshpots of Egypt."

Augur came in, nodded grimly, and shook everyone's hand without saying a word.

"Well, conspirator, what's going on?"

"The public procurement office is a great swamp."

"Shall we print that?"

"Yes. Don't you want to print what the sparrows on the Hausvogteiplatz are chirping about?"

"I think that's dangerous."

"Oh, you're all cowards. That's why nothing will ever become of you, Gohlisch."

"Nothing will become of me because I'm nice, dear sir, I'm polite, which is why people often think I'm drunk. You don't believe me? It's true. I was recently sitting on the trolley, and two people kept chatting over my head. The man was sitting on the foldaway seat. Go ahead, I can switch with you, I said. Oh, no thanks, said the man. Well, why don't you sit down? said the woman. Oh, no thanks, said the man. I get up anyways, and I hear him quietly say to the woman, 'Can'tcha tell, he's drunk.' If you offer someone your seat, they think you're drunk. Only loudmouthed brutes or snotty suck-ups make it to the top. You definitely can't be nice, otherwise people think you're dumb. Take it from the top down and you'll be sitting pretty."

"In this city," said Miermann, "In this country of cyclists, you have to buckle up and kick down."[19]

"Do you know that Käsebier's coming to the Wintergarten?"

"I have a date with Käsebier tonight. We're going to drink a glass of mead together. That's how it goes, you see, I may have discovered the guy, but who am I? A small-time journalist. For Käsebier to become famous, Otto Lambeck had to come to Berlin, Otto Lambeck, the great poet, and be offered one thousand marks for an article on Berlin, and meet that slimeball Frächter, who told him, 'There was something on Käsebier recently, Käsebier's a hot tip.' Do you know who Käsebier is? He's the man Otto Lambeck discussed on the radio. By the way, Frächter's publishing a book on Käsebier. It'll be ready for the Wintergarten premiere. He graciously asked me to collaborate, that is to say, write an article for it."

"Contemporaries on Käsebier," Miermann said with a smirk.

"Mr. Miermann, perhaps you can interview Käsebier for our Easter issue, ask him what he thinks about the battleship," Gohlisch said.

"Why not? It's just common sense, after all! You're just jealous because Frächter works harder than you."

"Or because he's more tasteless. I'm going to Aschinger's with Augur after this. A sumptuous repast awaits us there. I'll leave the gazettes to our beloved Dalai Lama."

"Farewell, farewell!"

"Heil and Sieg and catch a fat one."

"Kohler, my child," said Miermann once the two men had left, "you can't go on like this. You called up the *Allgemeine Zeitung* four times in a row the day before yesterday. They're starting to make fun of you."

"Who told you?"

"No matter. Don't embarrass yourself."

"You're quite right, but it wasn't the way you think. He promised to take me to see the Impressionists. He said eleven at first, so I waited. I called at twelve, he said that something had come up and he'd be there at one. I waited until one; he didn't show, so I waited until two. I called at two, and he apologized in the sweetest, most loving way, said he'd be there just after lunch at four. He didn't come at four, I called again at five and he'd already left, and I tried him again at seven. But then I was done too."

"You can't chase after a man."

"But Mr. Miermann, if I love him and he loves me, it's not chasing, is it?"

"He doesn't love you. Or perhaps—don't be mad at me, child—he wants a woman who's wealthy."

"He loves me. I'm not an idiot, I have at least an ounce of sense."

"You have sense?!?"

"I'd never run after a man who didn't care for me. But believe me, he loves me."

"Hm. I don't know about that."

"There are people who are like that in other respects. I know a very important man who was invited to dinner by a business acquaintance. We waited for him, and he didn't show. Couldn't be reached at home. Afterward, we found out that he hadn't come out of sheer mischief, simple madness. The last time M. was in Berlin, we took a taxi together; it's disgusting, really, our courtship only takes place in cars and cafés, never a day in Potsdam, never a boat trip. We never spend any time together apart from hectic car rides between the newsroom, the publisher's, and the sound studio. Oh yes, I wanted to say that the last time M. was in Berlin, we were in the car together when he suddenly asked me whether marriage would solve everything. I said perhaps, because I was too dumb to say yes."

"That's just a manner of speaking. Any man who desires or loves a woman like you would marry her."

"You're speaking like a man, Miermann, no offense. He wrote me this letter after he left me hanging yesterday. Isn't it a love letter? You have to hear me out. I'm not just a silly goose."

"Well now! Hand it over."

Miermann read the letter:

Dearest!
    There's always something, as Tucholsky says. And he's right. I haven't called you this whole afternoon—and not even this evening. I hope not—I kept you waiting, but I certainly didn't gamble away any trust I'd earned. I'm angry—at you! Here's what happened: I was racking my brains in the newsroom until six, got home at half past seven, was called away immediately, and was dragged into other people's business until late at night. Why was I angry with you? Usually, I bear my heavy workload, the yoke of public affairs, with composure, but as my thoughts turned to everything this evening could have been, I was vexed and troubled by the thoughts darting through my brain—and thus, vexed by you, the source of this conflict between reality and desire. But on a serious note: I must beg your pardon, for if I could know great delights in an evening spent

in my company…you must pardon me for this loss. Egotist that I am, I ask for patience! Let me get through the next few days, with their mad array of commitments. Can I be in touch then? I ask for probation. Will you grant it? Regards!

Your
O. M.-P.

"Yes, it's a love letter."

"There you go."

"But I think that man's a talented, vain careerist. Not for you."

"Maybe I'm unlucky in my choice of men."

"Girls like you easily make mistakes, but the worst is that you can never get away from it. Miss Timmer's in the same mess."

"But I'm very happy with my love. I can be glad by myself, I can suffer by myself; I'm not all that unhappy, I'm fulfilled. I'll work well in the coming days."

"That's fine, but get that man out of your head. He's rotten, believe me. Recently, he attacked our valiant Behm-Rabke and wrote that all travel writers write like Heine: 'The waiters in Göttingen have red hair.' He also said that Mr. Behm-Rabke might well travel around the world and dine with lords and marquis, but that he had no clue about the working class. Of course, he knows Primo de Rivera and Briand."[20]

"Well, it was rather gauche of Behm-Rabke to describe his encounter with Briand, and how Miss So-and-So, the minister's daughter, smiled, and how Sir Exandwye bowed to the lovely Madame Zed."

"Certainly. But Behm-Rabke's still no snob, he's a knowledgeable man. Perhaps a bit too serious. But to pick out a few faults and nail them to good old Behm, that's low."

"Picking out faults to nail someone down is a nice touch. I'm not going to defend him halfheartedly. But I can't stand it when you insult 'him.' I can insult him; you can't. After all, what's he done? How's he disgraced himself? So far, he's only made fun of Behm."

"Certainly. But Behm-Rabke sent in a correction."

"Mr. Miermann, you're funny today. You can't correct satire. This sounds like the mess I got into with Miss Ostau last winter. I've known Grete Ostau for years. She was pretty as a picture before she began wearing a monocle and became a flabby garçonne. A fat garçonne is such a terrible thing. Last winter, I went to the Phillippses', and there was Grete Ostau in the hallway. I said—very quietly—to Gohlisch, who'd come with me, 'Oh, she's gotten ugly.' The next day, Karl Philipp rang me up and said, 'Listen, Grete Ostau left immediately last night because she was so upset by what you said. She says you should call her and apologize for the remark and take it back.' I said that I was very sorry that she'd heard me, but that I couldn't take it back. Should I have called and said, Dear Grete Ostau, I may have said that I think you've gotten ugly, but I take it back, I'm wrong, I think you're very pretty? Meyer might just as well write, 'I may have written that I think Mr. Behm's an ape, but I don't think so anymore.' You can't correct something like that."

"Right. But it was completely different. Meyer falsely accused Behm of making huge mistakes. That's all Behm wanted corrected. But Meyer didn't allow the correction to be published. Instead, he wrote a very polite letter to Behm, and published his own letter. He's always that cowardly. You just won't admit it!"

"Certainly, Miermann, certainly. But I love him. I can't help myself. He's just a poor soul. I want to call him up so badly."

"Don't do it, my girl, don't do it."

"You think he's a funny fellow. But he's completely different. I happen to be reading Buddhist texts right now. He recently quoted a sentence from something I was reading. Is that just a coincidence?"

"Of course it is. Don't put too much stock in that, and don't get so hung up on him!"

"And how are you doing, Mr. Miermann?"

"She's an unusual woman. She's moving up in the world fast, is perhaps a bit overeager, knows everyone already, goes out everywhere, has an opinion on everything. A completely new type. She cut her hair in 1918 already. You're quite old-fashioned by comparison."

"Fine, fine, I'll walk through the streets for a bit."

She took the train to the Tiergarten. Crocuses, strollers, and buds on the bushes, colorful woolen dwarves with scooters and teddy bears under their arms.

They were unloading barges at the northeast corner of the Tiergarten. The herring had arrived. Tons of it—young, delectable, fatty, soused spring herring. Oilskin jackets, blubber, sea wind and salt spray, from the coast to the Alexanderufer at the Lehrter train station. There this democratic animal was unloaded, along with the bricks for new homes that they carried out of the barge's store hold on their backs.

Invalidenstrasse: museums for boys, rocks, telegraph machines, whale skeletons. Heidestrasse, August. The Prussian Building and Finance Administration. The District Committee for the City of Berlin. And then you got a summons to pick up your civvies, while the gunner... Four years later.

The seventeen-year-old was unforgettable. A strong Berlin boy. August 1918, Heidestrasse. Swung his suitcase toward the gate, "Well, guess it's off to the slammer now."

Now a tattered poster hung there:
"Hunger"
"unemployment, mass poverty..."
"save the proles"
"the banking system"
"international"
"dictatorship."

The District Committee building was painted in soft hues of pink and rose, war's storms hush and subside.[21] A window was open: it revealed a room with a white tiled stove, a red sofa, a walnut closet, a giant African linden.

The old city. Clinics, students, commerce, cramming for class, establishments run by the Christian Community next to small hotels. Women straight out of Zille stood there.[22] "Not an easy life either," thought Miss Kohler. And there were the workers who earned forty-two or forty-eight or fifty-two pfennigs an hour—provided they had work. 'Good fatty ham shanks' cost one mark ten. You could get a pound of pig's heads for thirty pennies. It was six o'clock. Fried liver and soup for seventy-five pfennigs. Bright underwear in shopwindows. Wishful dreams of silk undershirts, pink with yellow lace. Powder and makeup, secondhand stores and furniture on installment, pawnshops. Medicine and law met their ends here as "Natural Healing Clinics" and "Legal Offices": divorces to the left, criminal cases to the right. The Berolina was already gone from Alexanderplatz.[23]

The state had erected its bastions here, albeit with a few holes; ideas were being fought over with sharpened lances. Here was also the bastion of the law, which had no holes, because it was protected by state-sanctioned violence. And here was the bastion of gastric sustenance. Piles of slop. Mountains of pale red lungs, blackened kidneys, bloody cadavers, boxes of oranges, greenish cheese from France and reddish cheese from England, green salad and cauliflower from Holland. Trainloads of flowers, sacks of beans, peas, and rice, night after night, partly by the grace of God and partly by freight bill, partly miracle and partly science, partly earthly blessing and partly organization.

The day began at six o'clock beyond the heart of the city. Narrow courtyards, houses stuffed with people, sewing machines, wood planes and hammers and stampers. Shabby houses covered from top to bottom with gaudy signs. SHOE STORE, STOCKINGS FOR SALE, TROUSERS HERE, GARMENT DISTRICT. The unemployed went to get stamped, stood around, hocked suspenders, combs, glue, chocolate. "Three bars for a mark!" Old clothes hung for sale in the rag shop with a big sign that said, WE PAY TOP PRICE. Young lads stretched their limbs, wanting to go tramping, leave the big city and walk the country roads. It was March.

Schönhauser Tor. Here was Berlin, stretching out far to the north and east and west. The life of millions; when it was good, it was one hundred and fifteen marks a month because you couldn't always get a full-time gig, and you got ten marks for your old mother's pension, but then rent cost thirty. Or one hundred and fifty marks with riffraff and creepy-crawlies, up and down the stairs, twenty-five marks in spending money, husband, wife, and child working as door-to-door salesmen.

Next to the pawnshops was the Impound Distillery, garments "for strong women," stores for work clothes. The Blessing, a watch store. Old factories. In front, villas with staircases descending to the front yard. Soon came new, splendidly vertical buildings: red brick, sober, modern, severe. The balconies were there for soulfulness and longing. The flower boxes were painted, newly attached, wires drawn for scarlet runners and wild vines, dovecotes put up. Between Fatty Max's distillery and The Wet Triangle were shops with canaries and tree frogs—even live goldfish—and shops for ribboned lutes. Children played with tops and marbles, drew with chalk on the asphalt and played hopscotch. The older ones went about festively: little girls in black dresses, clutching songbooks and yellow roses wrapped in white paper; little boys in black suits with sprigs of myrtle in their button-holes. They had been blessed for the life they now waited to begin: first, for the apprenticeship that couldn't be had; then, for the rest. Old folks sat in doorways, tending to the littlest ones. One lost his balloon, it flew off. He cried. First spring pains. Oh, what in life doesn't fly away!

The Ringbahn station. Flocks of workers returning silently in the dusk, blue jugs in their hands.

Miss Kohler walked with them. On her way back into the city, she wept. Her mother was expecting her at home, in Blumeshof. Mrs. Kohler, the privy councilor's wife, was a quiet, exceedingly old-fashioned woman. She always wore a gray moiré band with a brooch around her bare neck. She still received a pension of about three hundred fifty marks a month. Her daughter's salary, three hundred fifty to four hundred marks a month, came on top of that. This was quite good. She had managed to rent out the apartment, which cost five thousand marks in 1914, so that it only cost her one hundred marks a month, and the renters often gave her some money for break-fast, electricity, etc. The apartment had once been very elegant. They had several antiques. The foyer was forty square meters large, "exactly as large as an apartment that would make me happy," Lotte Kohler often thought.

The apartment had three rooms that faced the street, one with three windows, the others with two. Next to them was a dining room of about seventy square meters. It was an enormous room, with walls covered in dark leather. It could seat sixty. Two candelabras, Dutch brass lamps, hung next to the oven, a brown monster. This arrangement had once been very elegant. The Delft vases and plates were arranged on the wainscoting. Mother and daughter lived here. The large window facing the courtyard had stained glass.

"The law clerk is staying," the mother said.

"Oh, thank God," said Lotte. The maid brought out some sandwiches.

The maid looked dreadful. She wore a blue apron. With five tenants and ten rooms, there was no time for white aprons.

The mother said, "I was at Aunt Else's this afternoon, and she told me that the young girls are chasing after her Erwin. Recently, she came home to find Miss Glaser walking down the stairs. What do you think of that?"

"Tasteless of Erwin. What else?"

"Oh, come on."

"It's a matter of taste."

"By the way, I had quite a bit of trouble today. Powitzer finally did bring his big dog into the apartment. Now Wanda has to walk the dog, on top of everything else."

"Hey, that's not on."

"That's what I said too, but what can I do? Won't you talk to him sometime?"

"Sure, but what if he leaves? Two rooms!"

"Two rooms! We can't risk it."

"No, we can't. You know, Mother, we should really give up this big apartment, but where would we find the money to move and renovate? It would probably cost five thousand marks. We can't get a decent apartment for less than three thousand marks in moving fees, and we'd have to pay two thousand marks for the renovation."[24]

"We simply can't. But the tenants are such dreadful work."

"We won't get what we need, which is a three- to four-room apartment."

"Oh, three would do."

"Of course. But we won't get it without a certificate, and we won't get that certificate. We should have gone to the housing office and put our names down for a small apartment right after the inflation. It's too late now."

"I don't know. Seven hundred marks is a lot of money, after all."

"Yes, and we're barely getting by."

"You're quite right. I don't know either."

"We have to repair things here and there. A big apartment like this costs money too, even if you don't have anything done."

"And the things the tenants ruin! The top of the mahogany table is completely destroyed. Miss Ciczpenski always put her hot pots on it without a cloth, and the grand piano is completely covered in stains, and Mr. Powitzer broke one of the Meissen figurines recently."

"Which one?"

"The cherubs at the anvil. I wanted to get them glued together again, I already went to the Meissen shop."

"But Mother! Those cherubs are ghastly. We should thank Mr. Powitzer for breaking them, and you want to spend money repairing them?"

"I don't want to go completely to seed."

"But really, the Meissen figurines are utterly useless. And you get upset at me when I take taxis."

"But that's quite unnecessary. We drove rarely, if ever. Your grandfather was of the opinion that young women could walk."

"That was in 1895, thirty-five years go. Why don't we sell some of the silver?"

"I would have liked to keep it for you."

"Come on, what will I do with silver for forty-eight people? That's just a burden. But we'll get far too little for it. No one wants rococo anymore. I'm glad that we sold the Grützner and the Lenbach during the inflation."

"Yes, yes, although your father was very fond of those paintings."

Miss Kohler went to her room. She was still reading a book that Meyer had lent her. *The History and Nature of Buddhism.* Was a woman really worth that little? So far from nirvana? So impure, so enmeshed in the wheel of life? Why did he preach asceticism to her—especially her!—when precisely the opposite was necessary?

Why was he so dreadful, so awful, why was she so terribly alone? Exploited, lonely, a laughingstock. She wept.

Mrs. Kohler sat in the dining room, busy with her accounting. It was an old habit from the days in which she'd managed a household budget of sixty thousand marks, and her husband had earned eighty thousand to one hundred thousand marks. Why didn't her daughter get married? She was very bitter. All the others had married, and married well, as well as anyone else! Something must be the matter with Lotte. If only she'd chosen Dr. Brandenburg! He's got a splendid income now; such a decent man. He would have taken care of her. But girls always do the wrong thing. They don't want the good men. And she couldn't give her a dowry anymore. Just furniture and a trousseau, and silver and glassware and porcelain for forty-eight people.

10

Premiere at the Wintergarten

ON APRIL 11, Käsebier appeared in a guest performance at the Wintergarten. It was already late in the season, but still feasible. Everyone who was to be seen at premieres in Berlin could be found in the foyer. Margot had brought along her newest companion, a foreigner, a man from the South American embassy with whom she could happily converse in French. *Plus parisien qu'une parisienne.* When greeting younger women, she said, *"Ma chère,"* drawling the final "e." She didn't think much of literature lately, and preferred attachés and diplomats with decorative names. Käte was there, looking very good. In a moment of decisiveness, she had taken a furnished flat, and clients were already streaming in. She wore a beautiful black georgette dress she'd borrowed for the occasion. Margot wore pink pearls the size of walnuts around her neck along with a sequined coat, the latest look from Paris. Muschler the banker was there with his wife, Thedy; the banker Reinhardt Hersheimer with his wife; Count Dinkelsbühl, the golf and polo player; Mr. von Trappen from the foreign ministry with Mrs. Gabriele Meyer-Lewin; and Waldschmidt had a box with Lambeck and his youngest daughter. Aja Müller was there, the playwright on her left, the bank director's son on her right. That is to say, one couldn't really speak of her *being* there; rather, she made an entrance, flanked by both, wearing a pink dress that was quite long. She seemed very naked, with an overly rouged face and earrings the size of African nose rings.

"Aja Müller's all long," Mrs. Muschler said to her husband. Her two companions were well coordinated. Fair and dark.

It was a special evening. The theater critics, rather than the *varieté*

89

critics, had come. Ixo was there, Miermann, Öchsli. Lieven shook hands with everyone enthusiastically and ecstatically. Frächter was the man of the hour, as he had convinced Blumentopf the agent to engage Käsebier. If not, he would have made a big fuss over Käsebier at a cabaret. Frächter had made sure to invite the theater critics instead of the *varieté* critics, a major difference in newspaper terms. *Varieté* criticism appears in the local section, but drama is both a science and an art, and belongs in the arts section. An article in the local section is insignificant if there are fewer than ten deaths, but in the arts section, even the smallest things are important. If a cabaret performer is discussed by a theater critic, one can be sure that he is ready to play Mephisto. In fact, the question of whom the *varieté* critics cover and whom the theater critics cover is an overall benchmark. These are nuances that Frächter knew about, and which mattered.

Gohlisch was there, as well as Meyer-Paris. Frächter saw to everything. The books were in the lobby. *Käsebier, a Singer from Berlin: Who He Is, and How He Came to Be*. Preface by Frächter. They were being snapped up left and right.

What a scandal, Gohlisch thought, instead of having Frächter send ten copies to my house, I have to buy one myself! He bought one for one mark fifty. Glanced at his article. Very good, he thought, but for free?! No way. What a disgrace! I'm going to get that back!

Voices buzzed around the room. Müller called out to Lieven, who was five rows over, "Well, sugar, you lovely doll, you! Want to steer your graceful body over to me at the break?"

Lieven cried, "My greetings to the fairer daughters of fair mothers."

Miermann said to Käte, who was sitting next to him, "He may know Horace, but only halfways. *O matre pulchra filia pulchrior*, o mother, fairer than your fair daughter. Gracious lady, dear Käte—may I call you that?—I'd like to greet you with a classical phrase as well. *Recepto dulce mihi furere est amico*. It is sweet to be wild, as my friend has returned."

"Sounds nice," Käte said. She was pleased by the attentions of this important man, but she thought him passé, so passé with his Latin allusions.

"Do you know much about music?"

"No, I'm completely tone-deaf."

"Me neither, we'll be able to write about it so much the better."

First, the famous girls flexed their behinds on stage and kicked their legs in the air; doubtless a healthy gymnastics exercise for fifteen- to sixteen-year-olds. But some of the girls were pushing forty.

Two times nine hundred eyes, more than half of them male, stared out of the darkness. Naked legs en masse are incredibly distressing, smiling en masse causes embarrassment, as it's unvarnished prostitution, but fifteen women to every two hundred men somewhat temper the matter.

Lively, up-tempo music began. People arranged themselves on top of one another, flew off seesaws, carried out exercises in dexterity and courage. The act was directed by a large-chested, dark-haired woman, a Jewish matron of forty-five to fifty years of age. She wore a pale green tricot and a short pink skirt. Poor devil.

Indians appeared, pulled paper through fire without letting it burn, made cut-up fabric whole again, and separated water and fire with their bare hands. The whole thing smacked suspiciously of false bottoms.

Miermann took Käte's hand, bent down, kissed her hand, then put his wide and unkempt right hand on her thigh. Käte pushed it gently to the side, very gently, overly gently, so as to avoid any insult.

One of the soap dolls in the women's dance band was making hungry eyes at the audience, striking poses and flaring her nostrils. If her ravenous eyes stirred the appetite of one of the ten thousand salarymen of this northern city, she would surely say that her father, an important public official, had disowned her when she was studying voice, as an officer had left her with child.

The intermission came. Gohlisch went looking for Frächter. He confronted him.

"Well, you scoundrel, someone should really light a fire under you."

Frächter took it as a joke. "How can I be of service, Herr von Goethe?"

"Don't give me a song and dance, you know what I mean. We may be on the galley, we may be galley slaves, but you're mistaken if you think we're doing it for the honor of the printed word. How much? Moolah, moolah, mazuma." He stroked his fingers with his thumb.

"You wretched swindler, you."

"But Mr. Gohlisch, I don't want to cheat you on your fee, how could you possibly think that of me?"

"I think all kinds of things of you."

"I just didn't dare to offer you twenty marks. That's the most I can pay you."

"And what did you get, *sir*?"

"Oh, barely a penny. And you can imagine how hard I had to work to collect all the essays."

"I'm no amateur, sir. I have decent penmanship. Here's the money, here are the goods. Tit for tat. I don't churn things out, which means I don't push prices down."

"Like I said, Mr. Gohlisch, do you want twenty marks?"

"Come on, twenty-five."

"Fine, twenty-five. I'll send it over. And I'll ring you sometime. I have plans for you."

Käte said to Miermann, "It would be lovely if you could introduce me to some journalists."

Miermann was thrilled and steered her toward Gohlisch.

"May I introduce Mr. Emil Gohlisch."

Gohlisch bowed and said, "*Berliner Rundschau.*"

Käte laughed. "Why do you introduce yourself with your newspaper?"

"Miermann was kind enough to introduce me by my real name. A journalist introduces himself by saying, '*Berliner Rundschau,*' or '*Berliner Tageszeitung,*' or '*Allgemeines Blatt.*' We aren't human, you see. We're a kind of—"

"Well, we're galley slaves," added Miermann.

"We've been branded," said Gohlisch.

Käte's smile was frozen in place. How can I manage to steer this conversation with Gohlisch toward gymnastics lessons? she wondered.

"We're all galley slaves," she said.

"What are you chained to?" asked Gohlisch.

"I'm a gymnastics teacher."

"That must be fun."

"It is. I'm hoping it will also be profitable."

"Do you work a lot?"

"A decent amount. I've got a very particular method. Part Mensendieck, part Loheland."

"I'll have to check it out sometime."

"Give me a ring sometime. I'm always at your disposal."

Miermann smiled. "You're industrious," he said as they continued along. They bumped into Frächter. Frächter greeted Miermann.

"How do you do, Mr. Miermann? Käsebier will be on soon. I'm telling you, a natural talent like that is rare, a child of the people, completely unselfconscious, naïve, a treasure trove for a fine essayist such as yourself. I've meant to call you for ages. How's your wonderful poetry doing? I recently saw your book *Heimweg* remaindered on a book cart. It should be reprinted."

"But Mr. Frächter. Protest poetry, these days."

"All the same, we live in Germany. There's still an audience for that. Not just the loudmouths make it here. Look, if a wonderful poet like Hermann Stehr has a following, why shouldn't Miermann have one?"

"The only people who read my books have gotten them as presents. Try giving them away for free with razor blades."

"But Mr. Miermann, most of the readers of the *Berliner Rundschau* always look first to see if they can't find the Miermann article."

"They get me for free there as well, as a newspaper supplement."

"I'd still like to talk to a publisher about your collection."

"Do what you have to do, but wait until I start writing songs about Käsebier."

Waldschmidt said to Lambeck, "D'you see anyone you don't see? *Tout Berlin*, so to speak. And this is all thanks to you; that is, thanks to us. That's the way it should be, you see, publishers and poets collaborating. I asked you to write an article about Berlin. You wrote about Käsebier. This evening is the result."

"I'm afraid that I can't take credit for the discovery. Mr. Frächter alerted me to Käsebier."

"Who's Mr. Frächter? I just bought a book on Käsebier. Edited by Frächter, introduction by Frächter. Did Frächter invent Käsebier? From time to time, young people pop up in Berlin whom you've never heard of. Three weeks later, they've made a name for themselves. Apparently, Frächter also negotiated Käsebier's contract with the Wintergarten."

Käte was now standing by Margot Weissmann.

"*Enchantée de vous voir*," Margot said to Käte, because of the foreign gentleman.

"*Enchantée*," Käte replied.

The gentleman said, "*C'était très chic ça! Très chic.*"

Käte said, "Yes, I thought so too. I'm eager to see Käsebier."

"Simply terrific," said Margot, "marvelous, fantastic, splendid."

"When will you finally come by?"

"But my dear, I most definitely will. I've meant to ring you for ages now, I've felt so guilty. But you know how it is. We've been completely swamped since we've begun looking for an apartment. We want to move back into the old west, and, on top of that, my cook is sick. Otto and I are lunching at the Bristol every day. Ghastly. I can't even tell you what we've been through."

"Good evening," said Muschler the banker, and stepped towards them.

"Good day," said Mrs. Thedy Muschler. "My dear, we barely see each other anymore. How in the world are you?"

"How nice to see you, I've meant to ring you for ages, I've felt so guilty," said Margot. "I've had so much on my mind lately, I've barely had any time to myself. My cook is sick."

"How dreadful," said Mrs. Muschler, looking at Mr. Schrade, the lawyer.

"Good evening," he said as he passed by. He grazed Mrs. Muschler with his hand, although it had been over for fourteen days now. Schrade had been a company lawyer. He had his notice slip in his pocket. On top of that, he was in debt. He was walking around with another young man.

He said, "Just keep your chin up. The moment you wear a stained suit, it's over."

"Perhaps," the other man said, "but I have unpaid bills. Can't we have dinner with Muschler tonight?"

"I think Muschler lost a fortune on the stock market today, one hundred thousand marks. He was being bearish, and all of a sudden, everything shot up."

"Goodbye," said Muschler the banker. "We're anxious to see Käsebier. *Au revoir, Monsieur.*"

"*Au revoir!*" his better half cried.

"I'll ring you sometime," said Margot Weissmann.

"I'll give you a call," said Käte.

"Let's give each other a call sometime," said Mrs. Muschler.

"Margot Weissmann has the most incredible luck," said Thedy, walking back to her seat with Muschler. "She invited a hundred guests and not a single person turned her down, imagine that! When I invite a hundred guests, I have to count on twenty cancellations. And she's vice-president of the motor club as well. You know, the dress she's wearing is probably by Marbach, and cost six hundred marks. Well, aren't I a fool, mine had exactly the same little wings, and I just gave it to Gerstel so she could remove them."

The lights were dimmed. They were no longer in Hasenheide, no—they were in the great world of the *varieté*. Childish delight no longer reigned. There were no more fluttering doves, no more silly plays; gone was the happy-go-lucky, well-meaning atmosphere. The chips were down. This wasn't just about the gig; this was about international fame. They had moved up from the green wagon and the meadow fenced off with rope, left the green wagon, wretched circus folk.

Spotlights swept over a framework of ladders, swings, rings, and taut nets. Three beautiful specimens in leotards grasped swings that were thirty meters above the ground, somersaulted in the air once, twice, thrice, grasped their swings again, returned, traded rings. They led hard lives in order to somersault three times in the air, without drink or love, with gritted teeth, working from dawn till dusk, without detours or adventures. Their performance was the only thing that mattered. They kept their eyes on the goal: to somersault three times in the air and grab the right rope. Since this was quite dangerous, a sturdy net had been strung up ten meters above the ground. Lambeck thought of Miss Kohler's words. "Ridiculous. It denies all humanity and, because of that, it's unbearably sad. Dexterity for dexterity's sake, as a way of filling your days, is embarrassing—it's not for fun, *recréation,* which implies rebirth, renewal. We slide back into the Middle Ages when we take someone else's mortal peril for an amusing diversion. It's the same as burning people at the stake in the village square." And Lambeck thought that it was instructive to see how nothing else, truly nothing else mattered apart from grabbing the right rope.

The next act was delightfully absurd. Several individuals attempted to toss four balls up in the air and catch them using candlesticks balanced on their noses. They also played ball with thoroughly unsuitable objects.

Then came seven people all disguised as children. The girls were in red silk dresses, the boys wore yellow silk suits. They upended tables with a huge, American-style racket, broke the legs off of chairs, rode bicycles on crooked surfaces, fell over each other, jumped over tables and benches, causing a wild, youthful ruckus until they left the stage, skipping and whooping.

The harsh *varieté* music, loud and brassy, subsided. The curtain went up again. A wonderfully gentle background, softest pink silk with silver and palest green; a foreign, completely quiet world. In front of it stood seven southern Chinese women, smiling, dressed in soft hues of blue and yellow. They were as beautiful as the night, as great flowers on ponds unruffled by any passing breeze, as ivy on crumbling walls. They began to dissolve, turning into strands of rubber. They coiled themselves like panthers, they stood on one another, they jumped down; oh, you couldn't call it jumping, they flew up and down, and a little boy spun himself head over heels twelve times, then quietly went to the side. A silver dragon softly glowed overhead, pale green lotus flowers on pink silk.

The East set.

And Georg Käsebier appeared, Georg Käsebier, blood of the blood of this city. Thousands of wrinkles danced around his eyes and mouth, wrinkles of derision, mockery, audacity, facetiousness, and that most delicate shame: the shame of emotion.—"Boy, Isn't Love Swell?"—"In Tent Two, by the Spree, Over a Cup of Coffee, That's Where I Kissed Lieschen for the First Time."—"Why Don'cha Wanna Go to the Fair with Him?" Wasn't this Berlin? Courtyard to courtyard? Man to man?—"How Can He Sleep with That Thin Wall?"

Wasn't this Berlin, from the west to the east?—"I'm dancing the Charleston and he's dancing the Charleston and she's dancing the Charleston—what about you?"—"I need dough and he needs dough and she needs dough—what about you?" But he didn't sing about getting stamped.

Käsebier was a kind man. He didn't like saying unpleasant things to people. He didn't want to think about the revolution being carried out in the west.

Everyone was delighted. It was a smashing success. Miermann thought he was terrific. His crudeness, his ugliness, no schmaltz, no kitsch. Delightful.

Ixo said, "Did I promise too much?"

Müller shouted over to Öchsli, "Capital affair. What? Pallenberg and Guilbert, right? My sugar rabbit, my little golden pig, my fivefold dearest life, I'm waiting for your call. Oh, you don't believe me? It's true. All seriousness aside. What's more serious than love? Shall we go out again, or don't you love me anymore? Me, the little forest fairy? And why not."

Öchsli shook his head.

"Ghastly woman," said Miermann.

"Dreadfully noisy," said Käte.

Frächter found his way over to them. Charming, thought Käte. She thought him good-looking. Cochius, the publisher of the *Berliner Rundschau*, very blond, very feudal, walked by. He greeted Miermann. Frächter joined them. Miermann introduced him.

"Ah, a pleasure," said Mr. Cochius. "You put this book together, a pleasure."

"Yes," said Frächter. "I wrote the preface."

"The preface, yes, of course, the preface. Putting the book together was just a manner of speaking. I read the preface, excellent, extremely interesting. One reads too little of your work, Mr. Frächter."

"I'm working on larger projects, and I'm currently preoccupied with organizational issues in the newspaper industry."

"Well, well. Isn't that interesting. Goodbye, Mr. Frächter."

"Goodbye, Mr. Cochius, very honored to meet you."

Frächter beamed. Miermann was grumpy. They walked away together. Frächter said that Käsebier was petit-bourgeois.

"What can you expect of capitalist art?" Käte asked.

"Quite right," said Frächter.

"I don't understand how a ballad singer can produce capitalist art," said Miermann.

"Our dear Miermann is a romantic," said Käte.

"Yes, unfortunately," said Frächter. "Käsebier is a private citizen. Bed and a few little sorrows."

"He has no élan, no revolutionary fervor. He has the chops to put on a stinging political satire, but he's stuck in the same old rut," said Käte.

Miermann told them that Augur had only received thirty marks for his dramatic revelations.

"What can you expect from capitalism?" Käte and Frächter said in unison, and looked at each other, enraptured.

Miermann said, "That was a particularly unconscientious company."

"You always see things from such a narrow perspective. I'd prefer an unsentimental capitalism to a sentimental one," said Käte.

"Quite right," said Frächter.

"But I can't walk anymore," said Käte.

Frächter hailed a taxi. "I'm also taking a taxi. Can I bring you home?"

He hailed the taxi, Käte got in, Frächter followed.

"Goodbye, dearest," Käte said, and waved at Miermann, who was left alone in the dark on Dorotheenstrasse. Miermann walked on, farther along Dorotheenstrasse, almost until the Brandenburg Gate.

She's driven away with Frächter. That armchair communist, Miermann suddenly thought with venom, how he scorns everything human. It's those folks who hustle hard, strive for the best jobs, have no creativity. And as if that weren't enough, they make us out to be dumb and laugh at us. Personal bluster as revolutionary élan.

Miermann laughed.

"Who laughs there?" said Gohlisch, in the voice of an old ham. He came down Dorotheenstrasse with Öchsli. "Do we still want to go to Siechen?"

"Fine," said Miermann. "Everything's fine by me."

"Huth's better," said Öchsli. "They have a wonderful wine from '21."

"Fine," said Gohlisch. "We'll knock back a few. But the master must command us."

Miermann said, "I'm not particularly in the mood for drinking, but whatever you say, Gohlisch, my son."

Gohlisch said, "I thought Käsebier was marvelous."

"A great artist," said Öchsli. "He's got wistfulness and longing; he's mischievous and mocking; he can do mirth, happiness, pain. Everything that's timeless and out of date. Of course, his voice is nothing special."

"He comes straight out of Glasbrenner and Kalisch.[25] But suddenly, he's not radical enough for Mr. Frächter," said Miermann.

"Who's Frächter?" asked Öchsli.

"The man of the hour," said Gohlisch.

"That may well be," Miermann said bitterly.

"But once everyone's forgotten about Frächter, they'll still be reading Miermann," said Gohlisch.

"Or perhaps only Miermann's name will live on," said Miermann.

They went to Huth, and drank a '21 Nierstein first, then Lieb-frauenmilch.[26] It was three in the morning when Miermann came home, drank a cup of the coffee that he always kept at the ready, and wrote his review.

11

Margot Weissmann's party

ON APRIL 15, Margot Weissman threw a party. The invitation said eight o'clock. In Berlin, seven thirty means seven thirty, but eight o'clock means eight thirty. The cloakroom was very crowded. Maids relieved guests of their furs and handed out numbers. The gentlemen all wore coats with beaver fur collars, lined with herds of mink and muskrats. Some of the women wore brocade coats. They hesitated for a moment, but then left them in the cloakroom. Only one older singer brought hers in. But the great disappointment had already begun in the cloakroom.

Thedy Muschler had been on the phone with Glauker for days.

"I'm beside myself! I don't have that pink georgette yet, though it's almost summer and I've been invited to Mrs. Adolf Weissmann's this evening. Am I to walk around in black tulle forever? What are you thinking? When I'm such a good customer! I was featured in *Fashion* wearing your black lace dress. I even sent you the photograph, and you're still making me wait? . . . Today after all, then? Let me think. *Déjeuner* at two thirty, bridge at five. So come around one thirty. But we have to be finished with the fitting in half an hour! And you'll have to deliver the dress by seven."

Thus Mrs. Muschler had telephoned, but the great disappointment had already begun in the cloakroom. And not just for Mrs. Muschler. A woman is always beautiful on her own. But many—well, that's where the problems begin. Everything looks entrancing in front of the mirror at home. Wearing pink and pearls, powdered at her own dressing table, every Eve can nod at her reflection and say, "Very good." But at the party, Mrs. Muschler was greatly surpassed by Käte in black taffeta, who looked like Messalina, not to mention Hannelore, a vision in pale blue ruched tulle! Even worse: half of the women present were wearing pink. Thirty women thought: Pink—what a mistake. I'll never use Glauker again! Mrs. Muschler thought.

Cards indicating dinner table pairings lay on a small table. "Dr. So-and-So is asked..." Her, of all people? But why? Completely off the mark. Oh, fine, it's all right. The seating chart hung on the wall.

I'm a second-tier guest, Dr. Krone thought. But Mrs. Muschler is sitting at my table. Her husband is sitting at the former minister's table. She'll ask me about her nerves, and then she'll go over to the professor.

Several very young women walked by, dressed in black, painted like devils. They were looking for some fun, with their husbands in the background. Like their grandmothers, they were good bourgeois citizens, and knew that this was the most pleasant way to live. After all, great love only leads to bohemianism.

Father stood next to Mother. "They could have put someone else at our Susie's table instead of Otto Peter. He doesn't have anything and can't do anything."

Mother said to Father, "I will certainly extend an invitation to Klaus Waldschmidt. He'll be inheriting the *Berliner Tageszeitung* one day. You have to make things appealing for young people these days."

The tables were decorated with pink carnations and silver ribbons. A large porcelain figure stood at the center of each table. The tableware had wide matte gold rims. This had been the fashion when Margot had married, in 1912.

Mrs. Muschler noticed that Margot had new silverware. Until now, she had owned Chippendale, just like the Muschlers. Now the silver was smooth and modern; odd, since Margot otherwise only liked decorative things.

To begin, there was salmon from the Rhine, with sauce périgord.

After the cream of chicken soup had been served, the hired waiter continually inquired, "Red or white?" Mrs. Muschler talked to the doctor about Käsebier and his effect on her nerves.

There was music after dinner. The young girls made sure to get close to the gentlemen. The struggle for survival is brutal. Margot Weissmann sang, "Lift up the sparkling cup of wine," while gazing at the marquis, who looked dashing—tall, dark, and slender. He was Catholic and married. His wife had remained in Spain with their many children.

A well-known art dealer stood in the corner, talking to Oppenheimer.

Oppenheimer said, "I'm kicking myself for waiting so long on the little Pissarro. Cassirer just sold it for twice the price to Mr. von der Mandt. I wound up giving my two kakemonos away to the museum, since I'm now only interested in China before the Song dynasty. But I've hung the Géricault, a nice piece of work, very inexpensive, from Paris. It's unfortunate that one really can't put up any German paintings. By the way, do you know what dear Georg is auctioning off? Paintings from the French quattrocento. Terrible, isn't it? He's also said to be auctioning off a Chippendale chair. The backrest is authentic. However, the front legs are questionable. At least, the left one is. I'd still put it next to mine. We've had to make more concessions in the past few years."

Mrs. Muschler joined them and said, "I recently snapped up an ancient stone bowl, truly first-rate. It's done in white and blue. I simply don't understand dear Margot with her Tang horses."

"Yes," Oppenheimer said. "I wouldn't put up whole regiments of them. She does have some beautiful pieces, though."

Otto Peter was eavesdropping on a conversation between two older women.

"Women are born to suffer," said one. "First our men leave us, then our sons."

"Yes, and we stay behind, all alone."

Otto Peter said, "But we don't have it easy either; all we want is someone to talk to, and we can never find anyone. It's hard to study all the time without someone to converse with. And it's difficult in general with women! We feel responsible. We can't trust ourselves."

Sweet Hannelore went unnoticed in her pale blue dress.

"These young fops are a disgrace," said her father.

Dr. Schrade's friend had at last paid off his debts, but after four months was still looking for work. He wanted to establish connections, but he seemed cowed.

"He looks lazy," Waldschmidt said to Cochius.

"Yes, utterly," said Cochius.

Really, all that was left was to end it.

The beautiful, rich Miss Camilla was in love with Dr. Krone, who limped heavily as the result of a shrapnel wound. But he didn't make anything of it, despite being very fond of her. Out of pride, he went over instead to poor, ugly, Gerda, the gymnastics teacher of Margot Weissmann's young daughter.

"Käsebier," he said to Gerda, "is a comic genius. Most people consider only tragedy an art. But I believe that comedy is a higher art."

"Camilla's having a rough go of things," said old Mrs. Frechheim, Thedy Muschler's mother.

Miss Kohler stood by herself. Yet again, Meyer hadn't called to say he couldn't make it, and she had bought a new dress for two hundred marks, even though Mr. Powitzer might still give his notice because of the dog.

The man of the evening, the forty-year-old industrial titan, G., a fine violinist with a famous East Asian collection, approached her.

"Is the evening a bit too chaotic for your taste?" he asked.

"Oh, no," she said, delighted.

"You seem nervous," he said. "I'm sorry that I can't spend as much time with you as I would like."

He led her into the sunroom. "It's cool here, and there's a daybed," he said.

Funny, she thought. Why doesn't he call it a sofa?

She lay down. He sat down next to her and placed his hands under her head. There was a womanly tenderness to this gesture. It was particularly charming coming from this calm, important man with an East Asian art collection.

She stretched out, making no sound. Music drifted in from outside. They were an island. His fingers quietly stroked her arm. After a few minutes, she stood up.

"Feeling better?"

She nodded, without saying a word.

The maids were passing out fruit salad, plates, and spoons. The men had gathered in the Italian Renaissance library by the liqueurs. Waldschmidt, who was on the National Council of Economic Advisors, was discussing the current state of affairs. The others were listening.

"We won't be in the black definitively for quite some time," he said, and helped himself to a Hennessy. Another man was discussing Bismarck and Ebert. He was an ardent young socialist.

"Ebert has accomplished far more than Bismarck by leading us out of chaos. You can accomplish anything in the heady days following a military victory."

Frächter was there. No one knew why he'd been invited. He was describing his impressions from his last trip to America.

"Machines," he said. "Machines, reducing the cost of labor, rationality. They're producing three times what we are. Here, everyone is busy complaining about how rotten business is, and people aren't even doing that poorly. I went to the movies on Frankfurter Allee on Saturday recently, and they were packed, I'm telling you, packed, and everyone was well dressed."

Waldschmidt said, "Our Dr. Frächter is still a young hothead—but too much steam will scald you. We have to recognize that workers are the first to feel the effects of any economic change."

"Certainly," said Frächter. "But sentimentality won't get us far." He thought little of empathy. "The best technical methods are what's right; America has triumphed. You're not about to become a Luddite, are you, Mr. Waldschmidt?"

"Yes," Cochius said slowly. "We allow a film like *Potemkin* to be shown but we're against filth and trash; shouldn't we protect our children?"

"But your own newspaper! Miermann!" Waldschmidt laughed.

"Yes," Cochius said. "Unfortunately, I have a different opinion from Miermann. England also banned *Potemkin*."

"Well, we don't know how to run our country," Frächter said.

Said Waldschmidt, the old cynic, "People need medals and titles.

You can address almost any manager in Bavaria as 'councilor,' and everyone's happy."

The young unemployed man wanted to say something, but Frächter took Cochius to the side and said, "Even the American newspapers are organized very differently. Large rooms, fifty typewriters to a room, everyone in the same place. You can keep an eye on everything."

Cochius said, "That's brilliant."

Frächter said, "Newspapers have to be fun, entertaining, you know. One day, you might lead with the culture section; the next day, with a murder; the next, with politics, but not politics all the time; no one wants to read that."

"Yes," said Cochius. "Quite right."

"And pictures," said Frächter. "Each article needs top-notch illustrations."

"We're starting to publish drawings now," Cochius said.

"But drawings? Why drawings? Photography, technology's your trump card! Mechanization. Why should the *Berliner Rundschau* have lower circulation numbers than the *Berliner Tageszeitung*? You're not going to dazzle anyone with your intellect. Intellect? Who wants that? Speed, headlines, sensationalism: that's what people want. Entertainment. Something sensational every day, splashed across the front page. Oh, I could liven up a newspaper, all right! Three issues a day! Journalists still quote Latin in your paper. On the front page: 'Schmeling wins; Germany crowned world champion.' I want to create a ladies' journal, a beauty page, a page with dress patterns, and publish society happenings with the names intact, so that you can actually catch the gossip and know that something's going on between Count Dinkelsbühl and Meyer-Lewin, that Mrs. Weissmann received the Marquese de l'Espinosa at home."

Cochius laughed. "That's good, very good. Who will publish the newspaper?"

"Rüttger, I think."

"I'd be glad to work with you. We need to restructure our paper."

"That's right. The old grind won't do anymore. You have to organize a sightseeing flight sponsored by the *Berliner Rundschau*, introduce Berlin to its most beautiful pair of legs, give away thousands of little houses, host a swimming competition with prizes. The *Berliner Rundschau*'s most loyal seeing eye dog; the *Berliner Rundschau*'s last buggy-cart driver. Publish pictures of the fifty most elegant stenotypists in Berlin, the oldest cooks in the city, the most successful female drivers. You have to infiltrate every milieu. The zeppelin shouldn't be called zeppelin anymore, but *Berliner Rundschau*."

Waldschmidt joined them. He said, "Are you discussing newspapers? Do you want to take out some ads? There's no point. I once did a survey of all the subscribers I'd lost on my paper in southern Germany, and asked them why they'd cancelled their subscription. Ninety percent said they received three times as much paper with the *Echo*, and that they were grocers, or something like that, and needed paper. Five percent said they preferred the *Echo* because of the nice new novel it had, and five percent—it may have been two—said that they were unhappy with the paper's politics. People would much rather receive blank instead of printed paper, it seems."

Short, bald, stocky Richard Muschler sat in a deep armchair. Next to him, on a tall chair, sat a handsome, elegant young man who had married the beautiful, aristocratic, and rich Miss Waldschmidt, and whom everyone considered very smart and hardworking. At least, this was what everyone assumed, since they couldn't imagine that wily old Waldschmidt would have given away his daughter to a man of no stature whatsoever unless he was hardworking. "I'd also prefer a hardworking son-in-law to a stupid, rich one," they all said.

This young man was Mr. Reinhold Kaliski, J.D.

Muschler owned the old bank Muschler & Son, whose offices were in the street behind the Catholic church, right by the house on the corner to Französische Strasse. Reinhold Kaliski, J.D., was discussing Käsebier at the Wintergarten.

"The show's excellent," he said. "Fabulous girls."

Oppenheimer joined them.

"I don't know," he said. "The Palais had different foxes, not to mention the Metropol. Too scrawny for my taste, too scrawny."

"I like that tomboy look," said Kaliski.

"Not meant for the home," said Oppenheimer.

"Nothing for me," said Waldschmidt, who had joined the group. "I like something a bit fuller with a slender waist."

"Remember that bird, Waldschmidt?" Oppenheimer asked. "That pretty girl. She started out at the Arkadia and went over to the Palais after doing some time with the Gerson girls."[27]

"I remember her, all right!" Waldschmidt laughed. "What a charming little thing. She definitely got her hundred thousand. Crazy Dicky once gave her a pink pearl that must be worth twenty thousand marks today, and an apartment."

"Oh, Dicky, good old Dicky! Life's harder for girls these days. They only work in banks and factories. It's sad."

"Don't you want to sit down, father?" Kaliski asked.

"Thanks, keep your hat on," said Waldschmidt. He continued along with Oppenheimer. They spotted Miss Kohler.

"A pretty woman," said Oppenheimer.

"A bit old fashioned and stuck-up," said Waldschmidt. "Her mother's an old friend of mine. We knew each other as children at Neue See. We went ice skating together. You know, old Blomberg's daughter, from the U. family, of course. Her brother later...,"—he made a sharp gesture across his neck—"her sister married a Baron Rygbart."

"She got the short end of the stick. He was a drinker, right? Now I remember! Kohler, who had the EGZ factory. Died in 1915. Left a huge fortune behind."

"Oh, people always exaggerate. His widow lost everything in the inflation. Muschler managed the money in part. Not particularly well."

Oppenheimer wasn't interested.

"Pretty girl," he said, moving toward her. "Nicely filled-out, and such a tasty morsel."

"Käsebier is a first-class guy, truly first-class, you know," Dr. Kaliski said to Muschler. "He should be managed."

"He's being managed."

"No, just in the south. Who lives in the south, anyways? I'm talking about the west. Make him big on Kurfürstendamm! Organization is everything! You have land. It should be used. How large is your terrain?"

"One thousand square meters."

"That's perfect. A large house. A pure pleasure palace. Look at how Haus Vaterland is doing.[28] But not that big by any means! Shops on the ground floor, on the left. On the right, Käsebier, up two floors, Käsebier's theater. Just Käsebier. Käsebier the entrepreneur. He can be a real host and entertain his guests. After all, he once managed a bar on Wiener Strasse. He was always in the southeast, and he prefers the Wintergarten too."

"What're you going on about? You're talking big! Who's going to build and underwrite it? I'm not doing it. I don't put my money into business ventures."

"I know some top-notch folks, believe me! We have to get a top-notch construction company interested. They'll give you a first mortgage at eight percent, the second at ten."

"That's very cheap."

"Kaliski can always get you the best deals."

"And what kind of guarantee would I have on my property? I'm a banker, not an entrepreneur. I don't like dealing in things when I can't be sure of the interest rate. What if the theater does badly?"

"Then we won't get the rental income."

"No, no, I don't like deals like that. I know about securities. But construction?"

"But Mr. Muschler, you're not just going to let the land lie fallow in a neighborhood like that! Think of what the Sachows next door made on their property."

"Well, that was a particularly favorable contract."

"Fine, point taken."

"But why? What are you looking to earn? What's your percentage?"

"Me? Not at all. Please, Mr. Muschler. I might ask to be allowed to handle the leasing."

The maids came by and passed around beer and lemonade.

"Shall we play a game of bridge?" asked Hersheimer the bank director.

"With pleasure," said Muschler. They went off into the adjoining room to play: Muschler, Mrs. Frechheim, Muschler's mother-in-law, Hersheimer and his wife. Meanwhile, Kaliski had taken a seat at a round table with some five other guests. They were discussing tariffs.

"I don't know why women never want to pay duties on anything," Commissioner G. said.

"Yes," said Mrs. Muschler. "My husband is funny that way too. The last time we returned from Paris, I brought back several new things in my luggage. A coat and a few hats and the like. I had removed the labels beforehand, but my husband didn't want me to."

"I don't know, I've never had trouble with the customs office," Mrs. Weissmann said. "We drove through Italy with our car, from the Riviera to Africa. We never had trouble anywhere."

The maids were now passing bread around. The unemployed young man said, "The last time I came back from Czechoslovakia . . ." but no one allowed him to finish.

Käte told everyone about bringing a few cold creams back from Paris.

"When the officers began giving me a hard time, I told them that it was my food, took out a little spoon, and had a bite." The group laughed.

"But you live in Berlin now."

"Yes, but I don't go out much, I have to work."

"Where do you hold your classes?"

"Until now, I've been having them in my apartment; you know how difficult it is with apartments right now."

"Of course, terribly difficult."

"A friend of mine had to pay seven thousand marks in moving fees," Mrs. Muschler said.

"Yes, and we had to pay six thousand, not even for something first-rate."

"The situation is dreadful," said Käte. Then Klaus Michael Waldschmidt sat down next to her.

"What did you think of Käsebier, fair lady? My old man was quite taken."

"I didn't find it to be all that. It's prewar art, petit-bourgeois, with no élan. There are so many good cabarets today."

"Aren't there, though? But I think Käsebier's a great artist. Doesn't that count for something?"

"Not these days. Käsebier's good at livening up shy men. He's a kind of superior stimulant. But really, the whole thing is only good for a society that hasn't understood anything yet. Look at the films from Russia. You avoid them, I presume? They're not so pleasant, are they?"

"Oh no, not at all, I love the Russians."

"Well, one can't exactly love them, either. You can't remain neutral these days, you need to know where you belong. We know where we belong. Käsebier doesn't."

"I don't think that you can view all art from a political perspective."

"Yes, you can. Those French lovers' plays set in the clouds are sickening. We can do that on our own."

"Oh, really?" He kissed her hand.

"Love must be beautiful, mustn't it?"

"Of course. Shall we dance?"

Lieven was talking about Käsebier with sweet Hannelore. He wanted to take her along to Hasenheide.

"Perhaps with my friend Susie?" she said. "We can ask her straightaway."

Susie was thrilled. So was Hannelore. A poet! they thought, A poet!

Hannelore's father and the parents were upset. Look at the girls, sitting with one of those literati.

Otto Peter sat in the corner, feeling lonely. He was nineteen years old. Hannelore was ignoring him. He considered whether he should shoot Lieven. He had seen Lieven kiss Hannelore in the sunroom. He had grabbed her by the armpit, that bastard. Hannelore and Susie stood together.

"He's divine," said Hannelore.

"Is he bold?" asked Susie.

"Yes," Hannelore said proudly.

"Did he kiss you?" asked Susie.

"Yes, just think, in the sunroom."

"Does he love you?"

"Certainly."

"We have to talk tomorrow, I'll tell you more then."

"I'll call you in the morning."

Otto Peter looked gloomy.

"Isn't that boy green?" Hannelore asked Susie, glancing at him. "He trembles when he dances with a girl. What a frightful bore."

Susie agreed. "I've no time for boys either."

"He proposed to me. On Geissbergstrasse. Whad'ya think of that! When we haven't even kissed!"

Susie was equally indignant. "Any sensible person would at least pick the Grunewald for that. What a bore! What a bore!"

Margot came over to the Muschlers and the Hersheimers. They discussed Käsebier.

Mrs. Hersheimer said, "I saw him at the Wintergarten, unbelievable."

"Fabulous," said Mrs. Muschler.

"A genius," said Margot.

"A God-given talent," said old Magnus.

Otto Peter said, "A true man of the people. Magnificent. He should go to London."

"Exactly," said Margot. "I met him recently when I was there with Meyer-Paris and the Attaché de l'Espinosa from the Spanish embassy."

"And what's he like?"

"A very simple man, of course, but very nice. He was very happy to meet me. We spoke to him backstage."

Beer, lemonade, and large platters with bread, salmon, cucumbers, eggs, and anchovy butter were being passed around. There were delicate spreads of egg, mustard, anchovies, and oil, as well as crackers with caviar.

Frächter joined them.

"My dear Frächter," Margot Weissmann said, stretching her bare arms out toward him, "I believe I haven't yet thanked you for your dedication in my Käsebier. Wonderfully witty."

She batted her lashes at him.

"A very amusing book," Thedy Muschler said.

"I'm so pleased."

Mrs. Hersheimer said, "Your introduction brightened up my whole evening."

"And the writing!" said Margot. "You write with the wit of the French. Nothing can surpass Parisian *légereté*, of course. Paris is so enchanting."

"Naturally. We are always so serious," said Frächter.

"Dearest colleague," Lieven said to Miss Kohler in the Louis XVI living room, "you know I'm only interested in little Hannelore Siebert and Susie Schneider. Perhaps the male death drive prizes the virgin."

"For God's sakes, Lieven, get up."

"Why's that, little Charlotte? What do you say to this one?" He pointed to the youngest Waldschmidt daughter. "She's living a double life, sneaking out of her parents' apartment three times a week to visit her boyfriend. I could imagine this woman in a few choice situations."

"I'm telling you for the last time, get up."

"Dearest lady, you're sitting here all alone," said Muschler, taking Lieven's place. "D'you see that girl in blue and gold? She's the best catch in Berlin." He pointed to the youngest Waldschmidt daughter.

"I can hardly believe that Waldschmidt managed to keep all of his money through the inflation."

"Well, it's common knowledge at the stock exchange."

"Well, then it must be so."

Muschler felt uneasy. He had the feeling she was making fun of him. Entirely understandable that no one wants Kohler, he thought. Clever, educated women are awful.

The man of the evening, the forty-year-old industrial titan, the important violinist with the famous East Asian collection, was strolling about with Käte.

"Is the evening a bit too chaotic for your taste?" he asked.

"Oh, no," she said, delighted.

"You seem nervous," he said. "I'm sorry that I can't spend as much time with you as I would have liked." He led Käte, who looked ravishing in her black taffeta, red hair, and copious fake pearls, in the direction of the sunroom.

Miss Kohler flinched. But then Monsieur de l'Espinosa asked him about Yugoslavian sheep exports. He answered clearly, smartly, giving numbers. Miss Kohler fell more and more in love.

Mrs. Adolf Weissmann walked through the apartment. Doctor Krone was sitting in a corner with Gerda, her daughter's gymnastics teacher.

Honestly, she thought. You invite a talented young man like that to a soirée where he could meet a few rich girls and make a good match, and he spends all night sitting with that thing, which will give him nothing. Some people just don't know how to get ahead.

It was four in the morning. Furs were being handed out in the cloakroom, cars were being ordered. Klaus Michael Waldschmidt accompanied Käte out. She found young Waldschmidt very pleasant.

Mr. Cochius said to Frächter, "I'd be pleased if you paid me a visit sometime. I've said so before."

Mr. Muschler said, "Well, Mr. Kaliski, I'll be hearing from you." Kaliski nodded. "I'll give you a call."

Lieven kissed Hannelore and Susie's hands. "I'll ring you sometime."

The man of the evening said to Margot, "Allow me to inquire tomorrow."

Krone accompanied the gymnastics teacher home.

"Once again, there were absolutely no suitable young people there," Mother said to Father as they got into the car with the two seventeen-year-olds. "Perhaps Klaus Michael, but he's the kind of man who spends all evening dancing with someone like Herzfeld."

Otto Peter sadly watched them go. At Zoo Station, he got out of his taxi and switched to the night bus.

I'll end up in a homeless shelter, the unemployed young man thought. Ten years ago, I thought I'd build something for my fellow citizens. I'm at the end of my rope now. I can't go on.

Oppenheimer accompanied Miss Kohler home.

"The moment you entered the room," he said, and kissed her hand. "You have such strange eyes!"

"It's quite warm outside already."

"Please, stay seated like that—no, like that, half in profile! I would have definitely married you if the thought had crossed my mind." And then he kissed her hand. "Spring is coming," he said. "Please give my greetings to your dear mama. I'll ring you sometime."

Miss Kohler thought about Oppenheimer. She walked up the stairs terribly agitated, awfully unhappy about the man of the evening and Oppenheimer.

Käte got into Klaus Michael's car, a Nash two-seater.

Käte said, "I'll sit a bit closer to you, it's so cold in an open car, my dear."

How easy, Klaus Michael excitedly thought. As he covered her with a blanket, he grazed her bare arm through the wide sleeves of her evening coat.

"It's quite surprising," he said, "how a bit of cold skin can be so thrilling."

Käte was thrilled by the young man's position, his car, his coat, his athleticism. Besides, she was tired from drink and the late hour, and thus found him brilliant. Young Klaus Michael drove her to his apartment. He noticed the bright glow of the area around the Gedächtniskirche over the Tiergarten.

"I've never seen that before, look how red the sky is. Like a glowing fire."

Käte thought, He seems to love me.

Mrs. Muschler sat in her bedroom, which was done in white varnished wood and decorated with pink carpeting and pink silk furniture. She dipped a cotton swab into Arden's precious Cleansing Cream to clean her face of powder and makeup. She looked very pretty in pink ostrich-feather slippers and glistening pink silk pajamas. She observed her husband in the mirror. He had a large stomach and was wearing pale green underwear.

"Mausi," he said, "Young Kaliski, old Waldschmidt's son-in-law, proposed a plan for using our land."

"For God's sake," Mausi said. "Does he know what state we're in?"

"Nonsense. Not a soul knows. Our reputations are spotless."

"What do we still own?"

"Nothing, except for the land."

"And Perleberger Strasse?"

"Two mortgages."

"And Niederschönhausen?"

"Same."

"So let's sell the land, move away, and live off the interest!"

"The land won't go for that much. I can only get back on my feet if I pull off a coup. If this construction project brings in ten thousand marks a year in profits, we'll make it."

"How will you manage that?"

"Kaliski wants to find me a developer who will bear all the risk and provide heavy guarantees."

"And Cannes?"

"Hey, of course we're still going to Cannes. We won't tank our credit like that."

"Well, naturally. We don't want to give people anything to talk about, after all. What would the Weissmanns say?"

"Who knows if the Weissmanns are doing all that splendidly."

"Come on, iron?"

"Iron's doing badly right now."

"But they're looking for an apartment in the old west."

"That doesn't mean anything. How Weissmann's doing isn't my problem. At any rate, there are still plenty of rich people around. That was clear tonight. Kaliski married very well."

"He's quite good-looking, too."

"You think so? I don't."

"Oh, don't keep the faucet running forever in the bathroom. You're making me all nervous."

"I'm always making you nervous."

"Well, the way you pace back and forth for hours in your underwear."

"I'm not as handsome as Mr. Kaliski. Oh, are you upset? But dear? It's fine. See, I've put on pajamas now."

12

A development project begins

WHAT Muschler had told Kaliski—that he'd never considered developing his property—wasn't true. The day after Margot's party, the two Waltkes dropped by to see Muschler. They proposed a project. It would be financed exclusively through mortgages, Muschler could keep his money. He wanted a guarantee on the rental income. They couldn't give it to him.

"You're wasting your time," Muschler said. But Erich Waltke came by anyway.

"Mr. Muschler," he said, "we'll build you something really swanky. Apartments fit for royalty. Five- and six-room apartments. A thousand to twelve hundred marks for a room. You can make a fortune off that."

"Aren't there plenty of empty luxury apartments right now?" Muschler asked.

"Not at all, where?" said Erich Waltke. "Everything's been rented out. People are paying up to ten thousand marks just in moving fees. You're mistaken, Mr. Muschler. Think of how much Köpenick made."

"Those were different times."

"But the city's still in need of thirty thousand apartments."

"Who'll guarantee the rent? I need guarantees. I'm a banker, not a building contractor. I don't pour money into dubious deals."

"All the same, I'd still like to show you the project we've put together." He unrolled the plans. "Below are garages. Each will cost a hundred marks a month. Then stores, then four floors of apartments. Earns twenty percent. No property taxes."

"And the many repairs I'll have to make?"

"They aren't prohibitive." He showed him the project.

"Very nice," said Muschler. "But I'm most concerned about the financing, you see."

Waltke left.

Waltke phoned up his brother.

"He's very concerned about getting a mortgage," he said.

"I'll ask around, shouldn't be hard."

Muschler called up the D. Bank. He borrowed money against bonds. Thirty Siemens bonds. Then he let it fly, went to the cashier, debited one thousand mark, and exchanged another ten thousand francs for Cannes.

Meanwhile, Kaliski was on the phone with Mr. Rübe, whose wife was the daughter of an important building contractor. Mr. Rübe was an architect. He was older, had a blond goatee, and sported black, decoratively trimmed velvet jackets at home.

Kaliski informed Rübe of his discussion with Muschler. Rübe was all for it. A project worth two million. His father-in-law would be the building contractor. He'd be the architect. His father-in-law could get a mortgage, no big deal. Kaliski would manage the rentals. Pronto, pronto.

Rübe threw himself into it. He visited the terrain and saw lots of potential. A theater, apartments, garages, shops. Each apartment would have five or six rooms.

Kaliski phoned up Muschler and asked for a terrain sketch. Because of this, Commissioner Mayer, old Mayer, who'd apprenticed under Muschler's father, learned of the plan.

"Good God, Mr. Muschler, what's all this about?" he asked. "Shouldn't we talk it over with young Mr. Oberndorffer?"

"'Course we can, but I'm not sure what you're expecting."

"He's an expert, after all."

"If the Rübes can't bear the entire risk, I won't go through with it, and if they do, I won't need an expert."

Old Mayer said, "Young Mr. Oberndorffer's always done everything for us. I feel we owe it to him."

"All right, fine," Muschler said good-naturedly.

Muschler called up Oberndorffer. "Hullo, Mr. Oberndorffer, how are you doing?"

"Well, thank you."

"And your dear wife?"

"Well, thank you."

"You know, I'd like to talk to you. We're thinking of developing the property on the Kurfürstendamm, you know."

"Wonderful, Mr. Muschler, I'd love to," Oberndorffer cried, over the moon.

"Not like that," said Muschler. "I've been speaking to a few folks who are going to do the whole thing for me and pay for it. I just want to get your advice."

Oberndorffer was deeply disappointed. He had done everything for Muschler; his furnishings, his summer house, he had provided him with estimates and assessments, and had worked very cheaply, sometimes below cost. Everything for a chance to work on the Kurfürstendamm property, everything for a shot at a big project, everything for a chance to finally show off his skills.

Now someone else had swooped in. He was beside himself. But he decided to get moving, and drove over to Muschler straight away. While Oberndorffer was in the car, Rübe was already on the phone with Kaliski. His father-in-law had a full proposal. He'd secured a first mortgage at 8.25 percent, and he'd assume the second mortgage himself at 10 percent—come on, these days, everyone's asking for 11 or 12. The first would be paid out at 98, the second at 97, all first-rate conditions.

Kaliski was passing Rübe's proposal along to Muschler just as Oberndorffer walked in the door.

"Good day, have a seat."

"So, what kind of shenanigans are you up to, Mr. Muschler? You want to build something? What?"

"A theater for Käsebier and a large apartment building with stores and garages."

"And which architect, if I may ask?"

"Of course you can ask, why not? Rübe."

"What, Rübe?"

"Yes, Rübe."

"Who's Rübe?"

"I don't know, the son-in-law of Otto Mitte & Co."

"What, and you want to sell yourself to Otto Mitte lock, stock, and barrel? Otto Mitte & Co. could cost you hundreds of thousands in extra construction fees."

"That doesn't matter, he's assuming the risk for the lease and the rental income. I couldn't care less."

"But Mr. Muschler, you're the client. You can't ignore the project costs."

"I'm not an entrepreneur, Mr. Oberndorffer, I'm a banker. I care about rents and profit. If Otto Mitte calculates a good profit margin and guarantees it, I couldn't care less."

"But something might be miscalculated. Then you'll end up with a poorly constructed building for too much money."

"Our calculations won't have any mistakes."

"What if something happens to Otto Mitte?"

Muschler laughed. "Do you know who Otto Mitte is? All Tegel and Weissensee belongs to him, not to mention half of Steglitz. Come on, the man's private fortune has been estimated at five million. Otto Mitte! The moment I heard that Rübe was Otto Mitte's son-in-law, I was relieved. When you build, the building itself isn't that important; the financing is everything."

"I'm not speaking out of personal interest, Mr. Muschler, I'm speaking in your interest. If the theater is beautiful, what a great advertisement it will be! And it's so much easier to rent out well-built apartments than badly built ones!"

"If Otto Mitte lets his son-in-law build everything and guarantees the rents, I'll be relieved."

"Have you already spoken to Käsebier?" Oberndorffer asked.

"Nah," said Muschler. "Why bother? We have plenty of time for that. First, the financing has to be taken care of. How can I negotiate with Käsebier before I have the go-ahead?"

"I'm warning you," said Oberndorffer.

"My dear young man, you don't have to warn me about anything."

"I'll draw up a counterproject for you that will generate much higher returns."

"By all means," said Muschler, "as long as you don't charge for it. Goodbye, Mr. Oberndorffer."

"Goodbye, Mr. Muschler."

Old Mayer handed the plans over to Oberndorffer. Old Mayer was concerned.

"I don't think we should close a deal with Mitte now, while Mr. Frechheim is gone," he said. "But they're offering very good conditions. And there's no risk."

"There's always some risk."

Oberndorffer got to work drawing up a project.

That same day, Otto Mitte phoned up a man at the Ministry for Social Welfare.

"Well, councilor, I'm having some trouble with the eighth floor of my high-rise on Fehrbelliner Platz. I'd already received verbal confirmation and planned on it. The foundation has been engineered for eight stories. This won't do. Please see to it. You can't give Otto Mitte any trouble."

The councilor was exceedingly polite. "No, no. That must be an error, dear councilor."

"That's what I thought too," said Mitte. "Look, I took care of what needed to be done a while ago."

The councilor said, "Do you know, dear councilor, that the Rail Service is planning a large housing development in Hohenschön-hausen?"

"Yes," said Mitte. "'Course. We toasted to that ages ago. So see to it."

"Certainly, councilor."

Mitte knew nothing about Hohenschönhausen. Karlweiss, he thought. Surely Karlweiss is building it. He called up Karlweiss the architect.

"I've got a few different projects floating around and was thinking of asking you to get involved. When could you pay me a visit?"

Karlweiss understood immediately, and replied, "By the way, I also wanted to invite you to join me on the Hohenschönhausen project. The forms will go out in the next few days."

"Just don't invite too many people. You know that the more you invite, the more expensive it'll be."

"There must be some folks outside the Ring, too."[29]

"Well, if you want to work with those folks!"

"When shall we talk?

"What about Thursday at eleven thirty? Is that all right with you?"

"Yes, that's fine. I'd prefer eleven forty-five."

"Very well. Goodbye."

13

Käsebier in sound, on screen, and as a table spread

IN THE meantime, Frächter had approached Omega Records and suggested that they record Käsebier, since there was now a tremendous demand for his songs. Frächter suggested that Omega acquire various rights to Käsebier's work. He wanted a 2 percent cut as a negotiation fee. They would release his four hits; each on its own, of course. "How Can He Sleep with That Thin Wall?"—"Boy, Isn't Love Swell?"—"If You Wanna Come with Me, Come with; and If You Don't, Go Your Way Alone"—"In Tent Two, by the Spree, with a Cup of Coffee."

Gödowecz designed a giant poster for Omega even before Käsebier could begin recording. He was currently booked up, preparing for his Wintergarten premiere.

"Hear Käsebier speak and sing—only on Omega!"

They finally reserved an afternoon to record him two days after the premiere. On the same day, Käsebier was scheduled for an afternoon film shoot at the Wintergarten for the weekly UFA newsreel. He had also been invited to a late breakfast at Mrs. Adolf Weissmann's at five o'clock. He couldn't keep things straight anymore and mixed everything up. The recording session was cancelled, since it was more difficult to cancel the film shoot, which was still silent. All there was to see was Käsebier's extraordinary acting, his distraught expression as he sang "How Can He Sleep with That Thin Wall?" The weekly news ran a segment, "Cowboy Games in South America," before him and "Il Duce Christening the Training Ship *Brigella*" afterwards; in between, two minutes of Käsebier.

The recording session took place the following day.

On Sunday afternoon, he sang on the radio for twenty minutes at 5:20, including a few old hits from the Biedermeier era, a real treat for connoisseurs. The Daily Profile in all the Sunday radio magazines was Käsebier. The photograph was by Miss Ilsemarie Kruse. She had been the first to photograph Käsebier, and now that she was earning ten marks per picture, she was doing brisk business.

Miss Isolde von Knockwitz had created silhouette portraits of Käsebier, one laughing, one crying, which were prominently featured in Sunday's *Berliner Rundschau*.

In addition to Gödowecz, Dietz the illustrator had also thrown himself on Käsebier. He had drawn a series, "Käsebier in Twelve Portraits," which appeared in the *Grossberliner Woche*.

Pankow, a young painter, exhibited a painting of Käsebier singing "How Can He Sleep with That Thin Wall?" in the Secession show. The painting was depicted in the catalog and mentioned dismissively in all of the reviews. The critic of the *Berliner Tageszeitung* even took twelve lines to rip it apart, a tactic that proved very successful. The *Völkischer Aufbruch* wrote, "Positively bestial—there is truly no other fitting expression—is the only way one can characterize Gottfried Pankow's portrait of this *Untermensch*. It is yet another snobbish painting of ape-folk, depicting them in their (im)purest form, amidst the civilization of Kurfürstendamm. *Brr.*" Another little-read, exceedingly genteel right-wing newspaper wrote, "Pankow dazzles with a portrait of the singer Käsebier, which deserves a place of honor in the Academy exhibition. The painting is well executed in its attention to pacing and hue." Pankow was elected to the jury. The critic of the *Berliner Tageszeitung* wrote another article mentioning the painting's thin, unskilled lines, a silly New Objectivity that made it look no different from a colored print. A savage little newspaper published an embittered article about the heights of snobbery, the downright barbaric appreciation of art, how ridiculous it was, a miserable portrait, just because it depicted a current celebrity; we should continue to favor fine floral still lifes and landscapes painted by great painters— because there were still great painters to be had.

Shortly thereafter, Pankow was commissioned to paint a portrait of Countess Dinkelsbühl, and his Käsebier painting was the only work of art sold in the show.

On Monday, the lunching ladies of Berlin held a big meeting to discuss two exhibitions. The first was to be a "table spread" in a department store, the other was a charity tea at a club, for which the ladies would also have to set tables. Countess Dinkelsbühl chaired the meeting. Countess Dinkelsbühl asked Mrs. Adolf Weissman for suggestions. Mrs. Adolf Weissmann wanted to put together a Käsebier table, decorated with the most famous lines from his songs.

Mrs. Muschler called out, "My dear Mrs. Weissmann, I've already asked for a Käsebier doll to be made for my table. I was counting on putting together a Käsebier table."

"My dear Mrs. Muschler, why didn't you give me a call? I could have told you right away that I had discussed this table with the countess quite some time ago," Margot said.

"I would have liked to put together a Käsebier spread as well," said Mrs. von Heyke, "but I think that we should do as our dear honored Countess says."

Countess Dinkelsbühl suggested that Mrs. Adolf Weissmann might like to set the Käsebier table for the charity tea, and Mrs. von Heyke could do so for the department store. Mrs. Muschler could put together a very simple table for Käsebier's coworkers; that way, the Käsebier doll would still be used.

"You'll do a lovely job, my dear Mrs. Muschler, you have splendid taste," said the Countess. "A table for *artistes*, dancers, and other circus folk."

The ladies agreed on the plan.

Mrs. Muschler said, "I'm leaving for Cannes in two weeks at the latest. I need to know about the tables."

"But certainly, my dear Mrs. Muschler," said the Countess.

Mrs. Adolf Weissmann wanted to do something very modern. "I'll put out blue glass plates for eight people, some bright vetches, and I'll make small tableaux of dolls based on 'How Can He Sleep with That Thin Wall?,' that could be quite charming."

Mrs. von Heyke, the manager's wife, wanted to use her antique Berlin porcelain set and prepare an old-fashioned coffee table with Bundt cake and bouquets of wildflowers. The Countess agreed. Then the discussion moved on to the remaining tables. Mrs. Thedy was beside herself. She left early.

"I have a fitting to get to," she said.

But the real reason was that she wanted to prepare a Käsebier table since it would garner the most attention. She phoned up her mother.

"Mama, don't you think Margot's behavior is simply outrageous? Of course *she's* the one who gets to have the Käsebier table, because it'll be the biggest hit. She's playing it up as if he were her godson. And you know that we're the ones planning a theater for him."

"Richard told me not to discuss it with anyone yet."

"Yes, unfortunately not, otherwise I'd have loved to say it straight to Margot's face this morning in front of the other ladies. She shouldn't get all high and mighty just because he had breakfast with her. We're building him a theater, that counts for so much more."

"Oh, please, Margot's making herself look ridiculous. Her parties are never good. I found Saturday's very disappointing."

"She always orders from the *traiteur*. Food only tastes good when it's cooked at home. I've always told Margot that she should get our Kriepke to help her out. That way, you know what you get."

"The turkey was dry."

"Of course it was."

"And she served compote."

"Yes, I really don't understand Margot. Compote is so terribly old-fashioned. And I'd like to see the Weissmanns serve decent Turkish coffee just for once. Margot is far too lax. She doesn't know how to handle her servants, she spoils her staff, and she doesn't put enough truffle on her turkey. Don't be upset about the table. You should have suggested another idea straight away. '*Souper à deux,*' for example."

"I thought of something similar, 'A farewell *souper.*'"

"Yes, see, isn't that charming."

"Isn't it, with white roses?"

"So call up Countess Dinkelsbühl, you know that she loves to hear from you, and tell her that you don't want to prepare the table for Käsebier's employees. They can't expect that of you, after all. What a stupid idea! Why didn't you say so straightaway?"

"Oh, I was too upset to say anything. Besides, I still need to order some new clothes for the trip."

"That's right, I don't understand why you want to walk around in that brown coat every day. Did you go see Marbach yesterday? You can only go to Marbach. Everyone else is no good. You want to use Frisko? I wouldn't do that. Everyone already wore that last year. Panama's a better bet. Did you go to Hammer's fashion show? I was there the day before yesterday. She showed a combination of beige, rose, and blue, enchanting and not even that expensive. Five hundred. Your cousin Nelly is a sharp one. She and Glauker have agreed that every time she comes in with her husband, Glauker asks for seven hundred marks, and then lets herself be bargained down by two hundred. Nelly says her Erich is so pleased with his bargaining skills that he buys everything on the spot. She knows how to do it, unlike you. You've spoiled your husband too much. You can never just squeeze money out of men. They want to give you presents. If you send him the bill, he'll agree to it. By the way, once I got home, I didn't like the shoes we bought together. Luckily, I discovered a small scrape just above the right heel, so I brought them back. They didn't want to take them back, but I told them that I simply wouldn't accept a damaged pair, and that if they wanted to keep me as a client, they would have to do it. So they did."

"I really must be going."

"By the way, just imagine, Gabriele Meyer-Lewin broke her leg, so they brought her to her sleeping car to Cannes in a stretcher yesterday. She'd already reserved rooms at the Palace. Dreadful, isn't it?"

14

Conversations; or, Love in Berlin

MEYER-Paris happened to run into Miss Kohler. He took her along in his taxi. Meyer became angry with the driver, who couldn't figure out a simple route, and decided to make him stop briefly at a stationery store. Meyer bought a Pharus map, showed him the way, and said, "Here, now you can get to know Berlin." Lotte thought he was over-doing it. But she was too thrilled to be sitting next to him to think any more of it. It was raining.

"It's raining," he said. "It's always raining when we meet." Once they arrived at their destination, Meyer insisted on subtracting the price of the map from the fare. The driver refused. Miss Kohler turned bright red.

She said to Meyer, "Please, don't make the driver pay for it."

She was embarrassed by Meyer, pleased that she still had her wits about her, but it was no use. A car narrowly missed them as they crossed the street.

"We were lucky," he said. "Otherwise, the midday papers would have already printed the news: 'Charming young married couple run over by Lützowufer.'" He looked at her meaningfully. "Come with me to Paris in April. Please do."

"With pleasure," she said.

"I'll let you know well in advance."

"And then suddenly I'll be standing alone in some train station, holding my luggage. You'll have forgotten about me, and there will be no one there to help me."

Meyer caressed her.

"No, I won't leave you alone." He kissed her on the mouth.

She couldn't keep quiet. She would have liked to speak with her friend. But she had to go to the office. Miermann and Gohlisch were there.

The money courier knocked. "Mr. Gohlisch?"

"Come on in."

"Here are twenty marks from Mr. Frächter."

"Thanks from the court of Austria," said Gohlisch. "We'd agreed on twenty-five."[30]

A messenger knocked and brought in telegrams.

Landsbergwarte. 1405—press—berliner rundschau. 46-y.o. clerk erich sahler minzke nordau-warthe region swallowed dentures lunch died despite immediate operation.

"What a telegram," said Gohlisch. "What correspondents we have! They'll telegraph us about some swallowed dentures, but we can't find out anything about the political situation. By the way, the *Völkischer Aufgang* recently published the following: 'A Mr. Gohlisch, whose name is really Cohn, a slimy Jew in the service of Mr. Cochius, discovered the simpering singer who is dragging our most precious goods through muck, and crooning of male loyalty in the jargon of red pigs.' Can I respond?"

"No, we don't want to associate ourselves with that tone."

"Why don't you take a look, Mr. Miermann, and see how well-written my answer is: 'My name is Gohlisch, and I am a German of noble birth. The name Gohland, which is identical to Gohlisch, was already held by a clerk at Charlemagne's court. My ancestors were hunting wild boar while yours were still living in trees and could only eat when the nut harvest was bountiful.'"

"That's so beautiful it should really be published, but a joke shouldn't tempt one to stupidity," Miermann said.

Augur walked in. Shook everyone's hand without saying a word, as usual.

"How are things, conspirator?" Miermann asked. "We're completely jammed up with the Lankoop and Itzehoe trials. What's there to expose?"

"I got wind of some funny business with an architect from the housing welfare office."

"Who?"

"Karlweiss."

"Well, if that isn't interesting. He's an extraordinarily dangerous man. I fear we won't be able to prove anything."

"An out-of-court settlement took place in Moabit today. Karlweiss is on the housing welfare association, and it's easier to get property tax money to finance his building projects, which is why many large construction companies got into the habit of involving Karlweiss, who's not particularly well-known otherwise, in their construction projects. Anyway, he had been part of the Steglitz housing office, where he rubber-stamped apartment divisions so long as he got the job. He was kicked out of the housing office, but he's still in the welfare association."

"Was anything proved?"

"Negative, one hundred percent."

"Then I don't want to publish anything. We already burned our fingers on Karlweiss once."

"But you can't prove stuff like this unless you send up a trial balloon."

"Official denials are always unpleasant, dear Augur. You can't imagine how much I'd like to publish something on Busch, who's on the city council. But everyone always says that he'd deny everything. And I don't want to put myself on the line for him. Gohland, our ur-Aryan, don't you have anything to say?"

"I'm thinking."

"Reflecting, rather, you're reflecting. Who still thinks these days, after all!"

"Of course I'm reflecting, I wouldn't dream of thinking."

"What did the companies who hired Karlweiss say?"

"They writhed and squirmed."

"I love to fuel scandals, but I need some facts first."

"I'm very suspicious of Busch," said Gohlisch. "But I must say that although everyone always claims that he feathers his own nest, he raises far more money for Berlin, tremendous sums. A bit of corrupt ingenuity is better than honest incompetence. And that's that. But Karlweiss? There's a thorny issue. Where's our coffee and grappa, and how's your little daughter?"

"Not much better, unfortunately, but the doctor says it isn't serious."

"You should ask Dr. Krone to come by."

"Oh, our doctor is excellent."

"I'm going into the city," said Miss Kohler. "Goodbye!"

"You're so cheerful today, my child, have you gotten engaged?"

Miss Kohler turned red as a tomato. "Oh, nonsense."

"She's obviously gotten engaged," Miermann said to Gohlisch.

"To our slanted-mouthed, bleary-eyed colleague?"

"Oh, nonsense. Goodbye."

"She's not denying it, look, she's not denying it. Goodbye."

Miss Kohler walked through the city. She bought herself two pairs of silk stockings and two pairs of pink silk panties. She would have liked to buy herself a silk nightgown, but she didn't dare. It seemed to tempt fate with its blissful intimations. Instead, she bought two sets of silken pajamas, but then thought that cambric would have sufficed.

Her shopping caused her a fair amount of trouble. Mrs. Kohler was a Prussian. She thought cake was luxurious, afternoon naps were dubious, taxis were simply a waste, and spent her evenings contentedly and lovingly mending white laundry. She was deeply shocked by Lotte's desire to wear colorful, let alone silk, underwear, and she only ever referred to them as "rags."

"If you want to wear those rags, go right ahead, but who knows *where* you'll end up yet."

"But Mother, why are you always mending our white linen? No one does that anymore. Besides, you still hire someone to do the work for you. It's not worth it."

"Let me worry about that. As long as I have something to say around here, nothing will go to waste."

Käte was at her wit's end. She was in debt. Despite having hordes of students, she still hadn't finished paying off the move or the new furniture. In addition, she had forgone everything in the divorce, even taken on the debt. She had wanted to get out. Mr. Herzfeld was what he was.

"I should have never married him," she said to Miermann, who felt that Mr. Herzfeld should have assumed the debt and paid her alimony, or at least given her a temporary allowance.

"You're at an economic disadvantage, and on top of that, you're a woman. I don't understand why you didn't take advantage of the laws in your favor. Woman are feeble creatures. All that talk of independence is nonsense, after all."

"You belong to a different generation," Käte said. "The debt is mine. I should never have married him. I wanted to be taken care of, that was my cross to bear. So why should he have taken on the debt? I wanted to leave him. Ultimately, he loves me in his own way. Why shouldn't I make it easier for myself to get away? And how could I take money from someone I'm completely indifferent to? No, I'm independent now. I don't want to feel tied down."

"Why not take money from him, just for a bit?"

"Absolutely not. I don't accept capitalist justice, where a man owns his wife."

"You've made up your own set of mores, though you don't even know if they're justified, and they make your life quite difficult."

"It's my only option. The notion that women should let themselves be fed by men is immoral. I don't accept presents, either."

"But surely you don't agree with those young girls who snap as soon as they're given silk stockings."

"Yes, I do," said Käte, half laughing. "Flowers and sweets are fine for women, but silk stockings are practically prostitution. Any other clothing is prostitution plain and simple."

"And what if you want to shower someone with love?"

"There are other means. I also think that there's something impure about unmarried people falling in love."

"???"

"They're focused on a goal. Love can only be completely pure and aimless if both parties are otherwise committed. In all other relationships, one thinks of, hopes for, and wishes for marriage, and defers the feeling of love."

"Years ago, we would have called that the transvaluation of values, but the younger generation doesn't read Nietzsche anymore."

This entire conversation took place in the small café on Mauerstrasse, as usual. It was one thirty. Käte had eaten breakfast. Miermann wanted to pay for both of them. Käte wouldn't permit it. She smoked one cigarette after another and got in a taxi. She drove to Waldschmidt at the *Berliner Tageszeitung*. Clever Waldschmidt had a soft spot for her.

In his office, it was business as usual.

"Welcome, welcome, dear child," Waldschmidt said, covering up the mouthpiece of the telephone. "One moment please, have a seat, I'm just on the phone. —Yes, councilor. —No, impossible."

He put down the receiver and said to Käte, "He talks so much that he doesn't even notice if you're not listening. From time to time, I pick up the phone," which he then did. "Of course, sir—no—no. Then I must have misunderstood you. We can gladly take the car. Goodbye. —Give my best to your wife."

The phone rang. "Yes, only up to ninety-eight. I'm capping it. No higher, by any means. They're not worth more than that."

A messenger brought in a basket.

"You see. I'll be at your service straight away. One moment, please." Into the telephone: "I'd like to speak to Mr. Otto. Mr. Otto? —I hear there's a strike in Nieder-Klappsmühl. *Entre nous*, they're quite right to strike. Abysmal salaries. What are they supposed to live on? It's dreadful. The workers are always the first to feel any fluctuations. But it's very unpleasant for us. If prices go up, we won't be able to continue exporting."—"So, my dear child, how are you doing?"

"To speak plainly, I need five hundred marks."

"But for heaven's sake, what's happened? Can't you use your savings if worst comes to worst?"

"What do you mean?"

"Well, don't you have anything left over from your acting days? An emergency fund?"

"I always spent the money I earned, and I went to Italy after the divorce."

"You can't afford that on a salary and lessons. You need a trust fund. But you just bought an apartment?"

"On installment."

"And furniture?"

"Also on installment."

"But that's dreadful! No safety net? You can't live like that."

"But that's how ninety percent of the world gets by."

"Well, yes, but not someone like you."

The phone rang. "How much do you need? —Whether I have fifty thousand available? —Is the deal certain? —All right, no, but twelve percent. No collateral at all? —What? A mortgage? I see. —Well, I'd be quite worried. And the taxes? Can you avoid getting taxed? Come over tonight for a bottle of Rotspon!" —"So, dear child, I'll loan you five hundred marks. You only need to give me back four hundred. I'll save that much in taxes anyway. Just write it down on your tax declaration."

"Of course, Mr. Waldschmidt. With pleasure. Many thanks."

"Not necessary. I'm glad to have seen you."

"The greater pleasure was mine," she laughed.

15

Frächter pays Cochius a visit

EIGHT days after the Weissmanns' party, Frächter called on Cochius.

Cochius was reserved, as usual.

Frächter began. "Mr. Cochius, we had discussed restructuring your newspaper. I'm not just a short-story writer. I'm not just a journalist. I did gramophone advertising for Omega for years, and I also worked for Mecker-Flossen for a while; fabulous water shoes. I'm no stranger to salesmanship. We need to make the *Berliner Rundschau* bigger. Even the masthead needs to change. Much bolder and larger. Hydrocephalic, so to speak. What's tradition good for these days? Locksmiths and dead lords. Just because a masthead is a hundred and seventy years old doesn't mean that it's good enough for 1929. On the contrary! I'll supply you with twenty new masthead designs. Your circulation needs to grow to at least one hundred thousand, then you can expand your classified section, but you'll only get more classifieds when your subscriber numbers are up. And you'll only get more subscribers if you advertise. If we offer a good deal to the management of the Tiergarten, they'll allow us to write *Berliner Rundschau* on every bench in white paint, but then! You should run a daily column: 'Berlin is talking about...' with everyone's names, very decent, of course, not too gossipy, but still! And raffles for your readers."

"Thank you, Mr. Frächter. You clearly have lots of ideas. What are your conditions?"

"A salary of thirty thousand marks, and a stake in the revenue increase."

"We could certainly agree on that. I hope that you can also use the most up-to-date management methods to streamline the business to cut expenses."

"Of course," said Frächter. "Your masthead needs new blood. Young blood! Your good old journalists from 1900, who haven't been swept up by the spirit of the times, write in a style that's far too elevated for today's readers. It's all the same to the public, after all. If we didn't have critics, no one would be able to tell apart the good paintings, films, or books from the bad ones. Newspapers receive as little criticism as silk stockings. The day after tomorrow, everyone will prefer reading about Mr. von Trappen or Käte Herzfeld's secret trysts rather than laboring through analyses of French politics. No one wants to admit it. But the job of the modern business expert is to awaken slumbering desires."

"Mr. Frächter, I hope your restructuring isn't too costly. I can't stress how tired I am of being bothered about taxes."

Frächter said, "You're quite right. One can't hand over responsibility to the capitalists on one hand and terrorize them on the other. I guarantee you'll make my salary back tenfold."

"You're making big promises! We're headed into the summer months now. But I'll consider whether you should join us this winter."

"Gladly," said Frächter.

"Thank you," said Cochius. "Well then, goodbye."

Frächter was a motor that ran at a thousand revolutions per second. He discussed founding a talkie company named "Käsebier" with a few people, to give him his big break, like Tauber.[31] His phone rang; it was ringing off the hook.

"Hello, Frächter here. —Good day, director. —Tomorrow, you think? —I'm afraid I'm going to Dresden by plane tomorrow, and I need to attend a conference in Hamburg on the following day. Just a moment, let me fetch my agenda. The third, the third. —Tauber, look at Tauber. Why can't Käsebier become the new Tauber? —His voice? Oh, that's the least of it. But we have to get cracking on the film; night shoots, day shoots. You have to see to it, it's got to happen faster. —What? Art has to grow? A film doesn't grow, a film gets shot. Goodbye." —

"Miz, get me the theater."

"Yes, what's happening with the loan? —You can't get it? My dear sir, I've already obtained a loan for the Titania publishing company and the Excelsior film company. —Director Breitfuss, who's with the trust bank, has gone to Geneva. Fritz Blumentopf, who wanted to introduce Fitzke to him, who's friends with Patz, who knows Kobalt from the Maris film company, told him that Patz is in Dresden right now because of a new talkie. I'm going to take the express train through Basel to Geneva, provided of course I can get a sleeping car, so that I can at least talk to Breitfuss. Let me take care of it. You'll get the loan. Goodbye!"—

"Miz, please connect me to the *Roter Stern*."—

"My dear Ohnstein, how are you? Listen, are you interested in a series of articles on 'The biggest deals since 1750,' ten of them? I'll do each for three hundred marks apiece. That's dirt cheap! People'll love it!"

"Of course, Mr. Frächter, what a fabulous idea. Could I see one first?"

"Gladly, I'll send one along today."—

"Miz, get me the shoe store."—

"Frächter. So you'll name the shoes 'Käsebier'? Excellent. Stick a big papier-mâché Käsebier in front of the store. Isn't that a good idea? —What? —Isn't it? I also hope it pays off. Ha, ha, ha. Deal."

He arranged for Käsebier to perform at private clubs. He became the director of advertising for the Käsebier cigarette factory, which had just been launched with an initial investment of fifty thousand marks. He launched the cigarettes Käsebier Melior, Käsebier Optimus, and Käsebier Bonus.

But although Cochius had thought it through quickly, he was not about to immediately hire a man—even an ace—for thirty thousand marks a year.

16

Financing the Käsebier theater

MRS. MUSCHLER was getting ready for Cannes. The Muschlers wanted to leave on the thirtieth of April. The sleeping car tickets and the hotel room had been booked long ago. They postponed their trip until the eighth of May, because Mitte had scheduled another meeting with Muschler on the sixth. In the meantime, Mitte had held other meetings. One with Karlweiss the architect. Karlweiss came to see Mitte.

Mitte said, "What's with Hohenschönhausen? Why don't I have the paperwork yet?"

"You'll get it. What projects do you have right now?"

"I have a big job for you. A property worth two million."

"What is it?"

"Oh, you don't know about it?"

"Out of the question."

"Well, it's Muschler's property."

"Isn't that interesting. Apartments?"

"No, much more."

"What everyone's doing right now—restaurants, movie theater, bar, café?!"

"Something like that."

"What is it, then?"

"First give me Hohenschönhausen, then I'll give you the Kurfürstendamm job!"

"You're not mincing words—"

"What of it? Why not? Mitte's always straightforward. What's with the fancy talk?"

"I'm just saying. What's the percentage on the construction if everything works out?"

"I was thinking three," said Mitte.

"Let's say three and a half."

"And you'll let me have a say in the prices."

"Fine," said Karlweiss.

"When are we going hunting in Rebenwald?" Mitte asked.

"I'd be delighted to join you this summer."

"I'm going to host a dinner there soon with crabs and May wine."

"I'll be there, thanks," said Karlweiss.

"Goodbye then."

"Goodbye then."

Otto Mitte had also talked to his son-in-law, Ekkehard Rübe.

"I'm sorry," said Mitte. "But I can't give you the job."

"Excuse me, Papa, but I brought it to you through Kaliski."

"I'm not excusing myself. I mean, who's Rübe, anyway? Do you think they would have come to you if you weren't my son-in-law?"

"Probably. Kaliski knows me."

"Oh, you and your Jews."

"Excuse me, that's a strictly professional relationship."

"It's all the same to me. I'll tell you the truth. I just got a job from my comrade in arms, Karlweiss, with property tax revenue. It's at least four times the size of your whole Kurfürstendamm thing. But I'll only get it if ... —D'you understand?"

"Understood. But you're throwing away my opportunity to work on a big project."

"Don't talk about throwing things away in that uppity tone and calm down. I'll pay you a negotiator's fee out of my own pocket, and we'll take the car to Rebenwald tomorrow. How's Jutta?"

"She's fine."

"And Eckbert?"

"Fine as well, as far as I know. How's your old lady?"

"She's busy with her club. Well, let it go. No harm meant!"

"See you soon."

Rübe was insulted, but since he was lazy by nature, he was content to remain head of the Zeuthen artist's association, sport a long blond goatee and a black velvet jacket and receive a respectable allowance from Otto Mitte.

Mitte phoned up Muschler and let him know that he'd chosen another architect. "Karlweiss. You won't care, anyway."

Muschler didn't care at all. All he asked for was a meeting on the sixth. It took place.

Muschler the banker and his dignified lawyer, Dr. Löwenstein, formed one party. Otto Mitte, Karlweiss the architect, and a solicitor, Matukat the assessor, were the other. Mitte presented a proposal with splendid financing and revenue estimates. Basic construction costs would come to one million, turnkey ready, and included the architect's fee. A hundred thousand marks on top of that for garages. The theater would cost 250,000.

"Don't forget the incidental costs," Muschler cried. "Interest rates. Damnum."

"Processing and legal fees," Dr. Löwenstein said.

"All in order," the assessor said again. "That'll cost ninety-seven thousand marks."

"If we're conservative in our calculations," said Muschler, "that comes to one hundred and ten thousand marks. So one million, two hundred and ten thousand marks in total. And what does the revenue look like?"

Otto Mitte read out the estimate. "One hundred and eighty rooms. Each room 1,000 marks a year equals 180,000 marks. Two stores equals 11,000 marks. Theater lease equals 50,000 marks. Garages equals 19,000 marks."

"Well, well," Muschler exclaimed.

Otto Mitte said, "Even with a land lease of twenty-five thousand marks! Well—and you'll get three thousand per month on the land?"

"Certainly."

"It's still phenomenally profitable. 20 garages at 75 marks equals 900 marks per garage per year, minus expenses, that's still 19,000 marks per year. Here, have a pencil, Mr. Muschler."

"Right, right," Muschler said.

"On top of that," Mitte continued, "we'll get extra earnings on gas. Garage renters will be obliged to buy their gasoline from us. Do the numbers again. Twenty liters at a ten percent markup comes out to 10,000 marks, which is 245,000 marks in adjusted net income. Now, to the interest rates: 68,000 marks on the first mortgage. We'll finance the rest through rental subsidies. 1,000 marks per room in subsidies equals 180,000 marks. Then we'll need another 230,000 marks at twelve percent for the second mortgage, which I'll contribute. So we've got 68,000 plus 27,000 marks. Add on additional expenses at 45,000 marks. That's 140,000 marks. Subtract that—245,000 marks minus 140,000 equals around 100,000 marks in adjusted net income. Well? With numbers like that, we can swing this thing."

"Then all I can say is, will we find renters?" asked Muschler. "Will we find someone to lease the theater? We haven't even spoken to Käsebier yet."

"We'll get him, all right," Mitte said. "And the rent? No big deal. There are no vacancies anywhere. There aren't any vacant five- or six- or four-room apartments. Not with this housing crisis! No way."

"You'll guarantee it?"

"I'll guarantee it."

"Gentlemen, please leave me your calculations."

"And the project?" asked Karlweiss.

"Oh, yes, the project. I'd almost forgotten. I'm traveling to Cannes now. I need to think everything over again."

"Don't wait too long," boomed Mitte. "You have to strike while the iron's hot. You won't get another mortgage of eight hundred thousand marks at eight-and-a-half percent so quickly, or find someone like Otto Mitte."

"Well, hopefully we'll reach an agreement."

"Goodbye and good trip," Mitte said in his boisterous manner.

"Well, what did they say?" Mrs. Muschler asked that evening.

"If their calculations are correct, one hundred thousand marks a year in net income."

"How heavenly!" cried Mrs. Muschler.

"I spoke to Oberndorffer yesterday as well. He said the project is a bad idea."

"Even if we can make one hundred thousand marks a year on it?"

"Times could change. The apartments cost four, five, and six thousand marks."

"That's not so bad. Our villa will be far more expensive, right?"

"Certainly, my lamb. Oberndorffer thought I should build one-and-a-half, two-and-a-half, and three-and-a-half-room apartments."

"Come on, you can't build working-class apartments, just imagine the fuss."

"Yes, I wouldn't even dream of it. But Oberndorffer said that people who used to have five rooms are now moving into two or three."

"Oh, nonsense. Our friends are all still living the same as ever. And Margot Weissmann is looking for an apartment in the old west, she wants to move to Drake or Rauch or Hohenzollernstrasse."

"That's hard to find."

"You see? That's what I said too. We saw each other today at Marbach's fashion show. The most divine things. Margot is also taking classes with Herzfeld."

"An interesting person. Brilliantly funny and pretty as a picture."

"Well, I don't find her all that good-looking."

"No, she is."

"Klaus Waldschmidt is courting her."

"He's a good catch. She should hang on to him."

"Margot said that first of all, Waldschmidt's old lady would murder her, and second of all, she's not even thinking about it. She wants to enjoy her freedom. You know, people say she's carrying on with Miermann."

"What, the old writer?"

"He's not that old yet. He's supposed to be very witty. Apparently, she frequents artists as a rule. Margot prefers to as well. Imagine, she's still friends with the attaché."

"Well, what's a small-time ambassador worth."

"But from Spain! Not from South America, like we all thought."

"Well, fine. I'll leave that pleasure to her."

"By the way, I still need to buy myself a hat."

"But Mausi, times are bad."

"You say that now, but if I realize that I need one once I'm in Cannes, it'll be much more expensive in Cannes than here."

"Well, fine, buy yourself one."

"You're such a dear. And if the house works out!"

"Well, we're not there yet."

17

A meeting in Baden-Baden

THAT EVENING, Muschler and his wife left for Cannes. Their children stayed in Berlin with the governess.

Oberndorffer was working on a project proposal, as was Karlweiss. Oberndorffer sent Muschler an extensive report: the Karlweiss project wasn't particularly well thought out. He'd wasted lots of open space. Out of 179 rooms, only 66—37 percent, in other words—looked into the courtyard. The rooms represented only 47 percent of the built surface area, because so much had been used up on hallways, stairs, and impractical interior courtyards. Almost every apartment was flawed: dark hallways and foyers with no ventilation, small rooms, awkward shapes. Oberndorffer wrote: "Luxury apartments of this sort should have only one problem: their price. If they have even the slightest failing, they will be unrentable." Oberndorffer, who was careful and reliable as always, offered this assessment to the best of his knowledge.

Oberndorffer's letter reached Muschler at the same time as two letters from the credit agency. It was of course ridiculous to make inquiries about Otto Mitte. But a businessman doesn't agree to a major deal without receiving some references: "Good for a credit of 100,000 marks." Once this was done, the matter was essentially settled for Muschler. But old Mayer and his associate Gustav Frechheim, Muschler's old, overcautious uncle, wrote that they couldn't disregard Oberndorffer's concerns.

"Have you ever known Uncle Gustav *not* to be a spoilsport?" Muschler asked his wife. "Here's what he wrote: 'I remember the housing crash before the war. You can lose far more money on houses than you can earn. Badly built apartments in Berlin are not uncommon, and then a theater! I think Oberndorffer's project proposal is much better, and ultimately it can't make a huge difference to Mr. Mitte whether he hires Oberndorffer or Karlweiss. Therefore, I think we should grant Oberndorffer's request for a third-party opinion on the plan. Oberndorffer has suggested Professor Schierling.'"

But events overtook Muschler before he could respond to this suggestion. Otto Mitte telegraphed that he could obtain a first mortgage of 900,000 marks, but first needed a definite answer as to whether Muschler could return for a meeting. Muschler telegraphed:

RETURN TO BERLIN IMPOSSIBLE STOP SUGGEST MEETING IN BADEN BADEN ON RETURN FROM CANNES STOP MUSCHLER

Mitte telegraphed back:

MORNING MAY 30 OK STOP BADEN BADEN HOTEL BELLEVUE

On May 29, 1929, Muschler & Sons ordered five sleeping-car tickets to Baden-Baden for Otto Mitte, Karlweiss, Matukat the assessor, Dr. Löwenstein, Muschler's lawyer, and Gustav Frechheim, the uncle.

The five men met at Anhalter Bahnhof on a lovely May evening. From there they traveled directly to Baden-Baden. Muschler came up from Cannes by car.

In Baden-Baden, the five men were picked up from the train station by the car of the Hotel Bellevue, where rooms had been reserved for them.

They sat down for their meeting immediately. A building contract was to be drawn up.

The great battle that Muschler was waging was, firstly, to get Mitte to guarantee the rental income. Secondly—and this was the most important guarantee—Muschler wanted a property lien in the amount of 250,000 marks to be recorded behind the first mortgage, representing the value of the land.

Mitte laughed. "Impossible. You're providing nothing but the lot and are getting a building put up by me for free that will generate one hundred thousand marks in rental income, and now you want another security that will leave me completely defenseless. Impossible."

But Muschler refused to back down, and asked for more: guaranteed interest on the value of the property in the amount of twenty-five thousand marks per year, which he insisted on in any case.

Mitte agreed to the second mortgage. Should the rental income fail to cover interest and depreciation, Mitte would defer the remaining payments.

"I'm a banker," Muschler said. "I'm not an entrepreneur. I can't bear a risk."

It was noon. Muschler said, "In case of foreclosure, the owner of the second mortgage will have to pay me the two hundred and fifty thousand marks. That's my only security. No, no, I'm not letting go of that. Otherwise the deal's off."

Mitte was an entrepreneur. He could never take on enough projects, enough risk, have enough to do. He had a head of white hair, he was worth millions, but he didn't have a retiree's soul. He was no heir. He was old Mitte: the most feared, most hated, most hardworking building contractor in Berlin. Before the war, he had built tenements on empty land according to the construction code set forth by the Wilhelmine privy councilors, and, just like the bureaucrats, had thought little of the people he was building for. He built courtyards up against courtyards, windows facing windows; his priority was fire safety. Bedrooms faced north in vain, living rooms opened onto southern courtyards that had never seen a ray of sun. He never went against the law. Even though children were cut off from all the joys of life, sunless creatures chased out of courtyards and stairwells where they were forbidden to play, with no lawns, no sandboxes, and subject to every danger—he couldn't have cared less.

Through the housing situation, today's society necessarily forces the lower ranks of the urban factory proletariat to sink back to a level of barbarism, brutality, callousness, and hooliganism that our ancestors left behind centuries ago. I would like to argue that this environment represents the greatest threat to our culture. The property-owning classes must be shaken from their slumber and must finally recognize that, even if they make great sacrifices, these are only a reasonable, modest price to pay to protect themselves against the epidemics and social revolutions that will result if we do not cease to oppress the lower classes in our cities through their housing situation, force them to become barbarians and lead bestial lives.

Otto Mitte had surely never read these words by Schmoller from 1886, but if he had, he would have laughed. He didn't try to make others happy. He submitted to authority. He did what the others did. The only reason he was worse was because he was more hardworking than the others. He built German Renaissance, he built Art Nouveau, he built Wilhelmine baroque. He took long, narrow properties that had been parceled up by a clueless bureaucracy, built them up as densely as possible, and was proud. He was made a consultant, he received the Order of the Crown, fourth class, he became a Prussian councilor of commerce. He donated money to the naval fleet. He was a pan-Germanist. He supported the annexation of Longwy and Briey, and when there was a call for garden cities after the revolution, he built garden cities. They were never first-class; he never worked with good architects, but always with people who had influential, moneyed connections to city government. But he built them. He was not a rebel. He was a salesman. He submitted to authority. He slapped the communist councilor on the shoulder and invited him out hunting, or over for a bottle of Rhenish, just as he'd bowed and scraped for the privy councilors of the Wilhelmine era. He built with property taxes, he built without property taxes, he built garden cities, he built houses with loggias, he built flat roofs—"Dreadful, but they're asking for it,"—he built steep roofs, he built row houses, he was not a rebel, he submitted to authority. That was Otto Mitte. Otto Mitte, a tough negotiator, for whom 150,000 marks was not an imaginary sum for which he would let two big jobs, the Kurfürstendamm project and the Hohenschönhausen project, slip out of his grasp.

"Let's get some grub," he said.

The others were ready for lunch as well. They ate at length, and steadily. Muschler had a kidney problem and could only digest Burgundy, but preferred to drink acidic water. Out of the blue, Mitte ordered a heavy Niersteiner.

"To yours," he cried to Muschler.

"Hear, hear," said Karlweiss.

"Let's knock one back for the president," called out assessor Matukat, a big, strawberry-blond East Prussian whose face was pockmarked with scars.

"Matukat, remember when we went hunting in Ikehmen and it took us so long to shoot down the big stag that was bleeding all over the place? Your old man brought out vats of Niersteiner. Remember?"

Matukat remembered.

"To yours," he said to Mitte.

"Hear, hear," said Mitte.

At three o'clock—Matukat and Mitte quickly knocked back a strong schnapps—they sat down at the bargaining table again. Muschler wouldn't back down. Mitte had agreed to the terms by six thirty.

I'll get it back during the construction, he thought.

Dr. Löwenstein read over the meeting minutes with great seriousness.

"Fabulous lawyer," Muschler said to Otto Mitte in quiet admiration.

Old Gustav Frechheim knew Baden-Baden. He suggested they take a short tour through the Black Forest: "Just an hour by car."

Mitte and Muschler thought this the idea of a doddering old man.

"Nah," said Mitte, "A little nightcap's fine by me, but no country outings."

They walked briefly through the Oos. There was still music coming from the dance floor of the Hotel Stefani. Slim, beautiful women were dancing in light dresses, fresh chestnuts perfumed the air, the olean-der had poured its pink blossoms over the gardens, and rhododendrons had grown into towers of petals. A sweet western wind rose from the Rhine valley, and the sun stood over the Black Forest.

"The train leaves at eight o'clock. If we're quick, we can still get tickets and be back in Berlin early tomorrow morning," said Otto Mitte.

"Don't you want to spend the night?" Frechheim asked.

"What, and be on the road all day tomorrow? No way. I'm not traveling during the day. My life isn't cushy enough to steal a whole day from our dear Lord."

"Let's go back and ask them to order our tickets," Muschler said.

They crossed the bridge and walked a little longer through the dust thrown up by the cars. Löwenstein was calculating his notary fees, Karlweiss was thinking about his commission, and Muschler and Mitte were discussing the contingencies once again.

"In one week," Muschler said, "the company N. Muschler & Son will notify you in writing whether we agree to the contract as per the proposal at hand. If we cannot come to an agreement, councilor, neither party will hold any claims."

"Yes," said Mitte. "But Karlweiss will need to be paid for his pro-posal, of course."

"By you, by you," said Muschler.

"But you're the principal," said Mitte.

They called Karlweiss over. "We forgot to negotiate what would happen if N. Muschler & Son decides to give the construction proj-ect to someone else."

"Well, my proposal must be paid for, of course."

"Why of course?"

"Because I've already done my work."

"Well, how much?"

"Four thousand marks."

"Well, look now, that's pretty steep."

"Given the project and the fee schedule, I should be owed a lot more."

"Let's say two thousand."

"Come on, we're not horse traders. Three thousand, period," said Mitte, the great councilor of commerce.

The sun set over the Vosges, over the Cathedral of Strasbourg. The wind subsided; the air was fragrant with jasmine, hawthorn, fresh chestnuts, oleander. The pines towered darkly in the dusk, the Oos babbled quietly. A charming nymph in a short dress came out of the woods next to the gently bubbling spring.

"Fine," said Muschler. "Three thousand marks, but I want a written confirmation of this agreement."

"Quick, Matukat, deal with it, play travel agent, get the bill," Mitte said a few minutes later at the Hotel Bellevue's reception desk.

The concierge bowed. "Rooms for the day, lunch, dinner, and wine."

Muschler wanted to see the bill: "They always miscalculate."

Otto Mitte sent off two telegrams announcing his return and arranging business meetings. Karlweiss did the same. Muschler placed a phone call to Berlin, noted down share prices, gave various orders, ended the conversation when the gentlemen were ready to leave, and drove with them to the train station. One suitcase, Dr. Löwenstein's, was missing when they got to the train station. There was a terrific commotion. Where was the valet? Muschler walked alongside the train.

"Bellevue!" he shouted, "Bellevue!"

Löwenstein cried, "If the suitcase doesn't arrive, I'll have to stay here. I have an appointment tomorrow, twelve o'clock, third district court. I wanted to look through the files in that suitcase tonight, where's that suitcase?"

—"Bellevue! Bellevue!"

Matukat said, "Well, I'd get off, but then I can't get on again." Muschler paced up and down: "Bellevue! Bellevue!" he shouted. Muschler went over to the valets. The valets helped him look.

"Half a minute left."

"All aboard!" cried the conductor.

"My suitcase is missing," Löwenstein shouted.

"Looks like a stray suitcase got in here," said a man sitting comfortably in a compartment. Löwenstein dashed over to him.

Short, fat Muschler was still shouting "Bellevue! Bellevue!" and racing around with the valets.

"It's here!" cried Löwenstein.

"Thank God," said Muschler. "Goodbye!" Karlweiss waved.

Muschler drove back to the hotel and made a phone call.

"Niedergesäss," he said to his chauffeur, "tomorrow morning at eight, we'll drive back to Cannes."

18

Schierling's report

ONCE MUSCHLER had returned to Berlin, Oberndorffer again suggested they commission an independent assessment. Oberndorffer had high hopes. His theater design was impressive, his floor plan far superior. If he got this job, he'd be made. In the back of his mind, he secretly dreamed of generous city government contracts.

Oberndorffer went to lunch with Gohlisch, Dr. Krone, and Augur on Kommandantenstrasse. Oberndorffer excitedly told them about his project and said, "Good sense will prevail."

"That's a fantasy straight out of the Bremen Ratskeller," Gohlisch said. "Everything prevails, not just the good."

"My dear friend," said Dr. Krone, "you seem quite young."

"But Schierling is such a capable man; you must know who Schierling is!" said Oberndorffer, a slim, young man.

"Even Schierling won't say a word against Otto Mitte," Gohlisch said.

"Even if the other project is that bad?"

"Mitte prefers it, and Schierling only does what Mitte wants. Believe me."

Augur nodded gloomily. "Mitte's said to pay half a million in bribes every year."

"You're being naïve. It's not quite that primitive, but unfortunately far more dangerous. Did you make inquiries as to whether Mitte has ever worked with Schierling?"

"No, I didn't do that," said Oberndorffer.

"You're going to stay on the galley forever."

"Good work will prevail," Dr. Krone scornfully laughed. "One of my patients died yesterday because of his mad follow-up appointments. I said the man was deathly ill, the head honcho disagreed with me, and I filed a complaint to no avail. Yesterday, the man got up, fell over, was dead."

"Bon appetit," said Gohlisch. "Four grappas and four coffees. I do hope you get it, but the great professor won't help you!"

Oberndorffer wouldn't be dissuaded.

"Come on, my project has one-and-a-half-, two-and-a-half-, and three-and-a-half-room apartments, while Karlweiss's just looks impressive."

"The content's not important," said Gohlisch. "Schierling gets work from Mitte, so he'll say what Mitte wants to hear. Oberndorffer versus Mitte! That's like Kazmierczak the foot soldier versus Ludendorff in the war."[32]

"But Kazmierczak was stronger than Ludendorff."

"But thinkers don't have coalitions."

"Right."

"Thinkers should drink grappa," said Gohlisch. "I'm drowning my sorrows."

As expected, Mitte made a big fuss.

"Well, I'll be damned, Mr. Muschler, what more do you want? I won't even consider working with another architect than Karlweiss; he's proven himself."

"But look, Mr. Mitte, your architect can be all the same to you. Oberndorffer is very reliable and exacting. His apartments seem better to me, and my associates are urging me to use him."

"What rubbish, Mr. Muschler. You've got socialist fancies, huh? One-and-a-half-, two-and-a-half-, and three-and-a-half-room apartments! What's that supposed to mean? Assessment! I'm enough assessment on my own, I don't need a professor!"

"But I'm paying for it! It would take a lot off my mind."

"Well, if you're just looking to ease your mind, Mr. Muschler, we can consult Schierling. But I'm not working with anyone but Karlweiss.

A young architect like that, just think of the doozies, he'll build rooms that are three meters tall and so narrow you can only squeeze three flies in them and no people. Nah, I don't like people I don't know! Fine, consult Schierling if it'll calm you down, even though you're only contributing the land. I've got just as much to lose. But Otto Mitte doesn't need his mind eased. Well, no hard feelings. Goodbye."

"Goodbye, councilor."

Mitte phoned up Karlweiss. "Professor Schierling is going to be engaged to assess the projects. It's just a formality." He laughed loudly. Karlweiss laughed too.

"Why is Muschler racking up extra costs?"

Oberndorffer's friends were right. Schierling's assessment twisted and turned, made general statements one could charitably interpret as a slight preference for Oberndorffer's project, wasted no words on the grave problems in Karlweiss's proposal, gave nothing away, and was otherwise useless. It almost seemed as if he hadn't even looked at the blueprints for the apartments and the theater. The assessment cost two thousand marks.

Oberndorffer was finally out of the running.

Muschler said to his wife, "Can you believe it? Mayer and Uncle Gustav's cautiousness have cost us another two thousand. As important as the project is! I'm charging two thousand marks to Uncle Gustav's private account. Why should the business have to foot the bill?"

The contract with Mitte took effect.

Mitte had delivered a remarkably bad building plan. Oberndorffer, whom Muschler had brought on as a consultant, pointed this out. Muschler asked for some changes, but he didn't consider them that important.

"I can only reiterate that when you're building, the building itself isn't that important. The financing is everything."

No one had spoken to Käsebier yet. Käsebier was on tour. Once the financing was in the bag, everything else would be a breeze.

19
Käsebier dolls and lawsuits

A CRAFTSWOMAN had patented a Käsebier doll made of four dust cloths. This hardworking craftswoman, Miss Götzel, had begun by making batik, which she had sold in huge quantities on the foreign market during the inflation. Later, when that wasn't working well anymore, she painted shoes. But above all, she made every type and kind of doll. She had no artistic conscience. "If the women want it, I'll make any old crap. Light blue rococo tea dolls with pink roses and tutus with silver trim." Now she was making dust cloths and had invented a Käsebier doll. Who had ever given away dust cloths as presents? Had they even been a product? Miss Götzel made sure that dust cloths became a product. During the Christmas of 1928, a department store sold forty thousand dust cloth parrots designed by Miss Götzel. Now she'd managed to make Käsebier! She hoped it would be a major event. She thought of Käte Herzfeld, the beautiful businesswoman. Since it was summer, no one was taking gymnastics lessons. Käte could manage publicity for Käsebier, visit shoppers, perhaps drive out into the country as well, be paid for her expenses, and take a cut of the revenue. Käte agreed. She wasn't tied down to Berlin. She still had Miermann. But she couldn't hang on to Waldschmidt. Everything else was background noise. The job was made for Käte. She was an unbelievably talented saleswoman. She had everything: she believed in her product—what she had was always first-class and everything else was trash—she had the gift of gab, beauty, sex appeal, a sharp mind, and the ability to calculate.

She was welcomed everywhere, she was lovable, and would immediately take on a slightly erotic tone that never became pushy. "Mr.

Persianer," she'd say, "you know that I love you; how many would you like?" She sat easily on desks, and would just as easily let herself be caressed every now and then. Miss Götzel had ten women sewing Käsebier dolls out of two brown, one white, and one flesh-colored dust cloth. They were quite original, and met the expectations they were held up to. That summer, a rubber Käsebier was also sold on Tauentzienstrasse and Leipziger Strasse, together with balloons and frogs.

But the best product turned out to be a Käsebier doll that could be wound up to sing "How Can He Sleep with That Thin Wall?" A patent had been filed, and the factory wanted to roll them out around Christmas. Twenty salespeople had already been hired.

During this time, you could hear "If You Wanna Come with Me, Come with; and If You Don't, Go Your Way Alone," in every beer garden. In every café, people requested "Boy, Isn't Love Swell?" Every jazz musician crowed it, every piano player plonked it out. Every gramophone jingled, "How Can He Sleep with That Thin Wall?" The songs rang out in every last hovel. They were sung during work breaks. They were sung on Sundays on the Müggelsee. The cook sang it while she washed dishes in the west of Berlin, and the courtyards of the east, north, and south rang out with "How Can He Sleep with That Thin Wall?" On Monday morning, every office worker said to his colleague, "Boy, isn't love swell." "Boy, isn't love swell," Käte Herzfeld said haughtily to Margot Weissmann. "Boy, isn't love swell," Gohlisch said ironically to Miss Kohler, to pull her leg. "Boy, isn't love swell," Miss Fleissig, Mitte's secretary, said to her colleagues. "Boy, isn't love swell," Aja Müller bellowed down the phone six times a day. "Boy, isn't love swell," said the workers making the Käsebier dolls, and the workers making the rubber Käsebiers, and the natty typesetter at the *Berliner Rundschau*.

Meanwhile, the Megaphon Corporation was suing Omega for malpractice, an omission concerning the slogan "Hear Käsebier speak and sing—only on Omega!" Years ago, Käsebier had sung a few lines on an old record by Megaphon, "In the Hasenheide." Megaphon's overeager manager had remembered this record, and had filed a lawsuit with the help of Dr. Löwenstein. I'm slowly turning into a

Käsebier expert, Löwenstein thought. As a result, Löwenstein gave a radio lecture on artist lawsuits.

Soon thereafter, Käsebier was facing plagiarism charges. Mr. Theobald Sawierski, of 7 Kameruner Strasse, declared that the opening words to "Boy, Isn't Love Swell?" came from him. It was June, and the papers jumped on the trial since they had nothing else to write about.

Gohlisch wrote a delightful editorial for the culture section in which he examined the words "boy, isn't love swell?" to see whether they could be plagiarized. Can the words "girl, I love you" be copyrighted? Is the conjunction of "girl" with "I love you" already a proprietary product? Is "miss, I love you" a Heine quotation or an everyday expression? He suggested trademarking the following phrases for hits: "Hey, don't walk so fast," "I wish the beer were better here," "Round the corner to the right, straight ahead to the left." —"Anyway," he concluded, "an expression as unusual and unique as 'Boy, isn't love swell' is certainly worth protecting. We eagerly await the outcome of this plagiarism trial, which will be of great importance to all poets."

Frächter wrote a larger piece in ten installments for the *Rasender Roland* evening paper on historic plagiarism trials.

Around the same time, Lieven stormed into the office again and informed Miermann and Öchsli that he had just finished writing a musical comedy entitled *Käsebier*, composed by the operetta composer Adams, in which Käsebier would play the lead roll.

"I have already prepared a notice for you: 'The famous playwright Lieven and the operetta composer Adams have just completed the musical comedy *Käsebier*, in which the famous singer will star in the title role himself, alternating with Pallenberg. The premiere will take place on September 4 at the German Artists' Theater."

Gohlisch said, "Let's say 'well-known' rather than 'famous,'" crossed out *famous*, wrote *well-known* above it, 12 pt. Feull., and brought the notice to the composing room.

Lieven forced a cigarette on Miermann. "Käsebier Bonus," he said. "New kind."

"I've already heard there are three: Käsebier Melior, Käsebier Optimus, and Käsebier Bonus. There's a poster hanging on the Friedrichstrasse train station so you can't tell anymore whether the station's called Friedrichstrasse or Käsebier."

"In one hundred years," cried Lieven, "it may well be called Käsebier."

"Or Lieven, perhaps?"

"Very flattering, but come on, what's Friedrichstrasse? A memorial to an incompetent king."

"Someone just told me that he was the only hardworking ruler who wasn't a Prussian, but a German patriot," Miermann said.

"At any rate, Käsebier brings people more joy than an absolutist monarch."

"Even I'll agree to that." The phone rang. "Goodbye," Miermann waved.

The first criminal trial in connection with Käsebier took place in June. A young unemployed singer, who did not bear the slightest resemblance to Käsebier and whose real name was Franz Leihhaus, had pretended to be Käsebier and had received an engagement of three marks a night plus dinner at a resort cabaret on the Baltic Sea. He had asked for, and received, an advance of fifty marks. He had swindled thirty marks from the widow of a privy councilor in similar fashion. The old lady, a very small, slender woman in black, testified: "Oh, I don't want him to be punished, he sang for me all afternoon and I'm usually so lonely." In contrast, the police statement given by the cabaret owner was quite heated and contained epithets such as "sneaky bastard."

The trial moved quickly. It was scheduled for nine thirty, so that the midday papers could run an account of the proceedings and the evening papers could announce the verdict: a month in prison followed by probation. The prosecutor pressed for five months, as the singer had signed his contract as Käsebier, which was a grave falsification of documents. The jury did not agree with this assessment.

The fake Käsebier was photographed in the courtroom and his picture was published everywhere.

Katter, Leihhaus's defense lawyer, had notified the entire press and was thus mentioned everywhere and pictured with his client. He became famous in one stroke.

The bar association, for whom Katter had been an unknown quantity until now, organized a disciplinary hearing on Katter and fined him three hundred marks for generating dishonorable publicity to his client's detriment. Katter the lawyer appeared quite contrite, but secretly laughed up his sleeve. As if he cared about the old judges! Moabit was Moabit, and he was famous now. He gladly paid up the three hundred.

The day after the trial, Leihhaus came to see Miermann at the *Berliner Rundschau*. He had no prior convictions, had been in dire straits as he was ineligible for unemployment benefits because of some formality or other, and thus, almost ironically, had decided to call himself Käsebier, whose glorification he found ridiculous and infuriating. Now his name had appeared in all the papers, his picture had been printed everywhere—in short, he was done for.

Miermann was truly scandalized. But what had happened couldn't be undone. He gave Leihhaus ten marks out of his own pocket and spoke to the court reporter.

"All the newspapers published his name," he said. "I can't be the only one to use a pseudonym."

"Why not? Then you would be one of the only decent men left."

"And in the editorial office, the others would notice that I'm using a different name from the other newspapers and would change it to 'Leihhaus.' You can count on that. I've seen it happen all too often."

"Leihhaus is really such a fantastic name. I'll admit it's difficult to hold back."[33]

As it happens, there were already two or three cabaret singers who were imitating and parodying Käsebier.

Once the film shoot had begun, rumors sprang up that Käsebier might go to Hollywood. But that hadn't come up yet. Käsebier was still on his successful German tour. Negotiations were pending with Copenhagen, London, and Budapest.

On a Sunday in July, Miss Kohler was lying on the terrace of a weekend spot near Berlin. There was an incessant din. Cars nosed up against each other. Little men, little women, less kit and caboodle.

The jazz band struck up in the afternoon, my God, what a summer's day! People shouted at one another from various terraces, made dates, went on joyrides, sailed, rowed, and produced an incredibly healthy, young racket. Miss Kohler had received a thick letter covered in familiar handwriting. It held the program and text for Käsebier's guest appearance at the Stuttgart theater. There was also a card. "Despite everything—Charlotte—I remain yours. Your M. P."

20

Käsebier seizes the moment

CONTRARY to what Mitte had said and promised in Baden-Baden, the first mortgage hadn't been granted by July. On July 24, he informed them that the relevant bank meeting would only take place on August 1. Karlweiss's proposal for the municipal building inspectors was also ready by early August. It transpired that the new design, which had a smaller theater occupancy and omitted a shop and several rooms, was 47,000 marks less profitable than the initial project. In addition, new shortcomings arose. Dark apartments, rooms that were too small. Apartments with kitchens and maid's quarters in the basement or the walk-down. One of the apartments had been listed in the calculation of expected returns as a three-room apartment. In fact, it consisted of two rooms, of which only one was usable.

Muschler announced that he wouldn't let himself be walked over like that.

Karlweiss said on the phone, "I've already discussed most of this privately with the building inspectors. There can be no more changes."

Muschler was very annoyed. He wrote Mitte: "I can only say that I will not stand and accept a fait accompli concerning preliminary discussions on an unapproved project." Negotiations dragged back and forth. On August 29, the Charlottenburg district office demanded a larger courtyard, but approved a sixth floor in exchange.

A new proposal was put together. New profit calculations were made. Muschler was extremely annoyed. Couldn't construction begin in the winter? Probably not? This meant he couldn't count on any rent for the summer of 1930. Meanwhile, Mrs. Muschler was moaning that the children would have to stay in Berlin for the hot summer.

Old Mrs. Frechheim, who telephoned her daughter every morning, had stirred her up. "You simply don't understand. Take Lotte, although she's quite ugly. Have you ever taken a good look at the pinkie on her left hand? It's unbelievable, completely out of proportion. That it doesn't send everyone running. But her husband just gave her a May-bach and let her go to Paris on her own. And you, you're supposed to stay in hot Berlin all summer? Ridiculous. You know, men are always complaining. If it were up to them, we'd never spend any money. They always see the downside. I don't understand you. Are you going to walk around in that brown coat every day? You simply can't wear it anymore. You've spoiled your husband too much. You can never get any money out of men. I'm telling you, go to the North Sea. To Bel-gium, there's a good crowd there. It's ridiculous, Evimarie and Peter desperately need rest. But first go to Gerson—you should only go to Gerson—and get yourself a nice bathing suit. Something good. You're never well dressed. How was your georgette dress yesterday evening? —Good? —I don't think it's all that perfect anymore. Go to Gerson and get yourself something."

Mrs. Muschler did everything her mother had advised her to do. She succeeded in traveling to Westende by the North Sea with the children, the governess, and the car.

On September 14, the building inspectors received a dispensation request. An impossible number of applications had to be put through. Karlweiss had portrayed everything as small matters. He had wanted the provisional building permit by mid-July. But by mid-September, it still hadn't arrived.

Käsebier returned from his tour in mid-September. It was difficult to get hold of him; he was performing in Hasenheide every night and was at Babelsberg all day for filming. He was playing the lead in a filmed operetta: *Gee, Love Must Be Swell*.

This filmed operetta had nothing to do with Lieven and Adam's musical.

It was a true Austrian operetta with a young archduke and a Berliner who kept making a fool of himself. Käsebier played the Berliner. The operetta featured delightful sentences such as "Follow me, my darling, and my heart will forever lie at your feet."

The big hit was Käsebier's song "All the Rich Have Money."

Although it wasn't his job, Otto Mitte arranged for a preliminary talk with Käsebier on September 16. Muschler gladly left it up to Mitte. Mitte spoke the language of the people; could boom and backslap; when necessary, he slipped his hat back on his neck and stuck a Gamsbart on it.[34] He'd go for a pint with Käsebier. Mitte would get it done.

Thus Mitte, Muschler, and Käsebier met on September 16 in Mitte's garden in old Steglitz. Mitte served them wonderful wine from the Rhine.

"Well, Mr. Käsebier, how's life as a famous man?"

"Thanks, kinda so-so."

"Why? Dissatisfied?"

"Ah, nah. Not at all. Who'd I be taking myself for!"

"Well, where d'you like it the best?"

"Cologne, what a great city, the dome and the Rhine and the evenings on the Rhine terrace, fantastic."

"More beautiful than great Berlin?"

"Not at all."

"Do you want to keep traveling around like that?"

"Not at all."

"Well, Mr. Käsebier. I'll make you an offer the likes of which Otto Mitte, his majesty's councilor of commerce, has never made. D'you know what a patron is?"

"What do you think, course I do."

"I'm a patron, a patron like you've never seen before."

"I'm against that."

"What, you're against Otto Mitte? Mister, do you know what you're passing up? You're passing up your lucky break. You're a smart man after all, Mr. Käsebier."

"Well. Look here—"

"Look, d'you want to stay in Hasenheide forever? Hasenheide's fine and everything, and the Neue Welt was great when the giant swing was there.[35] But if you want to get ahead, there's only the west. You've got to go west. There's a musical, *The Girl from the Golden West*. You see, if you've got a theater on Kurfürstendamm, you'll have it made. The audience out there loves folksy stuff, you know. Cabaret shows, naked girls, and all that jazz aren't doing it anymore. You— that's what they want today. Imagine having a theater on Kurfürstendamm, Käsebier's Parlor, or Käsebier's Beer Garden. That works. Rococo's out. Over. Out of the question."

"Yes," said Käsebier. "Sounds nice, but it'll cost a fortune."

"You pay thirty-five hundred a month in rent and make five hundred a night. You can tack a zero onto your prices, see: three marks, five marks, ten marks. In that tiny pit, that shed, in the Theater des Westens, they pay four, six, and eight marks, it's bursting at the seams and a soda costs one-fifty. Easy money. Are you in? Let's shake on it, why don't you leave that old dump behind."

"Are we making trouble?" said Muschler.

"Well," said Käsebier.

"Mr. Käsebier, what's there to think about? Easy money. What kind of risk are you taking?"

"Well," said Käsebier, "it's Hasenheide. I'd have to cancel the show there, and the ensemble. After all, you get used to things."

"Keep your best and fire the rest."

"Nah, I don't want to do that. Now? Nah, I don't want to."

"Why not? It's the law of the jungle. Every man for himself. Give them severance pay, you're a rich man now."

"Well, I guess I have a few pennies to rub together."

"You call that a few pennies? Ha, ha, ha."

"You've got to decide, Mr. Käsebier, we have to begin construction. You're fantastic, we want to build you a theater, and you're still wondering whether to accept the present? Well, how about another round?"

Käsebier said, "I'd like to, but I don't want to. I'll talk it over with my Kitty. Don't take it the wrong way, Mr. Mitte. But that's a big deal—and thirty-five hundred marks."

"Well, we can discuss that."

Käsebier left.

"What now?" asked Muschler.

"Don't worry, Mr. Muschler. Tomorrow Käsebier will come round. He'd have to be soft in the head to turn it down. Just calm down, Mr. Muschler. I'll start digging the foundation."

"To your venture, councilor, to your venture."

"To my venture," Mitte laughed, and washed down one more glass of heavy Rhenish wine.

That evening, Käsebier spoke with his wife.

They were sitting in their apartment. Dried laurel wreaths and photographs of Käsebier hung in the living room. Great hymns of praise pressed under glass and framed, newspaper already yellowed. Kitty didn't keep a maid. "Nah," she often said, "I can't do that, have everything so improper. Bringing me coffee every morning, doing the housekeeping, going out to get a nice piece of meat. Nah, I wanna know what I'm eating."

She had extremely blonde hair, wore stilettos and garish dresses. She was all for Kurfürstendamm: "A big fancy apartment, you know, where we can put up a new sideboard, and a new kitchen too, right? And elegant bedsheets with lots of lace and a fur coat, right? In Hasenheide, where every Tom, Dick, and Harry knows us, it's embarrassing, right? But in the west, we'd be high society, right?"

"Well, you could buy yourself a fur coat here too. The whole thing gives me a funny feeling!"

"Honey, I don't understand you. What d'you want? They're making a talkie for you. You're famous. You were at the Wintergarten. What's got you stuck on Hasenheide? You can become Caruso, Hindenburg'll invite you over, you'll sing for the king of England, after all, things aren't right around here anymore without a crown on someone's head."

"Y'know, Kitty, you'll weep for Wilhelm, you're mad about Lehmann, and I've got Bebel and Marx hanging in our parlor."

"You're just not into high class. I don't like the proletariat. I wanna be a lady. Remember, in Wiesbaden the police lieutenant told me, 'Madam, you belong in high society,' and I felt it too. I told him, 'Please mind your own business, lieutenant, sir,' but he was right."

"Well, Kitty-pie, what d'you expect, the bourgeoisie is a dying class."

"Oh, c'mon, it's still pretty nice to have a villa in Zeuthen or Grunewald. You've got no ambition! You're so famous, I want to get something out of it too."

"Well, what d'you want?"

"A car and a real parlor and embroidered sheets and country trips with a car and a gramophone and picnics and chilled punch! You could be as famous as Chaplin, lords could invite you to their castles, and you want to wither away in Hasenheide."

"I don't need to go to Kurfürstendamm just for a car."

But in truth, Käsebier had already been won over. When Mitte called the cigar store in the building the next morning—Käsebier was just getting around to having a phone line wired—and asked for Käsebier, the matter was settled within two minutes. "The rent, well, the rent! We'll see about that."

21

The construction fence

THE CONSTRUCTION fence on Kurfürstendamm was already up. It was impressive. In those years, construction fences were no longer just construction fences. They were "free space, available to rent for advertising." The doge of Venice was no longer letting Tintoretto paint his palace; instead, the laundry business on Leipziger Strasse and the wine store on Leipziger Strasse who were building on Kurfürstendamm let great artists paint on their construction fences. This was the contemporary fresco. Something was being built behind these fences by coincidence. Purely by coincidence. And a lot was being built. Every self-respecting store was tearing down the German marble from the Wilhelmine period because it was too ostentatious. They covered their walls with more expensive Italian travertine. Carved oak and German walnut tables were ripped out; smooth, luxurious Makassar ebony was used instead. Plaster was knocked off the walls and simple transoms installed, because there had to be construction, no matter the cost. The landlords of the Kurfürstendamm had succumbed to the frenzy of inflation. They destroyed ground-floor apartments, lordly apartments of ten to fourteen rooms, in which parties for sixty had been hosted a mere decade and a half ago: fish, turkey, ice cream, lieutenants courting the young daughters of industrial magnates, young sons of industrial magnates wearily thinking, Socialism or the South Sea? First editions, faïence, Wildean aphorisms, lawyers and undersecretaries making toasts, engagements celebrated with vast sums of money. These apartments were to become shops, shops rented out for fifty thousand marks a month, shops for cars, shops for clothes, shops for perfume, shops for shoes.

And Otto Mitte & Co. had installed quite a construction fence! Käsebier, painted by Scharnagl, stood three stories high. At the last moment, Gödowecz had tried to wrest the contract from Scharnagl, but Scharnagl was and remained the best commercial artist in all Berlin. His style, a kind of children's drawing, was immediately recognizable: "Aha, Scharnagl!" Scharnagl had asked for five thousand marks for the fence. Otto Mitte had agreed. Next to the enormous Käsebier were the words WHAT? KÄSEBIER? YES, KÄSEBIER ON KURFÜRSTENDAMM! All around him dancers skipped, acrobats climbed, one balanced on a tightrope, another juggled balls.

"Have you heard?" Mrs. Adolf Weissmann said to Käte. "Käsebier on Kurfürstendamm. I think it's completely justified."

"Me too," said Käte. "What a fascinating rise."

"An artist of that caliber!"

"All the same! He came from nothing, after all."

"He embodies the real Berlin. In Paris, the finest ladies marry people like that. By the way, I'm traveling to the races in Longchamps after all."

"How was it at the Muschlers'?"

"Oh, quite delightful. You know how she always overdoes things. Mounds of caviar as an appetizer, and quite ordinary people. I mean, who keeps company with the Muschlers? But they're building the theater! Thedy practically believes she's the wife of a theater director. She only talks about 'our theater.' By the way, she was featured in *Frau im Bild* together with Trappen, Meyer-Lewin, and Count Dinkelsbühl at the Red-White Tournament."

"Won't she be thrilled."

The construction fence caused a general stir.

Mitte began the excavation. Kaliski began his announcements:

"Magnificent luxury apartments on Kurfürstendamm with roof gardens, all amenities included. 4.5-, 5.5-, and 6.5-room apartments available. Contact Dr. Reinhold Kaliski, real estate and mortgages."

Kaliski phoned up Rübe once again for his commission. He demanded thirty thousand marks.

Rübe said, "As you know, I'm not doing the construction. I wasn't suited to the task, I spoke to my honorable father-in-law, and he gave Karlweiss the job. But I will naturally notify him of your demand."

"Demand? You call that a demand, when a man does business and wants to get what he's owed? Am I *meshugge*—excuse me—to hand over a project worth millions to Mitte & Co. for no reason? Am I a charity?"

"Don't get so upset, Mr. Kaliski, you'll get what you're owed. Twenty thousand marks isn't disastrous. I'll discuss it with my father in law."

"Oh, I'm already upset," said Kaliski.

Ekkehard Rübe spoke to Mitte. "I'll deal with that myself," said Mitte, and called up Kaliski. "Now tell me, dear Mr. Kaliski, you've got your rentals, what more do you want from me?"

"'Scuse me, Mr. Mitte, I've already told your son-in-law I'm not a charity. I'm an agent, in case you weren't aware."

"Muschler told me you were getting nothing except for the rentals."

"From Muschler, yes. I got the rentals from him, but what about you? Did I have to give you business for nothing? Can I help it if your son-in-law doesn't like the job? Just because he's an artist doesn't mean I'm one, and I'm not even sure that's the case. Karlweiss, people know, Karlweiss, the gentlemen at the building office—"

"That's enough, Mr. Kaliski. If you don't stop now, I'll hang up. I thought you wanted money from me, but now you're insulting me instead?"

"Excuse me, councilor, but I'm upset because I've been waiting on the commission for five months."

"I can only reiterate that Muschler told me you hadn't asked for a commission. He also told me you were Waldschmidt's son-in-law."

"I may be, but I've still got a real estate business. So Muschler thinks commissions are beneath him? Muschler, you know, Muschler, Muschler needs them badly! He was the banker for the EGZ factories and on their board of directors, what kinds of commissions do you think he got when he landed a contract worth millions for EGZ? Not too shabby. If old privy councilor Kohler had known about it, he'd never have trusted Muschler with his widow's fortune. Now she's sitting around renting out rooms."

"That's quite interesting, what you've told me."

"This is confidential, of course."

"Naturally. So, the commission, Mr. Kaliski. Five thousand marks."

"Councilor, you're known to be a generous man. Your son-in-law—he must have told you—promised me twenty thousand marks. A gentlemen's agreement. You don't need anything on paper for that."

"No, Mr. Kaliski, of course not. But twenty thousand marks is a lot of money. The building office is giving us an awful lot of trouble. The job isn't as good as I thought. Let's say ten thousand marks, and I'll have it disbursed to you tomorrow."

"Fine, done, it's not all that much, but it's important for me that you know I'm an honorable businessman. Goodbye, councilor."

"Mr. Kaliski, I'd be pleased to do business with you again. Goodbye."

Oberndorffer intervened once more. He informed N. Muschler & Son of his many concerns in a long letter. Once again, he listed his concerns regarding the specifics for the apartments. They wouldn't bring in the projected rent. The apartments had serious flaws, and such expensive apartments could only have one flaw, their price. Once again, he strongly counseled against the entire project. One and a half, two and a half, and three and a half rooms were what was needed. The demand for large apartments was already weakening. Not to mention the theater.

That evening, Uncle Frechheim and Mrs. Frechheim came to the Muschlers' in Grunewald. After dinner, they sat together in the study, English mahogany with green.

"Young Oberndorffer wrote me another letter with his concerns regarding the apartments," Muschler said. "In particular, he told me that apartments of that size will be unrentable soon."

"Margot Weissmann just saw something she likes, it costs six thousand marks just to move in."

"Fine. But not everyone's Theodor Weissmann. Have another cigar, Uncle Gustav, they're mild."

"But on the other hand, you can't build small-time apartments, you won't get any rent," the uncle said. "Good cigar," he added, sniffing at it.

"Apartments with four, five, or six rooms at least," said old Mrs. Frechheim, "if not grand ones."

"I agree with you, of course," said Muschler, "but times have changed."

"But not so much that we're building apartments for the proletariat on Kurfürstendamm all of a sudden," the old lady said indignantly.

"All the young couples are only renting four-room apartments these days," said Muschler, lighting a cigarette.

"Well, not among my acquaintances," said Mrs. Frechheim.

"I also think it's a ridiculous idea to build apartments with no stature whatsoever," said Thedy.

The maid brought in coffee on a silver tray, then wheeled in a tea cart which held a fruit bowl with plums, pears, and grapes, fruit plates, and a basket with glass shelves for bowls, fruit forks, and paper napkins. Next to the basket stood two bowls of sweets.

"Have some," Mrs. Muschler said to her mother. "They're real, bitter sweets from Hamann."

"I've discovered a new kind," Mrs. Frechheim said. "Liqueur pralines from Hildebrandt, exquisite, you must try them sometime. I'll have a quarter pound sent to you so you can try them."

The uncle said, "I do think the ceilings are much too low."

"What," said Mrs. Frechheim, "you're going to build low ceilings, too? Those rooms are at half-height, it's all mezzanine."

"That's how people are building these days."

"Isn't that ghastly."

"And rooms that small?"

"No, no, the rooms are very nice."

"No," said Mrs. Muschler, "you can't build discount apartments, people won't pay any money for those, really, how ghastly, four-room apartments are small enough."

"A proper stately apartment begins with seven rooms, three water-closets, a dressing-room, two baths, a winter garden—that's how it's done. People will leave this petty stuff behind soon enough," said Mrs. Frechheim.

"Who'd like a schnapps?" Muschler asked. "I have some real Benediktiner over here, or how about curaçao? To return to the house, Uncle Gustav, I received a reference for Otto Mitte today. These people are simply top of the line, I must say, and since they're bearing all the risk and guaranteeing the rents, nothing can really happen to us. It doesn't much matter what the building looks like."

"I don't know," the uncle said. "In the long run, only attractive apartments bear returns. But what's attractive today is ugly tomorrow. I find those modern, bare apartments dreadful, and my niece is always asking me, 'How can you bear to live in those overstuffed, dark rooms?'"

"Well," said Muschler, "there you have it."

They were standing in the hallway.

"It's getting cold already. You need your fur. Haven't you turned on the heat?" Uncle Gustav asked.

"No," Muschler said. "We're pretending it's summer, since we want to begin building."

"Always witty, our son-in-law, always witty," said Mrs. Frechheim. She put on her Persian lamb coat and got into the car with her brother.

"I have a bad feeling about this construction project," he said.

"I don't understand you. A Käsebier theater is a wonderful idea, after all."

"Your son-in-law still has inflation psychosis, as does everyone in Germany, by the way. They all have property ghosting around in their heads. The whole matter seems a bit fishy. I have a bad feeling about Mitte, too. You can't see straight with all of these people."

"I don't understand you, Gustav, Richard is such an entrepreneur. You've always been a spoilsport!"

"Dear Mathilde, don't you remember when Thöny and Schwarzbach collapsed? They also started a theater. After that, not a soul went there. No, I have a bad feeling about this. We've had the land for so long, we might as well have hung on to it for a little longer."

Mrs. Frechheim said, "Rumor has it Oppenheimer's carrying on with little Kohler. It's so dreadful today with the young girls. Now no one will marry her."

"Do you want to come to the opera with me tomorrow? I have tickets."

"What is it?"

"Traviata."

"With pleasure, Gustav."

"Then you'll pick me up with the car."

Uncle Gustav got out at Keithstrasse, where he had lived for many years.

22

The building inspectors

BY THE end of September, construction had progressed to the excavation of the foundation pit, but with no date yet in sight for the permits. In the meantime, Karlweiss had entrusted the complete execution of the Hohenschönhausen housing estate to Otto Mitte. Apartments for five thousand people were going up based on a completely absurd plan. The main space was reserved for interior courtyards and wonderfully spacious stairwells, which made for a picture-perfect façade. The apartments, by contrast, had two small holes for bedrooms, in addition to a bathroom, kitchen, and side room placed along a very wide, windowless foyer. The result would be that, year in and year out, wives and children would sew and play in that windowless space under artificial light.

On top of that, Otto Mitte's construction work was particularly costly.

So far, the Otto Mitte/Karlweiss business venture had gone smoothly. Apart from the Käsebier theater. There everything was still up in the air. No building permits had been granted yet. Consequently, the Mitte/Muschler contract had yet to come into effect, which depended on the issuance of the permits. On October 22, they received an answer to their request from September 14. Otto Mitte realized that Karlweiss hadn't been diligent enough and had underestimated the difficulties of going through proper channels. On the fifth of November, they received the permit for the basement. Two months had passed since Karlweiss had said he was sure to receive the construction permits any day now. By the end of November, when the frost had come, they still hadn't arrived. In the meantime, people who actually wanted to rent luxury apartments had answered the advertisements in the daily papers, only to back out when no one could provide them with a date. The whole business was now delayed for another six months. Instead of opening on February 1, the theater would open in the fall.

Käsebier had been unable to get out of his contract at Hasenheide before for April 1. This now proved to be a stroke of luck. He would remain in his gold mine until then. The colleagues he didn't want to bring to the Kurfürstendamm also had some breathing room, while the summer of 1930 would be free to do film work and develop new acts.

Mrs. Käsebier, however, had been eager to suit herself to the new apartment: she was dismayed that her fantasies hadn't yet materialized. She wanted to get to work on those lace curtains, and yet accurate window measurements were not to be had. She wanted a dining room with an elegant sideboard. How wide a wall would there be? She got no answers.

In early December, shortly before Christmas, Otto Mitte hosted a longer meeting on the "Käsebier Project."

Mr. Karlweiss gave the parties in attendance a lengthy lecture on the nature of the proper channels and the timeframe for going through them. He said, "When you hand a project over to the building inspectors on June thirteenth, it'll arrive at the municipal offices a week later, eight days later at the civil engineering department, and then June is over. On the second or third of July, it'll reach the drainage department, then it'll spend fourteen days with the deputation for structural engineering, eight days at the surveyor's office, eight days in the fire safety department, which means we're in August. From there, it goes to the city's buildings department—another eight days— then in September, it goes to the headquarters of the building authorities. Assuming everything goes smoothly, it takes four weeks, that is to say, October, to get to the structural inspection department, three weeks to land in police headquarters, four weeks to get to the ministry. Now we're in early December, which means almost half a year. The gentlemen always think we can plan today and build tomorrow. But getting the permits for a complicated project like ours takes six months if we're lucky."

"You could have said that in Baden-Baden!" Muschler shouted.

"I thought I could expedite the process, but for the additional requests from Mr. Muschler."

"Well, isn't that swell. I left everything regarding the construction up to you, and now—"

"Quiet, quiet!" Mitte cried. "We're not going to argue here, right, Mr. Muschler? Everyone's doing their best. This entire project has cost us more than we'll ever make on it."

"Well, well, councilor, aren't you clever."

"But I'm an entrepreneur, I want a job, I'm not a financier."

"All the same, Mr. Mitte, I don't know how the construction and financial markets will continue to evolve. In these times, we can't move things back by three-quarters of a year into fall."

"I often have to plan for stone or wood—or construction materials in general, for that matter—over a year in advance. We can surely plan over a few months. I don't quite understand, Mr. Muschler."

"I have nothing against continuing to pursue the permits and I want to check everything thoroughly once they come through, but right now I need free rein."

"That's fine," said Mitte. "I've survived many a go-round with the building inspectors."

"I'm afraid they'll halt construction again this time, and cost us many opportunities."

"What d'you think the building inspectors are there for, after all?"

"Too bad, this would be a good topic for my literary nephew," Muschler said, "but Oberndorffer should go by sometime."

"Fine," said Mitte. "I won't stop you."

Muschler had repeatedly requested that Oberndorffer approach the building inspectors on his behalf. Karlweiss had invariably replied that given his excellent relationships, there was more to be lost than gained from this venture.

In early December, Oberndorffer finally went to the building inspectors. An official received him downstairs. He had a gray walrus moustache and peered over his pince-nez at Oberndorffer. "Fill out this form, please."

Oberndorffer took the form: visitor's name and business matter. The concierge pressed another form into his hand, identical to the first. "Here, fill out this 'un too. You can keep *that* one."

Oberndorffer filled it out. "It would be more practical," he said, "if you used carbon paper."

"Yes," said the porter, and blossomed as if he'd just received two cigars. "Someone else said that once, we even tried it, but then they weren't accepted anymore. Anyways, those things're useless, we were given 'em a while ago and now they've got to be used up. So we've got to keep 'em lying around for a while, and then we'll throw 'em out."

Oberndorffer went up to the top floor, walked down a wide gray corridor, and arrived at room 213. Two clerks sat at the window. One was writing, the other was finishing his breakfast, and the third, an old man, was filing papers. Coarse twine and glue stood next to him. Oberndorffer went over to the man eating his breakfast. "Dispensation appeal Mitte/Muschler." The breakfasting clerk pointed with his thumb over his shoulder toward the fully dressed clerk sitting behind him. Oberndorffer turned to him: "I have an inquiry regarding the Mitte/Muschler dispensation appeal."

The clerk reached wordlessly into the card file in front of him, shook his head, turned around, got up, went to the file cabinet behind him, and looked: "'S'been passed along already, room 238."

"Thank you." Oberndorffer went to room 238. The man sitting there ignored him.

Oberndorffer said, "I have an inquiry regarding the Mitte/Muschler dispensation appeal."

"Just a moment," the clerk said. He looked around. "It's gone on to the head of the department."

Well, that was quick, thought Oberndorffer. He walked back down the corridor, took the stairs up two flights, made a right, then a left. He was standing in front of a window and the ladies' toilet. He turned around. The hallways were deserted. They had become independent long ago. They offered themselves up to Oberndorffer as cruel, echoless. Finally, Oberndorffer knocked at a door that said "Registration."

"Excuse me, where can I find room 314?

An affable East Prussian got up. "It's quite difficult to find. Go back down the corridor, walk up two flights, then round the corner and round again, and you'll be there."

Oberndorffer thanked him profusely and turned around. Finally, room 314. "Government and Construction Commissioner Hoppe."

Oberndorffer knocked. Commissioner Hoppe wasn't there. Oberndorffer stood in the hallway again. Not a soul to be seen. He knocked on doors at random. A clerk said that the commissioner was meeting with the head of the department; it could take a quarter of an hour.

What a lot of standing around, Oberndorffer thought. There was a bank in the central wing. Oberndorffer bought the midday papers and read them. After a quarter of an hour, he returned to room 314. Commissioner Hoppe was a measured man. "Dispensation appeal Mitte/Muschler has already gone to signature."

"Many thanks," said Oberndorffer. "May I ask whether it was approved?"

"You will receive an answer through regular business channels," the official said haughtily.

Oberndorffer wandered through the office building and reached the chancery division. Two clerks sat at the window; one was writing, the other was wrapping up his breakfast, the third, an old man, was filing papers.

Oberndorffer said into the room, "Dispensation appeal Mitte/Muschler."

Wordlessly, one of the clerks reached into the card file behind him, turned around, shook his head, went over to a file cabinet, looked: "'S'gone already. Headquarters."

"When, please?"

"Fourteen days ago."

"Thank you."

Oberndorffer stood on the street amid heavy snowdrifts. The wind whistled. "How can I get to headquarters? Metro. The metro is best."

He got to headquarters. The department head, Dr. Scheunemann, was a friendly man: "Dispensation appeal Mitte/Muschler isn't here yet."

"But how is that possible? It left the municipal offices fourteen days ago."

"Yes, that's how long it takes for the paperwork to reach us. Fourteen days isn't so long for the file cart."

"Why don't you send them by mail? Then they'd get there in a day."

"That would be far too expensive for the state. No, by mail, business would be much more expensive."

"But that's dreadful, all this rushing around for something like that. Is there no way of telling where the appeal is, so as to expedite it?"

"Well, it's like this," Dr. Scheunemann shrugged his shoulders. "I could just as well ask you about the whereabouts of a brick in a wall of one of your buildings."

The wind was sharp. Oberndorffer stood on the street. The snow had begun to fall thickly in wet flakes. Oberndorffer now had to get to the farthest reaches of Schöneberg because of the theater. The tram is far too dull, I'll get a taxi. No luck, thought Oberndorffer. Drove to Schöneberg, thought that it wasn't even his own building he was driving around for.

He asked the driver to stop on Tauentzienstrasse, and inspected the Christmas shopping. Nothing but Käsebier. Käsebier rubber dolls, windup dolls, balloons. Got in again. Käsebier's becoming more and more famous, he thought, but he's not that good. We overdo everything. This rubber stuff is awful. People have no sense of quality anymore, things like this could be done well too.

Oberndorffer arrived in Schöneberg. In a dark foyer, an old Berlin room, two clerks stood counting towels. One clerk was holding dirty towels and said, "Twenty-six."

Oberndorffer stood there: "I'd like to deliver a certificate to the head of your department."

"Yes, twenty-six. 'S'not there anymore," said the other one. "Now for the twenty-eight clean ones."

The first: "Yes, twenty-eight."

The other counted. Oberndorffer said, "Then perhaps you would be so kind as to pass on the letter."

The clerk continued to count. "Thirty, thirty-one. I can do that, put it over here."

Oberndorffer said, "Please give me a receipt."

The clerk counted: "Thirty-five, thirty-six. No can do. Send it by registered mail."

Oberndorffer said, "It contains important documents. I need a receipt."

The clerk said, "No can do. Send it by registered mail. Forty-one, forty-two."

"Every government office is required to register the receipt of letters."

"We're not required to do that. Send it by registered mail. Forty-four, forty-five."

"You're required to do that."

"There's a clause that says we don't need to register receipt. File a complaint or send it by registered mail, forty-eight. One, two, three..."

Oberndorffer left. He got out on Tauentzientstrasse. He wanted to buy himself a pair of shoes.

"Do you want the Käsebier brand?" asked the girl in the shop.

Oberndorffer let her show him the shoes. He would have preferred a different style, they were too gussied up for his taste. But in the end he bought them.

On Tauentzienstrasse, street hawkers cried into the snow: "Silk scarves, first-class silk scarves, three marks each," "Genuine Coty perfume, manufacturer's gone bust, a bottle for a mark," "Käsebier, the real rubber doll, something for the kids so they'll laugh and won't cry, you can squeeze it to your chest, put it in your bath..."

"You'll only find little Käsebier here, turn a small screw..."

"Three bars of chocolate for thirty pfennigs, from the famous Austrian chocolate factory. A nougat, a mocha, a marzipan, try a bar for ten, get three for thirty, for your own affairs, for your own person, for your own body, for yourself, for your own health, ten pfennigs, a groschen for yourself or the body of your child, your wife, for a groschen, ten pfennigs, for a..."

"Käsebier, the real rubber doll, something for the kids so they'll laugh and won't cry, you can squeeze it to your chest, put it in your bath. Käsebier, the real rubber doll..."

23

A Christmas walk

IN THE office, Gohlisch said, "I was walking down Leipziger Strasse today and wanted to buy myself a pair of shoes for Christmas. The shoe girl said to me, 'Would you like Bally or Käsebier brand shoes?' I said, 'I'd prefer Gohlisch style.' When she heard that, the girl turned pale and wanted to call her manager. If it had thawed, Miermann, Käsebier would never have seen the light of day! Now Käsebier has taken the universe by storm and conquered it. Will you venture into the storm with me?" he asked Miss Kohler.

He turned up his coat collar, pulled his hat deep over his face, and said to Miermann, "Adieu, Heil and Sieg and catch a fat one," and walked out, an old ham, with Kohler, who was large, slightly plump, and still wore a bun to match her boring face. She had on a simple brown coat. Off they went.

There was a Christmas market on Dönhoffplatz. Rock candy and gingerbread hearts.

"Silk scarves, three marks each."

"My dear lady, right here you can buy the wonderful Coty perfume, the wonderful flower scent. The manufacturer's gone bust, so we're selling off everything for a mark, genuine Coty perfume, the wonderful flower scent. What, it doesn't smell like lilies of the valley to you? It smells wonderful to me! Genuine Coty perfume…"

"Käsebier, something for the kids so they laugh and don't cry, you can squeeze it to your chest, put it in your bath."

"You'll only find little Käsebier here, turn a little screw and little Käsebier'll sing 'How Can He Sleep with That Thin Wall?' For twenty pfennigs, you'll reap millions in laughs at your favorite bar, at the regulars' table, just turn the little key and he'll waggle his head and sing, it's not witchcraft, it's not magic. Just turn the little key and little Käsebier'll sing 'How Can He Sleep with That Thin Wall?' You'll have so much fun with it at your favorite bar, at the regulars' table."

The Käsebier doll sang.

"Käsebier, the real rubber doll, doesn't burst, doesn't crack, it's indestructible," his neighbor said.

Gohlisch and Miss Kohler moved on.

"Lametta, Lametta, three packs for a groschen."

"Christmas candles, Christmas candles!"

They went into a linens shop.

"Something small?" the shopgirl asked. "Can I show you our latest? We have an enchanting flower bouquet made of dust cloths, charming, isn't it? Or here, our latest: 'Käsebier' made of four dust cloths!"

"Only Käsebier for Christmas," said Gohlisch. They bought the dust cloth Käsebier.

A chain of lights spelled out "No Christmas without Käsebier" above a fountain pen shop in which Gohlisch wanted to get his pen repaired.

"It's not worth repairing," the owner said dismissively. "The repair'll cost you three marks, it's an outdated model. Buy the latest 'Käsebier.' You can get a pretty good one for three marks."

"No," said Gohlisch. "This pen produced Käsebier. Am I Saturn, devouring my own children? Will I allow this pen to be killed by 'Käsebier'?"

"I'll give it to Miermann for Christmas," said Kohler, and pulled out three marks. "We still need cigarettes."

"Oh, right, cigarettes."

"Do you want Neuerhaus," the cigarette seller asked, "Muratti, or Käsebier? Käsebier Melior for five pfennigs, Käsebier Bonus for three, Käsebier Optimus eight pfennigs."

"Since what's good is better than what's better," said Miss Kohler, "you may as well get Bonus, if you want my advice."

"Give me twenty-five."

"Walk with Käsebier, write with Käsebier, dust with Käsebier, bathe with Käsebier, smoke Käsebier," said Gohlisch.

"Käsebier, the real rubber doll, doesn't burst, doesn't crack, it's indestructible. Käsebier, the real rubber doll, something for the kids so they'll laugh and won't cry, you can squeeze it to your chest, put it in your bath. Käsebier, the real rubber doll—"

Käsebier's songs drifted from the gramophone stores. Käsebier lights glowed against the darkening sky, scrolling ads: "Käsebier shoes are the best."

On the streets, balloons shaped like Käsebier. A blow-up Käsebier. A windup Käsebier.

Posters: "For your Christmas holidays: *Käsebier, the Musical* at the Artist's Theater with Pallenberg."

Käsebier fountain pens. One lady said, "We'll go to Käsebier on Christmas day, I still want to get tickets."

"Käsebier, the real rubber doll, doesn't burst, doesn't crack, it's indestructible. Käsebier, the real rubber doll, something for the kids so they'll laugh and won't cry, you can squeeze it to your chest, put it in your bath. Käsebier, the real rubber doll—"

Over in the shopwindows of the bookstore: Willy Frächter, *Käsebier*. Next, Heinrich Wurm's *Käsebier*, from the series Darlings of the Public. *The Käsebier Picture Book* by Dr. Richard Thame. *Käsebier Cartoons*, put together by Gödovecz. Otto Lambeck: *Käsebier, an Essay*.

Gohlisch and Miss Kohler were standing in front of the display when Lieven suddenly appeared before them.

"My friends!" he cried enthusiastically, "isn't this a tremendous symphony of fame? Nothing but Käsebier from earth to sky. Theater, music, comedy, banks, commerce, industry, the weavers and leather manufacturers and rubber goods and toys—everything's here. They blow their trumpets with full cheeks, beat the drums, let the cymbals ring and dance a great dance with balloons and dust cloths and rubber dolls and singing dolls and records and brogues and construction fences and brick walls, with carpenters and woodworkers and plumbers and installers, flags and scrolling script and glowing letters in red, purple, and green, and above it all, *gloria, gloria*, the fountain pen of the press. And I've been a part of it, I'm a child of my time, I acknowledge it, I belong to it."

"Why don't you write the Song of Songs of advertising, how we woo her, sleep with her, the old whore. How beautiful are your breasts, O golden neon Atrax, I could embrace your thighs, sweet radio, how your adaptor glows with its fig leaf, sweet…"

"But Gohlisch," said Miss Kohler, feeling somewhat foolish and embarrassed.

"You baroque jester," Lieven said, unsettled. "My compliments."

"Heil and Sieg and catch a fat one," said Gohlisch.

"Käsebier, the real rubber doll, doesn't burst, doesn't crack, it's indestructible. Käsebier, the real rubber doll, something for the kids so they'll laugh and won't cry, you can squeeze it to your chest, put it in your bath. Käsebier, the real rubber doll—"

24

The building

IN THE meantime, the building had grown, the scaffolding had risen. The walls were rising. Allocations had begun, the great race for contracts. Otto Mitte's Max Schulz, also called "Old Man Schulz," was in charge of awarding contracts. He had a beard like August Bebel and watched every penny. The installation companies sent along their representatives. Old Wurm from Wurm & Redlich came for gas and water. Schulz would have liked to give Wurm & Redlich the contract, "But you're too expensive, Mr. Wurm, what can I do, too expensive." No, Wurm & Redlich was out of the question. Max Schulz had to give the contract to Staberow & Sons, although he found Staberow quite unpleasant, a smart, modern Nazi who did business with a swastika in his buttonhole.

"Mr. Staberow, you may have gotten the contract because you're the cheapest, unfortunately, but I'm an old Social Democrat. Next time, please leave your brass outfit at the coat check."

"An opinion is an opinion," said Staberow.

"And an asshole is an asshole," said Schulz. I can get away with that, he thought, with a contract worth ninety thousand marks.

"'Scuse me, what did you just say?"

"Me? I just said that naturally, you have to accept our general conditions."

"On my honor, Mr. Schulz."

The heating folks came. The light installers came. Schulz didn't like big companies; they were somewhat more flexible, but he preferred working with the handymen themselves. He called up Nierstein and Hammerschlag, two electricians with a small business.

"No one's picking up," said Miss Fleissig, the secretary.

"We have their home number."

Miss Fleissig dialed it.

"Nierstein."

"Otto Mitte & Co. We have a job for you, please come by to provide a quote estimate."

"I don't exist anymore," said Nierstein. "I thought you knew that."

"No," said Miss Fleissig.

"Mr. Hammerschlag's bumbling around on his own now."

"Well, well. Many thanks . . ."

"They folded," Miss Fleissig said to Schulz.

"That's the way it is, if you don't hear from folks for three months, they've gone bust. Send the forms out to the others as usual."

The heating men were already waiting in the vestibule. Sanitary facilities and plumbing. The oil company representative for the fuel facilities in the garage. The staircase company representative. Outside sat old Böker, a locksmith and master craftsman with twenty employees. There sat Mr. Feinschmidt himself, from Feinschmidt & Rohhals, joinery and woodworking. He had come because of the doors and the parquets. Duchow, Duchow the carpenter was there, for the theater seats. Duchow walked in.

"We're not ready yet, Mr. Duchow," said Schulz.

"I just wanted to come in and say that I won't be passed over, Mr. Schulz."

"Nah, nah. Come on, you think Karlweiss's already drawn something up? Nah. Mr. Duchow, we've known each other for almost thirty years, you know, I've never worked on a project as nuts as this one. You should hear Dipfinger, our foreman over there. When he starts up in Bavarian, it's something else."

"There's nothing doing anymore, Mr. Schulz, d'you think people still want good work? No one cares anymore. It's no fun anymore, either. I work for Bollmann now. Bollmann raises my prices twofold. But d'you think he notices what I deliver? Couldn't care less. And then people think they're getting a deal. Slap some nice veneer on wherever you can, and use different wood to make the piece. No one notices. Who still double glues anything? Not a damn soul, right? I haven't done dry veneer in five years, but I'm still glad for Bollmann. He pays—badly—but he pays. Recently, a private client put me out two thousand marks. That's something for old Duchow, two thousand marks. Nah, Mr. Schulz, things aren't right anymore."

"It's the same everywhere. No matter who you listen to. I have to wear made-to-measure shoes, and recently my cobbler told me folks don't notice whether you give 'em cardboard insoles or decent leather, they don't notice nothing. They don't care if they get blisters on their feet or crippled toes, long as it looks nice and doesn't cost much."

"You know, Mr. Schulz, I recently repaired an old monster, a real old monster, about three hundred years old, southern German with intarsia work, a fine piece of furniture. You'll still be able to put your linens in that wardrobe in two hundred years. And no one wants it anymore. No one understands that kind of work anymore. You know, I made a modern desk recently, what a thing, it has flat legs, real flat legs, seems a bit shady. What a thing.

"You know, Koller the upholsterer, old Koller, also said that people buy chaise longues for 39.50 at Bollmann. They haven't got a clue. Every evening, they sweep the workshop, and when they've swept up the spare wool and dirt, they stick it right in the filling. You know, Mr. Schulz, people are so dumb, especially the women. They bounce on it a few times, look at the fabric and say, 'Gee, what a bargain.' They don't know nothing about the insides."

"Yeah, Mr. Duchow, it's not a pretty picture. And no one's learning anything anymore. What're the young kids learning these days? I learned how to lay bricks with Schmalz and his courthouse. We had to get in and lay those bricks exactly, down to the millimeter to make those vaults ... now they put iron trusses in everything. Everything's lazy."

"Sure, there's nothing decent anymore. D'you remember old Nagel, Mr. Schulz?"

"Still alive?"

"Well sure, he's been making window frames for Feinschmidt and Rohhals on Skalitzer Strasse for about fifty years now. Mr. Feinschmidt sits outside, goes out to deliver quotes himself sometimes, Mr. Fein-schmidt does. So I said to Nagel, Nagel, are you still making window frames? He says, sure. I say, has anything changed in fifty years? He says, nah, it's always the same, in the past I made two a week, now I'm making twenty. I say, well, that's the difference. He didn't think so. Nah, it's no fun anymore. But I'm running my mouth during business hours. You have work to do, Mr. Schulz."

"I'm always happy to see you, Mr. Duchow. And I'll keep you in mind. Oh, I meant to ask, do you still have your summer house in Hessenwinkel?"

"Oh, you know, it got much too expensive. The likes of me can't afford it. I shouldn't have bought it."

"What about your son? Is he in the workshop now?"

"The one is, Albert, but it wasn't good enough for Oscar. He worked at the bank and now he has a radio business, he's doing pretty well."

"Well, Mr. Duchow, that's the way it is with kids. Goodbye."

"Goodbye, Mr. Schulz."

Meanwhile, the building grew.

Dipfinger was angry with Karlweiss.

"'Scuse me, councilor, but I haven't gotten anything decent out of Mr. Karlweiss. He gave me all of his drawings at 1:100, as if I was a building inspector; I said, Councilor, surely one should be able to ask an architect for 1:50, but I can't get nothing out of him, no details, we've got huge problems. It's a total cock-up, a pile of shit!"

"You're right, I'll write Karlweiss a letter."

In the meantime, the frost arrived; by the end of January, the dispensation request from the building inspectors; on February 10, the permits from police headquarters. The carpenters were already installing large beams, the roofers were already up on the scaffolding, hammering at the roof gutters, and the gutter spouts were being delivered. The gas and water lines had been almost completely laid. The radiators had already been installed, though they hadn't all been hooked up yet. They hadn't started with the electrical wiring; the electricians were on strike. The stairs were being built, and the lock-smiths were already beginning to install the windows. But there was still no detailed drawing of the theater. The stuccowork hadn't yet been contracted, the furniture hadn't yet been designed, nor the fabrics or the lamps—all that was still up in the air.

It was already March, it was already April. Miss Götzel was already rolling out *nouveautés* for the coming fall.

No one cared about Käsebier anymore, new things had to be invented, you couldn't have the same thing two years in a row, so she designed a dust cloth Mickey Mouse. She had great hopes for Christmas sales, and indeed, she was not disappointed. In general, everything had turned to Mickey Mouse. Rubber Mickey Mouses and swim toys had become major products during the swim season. Mickey Mouses made of cloth, Mickey Mouse brooches. The sales representatives made offers to the shoppers.

"Well, and nothing new in Käsebier?"

"No one has Käsebier anymore," said Käte Herzfeld. "He'll be completely over come winter."

The premiere of the *Käsebier* talkie was a complete flop.

25

The housing turnaround

IN THE spring of 1930, something strange happened. No apartments had been available since 1917, for thirteen unfortunate years. The dramatic transformation of the population had not been outwardly visible. It had been impossible to change apartments. Back in 1918, people crawled into every last corner, became renters by necessity. Barracks were built and called emergency apartments. Apartments were divided up, shared bathrooms and shared kitchens became the norm. Young couples scraped by in furnished rooms; no one knew what the next day would bring. The war speculators and inflation speculators were subletters, or had stayed in their old apartments. People with nothing yesterday and everything today couldn't enjoy their good fortune; they had no rooms to fill with the luxury they had once dreamed of and now attained. Some of them built villas. Others sat around in two-room apartments in old Moabit, or three on Zossener Strasse, even though they could have long afforded to live on Kantstrasse by now. The formerly wealthy clung to their apartments as their only possession. A Serbian woman slept in the black music room; a student in the Renaissance study; a Hungarian had moved into the Romanesque dining room; and a Russian family lived in the rear. The landlady had retreated to a small room next to the toilet or had rented out the entire apartment, asking only to be fed in return. Young couples from 1916, 1918, and 1919 with two children were stuck in the same three-room courtyard apartment that had seemed a godsend when they married, although it was nothing more than the rear section of a ten-room apartment arranged along a long, dark corridor, with no balcony, and a kitchen that was a former bedroom with a gas stove. In 1924, when they could see straight again, it transpired that this disaster of an apartment cost two hundred and fifty marks a month while their parents paid the same amount for their six-room apartment, which was furnished with every convenience.

The young couples moved out. In 1926, those married in 1918 had the right to their own apartment. But the older people stayed put in the large apartments. They were still renting them out. Rent money had replaced pensions. Rental income had turned into earnings. Around 1927, something like a housing market finally emerged—but only for apartments larger than four rooms. The command economy relaxed. Apartment agencies blossomed. All the same, obtaining an apartment was a difficult and tediously acquired secret science, a business similar to obtaining foodstuffs during the war: there was the white certificate, the certificate of eligibility, the certificate of priority, one had to pay moving fees and a construction fee subsidy for the apartment. People paid between twenty-five hundred and ten thousand marks for an apartment. Then there were renovation costs. Muschler and Mitte couldn't imagine that things would ever change. No one could.

The turnaround came suddenly, at the end of 1929. It began on Kurfürstendamm and on Hardenbergstrasse for apartments larger than twelve rooms. A handful of signs could be spotted, the signs every Berlin child is familiar with: the top eighth red, the rest black, APARTMENT TO LET.

It was late February when Muschler saw a sign like this as he was driving from the office to Grunewald, over Kurfürstendamm to Fontanestrasse.

"Niedergesäss, stop for a moment." Muschler got out. Looked at the sign. "Well," he thought, "it's fourteen rooms, who needs that these days? Oh well."

"Niedergesäss, let's go home."

But more appeared in a flash. This wasn't an isolated incident anymore, and it hadn't taken hold of just the top tier. It was as if large apartments had cholera. Their inhabitants were fleeing. The pandemic raged. Fourteen-room apartments had been under siege yesterday;

ten-room apartments had their turn today; tomorrow, the eight-room would have its day, and the day after tomorrow, six rooms over two thousand marks. Two thousand marks seemed to be the cutoff. At two thousand, the water pipes weren't contaminated. Come April, people who had paid moving and renovation fees in January and February and given their broker a few extra hundred shook their heads in disbelief and called themselves asses.

A product that had cost six thousand marks in February could suddenly be obtained for free. A big apartment was no longer a source of rental income, a big apartment was no longer interest-bearing capital: big apartments were big problems.

Muschler looked at Kurfürstendamm. Signs on house after house. A dead city—cholera had passed through. Or was it like an American gold mining town where the gold had run out? To let, to let, to let, house after house? All the shops were closed. House after house. The liberal, *laissez-faire, laissez-passer*, suddenly cried for the state.

"Mr. Mitte, one can't simply let buildings go to ruin," Muschler said on the phone. "The state should take responsibility! And what's Kaliski doing anyway, do you know? —Just five percent of the apartments have been rented? Well, he's not advertising at all! My wife said that his wife wants to divorce him. It'll be completely over if the Waldschmidt fortune is pulled out of his business. Then he won't be able to advertise at all anymore and we'll sit here looking like fools with our contract."

"Well, we can still manage to get out of the contract. Let me take care of that. But Kurfürstendamm isn't a residential neighborhood anymore."

"And the Sachows next door?"

"Different economy. We missed the boom, that's the way the cookie crumbles. I'll see it through, Mr. Muschler."

"Me too, Mr. Mitte."

"Well, there's no risk in it for you, just for me."

26
Kaliski gets the boot

WALDSCHMIDT'S daughter was never involved with the right men. Waldschmidt was fond of saying, "It's already hard enough to hire the right men, and there are none at all to marry."

Miss Ella Waldschmidt had had a dismal love affair in 1924. Dr. Kaliski courted her the same year. He was invited to the Waldschmidts' house. He was particularly handsome, had a doctorate in economics, and his origins were unplaceable. He said clever things, was just a bit too brash at times.

She had first noticed this on an excursion when he shouted at the waiter, "Where's the food, for God's sake? Close the curtains, the sun is shining right in our eyes!—Well, now it's pitch dark. Open the curtains again! Bring out the place settings at least!" He'd gotten on her nerves back then. But she married him anyway. She was thirty years old. Her father, who thought Kaliski was very clever, advised her to marry him, since he was the same age. It turned out that he was from Poznan. He was unrefined. Quite unrefined. He came from a very different background. He brought a Gobelin tapestry into the marriage, a girl making wreaths of roses for the trumpeter of Säckingen. "My mother, God rest her soul, embroidered this tapestry. We have to put it up. She was a real woman!" he said, quietly reproaching Ella.

He did not think that spending money was a matter of course. He asked, "What did it cost?" about everything. Mrs. Kaliski endured this for four years. Then she found out that he also had a girlfriend. She asked to be shown her. The girlfriend made his tastes clear. The very fat, small, and vulgar girl in a bilious green coat with white fur was the last straw.

Mrs. Margot Weissman told Ella, "Why don't you get divorced, after all, what do you want from such an impossible man? Your father is clever enough, he'll save your fortune. You'll keep the child. Be sensible."

"I feel sorry for him," said Ella. "Then he'll have no money at all, what will become of him?"

"He'll make it again."

What do strangers know? Ella thought. Margot is so energetic and always thinks that what *she* does is the right thing.

"Yes, yes, Margot," she said, bid farewell, and drove over to Aunt Eugénie.

Aunt Eugénie was sixty now, but what a woman! She still wore flowing feather hats and brocade coats. Her apartment was a museum; her furniture was from the early film era, in which films largely involved furniture toppling over. Étagères with Meissen figurines stood everywhere.

"How lovely to see you again," she said, closing and opening her eyes in a manner no woman could still master, "Come here, let me embrace you." She stepped off the raised platform on which she was sitting and reading, or writing her many, endlessly long letters *au courant de la main*, a vast correspondence with people of all nations. She spoke the broken German of diplomat's wives and cabaret singers. She rang for the maid.

"My dear, my niece has come. Tea on the terrace. *Qu'est ce que c'est, mon enfant?*"

Aunt Eugénie knew the world. Who knows who had come through this house on Tiergartenstrasse! Not all of whom Aunt Eugénie spoke, but most of them. She had surely had many relationships in the manner of Prévost, but not even to herself would she have admitted it.

The maid opened the portiere. "Tea is served."

Ella accompanied Aunt Eugénie to the terrace. This was where Berlin ended. These gardens, which led off from their houses' southern walls, were still the most beautiful in the city. The old white greyhound, that dumb, elegant creature, lay on the long terrace under the red-and-white awning; the tea table was set; and a sweet scent wafted from the roses. Aunt Eugénie wore a silver-gray silk dress decorated with real lace, a heavy pearl necklace, and large diamonds in her ears. Outside on the terrace, she wrapped herself in a large white scarf made of embroidered crêpe de chine. Ella thought, I'll never look that good, and I'm underdressed again! And her posture, and the tea table!

"Your tea table is always enchanting," Ella said. "The porcelain and the roses!"

"Yes, the Wedgewood is delightful. Just think, yesterday my dear Thérèse broke the last cup of my good Limoges. I was devastated. Help yourself to the brioches, or would you like some jam? I see you're looking at my *boutons*, I was at the opera last night and haven't taken them off yet. You say roses, but the ramblers are not so nice this year, far from it. I should keep a regular gardener, but I can't afford to anymore. But now to you, *ma chérie*. What's on your mind?"

"I want to leave Reinhold."

"But of course, my dear, that's no matter these days."

"But I feel sorry for him."

"Well, you'll have your reasons, or are you still in love with him?"

"No, but the child."

"All the same, *mon enfant*, I beg you, he's impossible. When I invited you over for breakfast to celebrate your engagement, he stood in front of my little Van Dyck and said, 'Must be valuable, a picture like that.' I thought, how can my brother give his daughter away to such a man?"

"My dear aunt, he doesn't understand the slightest thing about art, but that doesn't matter."

"Certainly not, but the *niveau* matters, my child. The Duc d'Aubreyville threw himself at my feet in Ostende and I paid him no mind, and you know that Professor von Lossen was a childhood friend of mine. I know the world, *ma chérie*, you can be friends with whomever you like, but marriage is a question of milieu and *niveau*. Kaliski does not have our *niveau*. I will congratulate you once the divorce has been settled. He does not belong in our family. The worst was the letter from his sister in Schrimm, in which she wrote that she had always hoped that her brother, who was the pride of the family because he was an academic, would marry well, but that marrying into the Waldschmidt family was almost too much for the Kaliskis from Schrimm, despite being the first family to settle there. I felt this was decidedly over the top."

"Times have changed. War, revolution, and inflation."

"Certainly, and my dear brother is a brilliant man who said to me that it would be good for new blood to come into the family, and your little boy is a darling."

"Yes, dear Peter turned out beautifully."

"But Kaliski is simply dreadful. I don't know, perhaps you didn't make the right inquiries."

"We wouldn't have learned anything, dear Aunt. Father may be very clever but he always says that you only come to realize what's important once it's too late. No one wants to impede an engagement."

"That's certainly true. I don't enjoy saying anything unflattering when I'm asked about a match. If the match is made, I'll have been indiscreet, which will lead to a lifelong rift with the people in question."

"You say that father spoke of degeneration; that's a problem too. Our Klaus Michael is only interested in golf and Rot-Weiss, talks about Wimbledon and cars and horses and champions. Father would have preferred a real businessman."

"But he was a bit too much of a businessman, dear child. Get divorced and live with me for the next quarter of a year, or go on a trip. And *tenue*, Ella, *tenue*, maintain your *dehors*, you're a Waldschmidt. Goodbye, my child, *bonne chance*."

"Goodbye, dear Aunt." She kissed her hand.

That evening, Kaliski came home. Ella was sitting on the sofa.

"Well, doll, are you mad?"

Ella started; he was so terrible!

"I wanted to let you know that I've decided we should get an amicable divorce."

"Amicable, what's amicable about that?"

"You've betrayed me, dear Reinhold."

KÄSEBIER TAKES BERLIN · 199

Ella was discreet. But Margot Weissmann told Mrs. Muschler.

Mr. Muschler decided to terminate Kaliski's contract. "I couldn't care less if I were making twenty-five thousand marks in interest on the property and didn't have to pay interest on the second mortgage, but I do care since the rental income doesn't even cover the interest on the first mortgage or the expenses, and I don't know what will become of the theater since the Käsebier film was such a flop."

And so he canceled the contract, on the grounds that Kaliski hadn't sufficiently advertised the rentals. Kaliski fought back. The apartments should have been finished by the spring of 1930, but they would only be done in the fall. Luxury apartments could only be rented out right before they could be moved into, and the economy had gone through disastrous changes.

"For years, you tried to raise money and build on your terrain," Kaliski wrote Muschler. "The biggest firms turned you down. You received this risk-free deal purely through my connections to Mr. Rübe. I did not ask for a commission, but contented myself with your binding promise to give me the rentals. These apartments were offered to thousands of interested parties. The fact that the renters decided against renting wasn't just because of the price, but also due to the terrible floor plans and unfortunate apartment design.

"Despite these problems, which make leasing significantly more difficult, I spent several thousand marks on advertising. I will not take you to court, since I am not an idealist and do not intent to 'seek justice,' but the injustice remains."

Muschler was unmoved. If Waldschmidt's daughter got divorced, Kaliski would have no more money to advertise the apartments. That was enough for him.

Being fired, Kaliski thought, is a disgrace. His contract, which ran until the first of April, should have been extended since the construction was so far from complete. But there were larger things at stake in his divorce, and he accepted the harsh termination, which robbed him of his commission, without much of a fight. He no longer belonged. He sank back into the mass of small-time Jewish agents and brokers. The great match he had made had unraveled. He had to start over again. He went to Mr. Klass, who gave him rubber Mickey Mouses to sell. When Kaliski asked Klass what had happened to Käsebier, Mr. Klass said, "That product's finished, over. We need fresh wares for winter, fresh ones! That's essential."

A few weeks later, he wrote another pointed letter to Muschler through a lawyer. "You told Mr. Mitte that Dr. Reinhold Kaliski's business was facing complete financial ruin. I hereby deny this and would like to note that, in light of these falsehoods, I reserve the right to make the source of these rumors legally liable for any possible arising damages."

You've got to be joking, Muschler thought when he received the letter.

Three days later, the papers printed a notice that Dr. Reinhold Kaliski, real estate and mortgages, was declaring bankruptcy, but that the firm would pay its outstanding debts in full and that no one would suffer damages. No one had expected anything less. Waldschmidt, of course, had stepped up.

27
Rohhals of Feinschmidt & Rohhals shoots himself

IN THE meantime, the building was growing. Schulz was on call. Miss Fleissig was on call. The details for the theater had finally arrived. The contracts for the stuccowork were ready to be given out. The interior was being plastered up where the lighting had been installed. Messengers came and delivered floor samples; messengers came and delivered sample door and window handles. Schüttke's carpentry shop was already delivering doors and window frames to the construction site.

Feinschmidt & Rohhals hadn't received the contract. They had been too expensive.

"What can I do?" said Mr. Schulz. "I'll get for less. You know that I like working with you, but business is business, and I have to watch expenses."

Feinschmidt told Rohhals, "The contract could have bailed us out, but how can I operate with these losses? I've calculated everything down to the last penny. We have forty thousand in outstanding debts, which includes an assured loss of twenty thousand to illiquid firms. I don't know what will happen. Taxes are eating us up. Who can bear capital taxes? Otto Mitte and Co. has always worked with us."

Rohhals shrugged his shoulders. He was tired of fighting. "If even Otto Mitte and Co. won't work with us anymore!"

Schüttke's carpentry shop was already delivering doors and window frames to the construction site.

Karlweiss had finally settled on a design for the theater. Lots of wood, more like a beer hall, something comfy. Duchow was among those asked to do the carpentry work.

Duchow came to Schulz, "You know, Mr. Schulz, it's none of my business, but I'd rather make something good than something bad. Take a look at these drawings, I'm supposed to turn them into a carving. That there's supposed to be embellishment. Now look at it, Mr. Schulz. Up close it's nice looking, one of them modern affairs. Now take a look from far away. What's it look like to you now?"

"Like a naked man lying down, sort of on one elbow, propping himself up on something."

"Yeah, on a platter. And I'm s'posed to send it off like that to get done? The foreman's fiddled around with the drawing so it looks fancy up close, but from far away it's just plain dumb. You want me to send off the naked fella?"

"Yes. The project's in so much hot water, the only thing that matters is getting it done. Mitte's backing the project, and there's nothing to rent! And what'll happen to the theater, God only knows. Doesn't matter anyway, since Mr. Karlweiss isn't upset!"

Oberndorffer came to see Duchow a few weeks later and saw the model. "What kind of funny thing is that?"

"Paneling for the Käsebier theater."

"Lots of dying gladiators?"

"What, doctor?"

"Dying gladiators, it's an ancient motif, a naked dying man with a shield."

"See, Doc, I was right! I always thought it looked like a naked fella with a platter. S'posed to be decorative."

The glaziers came and put in the windows. In the meantime, three new apartments had been rented out to a Russian, a Baron von Schleich, and an odd woman with no profession. But that was meager progress.

Dipfinger was furious with Karlweiss, that "dirty bastard with no conscience," but what could he do. Mitte shrugged his shoulders. Who knew if it had been worth trading this miserable Karlweiss project for Hohenschönhausen, he thought. In all likelihood, he'd still be compromised. A lot was slipping through the cracks.

Dipfinger said, "Look here, councilor, he didn't even draw the windows right. They've been split up differently on the Kurfürstendamm side. Now we've learned there's not enough space for the doors, so we've gotta cut off the moldings. There's one piece that won't do, we'll have to get Schüttke to work it over. This here's a piecemeal job slapped together by a shameless architect."

Mitte said, "I'm not exactly thrilled with what Karlweiss gave us. The rooms are so badly planned that no one wants the apartments. A few missing door and window moldings won't matter now, dear Mr. Dipfinger. Just get it done somehow."

New problems kept popping up. Doors had been installed so that beds couldn't be put in the bedrooms, there was no space for cupboards in the kitchens, and there were no sinks in the bathrooms. The rentals weren't progressing.

The painters began their work in July. There had been a heated battle over the painting contract, and Schulz had managed to award it for two thousand marks less than the lowest original bid.

In mid-summer—it had been a very rainy summer—the Käsebier production company released its new talkie. A military farce.

"Dreadful," said Gohlisch worriedly. "In the evening edition, I gently but clearly and lovingly pointed out its mindless premise. It's becoming clearer that Käsebier has no taste at all. He picks the dumbest scripts."

The evening papers came in. "Ah, here's Gohlisch," said Miermann, "and here: 'The old carpentry firm Feinschmidt and Rohhals declared bankruptcy today. Forty-nine-year-old co-owner Franz Rohhals shot himself.' Franz Rohhals was in my class at school, he was a good fellow. Isn't it awful. Imagine what's behind news like that!"

Oberndorffer sat at the regulars' table. "Today, Rohhals of Feinschmidt and Rohhals took his own life. Do you know who that was? Feinschmidt and Rohhals used to work for Schinkel. They did the woodwork on the theater. Schinkel once wrote, 'My honored master carpenter Rohhals showed me exquisite work today, which, I hope, will rapidly allow us to receive the outstanding permits from the highest office.' I looked it up today when I saw the news in the papers."

"You know, the building doesn't matter anymore when you're building," Krone said.

"And the content doesn't matter for newspapers anymore," Gohlisch said, and stood up. "Heil and Sieg and catch a fat one."

Miss Fleissig said to Schulz, "Just think, Mr. Schulz, Feinschmidt and Rohhals declared bankruptcy today, and Mr. Rohhals took his own life."

"What?" said Schulz. "That's terrible! Do you remember, Mr. Feinschmidt came to see me a few months ago for the Kurfürstendamm project, and then Schüttke was cheaper, so I went with Schüttke? Now there was a great business! Their work is priceless these days. They made everything that's quality in Berlin. No, it's not pretty these days. It's not fun. Everything good's been ruined. But Miss Fleissig, you know Schüttke was cheaper, I couldn't justify it. We've got to watch expenses, after all! Otherwise we'll go to the dogs ourselves. It's the taxes; the economy simply can't handle them."

28

Meyer-Paris goes to America

IT WAS summer.

Margot Weissmann was getting ready for La Baule.

The Muschlers were in Salzkammergut.

Mrs. Frechheim was in Gastein.

Uncle Gustav was on the Isle of Wight.

Miss Kohler received a thick letter covered in familiar handwriting. She opened it. It contained the program and the text for a Käsebier play in Stuttgart. There was a card as well. Completely blank. Just "M-P."

The Rhineland had been liberated. Miermann traveled to take part in the festivities. He was over the moon. The beautiful landscape, the lighthearted people, the wonderful weather, the Rhenish wine; the lovely girls filled him with bliss.

Frächter asked Gohlisch whether Miermann's reports were meant ironically.

Gohlisch replied that Miermann was utterly thrilled, and that the only worry to trouble his heart was whether it was preferable to drink a wine from 1921 or 1911 in Trier or Mainz.

Käsebier was on tour. Berlin was empty.

M-P came to Berlin in July. Miss Kohler thought it over for a day, then called him up. He claimed that he had no time, so she walked over to the office to see him. He solemnly pressed her to his chest without saying a word.

"In four weeks," he said. "In four weeks, I promise. I'm going to the South of France. We'll visit Arles, Nîmes, Avignon."

"Really?"

"Yes," he said, with sad dog's eyes, which in his funny head she found sweet. "We'll go this time for sure. I've thought about everything a lot this year, my dear." He kissed her hand. "I just have to travel briefly to Leipzig for a radio show."

He sent a card from there. "Yes, here—why are you not here *now*? I've put my cares aside and am celebrating the first completely free hour I've had in a long time."

Miss Kohler wrote, "Since I haven't seen you in almost a week, I have, by heavens, the feeling that you are not real, only a spiritualist's apparition. You will see that it is therefore vital to make yourself appear once again. Right now, an acquaintance wanted to pick me up for an evening walk, but I said that I had 'things to do.' The 'doing' consists in writing you a letter on Möve letter-paper..."

He sent no word.

She wrote him, "If I were to avoid you, as my so-called pride dictates, a human relationship that could still offer both parties stimulation, clearheaded conversation, and joy would be destroyed. It seems to me that we are both wandering and climbing. I would be happy if we could—to conjure a bold image—sometimes be a bench for each other from which we could enjoy the views over the valleys and peaks. I therefore ask that you not let feelings of displeasure over this lowly womanly behavior take hold; please try to view me in a more generous light. A coarsely cut rope is perhaps easier to repair than an unraveling silk thread."

She wrote him letters like this every day, but didn't always send them. Instead, she went to a small café on Markgrafenstrasse every day at three o'clock, on the off chance that Meyer-Paris would be drinking his coffee there. Sometimes, she found him. His reason would leave him the moment he saw her. She wrote to him in the same grave style in which he spoke to her. Every time he met her, his gaze was filled with great, festive solemnity.

"I will come by with a finished program. In Paris," he said, "in a few weeks. I think that everything will be much easier in Meudon or Versailles."

"But why is it so hard? Perhaps because you resent *me* for what *you're* doing to me?"

The rhododendrons bloomed in great mountains of yellow, red, and purple in the Tiergarten. The girl Kohler walked through the Tiergarten. Every time a man approached her, she quickly walked away. She sat in the café, waited, ordered coffee, sometimes a chocolate marshmallow. She had to be at the office by half past four. Meyer didn't show.

Gohlisch was tacking up his latest watercolor over his desk, a lake in Brandenburg with a sailboat. Miermann was grumpy:

"Frächter's put out a book, *The Newspaper Business.*"

"It's the most cold-blooded thing I've ever read."

"Everything that's indecent, he calls the essence of capitalism."

"He wants Fordism to satisfy consumer needs, rationalization, collective work."

"Rationalization! It's always the same," said Miermann. "Are the people there for the machines, or are the machines there for the people? The machine is an incredible boon. Man is no longer a packhorse. But in return, the machine controls him. They're inventing increasingly foolproof methods to wean humans off thinking and habituate them to mechanical tricks."

"On the other hand, they're saying that soon there won't be anyone with enough training to operate complicated machinery."

Miermann said, "For years, they said that mechanization—only mechanization—could bring us forward. They spent millions to get machines into businesses, and thousands of people who wanted to earn their hundred marks through honest work were let go. Suddenly, we had a crisis. Then they said rationalization was completely wrong, we should hire more people, all rationalization gave us was unemployment."

"As my father used to say, you can't just put people out on the streets," Miss Kohler said.

"That was early capitalism, things look different now," said Gohlisch.

"Frächter, the servant of capitalism, that's right," said Mierman.

"What do you have against Frächter, anyway? I think he's just a pompous fool," said Gohlisch.

"No," said Miermann. "He's dangerous. He's a speculator. He

supports every trend that should be stopped. He likes to bluff. He likes hoopla. He scorns intelligence. He thinks it's silly to think something of culture. He talks about sports and worships the micro-cephalous. I know Frächter."

"From where?"

"I've known him since 1917. When I was a reporter for the *Berliner Tageszeitung* in Bern during the war, he was a German idealist, doing a little espionage on all sides. I met him again in Munich in 1918. He had since founded a newspaper, the *Sun of the East,* and had become a spokesperson for various -isms. He was against money and warfare and believed in the human soul, he wanted 'community' to embrace the world, like Schiller's millions under the starry canopy: 'Man, brother, the crown of creation.' He gave his disciples explanations for the connection between the war, the Russian Revolution, and the world to come. 'France, England, and America are done for, their edifices are collapsing.' I can still hear him today in his room in the boardinghouse by the Victory Gate. All the girls listened to him. 'Everything to do with knowledge and rationality will be destroyed.' The rational man was a dead man since the death knell had sounded for human exploitation, the worship of plenty, the thousand dozen a day. Instead, we had the rise of observation and intuition, the East, Buddha. But India wasn't far east enough for him, so he said, 'Maybe Laozi.' He wore black peasant blouses and let his hair grow to his shoulders. He put up pictures that were jumbles of brushstrokes. 'That's what we are,' he said, 'chaos.' He wrote a kind of *Sonnenspek-trum* and called it 'Love.'[36] Back then, he was writing plays."

"*The Son,*" cried Miss Kohler.[37]

"No, *Lassalle,* who shoots his father."

"I knew it!" cried Miss Kohler.

"No, not because of the house key like in Hasenclever; it was more symbolic, because we had to get over the guilty fathers who were capitalistic and mechanistic, and who had presumptuously taken steam and electric power for life itself. Later, he would worship ma-chines through communism. Today, he does so through capitalism."

"Have you read the play?" Miss Kohler asked.

"He gave a reading once, what do you expect!"

"I think I'll order a coffee and a grappa now," said Gohlisch. "Cake?"

"No thanks. So what's with Frächter's play?"

"The play featured never-ending debates between a general, a capitalist, a gentleman in blue, a gentleman in gray, a gentleman in yellow, and a 'Führer.' He was the Führer, of course. After the murder, he ran away with a girl in order to build a new world. The girl was a noble thing. She was supposed to keep her hands folded over her body, wear a blue robe, have a blonde face straight out of Holbein, and do nothing except give birth to the New Man. He was an antifeminist, because his ideal was the 'Hero,' the embodiment of logos and eros."

"Erooos," said Miss Kohler, "oh, that whole Blüher nonsense."[38]

"He didn't find women spiritually mature enough. He tried to pick them up, started doing that at fancy-dress balls. He didn't think much of marriage. A man had to remain free; he supported matriarchy. He looked down on people who coveted marriage, standing, or income. He had a lover he called Sonja although her name was Margot. He lived with her on the money he'd received through a dispute settlement with his publisher. No one else had gotten as much money out of the publisher as he had, because he always signed extremely clever contracts. He wrote for all kinds of newspapers, was apparently involved with a film company at some point, and now Cochius is mad about him."

"They met at Mrs. Weissmann's party," said Miss Kohler.

"Yes, it seems like a lot of people met there," said Gohlisch. "The great Käsebier theater is supposed to have been conceived there too."

"That's possible," said Miermann, "but I was the one who introduced Frächter to Cochius. I remember it as if it were yesterday; it was after Käsebier's premiere at the Wintergarten. Frächter called it 'capitalist art' and drove off with a friend of mine."

"Why didn't Frächter become a Nazi intellectual?"

"He could have," Miermann said. "It's simply chance that he hasn't, but he probably still will."

"An unhappy man, really," said Gohlisch.

"Well, if you want to put it like that."

"What does he get out of all his ventures?" asked Gohlisch.

"He'll marry someone very wealthy," said Miss Kohler.

"He certainly won't fall in love."

"Poor sod," said Gohlisch.

"By the way, you mentioned Käsebier before. Where is he, anyways?" asked Kohler.

"On tour, of course," said Gohlisch, "through all of northern and western Germany."

"A week in August in Baden-Baden?" said Miss Kohler.

"Well, what else?" said Gohlisch. "Miermann," he continued, "you may have just called Frächter a traitor, but I'm also a traitor. I'm a traitor to my class."

"How can you say that?" Miss Kohler cried. "Have you ever written a single line that could harm your class?"

"The *Berliner Rundschau* is a liberal right-wing newspaper, a leftist German People's Party. I went to a social democratic primary school."

"You're a German romantic," said Miermann.

"Does party politics have to be everything?" said Miss Kohler. "If so, you belong to the party of loners."

"I want to write a book," said Gohlisch. "*Hölderlin and the Rubber Collar,* a fusion of socialism and classicism."

"Why combine socialism and classicism? Why socialism? The collectivization of the means of production, the unbelievably unfortunate distribution of goods—in Argentina, they fuel their locomotives with corn—has nothing, absolutely nothing to do with this monstrous goading and division of our society into bourgeoisie and proletariat. I think that the socialist ideology, which is committed to *one* scientific theory that has certainly not yet been established as correct, is an impediment to impartial scholarship. 'Hölderlin and the Rubber Collar' could be the party for intellectuals."

"Don't forget, my children, that the Nazis think they're 'Hölderlin and the Rubber Collar' too," Miermann said.

"Nonsense," said Gohlisch. "Fascism is just a party for power."

"Form as content," said Miermann.

"To come back to Frächter," said Miss Kohler, "after his past and all his jabbering about capitalism, how can he a) publish such a pro-American book, and b) become such a thoroughly rationalizing business dictator?"

"It's a springboard to him. I don't find it all that odd; it's the fight for survival. His love of machines is just as Soviet as American, of course."

"Collectivization," said Gohlisch, "requires the initial step of greatly increasing the volume of consumer goods, which we're now calling Americanization."

"The inefficient distribution of surplus," said Miermann, "is the problem. They say collectivization is the solution."

"I don't believe that hatred will create a happy world," said Miss Kohler. "I simply don't. What we're seeing in Russia, compared to western Europe, seems to be a deterioration of living conditions fueled by ideology. The ideology of Christianity in the Roman Empire was just the same. But that's the opposite of historical materialism."

The phone rang.

"Very thoughtful, very kind," said Miermann. "Thank you!"

Miermann turned: "That was Hoffmann from the *Allgemeine*. He sent along Meyer-Paris's apologies for not saying goodbye. He didn't have enough time. Why didn't you tell us that Meyer-Paris is going to America?"

"What?" said Miss Kohler, and went pale. "I don't understand."

Miermann and Gohlisch looked at each other.

"Meyer-Paris is going to America for his paper; in fact, he's already left."

Miss Kohler opened the door and walked out without saying a word.

Gohlisch went after her: "Where are you going?"

"Just leave me alone, please," she said to the well-meaning man.

She called up her friend Miss Wendland.

"Something dreadful has happened."

"Has he left again?"

"Yes," said Miss Kohler, crying.

"Do you want to come over?"

"No, please come here as fast as possible."

"Where?"

"To the café on Mauerstrasse."

"Fine, I'll be there straightaway."

"What should I do?" asked Miss Kohler.

"Take a trip, definitely take a trip."

"Where to?"

"A nice hotel, a nice place. Go to the Black Forest, or might I suggest a cheap, small B and B in Schierke, it's always lovely there."

"I'll write them. But I can't go alone. Can't you come along?"

"No, I'm afraid not. I'd like to very much."

"Maybe it's not true after all."

"I'm sure it's true."

"I have to ask him again."

"Do you have to put yourself through that humiliation?"

"It's not a humiliation. I'm like a dead woman, beyond everything. Nothing else can touch me."

"I'm asking you, please don't do it."

But she did it anyways. She called up the *Allgemeine*. He was still there. She wrote a letter. "Dear friend, I can tell that you have reservations, and perhaps you'd prefer that I tell you to travel alone. But there is a moment where pride runs ashore or rather, when personal certainty trumps any feelings of pride. Barely four weeks ago, you said you would come see me with a finished program in hand, and, fool that I am, I waited for your finished program and your Kingdom of Orangia.[39] And all this time, the person in question already has the tickets for his voyage. That's a bitter pill to swallow. But because I'm not going to pretend, I'll come to you, put my arms around your neck, and once, just once, lay my head on your shoulder, speak from my innermost soul, and tell you that the few conversations we would have on such a trip are existentially necessary to me. Eight days somewhere. I won't bother you. I'll be very quiet."

She received no answer.

She phoned up the *Allgemeine* the following day. She picked up the receiver and said, "Dönhoff 7630."

"You've reached the main desk of the *Allgemeine Zeitung*."

"Could I please speak to Mr. Meyer-Paris?"

"Just a moment, please."

When he picked up, she hung up.

She phoned up the *Allgemeine* the following day. She picked up the receiver and said, "Dönhoff 7630."

"You've reached the main desk of the *Allgemeine Zeitung*."

"Could I please speak to Mr. Meyer-Paris?"

"The gentleman is currently not available."

"Is he still there?"

"Yes, probably, he was on the phone just a few minutes ago."

"Oh, in that case I'll try again later."

The third day she phoned the *Allgemeine Zeitung,* the girl said, "Mr. Meyer-Paris is no longer in Berlin, he left for Hamburg last night."

She managed to choke out, "Thank you."

She burst into the hallway, put on her hat, ran outside. It was pouring rain. She hailed a taxi. The money I'm spending, she thought.

"Hapag, please."

The chauffeur drove her to Unter den Linden. She stood in the Hapag like a madwoman, hat askew, eyes swollen from crying.

"Which ship is going to Hamburg tomorrow?"

"What?" said the clerk.

"I mean, from Hamburg to New York."

"There isn't one."

She ran out without saying thank you. She stumbled up the street to the North German Lloyd company. A gentleman who thought he was dealing with a deranged woman stuck a pince-nez on the tip of his nose and kept an eye on her as he looked through the records.

"A ship left this morning. But there was no Mr. Meyer from Berlin on it. At any rate, he didn't have a reservation, but it's possible that he boarded the ship early today without a reservation."

He was gone. Stunned, she walked through Neustädtische Kirchstrasse to Dorotheenstrasse in the awful weather, sat on a stone ledge, jumped up, and drove to her friend.

"I'd like to shoot him. Why can't we shoot people?"

"Because you're not a maid who can't control her temper."

"Is he allowed to make me this miserable?"

"But you can't shoot him or chase him down. Have a seat and write the little B and B in Schierke."

Three days later, she packed up while her girlfriend kept her company.

"Take a look," said Lotte Kohler, "at the nice note the B and B sent me. We are looking forward to welcoming you."

"You're so miserable," said Wendland, patting her, "so miserable that you're even touched when a hotel is delighted to welcome you."

The next day, she said to Wendland, "I'll tell you something. It's over with Käsebier too."

"Why's that?"

"I just have a feeling. Everything began with Käsebier; now it's ending with Käsebier."

"You've gotten your sense of humor back!"

"Till soon, Kläre, till soon. I'm a hopeless case. But I'm trying to change. Look at me."

"You cut your hair?"

"My braid is gone."

"Hopefully, something else will be gone soon too."

"I'll try my best."

"Best of luck. But for God's sakes, don't fall in love, don't fall in love."

"A burnt child fears the fire. You know, Miermann recently said that if I'd come from different circumstances, I would already have five children out of wedlock and wouldn't be getting any alimony because I wouldn't know who the father was. And a goose like me managed to get her PhD."

29

Frächter takes the paper into his hands once and for all

FRÄCHTER took the paper into his hands once and for all. Rumor had it he was receiving a salary of thirty thousand marks, a bonus of twenty thousand marks, and a stake in the holdings—sixty to seventy thousand in total.

First, the masthead of the *Berliner Rundschau* was changed. Next, an illustrated supplement was added with a cosmetics and tailoring section. Then, a section entitled "Berlin Is Talking About...," which a man from the tabloid *Aus der Gesellschaft* wrote for a hefty salary. Next, two large photographs were added to the daily front page, which was by now one-tenth advertisements. Finally, every fifth employee was fired and the remaining salaries reduced by a sixth. Öchsli, who had quietly stood by as his salary was halved, quit.

When Frächter received the lists of employees who could be fired, he crossed out the accountant Dienstag's name. The man sitting with him said, "Not Dienstag, he works enough for two."

"Then we can cut two jobs in his place," said Frächter, and fired two people instead.

But the children's party at the zoo left everyone transfixed. As a matter of fact, the Sunday papers had twenty additional pages of advertisements for children's products. Balloons, flags, and lanterns were handed out. They were all emblazoned with *Berliner Rundschau*. Fifty thousand children were there. Afterwards, the monkeys didn't touch a morsel of food for days.

Frächter was very pleased.

In July, the Kaliski/Waldschmidt divorce was finalized. Miss Ella Waldschmidt drove with her governess and child to a hotel on Lake

Carezza. Frächter, who had heard about the divorce, followed her. Miss Ella was leaving the dining room with her governess and son when the waiter handed her a business card.

"Willy Frächter, publisher of the *Berliner Rundschau*."

That afternoon, he went for a walk with Miss Waldschmidt around Lake Carezza. He danced with her that evening. She had enjoyed getting dressed up. For the first time in ages, she was dressing up for a man. She considered whether to wear the black or the *bleu*, had her hair washed at the salon, and bought a new perfume: *Narcisse noir*. Thus revived, she met Frächter. Frächter still looked very good. He was the rare German intellectual who dressed well. In his tuxedo, tall, mostly slender despite some pudginess here and there, dark blond, blue-eyed, his intellectual bearing stood out amidst the group of wealthy people. For Ella Waldschmidt, delicate, nervous, and unnoticed by most men, this encounter in the grand hotel was an event. Frächter showered her with graceful attention. "You beautiful, lonely woman," he said, and raised his glass to hers, staring into her eyes until she blushed. After dinner, they danced. He danced very well. He was already holding her close by the second dance. After the fourth, he retrieved her furs, went with her into the summer night, and kissed her hand. When they returned to the hotel, he pointed to the façade and asked, "Where's your room?"

She showed him the window, already blushing. They spoke until morning in the hallway. She told him about her marriage. He understood her. Said intelligent things. He was a worker. Women? He'd never had much time for women. But her... He looked at her. There were no more doubts. If he had been leaving the next day, he would have embraced her that evening. So it happened. He was in love with her because of his ambition. True feelings could no longer be distinguished from artificial ones. This was only apparent in one aspect: the feeling didn't change him; love didn't bowl him over.

Eight days later, they secretly got engaged. They planned to marry in August. Frächter would become Waldschmidt's son-in-law.—

Summer passed. It was impossible to rent out the apartments on

Kurfürstendamm. Oberndorffer, who saw Muschler sitting in a café on Kurfürstendamm one hot August evening, couldn't stop himself from saying, "Well, it would have been better if you'd built one- and two-room apartments. The bachelor apartments designed like that have all been rented out."

Muschler admitted this was true. But the construction wasn't fully finished yet, so one had to wait. Everyone was waiting these days. All the same, it would have been smarter. The theater would open on September 1. One would have to see. The current situation was exceptionally disadvantageous.

In the café, they were playing "How Can He Sleep with That Thin Wall?"

"It's disgusting, no one can stand to hear it anymore. They should turn off the radio," said Muschler. "Waiter, turn off the radio, it's awful."

"Terribly sorry, but I can't turn off the radio, they're playing the 'Thin Wall' by Käsebier. The gentlemen at the next table also said they can't stand it anymore."

"Oh no," Muschler, who had just recognized it, said quickly, "I wouldn't say that, he's a great artist."

"Sure," said Oberndorffer. "They just took it too far in Berlin, as usual. It's a bit annoying now."

"Well, he'll perk up again on Kurfürstendamm," Muschler said.

Augur came into the offices every day. Gloomily, his head bowed, his pockets stuffed with newspapers—a Cassandra—he would deliver daily prophecies of yet another city councilman's downfall, and, just like Troy, they fell.

"Well, Augur," said Miermann, "what's new with the election?"

"Do you know who's supposed to have paid for the poster of the German Nationalists with Sklarek on it? The Sklareks!"[40]

"How's that possible?"

"Because the Sklareks gave huge sums to the German Nationalists—who haven't they given money to?—and because the printing costs were paid for with a Sklarek check."

"That's outrageous," said Gohlisch.

"I fear," said Miermann, "we'll end up with a completely radical-ized Reichstag."

"Dissolving the Reichstag is a huge blunder on the part of the Social Democrats," said Gohlisch.

"What else can we expect from a party of weak-minded prats?" said Augur.

"How's your daughter doing?" asked Gohlisch.

"Not so well at the moment, the doctor said that we should send her to Switzerland once her health improves."

Miss Kohler sat quietly. The two renters had left. What could she do? In the front room were now two homosexuals who walked through the apartment in women's nightgowns. In back was a young man who brought back a different girl every night.

Their home had become a brothel. If the doorman got upset, he could report Mrs. Kohler to the police at any moment. She had long since stopped telling renters, "Ladies may only visit by day, please."

They were sinking; they could swim all they wanted, but they were sinking. The apartment cost five hundred marks a month. They couldn't afford to let the young people give notice.

30

A child dies, a man despairs

IT WAS four thirty in the afternoon on July 31. Miermann, Gohlisch, and Miss Kohler were sitting in the editorial offices again. They were discussing a speech that the leader of the Stahlhelm had given in Leipzig.[41]

"Well," said Gohlisch, "at the Stahlhelm rally in Berlin, he drove along Unter den Linden, studied the map of Berlin intently, and looked for the Lustgarten. Once he had found it, he stood there with three gloves, two on his hands, the third held in front of him like a kind of marshal's baton."

"Gohlisch, is that true?"

"Just do me a favor and order coffee," said Miss Kohler.

"With cake?"

"Without," called Miermann.

"With," Lotte Kohler.

Gohlisch went to the phone and ordered. "Three coffees, but hurry up, pretty thing, and three grappas for room eight, *Berliner Rundschau*."

That instant, a young messenger came in and announced a gentleman who had followed on his heels: Mr. Förster.

Miermann was about to say, "Please ask him to wait next door," when the man entered. He was very long and gaunt, had rather bony hands, and wore a yellowish linen jacket and a wide green scarf bound as a tie along with trousers that were too short.

"Gentlemen, please allow me to put down my suitcase. My name is Förster, police constable. I have some important documents to show you. I have a clock that will allow you to read off the election results."

"What?" said Miermann. "The election results? Very interesting."

"Yes," the stranger said. "I worked on it for a year until it was ready, but now it works. It doesn't show the time anymore, just the election results."

"An odd clock," said Gohlisch. "How do you read it?"

The stranger stood up and walked over to Gohlisch. He showed him a golden pocket-watch: "Here you can see one hundred and ten votes for the National Socialists, one hundred votes for the Social Democrats."

"I see a twelve," said Gohlisch.

"Sir, can you not see one hundred and ten in small, blue letters over the twelve?"

"Have you come to show us the clock?"

"Certainly, the clock, certainly! I've been collecting old newspapers on Wittembergplatz, but I was once a police constable. The police work under unbelievable conditions. Here, this entire suitcase is full of material, I'm in the process of writing my memoirs, I'm just looking for a publisher. I contracted a serious illness for fiscal reasons and am receiving no remuneration!"

"That's disgraceful," said Gohlisch.

"Isn't it? Listen, I'm a man of the old school, my great-grandfather was hanged by Frederick the Great. Gentlemen, I had a criminal case to solve, a mysterious murder among the reeds of Buchsum. I was looking for the body when my supervisor said, 'His girlfriend will know everything.' I got on my bike, rode over, took along a bar of chocolate and went to see the girl. The girl was crying, I comforted her, squeezed her knee, I'm a man of the old school, and, to cut a long story short—after all, we have a lady present—the gentlemen can picture the situation, she confessed to me—in bed, apologies—the name of the murderer. I filed a report and fell ill. And the government, gentlemen, the state, where can we seek justice? The Jews have been bribed by the Catholics. The Jews—"

Miermann and Gohlisch looked at each other.

Miermann interrupted the stranger and said, "Won't you write your business down for us, we have work to do, I'd be happy for it."

Gohlisch stood up: "Please follow me outside. The man has work to do."

With great long steps, the man stood up.

He pulled out his watch again and said, "My clock, gentlemen, shows a dead man. I'd like to shake your hands. One of you, I won't be seeing again."

He left.

"Well," said Miermann, "that was uncanny."

"Dreadful, yes."

Gohlisch came back.

"Is he outside?"

"I got rid of him."

"Don't kid around," said Miermann.

"Are you superstitious?" Gohlisch asked.

"I don't understand where Augur is hiding with the news."

"I don't either."

"I'll give him a call."

Gohlisch got on the phone.

"This is Gohlisch. Hey, conspirator, where are you with the news? Are you only going to come out of hiding around midnight?"

"I'll send them along," said Augur. "I can't come in, my daughter has died."

"I'm terribly sorry." Gohlisch hung up.

"The child is dead?" said Miermann.

Gohlisch nodded.

"That shouldn't have happened," said Miss Kohler. "We're sitting around here chatting about Stahlhelms, Nazis, Socialists, corruption in the Berlin administration, elections, elections, and then a child dies."

"I don't know," said Gohlisch, "why I didn't try to help."

"You never know until it's too late," said Miermann.

"I mentioned something to Dr. Krone once," said Gohlisch.

"Sure, sure," said Miss Kohler. "But the death of a small, gentle, young, wistful creature was unnecessary, it was so much more important than all this nonsense, much more. I didn't try to help either."

"Yes," said Gohlisch, dejected.

"Yes," said Miermann.

They sat and drank their coffee.

Miehlke came in, asked what was going in, too little room, gotta cut. "Doesn't matter," Miehlke said, "cut, cut." Ten percent of Siemens workers were to be fired. Schiele had moved to the Farmer's Party. 272,000,000 railroad commissions. Earthquake in southern Italy. Big clashes between Communists and National Socialists.

The phone rang. "Layout, gentlemen."

Miermann and Gohlisch disappeared in the composing room.

The next day, Miermann and Käte sat together in an unused room. Miermann told her that Augur's little daughter had died.

"What?" said Käte. "And you all watched as the child slowly wasted away from tuberculosis? It didn't occur to you, Gohlisch, or Miss Kohler to help out?"

"I'm upset with myself too."

"What do you mean, upset with yourself? It's terribly easy to be upset with yourself. It was your damned duty and your responsibility to intervene. You should have gone, sent for a doctor, or seen to it that the child was sent away. Letting yourself go and standing by as someone croaks, that's lovely, all right. If *I'd* have been there, it wouldn't have happened."

Something swelled up in Miermann. Maybe, he thought, she would have seen to everything with her energy and confidence, maybe I should have behaved like that, been a man. But her, a woman?

"You're very convinced of yourself," he said out loud.

She pulled back. "I think that someone should have intervened. And I would have!" She stood there, a blazing Judith.

"Käte, you know that I love you."

"And I you," Käte said, tongue in cheek.

"Please, be serious."

Käte understood. "I'm quite serious, my dear," she said.

"I want to ask you about something that's been on my mind. I saw you yesterday with young Waldschmidt."

"Yes?"

"I mean ..."

"Yes."

"Käte, really? You have a boyfriend?"

"What, just one? How many do you want to know about? One, two, three, four? Pardon my candor, but I can't stand people who tell themselves stories."

"But why? A creature so beautiful in body and spirit?"

"Can't you understand? I married too young. I did *not* love my husband, as you know. I could have made a wonderful lover, but I became a cold thing instead. It's a thorny problem. I started up with others. I had unhappy relationships between three and five o'clock in the afternoon. I fell in love again and again. I couldn't stand anyone in the long term, but I didn't want to, anyways."

Miermann sat there with an uncomprehending face:

"But many?"

She guessed his thoughts: "I've never toyed around, I've also never acted a part for someone. Ugh! You can't reproach me for leading you on. I find flirting vulgar, and then *tout excepté ça*. No, if someone's fallen in love with me and I am perhaps to blame, then I am involved with him. I call that decent behavior. Everyone cheats on their wives in their minds, in their dreams—I think that's just cowardly. Have you never cheated on your wife? If you say 'never,' you're a liar, like this whole bourgeois society."

"Dear Käte, I don't believe you're coldhearted. Don't think emotion is shameless. You should dare to claim your clever heart. I can't imagine that you wouldn't be happy if a young, intelligent man came along and made you his wife."

"I think marriage is crazy. I couldn't stand it, even with someone I was completely in love with. I have to be free."

She was incredibly beautiful. In that moment, Miermann followed the dictate of his generation, which forbade a man from appearing small, helpless, and afflicted in front of a woman, for fear of ridicule. "Free?" he said with an attempt at male scorn, and embraced the shrouded woman. He expected to encounter resistance. He didn't. He had hoped to be freed, but he was embarrassed. They had both grown serious when they left. Though she found him unappealing, she needed tenderness, a kind word to become human again. He had failed. It had been rape. She would never forgive him.

It was five o'clock in the afternoon. He went back to the office. Miss Kohler was in the room. Miermann looked pale.

"Is something the matter?" she asked. "Shall I order you something? Perhaps an iced coffee, in this heat?"

Miermann asked, "How old are you?"

"Thirty-three," she said.

"You know women in their thirties?"

"Maybe. War generation."

"Something strange happened to me. She told me that she's had many affairs since her divorce, and that she takes them lightly."

"Maybe she's cold, maybe she's looking for something."

"Do you understand it? I can't."

"Yes, I do."

Miermann shook his head. It was very hot. The windows were closed, the yellow summer blinds pulled down.

"But look, Miermann, such an intelligent and sensuous woman, as you always say, must be looking for great love. Mustn't one perhaps go through many beds to find it?"

"She says everything else is just a fantasy."

"A courageous woman. She knows that you can love many people, you can love them in succession, but you can also love different people at the same time."

The phone rang. Mielke came in. "When are you coming in for layout? What're we keeping? We've gotta cut."

"Where's the overset, Kohler?"

The funeral took place on August 4 in the Wilmersdorf crematorium. People stood in the portico of the cobblestone courtyard, wearing black clothes in the August sun. Many had come. Öchsli was there, Lambeck, and five small girls with brown and blonde hair carrying bouquets. Surprisingly, this did Augur some good. Augur came with his wife. He looked around sadly and supported the small, inconspicuous, miserable, overworked woman, who was crying, stunned. The organ played "*Es ist bestimmt in Gottes Rat.*" The child's coffin was completely covered with pale white and pink roses.

Miermann held the eulogy.

"Little Eva-Maria Tradt, today we lay you to eternal rest. Dear mourners, what can I say over the coffin of this little elf, this half-fledged woman-child, what can I say to her parents that will not tear their wounds open anew, since the pain is so overwhelming, since innocence itself has left this earth? This little girl was a marvel of grace, her little girlish footsteps pattered through the house. Her classmates adored her, here are a few of her little friends who have brought her flowers. Her soul held nothing but the longing of butterflies and the goldfinch and the cowslip. Her heart held love for her parents, her teacher, her little playmates, but her young mind desired to learn and do much. She was a clever child, a gentle soul, a loving heart. What, dear, good parents, honored Augur, good, dear mother, is better than that?

"We must think of ourselves, but not of her. For her, life would have been a disappointment; she would have suffered without end. Her delicate body would have been unable to bear the painful burdens heaped upon her heart, her soul unable to grasp them. The heart's betrayal, deceived trust, the loneliness of city life would have dragged her down. She would have cried out and pleaded for salvation because such flowerlike beings are ruffled and uprooted by the storm of our time. This time is harsh and relentless, and we force little elves to face life, so that life's millstone can grind them to bits.

"Heavenly little angel, you flew through life for a few sunny children's days, you were sheltered from sin, shame, suffering, pain, sorrow, need, from the terrible problems of our time, against which life's joys seem feather-light.

"You have been received by the great rapture. You will join the eternal choir as a heavenly seraph. We below, all of us sinners, who have lied without need and betrayed, who have bowed to power, closed ourselves off from the good and sought our advantage, we who have not loved our neighbor and have closed our doors and eyes and ears to his need, we will need to wander through many circles before we meet you again. For we have sunk so low that the clocks no longer tell the time, but someone has invented a clock that shows election results. We no longer notice how time flows from night to day and from day to night, the sun setting on the horizon and rising at dawn, the awakening of the birds and the opening of flower buds, but we need clocks that indicate the day's business, seismographs that track the collapse of parties.

"We have fallen so far, we have grown so ugly!

"But you are in the realm of the blessed. Because a life like yours, begun in heavenly lightness, without the pains of motherhood, of womanhood, of love, is not over yet. Love will never cease, love for you, little elf, from those who are banished from your sight, the unworthy, the unrepentant, woven into the wheel of life. You have found the river of knowledge. You will live eternally. Be blessed, as you were a blessing. Amen, amen."

"You are the calm, the restful peace,

"You are my longing and what makes it cease..." the organ played.

Most of those present found Miermann's speech strange. He, who was so highly educated, had mixed up all of his references. He had taken what he needed from Greek mythology, from Christian theology, and from the teachings of Buddha to prove that this child would live on.

But this was not the only thing that struck them. It was how moved Miermann was, how vehemently he confessed to his own sinfulness, how he sought a path, how helpless he was in the face of death, a fact he was perhaps still unconscious of. This intelligent man, so deeply connected to the events of the day, stood there, a short, fat man in a frock coat, whose collar was covered with dandruff even today, and cast off his cloak and his pride before God and confessed. Although everything he said was universal, although it touched on religious traditions across two millennia, it sounded intensely personal to those who knew Miermann. Gohlisch and Miss Kohler felt it was a resignation. This was more than the caprice of a journalist bowled over by the mood of the day: this was repentance, a great longing for the void.

Everyone shook the poor parents' hands. "You too, Mr. Lambeck," said Augur, touched. Lambeck led the poor parents out.

"I think my little girl will become an angel, I know I'll see her again," the wife said. "She was so beautiful. She was the perfect child," and sobbed heavily when she saw the little living friends.

Miermann, Gohlisch, and Miss Kohler began their day's work at the office.

"I can't write today," said Miermann, and phoned home. "Emma, I'll be home late, don't wait up for dinner."

He went to the little Geroldstube, ordered a bottle of wine, and sat there for several hours. Then he walked through the dead city.

Sparse streetlights burned on Zimmerstrasse. A few miserable-looking girls stood on Markgrafenstrasse. A couple was fighting. A man yelled, "You damned whore, fooling around with a married man," a woman sobbed loudly. Then everything went quiet. I don't want to go west yet, thought Miermann, Everyone will be cheerfully sitting about on Tauentzienstrasse and the women are pretty. I don't want to see that. —He went back down sad Zimmerstrasse, over dead Leipziger Strasse, which was brightly lit up by arc lamps and looked like a film set that would be torn down the next day. He crossed the Spittelmarkt, walked along the water until the Waisenbrücke, and looked at the silhouette of the town hall spire against the red sky. He went over the bridge and along Stralauer Strasse. He could hear only his own steps. He stepped into the Grosser Jüdenhof for a moment. The large tree cast a shadow over the old houses; light shone from the windows. Miermann felt incredibly homesick. The strains of "Be Honest Truth Thy Guide" came from the parish church. Miermann hugged the tree, "Help me," he said to the tree, "Help me." He was not ashamed in front of the tree, this tree was good, it sheltered him, it did not expose him to scorn, it did not demand any posturing, irony, or industriousness. "You dear," he said, and patted the tree. He walked back through old, narrow alleys. They want to demolish all of this—all of it. It's all supposed to become office buildings, he thought. The buildings on the Molkenmarkt were already empty. I knew this city, he thought, when it still looked like a city, when they hadn't torn down house after house yet, when wool was still stored in Hohes Haus and the horse carts stood on Klosterstrasse, the Hollmann school was still at Hackescher Markt, and there were gardens everywhere. There's no more space left for mankind or its longings. He wandered farther, came to the Schlossplatz, and walked along Französische Strasse. He encountered no one. He had returned to a derelict city after a thousand years. The houses were unoccupied, and sometimes only an old God stood out front wearing a uniform with braided trim, holding the keys. Never again would people breathe here. Laughter had died when the people had perished. He alone was awake. He was tired, the soles of his feet ached. "Tired feet," he thought. "The mildest work is washing feet. We have stopped wandering, we no longer have tired feet, we have no one to wash them for us, our hearts betrayed, our trust deceived in the cities."

There were people, trolleys, cars on Friedrichstrasse. He took a taxi. "Potsdamer Brücke," he said. He got out, walked along the canal. The scaffolding of the Shell house rose up in the air. He spoke to the guard:

"Such beautiful houses torn down here."

"But it's good after all, those old dumps," said the man. "There's work, and a big house from a foreign company brings in cash."

"I think it's a shame," Miermann insisted.

"Oh, no, sir," said the man.

"The people of Berlin think nothing of tradition," thought Miermann. "They like tearing things down and hullaballoo and ta-ra-ra."

Miermann couldn't go home yet.

On Würzburger Strasse, he thought, there's something bleaker, more meaningless than this street, something more hopeless than these houses that were built so lovelessly. He hailed a taxi. "Friedrichstrasse," he said. He got out, went past the girls, hot dog sellers, pimps, construction sites, and torch flames, and into a bar. A den of vice in faux Chinese style, wooden carvings, dragon heads, colorful lanterns, many women. A few coarse but pretty girls in low-cut dresses danced with lanky young people. A blonde in black sequins sat down at his table.

"Well, sugar."

It was a man. Miermann was disgusted. But he didn't want to raise a fuss.

"I want a curaçao."

"Don'cha want a bottle of wine? I'll be nice, too."

"A curaçao, please."

He paid and left. Continued on, saw a young strumpet in a skimpy skirt.

"Come," he said. Took her along.

"Where'dja wanna go?"

"To a café."

"I don't have a lot of time."

"I just want to drink a cup of coffee."

"And then?"

"You can go."

"Oh, you're one of those perverts? Well, fine."

He went into a café with her. "Order whatever you like," he said. She ordered cake and whipped cream, stuffed herself like every other little girl in Berlin. Miermann kissed her and gave her five marks, and she was on her way again.

In the dance hall on the corner, a girl in a twenty-mark red silk dress was splayed over the podium singing a love song. She was in a bad mood. Below her sat young men, blond and greased up. There was screeching from the next street over. "Can'tcha do something else than arrest a poor girl," a woman in a uniform of black silk shrieked; over it she wore a thin coat trimmed with gray goat. "I wasn't even working, I was going to my friend's birthday party." The shrieking subsided. The "U" of the underground shone in the night.

It was already light and the night was long over when he ended up in a basement in the north. Long tables, wooden benches, a piano player, streetcar workers. A dark crowd of misshapen, pale girls with red mouths wearing bright knit cardigans, and men with sport hats.

The next day, Miermann received a letter by registered mail:

"Dear Mr. Miermann! Unfortunately, it is no longer possible for us to uphold our current contract with you. It will be terminated on the first of October.

"Berliner Rundschau Publishing Company, sgd. Frächter."

"Look here," said Miermann. "I've been here for eighteen years. Now, suddenly, right now, when everyone knows that jobs are scarce, even for the best people! What are we? Freelance writers? Journalists? Politicians? No, dear Gohlisch, we're small-time employees, you see. We can go to the labor courts like a maid, a servant who's fired on the fifteenth. Are you an artist, Gohlisch? You think so? You're not! You're a poorly paid employee. Nothing more than a poorly paid employee. The free man is going to the dogs. They'll say, Are you surprised? This is capitalism, this is what it looks like."

"He didn't need to do that," said Miss Kohler. "Not everyone behaved or behaves like that. Those who've built up their own business treat their workers like colleagues. Only careerists are that heartless."

"Not just," said Miermann. "Heirs and retirees who become entrepreneurs are bad news too. The worst—and by the way, it's the same in politics—is that those who have power are those who seek power, and those who seek power are not decent people."

"You should talk to Frächter," said Gohlisch. "But it won't help."

"I'll say, *Sun of the East*, d'you remember the *Sun of the East* from 1918?"

"Don't fly off the handle. You're right, but you have a wife; it's not Napoleon's seven, but you have two reasons to give in."

"Everyone can do that," said Miermann. "But I can't. I've spoken too much about the freedom of the press, I've defended freedom of expression thousands of times. I've tried to never make compromises in someone's favor or harm. And I'm supposed to go and ask the renegade Frächter for two hundred marks? I can't do that. Tomorrow I suppose I'll have to speak with an outside representative? I'm supposed to remain a free man if I go begging for two hundred marks? And I'm supposed to get by on a salary of three hundred marks a month? I can't do that."

"Frächter will tell you that ninety percent of the German population has to get by on a lot less. Go to Frächter, but not today."

31

Miermann goes on strike

MIERMANN made a plan of attack. He went on strike. For eighteen years, the readers of the *Berliner Rundschau* had been used to reading the little Miermanns. Miermann had written between twenty and fifty lines of finely polished prose on the day's events for eighteen years: cabinet crises, presidential elections, the Krantz affair,[42] the Haarmann trial,[43] the battleship debate. Miermann stopped writing. He waited for his readers and his publisher to respond. Miermann had been deeply loved by his readers over the years. He had three thick binders stuffed with letters from readers. He had received packages during the inflation, wine and sweets. He was betting on those three thick binders.

Every day, Gohlisch asked him, "Has anyone written?"

"No."

Miss Kohler asked and waited.

But nothing came.

Miermann said, "No mass will be sung, no Kaddish recited. Nothing will be said nor sung on my dying day. By the way, this has only happened to me since my 'Käsebier' stopped working. The nib burst yesterday."

After four weeks, a friendly woman inquired whether Miermann was sick.

Gohlisch, who had noticed the strike on the second day, said to Miermann, "I'm curious to see what will happen. Öchsli said that he was sadly quite certain of the consequences of such measures."

On August 28, it transpired that even Heye hadn't noticed

Miermann's silent protest, let alone the publisher. No one had noticed. Perhaps they would have if he had remained silent for several months, but even that was highly questionable.

32
Käsebier returns

WHILE Miermann was still on strike and the atmosphere at the *Berliner Rundschau* made any kind of intellectual collaboration impossible, Käsebier returned to Berlin.

Frächter made an editorial intervention and demanded that Käsebier be put on the front page.

"Käsebier after His Show in London."

"Käsebier Boards the *Leviathan*."

"Käsebier Returns to the Continent."

He was treated like a blimp or a firestorm or a tornado.

"Käsebier Comes to Cologne."

"Käsebier Comes to Berlin."

In fact, his show in London had been a complete flop. The London press unanimously agreed that he was a local celebrity and could not be exported. His guest appearance had greatly damaged the exchange between German and British artists and art. Influential German artists were completely appalled by this thoughtless and poorly prepared guest appearance, which had been orchestrated by Frächter's friend.

The London correspondent of the *Berliner Tageszeitung* sent Waldschmidt a private report.

Among other things, it said, "Unfortunately, I must report that the *Times* had only very nasty things to say. 'It can only be considered shameless to invite London's high society to partake in the offerings of an extremely mediocre bench-singer. Pronouncing this lovely and amiable dilettante of the same caliber as Raquel Meller, Guilbert, or even Marc Henry (a rather average artist), indicates a strong bias for one's own nation.' We should publish these opinion pieces in Germany. Misguided guest shows hurt us more than they help us. Above all, they hurt German art that is truly great."

But barely anything was published on these reactions. There were tremors at the *Berliner Tageszeitung*. The *Berliner Rundschau* reveled in "Käsebier's Triumph." But the Käsebier economy was over for good. The toy and rubber industries and Miss Götzel weren't the only ones who had turned away from him. His records were no longer in demand. Käsebier's songs were replaced by new ones, and in locales that had once played only "How Can He Sleep with That Thin Wall?," one could now hear "Three musketee-heers, three cavalie-heers," or "In Paris, in Paris, the Girls Are So Sweet" from *Under the Roofs of Paris*.

He was over for the film industry—his films had been too bad—and there were no journalists left to discover him. The only thing that proved lasting were the Käsebier woven shoes, which sold steadily all summer long. The large papier-mâché sculpture of Käsebier was still standing in the shopwindow, but the Käsebier cigarette factory—"Käsebier Bonus, Melior, and Optimus"—had gone bankrupt after a year. Its sign on the Friedrichstrasse train station had rusted, and was now being removed to make way for a new one: NICOBAR, THE NICOTINE KILLER.

Meanwhile, Käsebier had terminated his contract with Hasenheide for the first of April.

They were keeping the apartment until October 1. Mrs. Käsebier had wanted a five-room apartment, but Käsebier insisted on four.

Although the apartment on the Kurfürstendamm had first seemed like paradise, Mrs. Käsebier shed quite a few tears. She was used to eating in the kitchen; she didn't want to give up her habit. But as was standard in modern apartments, the kitchen had been pared down to the minimum. Its coziness would have been ruined by carrying plates back and forth, and she did not want to give in and get a maid. She tackled the kitchen problem several times, finally demanding that the kitchen be moved into a more spacious room. The construction management refused. Deciding on wallpaper, curtains, and furniture left her with no piece of mind. She got new furniture for the living room, study, and dining room, but decided to keep the bedroom as it was. She had been very happy in it, she was superstitious, and she wanted to keep something as a reminder of the day that all their debts had been paid off.

Käsebier, on the other hand, rehearsed and rehearsed and had more stage fright than ever before, even more than in his earliest days. He, who was so unpolitical, wanted to keep his show focused on human interest topics in these tumultuous times.

Margot Weissmann, who had just returned to Berlin, invited everyone to her apartment on September 3 for a housewarming party at which the latest sensational news would be announced: Frächter's engagement to Mrs. Kaliski, née Waldschmidt.

Mrs. Muschler had already ordered the first winter look, a white georgette dress, for the Weissmanns' party. Muschler agreed to it, although he was doing quite badly. The complex on Kurfürstendamm, which was still mostly empty, wasn't going to pull him out of the hole as he had hoped. It was more than doubtful whether Käsebier could manage three thousand marks a month in rent. In addition, Muschler had gotten involved in rather dubious business investments, even as his private banking had suffered. The stock market was turning ever more bearish with the rise of the National Socialists. If Kurfürstendamm had still been an untouched plot of land, Muschler could have sold or leased it off. The partnership between the associates often grew heated because of the construction project.

Uncle Gustav said, "I was against it from the start, but you always know better."

"It'll be a great business venture if we can hang on to it," Muschler said.

"But we can't," said Uncle Gustav.

"You're always a pessimist," Muschler retorted.

"I've always been proven right, unfortunately."

"But you believed in the mark."

"No one could believe in the madness of inflation."

"Well, I guessed right that time."

"Maybe in abnormal times, but you're not prepared for a normal crisis."

"Well, we'll see."

"All too soon, I'm afraid."

Mitte anxiously watched these developments. The sanguine Mitte, that eternal optimist, was counting on Muschler to go bankrupt. This would relieve him of his obligations. But even then, he would first have to pay Muschler an owner's mortgage of 250,000 marks as well as the property transfer tax, and he was completely illiquid.

33
Miermann dies

SINCE neither his publisher nor his readers had noticed his silence, Miermann decided to speak to the publisher on the twenty-ninth.

"I'm going to see Frächter now," Miermann said.

"Chin up and best of luck."

Even a month ago, Gohlisch wouldn't have dared to say that to his venerated editor. But Miermann had changed. He had changed in such a way that Gohlisch could now say "chin up" to him.

But before Miermann went to Frächter, he glanced over two articles, one by Gohlisch, one by Miss Kohler.

"I'm going to order coffee," said Gohlisch.

"Ah, leave it," said Miermann. "I don't want one."

"What about a grappa?"

"That's kind of you, but I don't want one. Dear Golisch," he said, "your manuscripts! You simply can't say: 'The political audacity of the German Nationalists allows them to speak about weak wills and so on, despite the clear state of affairs under a gloomy sky.' However, 'clear state of affairs under a gloomy sky' is the most beautiful thing I've read in a while."

He cut, reorganized, added punctuation, straightened out thoughts, lifted ideas out of the confusion of dim intuition and brought them into the clarity of enlightening prose, and only then did the articles by his faithful students Gohlisch and Kohler first become themselves: a good Gohlisch, a good Kohler. Indeed, Gohlisch and Kohler had gotten into the habit of writing articles as if they were composing private letters to Miermann. Their articles became good as they thought of his kindhearted, loving critique. This was also the case on the day Miermann sent both of their articles into the composing room and went to see Frächter.

Frächter had gotten a haircut. A buzz cut. A small bald spot had become noticeable. Nothing still resembled the man who had frequented the Romanisches Café a year and a half ago. Across from Miermann sat a slightly plump citizen, wedging in his monocle from time to time, with a salary of thirty thousand marks and royalties up to fifty thousand marks.

Frächter began, "I deeply regret this conversation. Believe me, if I could have my way, I would gladly give you a handsome salary."

"Mr. Frächter, you know as well as I do that a man in my position requires a different standard of living from a low-level office employee to retain his professional point of view."

"Certainly, but we can't pay you more. The economy is forcing our hand."

"What's it forcing you to do? Dumb down your newspaper and fire people who have worked for you for eighteen years?"

"Yes, that's what times are forcing us to do! What you call dumbing down, Mr. Miermann, I call blooming. Newspapers need new blood. It's not good for people to work here for too long."

"Mr. Frächter, have you ever taken an interest in your audience?"

"No, Mr. Miermann. It's unnecessary. Our readership notices nothing, unfortunately. Every year twenty thousand graduates leave universities having learned how to write essays in German. They'll write for ten pfennigs a line. I might be exaggerating, but the days of the hotshot journalist are over. It depends on the position of each newspaper, not each individual."

"You're quite right, that's why German journalists are held in such high esteem by the foreign press. The publishers are trying to raise the level of German journalism higher and higher since education is nonsense and getting to the bottom of things is ridiculous, but all the same, Mr. Frächter, it'll be hard to avoid limping after the tabloids. I'm willing to print 'Capitalist Rapes Girl,' or 'Rain for Eight Weeks, Socialists at Fault.' But I'm not sure I can start straightaway."

"Mr. Miermann, you're telling *me* how to run a paper? Our

circulation figures are rising and rising. Our street sales jumped by twenty thousand the day we premiered the most beautiful legs. The cosmetics page is unbelievably popular, and you can't imagine for how little money Mr. Schulz puts it together for me."

"I can give you German politics on the cheap. Perhaps I can even give you articles that are cheaper by the dozen."

"Mr. Miermann, you've talked yourself into a rage. This is not advantageous to our negotiations. I propose a fixed salary of three hundred marks."

"For how many articles?"

"Well, the usual!"

"That's twenty-five marks an article?"

"Then just write less. By the way, you can leave immediately if you are unwilling to accept our conditions."

Miermann climbed the stairs to his apartment on Würzburger Strasse. Emma, his wife, didn't ask why he'd come home so early. She never asked him anything. She considered herself a simple housewife. She went into the kitchen and washed some radishes.

Miermann sat on the sofa and felt as if he had nothing to do. Miermann, who usually came home and asked, "Is there mail? Did someone call?" who was on the phone immediately, reading brochures, sitting at his desk, now sat quietly on the sofa, and looked out the window toward the west, gazing at the setting sun.

Emma went over to him and said, "It'll be all right." Miermann pulled her down on the couch and put his arm around her shoulders.

"I love you very much, you know," he said.

They ate their dinner—bread, butter, cold cuts, tomatoes, radishes—and drank beer.

"Shall we go for a walk? It's terribly hot this evening."

Miermann went out with his wife. Dreadful, he thought. Würzburger Strasse, Geisbergstrasse; all of these brutal, hideous boxes for people. He felt as if the buildings were falling on him. And all the houses were full of nothing but worries from top to bottom without hope, belief, or knowledge. "They sleep much as the oysters live and die."[44]

They encountered two Galician Jews on Motzstrasse. They wore silken caftans and soft black hats. One of them had a long black beard, the other a long red one.

"Have we become that much more beautiful, you with your blonde hair and blue eyes, and I with my books on romanticism and classicism? People don't know what beauty is anymore."

They arrived at Nollendorfplatz.

"Shall we have an iced coffee?" he asked.

"Oh no, I don't need one. Let's leave it."

"Surely we can still afford an iced coffee?"

"Well," Emma sighed. She was already budgeting in spirit, and was adjusting to the smaller income. The iced coffee was two lunch sandwiches.

They entered the café, sat down, and drank the iced coffee. They sat there for a long time. After an hour or so, it got very crowded. The waiters couldn't keep up with the orders.

All of a sudden, a man began to shout loudly, "This is outrageous! I've been sitting here for an hour and no one's come. What kind of business do you call that?! I didn't come here to wait. I told the waiter three times, 'A chocolate milk, an iced coffee,' but he hasn't brought them, he hasn't come back! No one's moved, no one's come, I'm sitting here like a monkey! It's outrageous!" He was frighteningly red in the face as he slammed his fist on the table and pounded his walking stick on the floor. "It's outrageous! As if I wasn't going to pay! What a state, what a state—look at how we're treated!"

Everyone present was deeply frightened by the man's unrestrained shouting. The manager was summoned. He was very polite, and said placatingly, "My dear sir, you'll be served straight away. What will you have?"

But the man wouldn't stop screaming. His wife tried to calm him down, but he became more and more enraged. It was deeply alarming. He grabbed a chair and banged it on the floor.

"I don't want anything anymore. If you still think I want something, I've been waiting for three hours and now I've snapped. Enough is enough. I don't want anything anymore. It's over. I called, the waiter simply didn't come, he left us sitting there, didn't wait on us. It's outrageous! Outrageous!"

Miermann said to his wife, "He came straight from a political gathering."

The manager said apologetically, "Every evening, when the movies are done with the *Roofs of Paris*, we're slammed for fifteen minutes. I can't hire more waiters just for that."

Everyone made soothing gestures. After a while, Miermann and Emma got up and walked down Kleiststrasse. Just before the first crossing, Miermann suddenly said, "I feel sick!" At once, he staggered and fell. Emma, frightened, knelt down, propped him up, and held his head. He squeezed her hand and moved his lips. From them came words unspoken for thirty-five years, the age-old dying prayer of the ancient Jews: "*Shmah yisroel, adonoi elohenu adonoi echod.*" "Hear, O Israel, the Lord is our God, the Lord is One."

"Amen," said Emma.

"Come," he said.

But she had to let him go. She cried out for help.

A taxi driver got out of his cab and brought Miermann to the doctor who lived in the next house over. He pronounced Miermann dead. Emma wanted to take her husband home. The chauffeur lifted him into the car. As he lay silent next to her, Emma grew fearful of the man with whom she had shared twenty-four years of her life, and opened the window to the chauffeur. The breathing stranger was a comfort next to the corpse. Emma cried. If he could only have taken her with him! What would she do in this life without any duties?

She was soon at home and called her doctor. He arrived, diagnosed a heart attack, and left instructions. Emma stayed up with the man she had loved. It occurred to her that she should exact revenge upon those who had wronged him. Miermann's old fighting spirit awoke in her, and she called up Öchsli. She told Öchsli what had happened and added that Öchsli should announce it to all the papers but make sure that the *Berliner Rundschau* didn't catch wind of it. Only after she had undertaken the revenge of a journalist's wife did she surrender to her grief, the recognition of her boundless loneliness.

"Come," he'd said. Shouldn't she come, mustn't she come, wasn't it her duty to come? She was half mad when Öchsli came to see her in the morning and made sure she went to bed.

All the morning papers except the *Berliner Rundschau* reported on Miermann's death. Every newspaper dedicated at least twenty lines to him, and the *Berliner Tageszeitung* ran an eighty-line essay. There was no word in the *Berliner Rundschau*. As expected, this caused a greater upset than Miermann's death.

"I don't understand what kind of news service we have," Frächter said to the editor in chief of the local news. "How can we not know about the death of the most important editor on staff?"

The old curmudgeon said, "If you take away all my colleagues . . ."

Someone in the arts section who had heard that Miermann had died on the way home from a party angrily said, "With my salary, I can't afford a tuxedo or frequent the circles in which one learns of such things."

A midday paper contained dark hints of suicide. The radical evening papers printed large headlines:

DRIVEN TO DEATH!

Meanwhile, Heye had written a very moving obituary.

But the fake news had to be disproved. Frächter, worrying that word of the firing might get out and be shouted from the rooftops, wired Emma a thousand marks, since he assumed that this had likely been arranged by her. Then Frächter had an extra bone to pick with the head of the wire service.

The funeral was arranged for September 2. Emma, who had heard her husband's last words, wondered if it might not be better to bury him next to his parents at the Jewish cemetery in Weissensee. But Miermann had left Judaism behind long ago, and in his will she found clear directions that he wished to be buried in the Waldfriedhof cemetery.

Thus it was arranged.

It was a beautiful summer day: birds sang, butterflies flew about, all the flowers were bright and perfectly lovely. Being laid to rest here was a fitting departure. As expected, many people had come. Many of his female readers, who hadn't paid attention when it had been vitally necessary, now came and brought flowers. All of his colleagues were there: Frächter from the publisher's office, Miss Käte Herzfeld, Miehlke from the composing room, the theater critics, politicians, relatives, friends, Dr. Krone, Oberndorffer, Lambeck, and Mr. and Mrs. Tradt-Augur. Lieven went around and shook everyone's hand with great feeling. Aja Müller wore her black hat far back on her strawberry-blonde head and flitted from one distinguished guest to the next. It was an elegant society event. She made her rounds and was pleased by who she met. It was no different from an evening at Margot Weissmann's. Lieven made sure he was in the vicinity of Möglein, the theater director, and Heinrich Wurm in Frächter's. The organ played Bach. Frächter slowly stepped forward, and said:

"Dear friend, we stand before your coffin deeply saddened. Today, we are bringing my closest, most treasured colleague to eternal rest..."

He spoke of his friendship with Miermann and delivered a subtle analysis of his character. "He was," so Frächter said, "a truly great editor, a man who always stood behind an issue, a man who treated the work and words of others like his own. This was his great modesty, a modesty derived from great knowledge, a true *universitas*. His books and poetry may have remained unread, but he was ever more widely read as a journalist: he was a journalist by calling, not by profession."

Every word could be underlined.

"We publishers," he concluded, "we publishers know that the writer, the journalist, the mind is everything for the company. We publishers—businessmen, as it were—are merely the handmaidens of the journalist and the spirit. Ultimately, content matters most: it is the core, not the shell. And so I bow to an exemplar of the spirit, a paragon of journalism, one of the last, wise, true servants of the written word, who grow ever rarer and rarer. Peace be with him!"

Many others spoke after Frächter, mostly presidents and deputies. A deputy of the association of independent academics, at which Miermann had often been a guest speaker; a deputy of the Berlin magistrate's office; the president of the Berlin theater critics' society;

a deputy of the theater association; a deputy of the German writer's guild; a deputy of the national press union.

They all said the same thing: "Mr. Georg Miermann belonged to our association since 1899 and was an active member. He was always available when his advice was required. We and our members will miss him greatly, and we thank him beyond the grave for all the help he gave us."

In the meantime, the journalists jotted down the names of the attendees.

At last, Lieven stepped forward and said: "My friend." He gave an eloquent and thoughtful speech intended for the theater directors, the publishers, and the beautiful women, for the note in the evening papers: "In the end, Lieven, the well-known playwright, delivered a lengthy speech in recognition of the great journalist's work."

Gohlisch and Miss Kohler visited his grave. They thought of Miermann at Augur's child's funeral, and of this vanity fair that had sprung up between the trees, birds, flowers, and the dead man.

"The only people who spoke were the kind he couldn't stand," Gohlisch said.

"As always, you're completely right," Miss Kohler said.

Frächter stood in front of the cemetery entrance and generously offered Gohlisch, Miss Kohler, and a few others who had joined them a ride home in his car.

34

The grand opening of the Käsebier theater

THAT VERY same evening, the Käsebier theater had its grand opening. Suppliers from all across Berlin delivered incredible floral arrangements. The show began at eight forty-five. The great arrival began at eight. Almost everyone who had attended Miermann's funeral that morning was present. The Muschlers shared a very large table with the Frechheims and a few other friends. Margot Weissmann came with her Spaniard. Aja Müller was there with her latest. Frächter with his fiancée, Ella Waldschmidt—the wedding was in three days—, Gohlisch, Lambeck, Lieven, Countess Dinkelsbühl, Mr. von Trappen, Hersheimer the banker, Käte Herzfeld, Gabriele Meyer-Lewin. Miermann was missing. Young Schrade had finally gone under. It was a muggy summer night. Aja Müller looked grand.

"Aja Müller in very long gloves," said Mrs. Muschler.

"Like Yvette Guilbert in her younger days," said Uncle Gustav.

"Everyone's here," said Mrs. Muschler, very excited.

"Well, at the opening," said Muschler, skeptical.

"Look, even Lambeck!"

"Lambeck, so what, Lambeck? The theater critics haven't come. D'you see Ixo or Öchsli?"

"Yeah, you're right."

"They'll still come, I'm certain."

Gohlisch was standing by himself. Finally, he spotted Käte Herzfeld.

"Good evening, Miss Herzfeld," Gohlisch said. "We saw each other not too long ago."

"A terrible occasion," said Käte.

"I owe him so much."

"It's such a shame. Somehow he couldn't cope with life, but he was a wonderful man."

"Yes," said Gohlisch pensively. "You know, only the vaudeville critics came."

"How interesting! Öchsli isn't there, and neither is Ixo?"

"I don't see anyone. They sent a third-rate crop of young kids. No art critics, either."

"That's quite interesting. You know, Mr. Gohlisch, I'm beginning to think he's complete garbage."

"I think that's unfair. Of course, he's not as important as he was made out to be. But it's not his fault others overestimated him."

"Oh, he's just a foolish man without a clue about the present. What use do we have for a cabaret that's not political?"

Aja Müller shrieked, "Gohlisch, my duckie, my peacock feather, my golden pheasant, why don't you call me anymore? Don't you love me?"

Ella Waldschmidt greeted Käte Herzfeld: "How are you doing?"

"Thanks, as well as to be expected in such times."

"Of course, of course. Give me a call sometime."

Frächter looked like he'd arrived.

The Käsebier literature had been put out in the lobby. Willy Frächter, *Käsebier, a Singer from Berlin: Who He Is, and How He Came to Be*. Next to him, Heinrich Wurm, *Käsebier* from the series "Darlings of the Public." The Käsebier picture book by Dr. Richard Thame. *Käsebier Cartoons*, put together by Gödovecz. Otto Lambeck: *Käsebier, An Essay*.

Frächter stood with Gohlisch. "I don't feel comfortable about that book sitting out there," he said. "I'd much rather disown it."

Gohlisch sat with Oberndorffer in the concert hall.

"Well, how do you like the room?" Oberndorffer asked.

"I don't know, there's so much wood, and all these carvings from 1918."

"Oh well. Take a look around."

The edges of the ceiling had been painted in hues of silver and

gold. Below, the room had been paneled with carved wood. A piece
of cornice ran around the ceiling in zigzags from 1918, and large lamps,
golden semicircles connected to silver rectangles, flanked the stage.

"Aren't those carvings odd! But I had nothing to do with it."

"Well," said Gohlisch, "we're galley slaves, after all."

Öchsli arrived too late. "Hullo Gohlisch, how're you? I ended up
coming, I thought it cruel they left Käsebier to be torn apart by our
newest scribe."

Käsebier appeared in front of the curtain and greeted his guests.
But Berliners are stiff; it didn't work. They laughed a little. But no
one called out a kind word. There was no rapport.

A few dancers and a shadow artist came on, followed by an ec-
centric man on a unicycle who dashed on and off stage loudly ululat-
ing, and cycled over a round tabletop in an exceptionally amusing
fashion.

A very competent singer sang a few songs, but everyone had heard
something similar before. It was rather poor planning to put on such
an effective ghost scene before the break. A midnight spook in which
a skeleton danced the foxtrot.

During the break, Waldschmidt said to Lambeck, "We're facing
very difficult times. I don't feel good about the future. Only a grand
coalition can lead the government. Everything else means chaos. It's
looking very bad. We've all lived beyond our means, especially eco-
nomically."

Lambeck nodded.

"If the election results in a minority for the grand coalition, our
only option will be dictatorship. And who knows how other countries
will react to a radical election. Credits may be revoked."

Meanwhile, Käte was standing by Margot Weissmann.

"*Enchantée de vous voir*," Margot said to Käte because of the foreign
gentleman.

"*Enchantée*," Käte replied.

"No atmosphere today," said Margot. "Weak program. Boring."

"Yes, I think so too, it's been quite some time since I've found
Käsebier interesting. When will you finally come visit me?"

"Darling, well, of course! But you must come over to my apartment first, tomorrow evening. We're inaugurating our place. I think it's turned out very nicely."

"Good evening," said Muschler the banker, and stepped toward them.

"Good evening," said Mrs. Thedy Muschler. "My dear, we haven't seen each other all summer! How are you?"

"I'm so glad we bumped into one another, I've been meaning to call you, I've felt so guilty."

"We'll see each other at tomorrow's party, I'm looking forward to it," said Mrs. Muschler, looking at Mr. Katter, the lawyer.

"Good evening," he said as he passed by, grazing Mrs. Muschler with his hand.

"Goodbye," said Muschler. "We're very excited to see Käsebier."

Au revoir, monsieur.

"Let's ring each other sometime," said Margot.

"Give me a call," said Käte.

"Let's call each other sometime," said Mrs. Muschler.

Then came girls who threw their legs up in the air and a small scene out of a film studio. Two jazz pianists on two pianos. And then: Käsebier.

Käsebier was the same as ever. This time, he sang an old popular ballad. It was very funny. But people had expected much, much more.

Everyone thought it "very nice." But the program was far too long. Part of the audience got up and left during the second-to-last act. Käsebier gave a short speech after the last act. "That was well meant," the audience thought condescendingly.

"Miermann wasn't here," said Öchsli.

"Yes," said Gohlisch. "He'll be greatly missed. I thought it was very pleasant, by the way."

"Yes, me too. Käsebier is such a good man."

"I suppose that's not enough."

"Just watch, all the young kids'll write that he's avoiding the tough questions of our time."

"Yes, very likely, and perhaps with reason."

There was a large crowd at the corner of Kurfürstendamm. Word was a brawl had broken out. A truck covered in red flags rolled by, with young people screaming incomprehensibly hanging off the sides. The street steamed with excitement. Large election posters hung everywhere. Young people in uniforms with sticks on their shoulders marched by. Big words boomed: "Down with Capitalism!"—"For German Freedom!" But behind this big brouhaha was everyone's gnawing worry: whether they could keep their place—big or small—and hold on to their station in life.

Gohlisch and Öchsli took leave of one another.

The Muschlers drove home.

"A total flop," Muschler said.

Käte, who drove home with young Waldschmidt, said, "Käsebier is so touching." She was sorry that she would no longer be able to discuss this fascinating rise and fall with Miermann.

The big engagement and housewarming party was to be held the following evening at Margot Weissmann's.

35

Muschler declares bankruptcy

MISS KOHLER went to the office on the tenth of September and read the papers as usual. "The company N. Muschler & Son ceased all payments today," the business section announced. She started, but only slightly; she didn't think this event could affect her. She felt sorry for the Muschlers. "Terrible," she thought. "Bankrupt. Terrible." To her, bankruptcy seemed like the most dreadful event of a businessman's life. In her mind, it meant being chased out of your house, abandoning your cupboards and clothes. To owe others, many others, perhaps unwittingly. She didn't know that there was a long road from debtor's prison to the endpoint: the triumph of the debtor and the breakdown of the creditor. But she still asked Gohlisch if she should do something. Gohlisch directed her to a businessman.

Shy and slightly embarrassed, Miss Kohler asked Dr. Barein if the situation was bad and whether her securities were at risk—after all, her mother kept her remaining assets there.

"Do you have a list of security identification numbers?" Dr. Barein asked her.

"A security identification number? I have to confess, I don't know what that is. Mr. Muschler always managed everything for us."

"Go home straightaway, make your inquiries, and retrieve your share certificates immediately."

Miss Kohler was choked with fear. She drove home and told her mother what had happened.

The brave woman said, "Then I'll open a guesthouse."

She still thought people could get by through hard work and thrift.

"We can hardly rent it out in this state. I just want to make sure

I can retrieve our securities. Do we have a list of security identification numbers?"

The mother didn't know what that was either. "Oppler will know, he's on the judicial council," she said. Miss Kohler briefly spoke to old Oppler on the phone. She felt uneasy about involving him in the matter. He had never demanded anything from them. He had known the family for forty years and had earned hundreds of thousands through old Kohler.

Old Oppler said, "Of course you have a list of security identification numbers. Drive over immediately and make sure to get your certificates. Cash assets as well?"

"Yes."

"How much?"

"About four hundred marks."

"That'll be gone now."

"Oh God. That's not possible."

"Drive over immediately."

She drove to Französische Strasse. The chestnut trees were beginning to turn. The dome's beauty belonged to another era. If the church was open, Miss Kohler thought, I'd go in and rest. Across the way stood a house made of red sandstone from the Main, a grandiose palace in Italian Renaissance style. No expense had been spared on the building; the steps of the stairs were of white marble; the stairs were covered with red carpet; the walls were made of dark marble; the bannisters were bronze. Several cars stood in front, chauffeurs were huddled together chatting. Inside, chaos. She heard voices, doors. "Unbelievable!" said a man approaching Miss Kohler. Old Mayer, whom she'd known for many years, a dignified, respectable older gentleman, descended the stairs.

"What's going on, Mr. Mayer?" Miss Kohler asked.

"What's going on?" he cried, upset. "We're broke!"

In the cash office, she was engulfed by an agitated swarm. There were workers: a man who made letter paper, a small-time printer who was supposed to receive a thousand marks. An older, elegant-looking gentleman was vehemently demanding his deposits back; a young doctor his savings. The little people stood there, fearing they'd lose what they'd worked for, people who'd managed to save a small chunk from the inflation and were afraid once again. Miss Kohler spotted Löwenstein the lawyer. "What now? What can we do?" she asked.

Löwenstein shrugged. "I've lost my money too."

Miss Kohler said, "We can't lose that money, it's the last we have. My father, you know—I think it was twelve million."

"Well," said Löwenstein, "well."

"Where's Mr. Muschler?" an ordinary man cried. "Where's that Muschler?"

"I want my money back!" a woman sobbed.

Miss Kohler went over to the secretary. "Miss Fischer, what's happened to our certificates?"

"Gone," said Miss Fischer.

"Even those with security identification numbers?"

Miss Fischer shrugged her shoulders. "My savings are gone as well."

"Can I speak to Mr. Frechheim, perhaps?"

Miss Fischer went into his office.

Frechheim came out toward her.

"What's happened to our securities?" asked Miss Kohler. "We had them in a custodial account."

Frechheim said, "The accounts are here." He had become an old man overnight.

He went with her to the waiting crowd. "Where are my savings?" someone shouted. "Thieves, scoundrels, crooks. I'm going to go and file a complaint!"

Frechheim said, "No account holder will be disadvantaged."

"But the savings aren't there, are they?"

"The bankruptcy trustee has full authority over everything."

Miss Kohler went over to Miss Fischer once again.

"Miss Fischer, please, tell me the truth."

"Mr. Muschler tapped into the accounts, all of the securities have been mortgaged."

"All of them? And where are our Siemens bonds?"

"Pledged for cash long ago, last year already, before the family went to Cannes."

"I don't understand. I need to speak with a lawyer."

"The family intends to reimburse the funds."

"I demand to be given either the certificates or their monetary worth. I demand it. Where's Mr. Muschler? What about the house? Or Mrs. Muschler's jewelry? Aren't they collateral?"

Miss Fischer shrugged. "Mr. Muschler said it was all his wife's private property. There have been terrible fights around here. Mr. Frechheim didn't know anything, you see. Everything came out when the banks made large demands and Mr. Muschler couldn't pay. We've seen it coming for a long time. We haven't received our salaries for a month. You'll need to report your claims."

Miss Kohler left. We'll have to go through it all over again, she thought. I'll need to speak to the landlord, to ask him to let us rent the apartment for less, or let us out of the contract. We'll have to give up the apartment! What will Mother say? But we can't slide into poverty just because of the linens and the silver and the porcelain. We need a large apartment because of the closets! That's just mad. As a child, she thought, I always circled the curtains and tablecloths I liked most in the Herzog, Gerson, and Grünfeld catalogs. Now I don't want to own anything at all! I want to be as mobile as possible! But how will Mother take it? An auction! Giving up the apartment! For her, it will mean nothing less than the abyss, the end.

She spoke to her mother.

"Won't we receive a move-in fee for the apartment?"

"Out of the question, Mama. We have to try to convince our landlord to let us out of the contract."

"And where will all the things go if we rent two rooms?"

"We have to try and sell them. We'll need to anyways, so that we have money for the move."

They made an appointment for a man to come by. He glanced through the ten rooms and declared that an auction wouldn't be worth it. No one would want the huge buffet table in the dining room. They would be lucky if someone took it away for free. And the chandeliers were worthless—maybe good enough for the scrap collector!

Miss Kohler was embarrassed at how shabby everything was. Nothing had been renovated in ten years. The wallpaper was dirty, the ceilings blackened with soot.

The man began in the hallway. That iron umbrella stand: wasn't it trash? Those cloakroom hooks were hideous: fit for the scrap heap. He went through the rooms.

Mrs. Kohler said, "Please forgive the fact that beds are standing in all of the salons. We've been renting out the rooms, but we can't go on like this!"

"Oh," said the man. "Doesn't bother me. I can already see it's not much."

"It was once very good furniture," said Mrs. Kohler, making an effort. But the man knocked on the large buffet in the dining room. The painted plaster, fake early Renaissance! The brass chandelier with the faded silk pull-down lamp in the dining room was just as dreadful as the iron chandelier in the study! He'd give them five marks for the giant mahogany mirror.

The furniture in the music room, which was from 1910 and upholstered with green damask, was in bad shape and the fabric was torn. No one wanted the imitation rococo chairs in the '90s salon anymore, and the cloth was more gray than pink. Not to mention the bedroom! The vanity with the colorful washbasins had been Mrs. Kohler's great pride in 1897. But who still wanted to wash themselves in sinks where the spout poked out of the middle of a La France rose? There was walnut furniture. No one wanted a Danzig baroque armoire from 1904 in their study anymore, no one wanted a sofa-cabinet—which should have been refurbished long ago—in their salon.

"The carpets'll do, but they're all too large," the man said.

"And the grand piano?"

"The grand piano's maybe worth four hundred marks."

Mrs. Kohler cried out, "In its time, that instrument cost four thousand."

The man shrugged.

Like a fat grim reaper, he walked through the apartment and mowed down everything with his gaze. The Turkish smoking table was nixed. The velvet and silk curtains, the draped shades, the net curtains, the dining room cupboard filled with crystalware, the twenty-four differently colored wine goblets, the little armchairs upholstered in green silk, the cupboard with Meissener figures in the music room, the leather armchair decorated with chestnut leaves, the oak standing lamp. —The vast quantities of rococo-patterned silver could only be sold in bulk. No one wanted rococo silver anymore.

Does nothing last? Miss Kohler wondered. If we were buried alive, like in Pompeii, would nothing be worth excavating? Is everything we've done worth nothing?

The man stopped: "The Biedermeier room might bring in a hundred marks."

"But I'd like to keep that for myself," Miss Kohler said. The only things worth anything in their entire household, ten full rooms, an elegant apartment in the old west, were: a Dutch baroque armoire from 1700 with Delft vases, a place setting for twenty-four people from the Royal Porcelain Factory, a commode from 1790, the carpets, a few embroidered linens. That was it. Everything else was unusable in these new times. "It's not worth auctioning this stuff off. It won't bring in any money."

The man disappeared.

"That man doesn't know anything," said the councilor's wife, half-convinced, half to console herself. "Look, Aunt Amalie always had an eye on the buffet with the silver and glass inlays. It must be worth something."

"You know, Mama, why don't you call up Aunt Amalie. Let's give it to her."

"It'll be too large for her small apartment."

She did call her up. It was too large for Aunt Amalie. But she'd ask her daughter.

That evening, Aunt Amalie called back and told them that Annelies had laughed. She had a box for her silver; that was enough for her. That's the way it was with kids these days.

Miss Kohler went through the apartment, looked at the salon with its many rickety tables and chairs, the sofa-cabinet with its mirror, the table fully decked out in Gobelin. Nothing held up anymore when examined objectively.

What great bourgeois wealth miserably squandered! Could one—just one—beautiful piece still be found? A piece of Bulgarian embroidery lay on a table, a soulful oasis next to the bronze bust of a long-haired girl wearing a crown of water lilies. The icebox might be worth something, but it was too big as well. Men had worked hard to stuff their houses from top to bottom with shabby junk, so that nothing would have to be borrowed for parties with fifty guests. And yet hadn't Lotte had a wonderful time before the war? Hadn't she been just as blind to reality as everyone else? Hadn't she thought it more elegant the bigger the rooms, the larger the buffets, the broader the chandeliers, the more ornate the crystal, the more richly stitched the table linens? It was only elegant when the porcelain was trimmed with cobalt or gold, when the cigarette boxes were made of silver and the room was decorated with bronze busts, vases, and porcelain—far more than the eye could take in. Hadn't she thought their elegant, classical house in Blumeshof, with its curved white wooden staircase and the red velvet handrail, inferior in 1911 when everyone was moving to Kurfürstendamm and Kaiserallee, into buildings with entrances decorated with baroque plaster, bronze sphinxes flanking the stairs, and spinach-green and strawberry-pink murals?

Her mother was weeping over the debacle in the dining room. "If my husband could see this!" But Miss Kohler had cut off her braid, shortened her skirts, and cast off her longing for a full closet of linens. To be mobile, light! The ideal: two small rooms surrounded by greenery! That is, if things couldn't get worse; what if hard work and thrift no longer sufficed? A mortal fear suddenly crept over her. What if she lost her job? Her life was still secure—minimally, at least—but nonetheless secure. What then? Wasn't it better to keep things for the pawnshop? To have something when one had debts at the baker's, the butcher's?

Thus, ten years after the death of Privy Councilor Kohler, a man with a fortune of twelve million, his daughter sat in their ten-room apartment.

The brown bronze lamp burned. Her father had received it for some anniversary or another. Now she could throw it out, or maybe donate it! She went through the corner room into her bedroom. The dining room carpet may have been a lovely Bukhara, but it was threadbare. The goblets may be ugly, but hadn't they all happily drunk wine from them? Everything flew through her mind in a jumble.

The rubber Käsebier doll that Gohlisch had given her last Christmas sat on the sofa in her room. "Käsebier, the real rubber doll, something for the kids so they'll laugh and won't cry, you can squeeze it to your chest, put it in your bath." Maybe Muschler will get a good deal on the house and avoid bankruptcy, she thought.

That same day, Mitte and Muschler held a meeting. Mitte, Matukat, Muschler, Dr. Löwenstein, and Frechheim were present. Frechheim wasn't speaking to Muschler anymore. He had decided that he wouldn't let Muschler end up behind bars, but otherwise he was done with him. They were discussing the next steps for the Käsebier theater.

"What a good deal," Muschler said to Mitte. "I want to be the second buyer too!"

"I don't, with your fancy-schmancy Käsebier theater," said Mitte.

"Why not? Why not?"

"Come on! The poor sod! No one's going to go. First you lured him out of Hasenheide, now he's sure to go to the dogs here."

"Well, what about you?"

"I've acted in your interest. Who does the building belong to: me or you?"

"Well, he'll still be able to pay the lease."

"Nah, I don't think so!"

"Go right ahead and talk it down. I'd also like to get a building worth a million for a mortgage of two hundred and fifty thousand!"

"What about the property tax?"

"Another hundred thousand."

"Do you think the bank will let it stand?"

"The bank has got to let it stand."

Mitte thought. He didn't have 350,000 marks in available funds. If it came to a foreclosure and a forced sale, he'd have no chance with the second mortgage. Muschler thought that the two-hundred-and-fifty-thousand-mark mortgage might be enough to delay the bankruptcy.

Löwenstein said, "If it goes into foreclosure, someone could get a good deal and buy something worth a million for three hundred and fifty thousand marks."

"Well, we won't let it get that far," Mitte said. "Otto Mitte and Co.'ll buy it, but I think you can hand it over for a little less, Mr. Muschler. A house with a theater that's broke, and no renters for the apartments!"

"If you pick such a genius architect!"

"Nah, don't pin this on Karlweiss. The economy's changed. I can't even say what the building cost me. The whole affair started with our recently defunct Kaliski!"

"How much did Kaliski cost you?" Muschler asked.

"He got ten thousand marks for brokering this fine deal."

"What?" Muschler and Löwenstein exclaimed. "He told us he was satisfied with the rentals."

"Well, he told me a different story."

"Look at what's coming out now. But the law's still the law, and a contract is a contract."

"Can't get blood from a stone!"

"What do you mean?"

"You can go peddling around Berlin, but you won't find any buyers right now. I'm offering you fifty thousand marks to take over the Käsebier theater."

"'Scuse me, councilor," said Muschler. "We've got a contract on the mortgage."

"Just wait and see who'll pay. Otto Mitte and Co. won't. I'll give you fifty thousand, that's it."

They parted ways.

News spread through Berlin that there was a deal to be made; the

Käsebier theater was up for sale! Brokers were running about, phones were ringing off the hook. This was the deal of a lifetime!

"We'll split the broker's fee," Schabe told Peter.

"Why split it? I told you about the deal," Peter said to Schabe. "I want at least two-thirds."

"Why's that? You won't be able to get anywhere without my connections. I know all the rich buyers interested in a deal like this."

"Well, if you manage to bring it in, we'll split it."

Frechheim gave his nephew Muschler a piece of his mind.

"You've got some nerve, doing business behind my back! It's a disgrace. You've dragged us all through the mud: your name, our name."

Muschler shrugged.

"Oh, you don't care?! Names don't matter to you anymore?! And why not? Where are your savings? You scoundrel!"

"How dare you!"

"You mortgaged the accounts! Took other people's money! You could go to jail. And this crazy building! Idiotic! You think you're so smart!"

Uncle Gustav sat down, exhausted. Muschler sat there calmly.

"The family will cover it."

"If they can. And what will you do with your villa?"

"It belongs to Thedy."

"As long as I have something to say, Thedy will pawn off her villa and her diamonds! Don't you have any sense of honor? It goes without saying that I'm giving everything up—the paintings and furniture in my apartment on Keithstrasse. Are you a crook, or were your father and grandfather respectable, honest men, bankers who dined with Rothschild?"

"You'll have to talk to Thedy."

"I certainly will."

But that didn't change much. Thedy insisted on keeping her property. She would certainly give up the villa and some of the furniture, but she was under no obligation to do so. She stressed that she stood under no obligation. And the diamonds were out of the question. They were in part old Frechheim family heirlooms. She wouldn't even consider it. Worst case, they would move to Switzerland after the settlement, she said.

Muschler, who was easygoing and liked his comfortable life, agreed with her. It would be much more comfortable to move to Switzerland with debts than to become poor.

"You're quite right, why should we scrape by in Germany where they tax everything away!"

36

The creditor meeting

THE FIRST creditor meeting took place on Monday, September 15. The enormous political excitement over the election results was mixed with people's distress at losing the money they'd worked for, saved, and invested.

The meeting took place in Berlin-Mitte, on the third floor of the district court. It was held in the wood-paneled room of a wonderful house that, with its curved stairs, rococo balustrades, and rose petal decorations, had the feel of a dance hall. Miss Kohler arrived very early. But people were already clustered about, cornering each other, and furiously airing their stories.

"Three days ago—just imagine!—three days ago, I brought him two thousand marks and he took it," said a small-time businessman. "Just imagine, he took it. It would have been only decent if he'd made up some excuse and sent me back my securities."

"He won't even have bought them, that bastard."

"He used them up! Just used them up!"

"He's still driving his car," someone shouted.

"And what a car!"

"Someone's got to be paying taxes on that!"

Duchow the carpenter was there. He was there: tiny, old, and gray, and shouting in a high-pitched voice, "We've got to fight like lions! Like lions, we've got to fight." He shook his sparsely-haired head.

Dr. Krone stood there: "I'll go to the state attorney right away if my certificates are gone. Right away! You think I'll put up with this? First the state cheated us, now the bankers. Every five years they steal our savings. It's plain theft! I have major expenses; I need a new apartment. That's why you have money lying around. And now the certificates are gone. Simply gone. I've already asked twice for them to be sent by registered mail, and all I hear is something about a bankruptcy trustee. They may as well go ahead and bolshevize everything, then we'll know where we stand."

Oberndorffer, who had run late, came hurrying in: "Has it started yet?"

"What's your business here?" Dr. Krone asked. "Lost your savings too?"

"No, a fee. Good day, Mr. Duchow. Have you lost money as well?"

"Yes, five hundred marks. That's money too. Last year, I lost two thousand marks to a client. That's a lot of money for old Duchow. Ah, it's no fun anymore, Mr. Oberndorffer. No one knows how to recognize quality work anymore, and on top of that, you lose money. Us two, Mr. Oberndorffer, we're artists with god-given talent, and no one knows what to do with us anymore."

"God-given?! Mr. Duchow!"

"Well, you know what I mean."

"When you build," said Oberndorffer, "the building doesn't matter that much; the financing is everything. Here's our financing."

"Should just bolshevize everything," Oberndorffer heard Krone say.

"My entire fortune's gone," said an old lady, crying. "Everything I saved from the inflation."

Lawyers and representatives of major companies arrived. The meeting was opened. Böker the bankruptcy manager, a blond man with a goatee and a belly, delivered an overview. He read out a list of assets and withdrawals.

When the withdrawals moved to personal listings, and he read out, "Withdrawal by Richard Muschler, seventy thousand marks," indignation mounted. "Other people's money!" "Of course!" "Our money!" "Disgraceful!"

"That covers my life insurance," Muschler shouted. But it was no use. He was forced back into the corner. Frechheim had withdrawn ten thousand marks. A creditors' committee was formed.

"Who do you represent anyways?" one shouted.

"Me? The import and export union."

"That's impossible. I represent them."

"Sir, how dare you!"

Others intervened, trying to placate them. No one could get to the bottom of the matter.

A fat man yelled, "What's the bankruptcy manager earning?"

With great gravitas, the judge replied, "That is legally predetermined. You can consult the bankruptcy code. This is not the place for such discussions!"

"How much are you asking for anyways?" someone said to the fat man who had asked the question.

"Ninety-three marks."

Everyone laughed.

"Ninety-three marks is money to me," said the fat man. "Maybe everything's peanuts to you if it's under a million."

Dr. Krone wanted to join the creditors' committee as a midsize creditor.

"But you're not a businessman!" a lawyer rejoined.

"Oh, the gentlemen wish to be amongst themselves," the fat man called out.

"Yes, that's right," said Duchow.

And the printer said, "The large creditors will call the shots on the assets. The little ones'll be left with nothing."

"That's right."

Someone cried, "How did Messrs Muschler pay for the factory in Schleiz they recently bought?"

"We don't have a factory in Schleiz," Frechheim called out.

"It's called Textol A.-G., but Mr. Muschler's behind it. I want to know whether the factory will be liquidated."

"That's a question for the creditors' committee."

"I want to know whether the factory will be liquidated."

He received no answer.

"And what's with Mr. Muschler's Swiss bank account?"

"I want to know what's with Mr. Muschler's bank account, otherwise I'll report him for bankruptcy fraud!"

"D'you know who's going to chair the creditors' committee? Karlweiss, that crook."

"Really," said Oberndorffer. "Isn't that wonderful."

"Look at what we have here," said Duchow. "A nursery, a real nursery. The big 'uns'll take the pants off the little ones."

"What will happen to Käsebier?"

"He's yesterday's news."

"Is the theater doing that poorly?"

"Käsebier told me he'd come up short the first month. You know Berliners. As a rule, they only go for the first month. So if they don't even walk in the door the first month, it's over."

A few gentlemen stood together. Lawyers, Karlweiss, a representative for Otto Mitte, representatives from other large firms. They were discussing the creditors' committee. In the back, where the benches were, stood Duchow, Oberndorffer, the fat man, Miss Kohler, Dr. Krone, and the employees who hadn't been paid in a month—a fact no one had known.

That same day, Mitte said to Muschler, "Shouldn't we go to the court registry and examine the mortgage registration?"

"Why bother? We have the contracts."

"You never know."

"I don't know if I'm coming or going and you want me to waste a whole morning at the local courthouse! I want to be helpful, of course."

"That's what I think too. You know what'll happen if it comes to foreclosure?"

"Fine," said Muschler, exhausted. "I'll pick you up with the car."

The following day, Muschler drove by Mitte's office on Schellingstrasse.

"Well, Muschler, can't let your head hang, could happen to anyone! These days! Gets some earlier, some later!"

266 · GABRIELE TERGIT

"Oh no, no," said Muschler. "I'm not letting it hang."

They had to walk quite a way in the Charlottenburg courthouse before they found the right room. Mitte and Muschler inspected the property register.

Muschler was still scrutinizing it when Mitte began roaring with laughter. "Hey, Muschler," he said, and thumped Muschler on the shoulder, "your precious Dr. Löwenstein forgot to write it in."

Muschler said, "That's impossible, councilor. Löwenstein knew how important this was to me."

"You bet! We spent a whole day negotiating it in Baden-Baden."

"That's impossible. Such a respectable lawyer? Löwenstein doesn't forget things like that."

"Well, shall we ask a clerk?"

The gray-haired clerk peered over his glasses.

"Real estate mortgage for Mr. Muschler isn't here."

"It has to be!" said Muschler, furious. "Wait and see! I'm holding Löwenstein liable."

"Till you win *that* lawsuit!" said Mitte.

"Please, I'll keep at it until I'm foreclosed."

Muschler couldn't be spoken with. He drove to his office and called up Löwenstein immediately.

"And my savings, Mr. Muschler?" Löwenstein asked.

Muschler hung up. The overworked lawyer had dropped the ball. There was nothing left to do. That line of defense had vanished. The bankruptcy wound its course.

37
A visit

THE DAY before the auction preview, Waldschmidt paid Frechheim a visit. They had known each other since childhood, but for the past twenty years they had seen each other only at parties, premieres, and races. It hadn't occurred to Waldschmidt to visit someone just for the sake of it in years. It was absolutely crazy, to visit someone for no reason. Suddenly, just after he had left the office, he asked his driver to stop on Keithstrasse. On the stairs, he thought, I'm simply barging into Frechheim's place. He'll think I'm here to offer him money. But he had the feeling that Frechheim might be contemplating suicide. And he was right.

"Ah, Emma," he said, "is the master of the house home?"

Waldschmidt entered the dark study. Frechheim sat there, cowering in the corner.

"Don't even think of it!" Waldschmidt greeted him. "My dear Frechheim, why? A man as clever as you! It would be cowardice."

"Muschler dragged my name through the mud with this affair."

"People can make distinctions."

"In Berlin? Where the scum floats to the top and the decent folk sink? You see, Muschler had no sense for business. My wife, who died so early, and I always asked ourselves whether something would harm or aid the company. Although Muschler bears the company name, N. Muschler and Son is his Hecuba. N. Muschler and Son might as well be a big credit line."

"Yes, that's the way it is these days. At the Weissmanns' house-warming recently, I spoke to Theodor Weissmann. He said, 'If things get worse, I'll shut down the company' the way you'd say, 'I must order myself a new pair of shoes.' When I remarked that he had such a great fortune and asked how he could even consider it, he answered, baffled, as if I came from the moon, that his private wealth had nothing to do with the factory."

"Dear Waldschmidt, that's the difference between our generation and the one that followed us."

"Trust funds, trust funds, dear Frechheim, polo, golf, and an income; none of them are businessmen anymore."

"In the old days—surely old Weissmann felt this way once—your company was your pride and joy, the thing you saved for and put every spare penny into. The capitalists reaped the rewards because they took risks. But these people who treat their business just like a stock that provides them with an income—those men are ripe for bolshevization. His private funds have nothing to do with the company! Just like my nephew Muschler! It's a sign of particular decency today if you emerge impoverished from a bankruptcy and don't heal yourself with the money of your creditors."

"But that's old-fashioned now; I'd prefer going bust to a big windfall."

"You know that the house I live in belongs to old Mrs. Gerhard. That's another story; the house only has three apartments. The first is already free to let. If I move out, the second apartment will be empty, and the house will have to be foreclosed. Ever since my blessed wife died, that apartment has been too large for me. I just didn't leave because I felt sorry for the old woman—and now I'm auctioning off my affairs."

"That's not easy either."

"No, I'm attached to my possessions. My beautiful Roman glassware, and who wants real Renaissance doors these days, who can afford to install them? I would very much have liked to keep my desk clock with the glockenspiel, and the beautiful bronze by Kruse, and the lovely Krüger."[45]

"Well," said Waldschmidt, "we're attached to many things. Right after the Nazis were elected, the Americans canceled a big loan I had obtained."

In that moment, Waldschmidt wondered how he could blurt out something like that. Had he suddenly become a woman with his gossip, just like the ladies on the telephone?

Frechheim was deeply shocked. "It's sad to hear that everyone's doing so poorly."

Waldschmidt laughed. "Well, I'm still doing all right, but I thought that would comfort you! I've had to let some of my employees go though, and it's as bad with one as the other. But I have to pay my employees twice as much as in 1913 because of taxes and healthcare. We're going nowhere! We're all standing on the barricades, dear Frechheim. It seems to me that everyone's equally brave. One man falls, the other is unscathed by the bullet—at least for now. But we're all fighters."

"The old guard," said Frechheim. "But my honor as a businessman has been sullied. That man, that Muschler!"

"It happens to everyone," said Waldschmidt, and thought of the dancer his son wanted to marry. The two men parted ways warmly.

Who'll visit me when I go broke? thought Waldschmidt. He thought; there was no one.

By the time he stopped in front of his beautiful villa on Stüler-strasse, he had realized something: the fact that he was completely alone. He had business acquaintances, colleagues, a wife, and children. Some of his colleagues liked him. But friends?

Waldschmidt called Commissioner Levy. "Please put in a bid for the clock and the bronze Kruse bust." He wanted to buy them for Frechheim. But later, he felt embarrassed and didn't send them to Frechheim. The visit had been foolish enough.

38
The auction

AUCTIONS in west Berlin are quite an affair! The well-heeled do all their shopping there. Buying something in a store run by experts, a place that contains carefully culled, beautiful, high-quality goods—anyone can do that. But going to an auction and recognizing what's cheap and what's expensive—now, that's a task. It requires in-depth knowledge of all products in the interior furnishings business, which no one possesses to such a degree as the wife of luxury. Those constantly buying porcelain and toasters and cocktail glasses, replacing their curtains and repairing their Persian rugs, whose mothers already asked them as children what they thought of Aunt Herta's new tea set—they know.

Margot Weissmann phoned up Countess Dinkelsbühl. "Have you heard, dear countess, Frechheim is having an auction! His wonderful glassware and the other things! There's a preview tomorrow."

"Poor Mrs. Thedy! Shouldn't we give her a call?"

"I think she'd only find it unpleasant. After all, her husband has been seriously compromised! Shall we drive over to Frechheim together?"

"Gladly, it's been quite some time that I've been looking for a baroque armoire just like the one Frechheim has in his hallway."

"One can buy things for so little at auctions."

The preview took place in the apartment on Keithstrasse that Sunday.

The cars waited downstairs.

Auctions have a particular atmosphere. The gloomy mood of dissolution, abandonment, and death is dispelled by the parade of elegant cars before the door and the even more elegant women in the rooms. The smell of dust and dirt is overwhelmed by Caron and Houbigant and eau de cologne and the scent of gaiety a well-groomed woman spreads wherever she bestows her smile.

Käte Herzfeld was standing upstairs with Oppenheimer and the prominent art dealer when Countess Dinkelsbühl arrived with Margot Weissmann. Hersheimer the banker arrived with his wife a minute later. Mrs. Hersheimer was wearing a black knit coat and a Persian lamb fur. But Margot Weissmann was already in bottle green and broadtail. Countess Dinkelsbühl, a charming apparition, wore a brown suit. Käte was also dressed in black and Persian lamb. Frächter came with his wife, as they still needed a few things for their apartment.

"Käte, you look wonderful," Margot said. "I meant to ask you at my party, are you still going to Arden?"

"No, I have a masseuse who's simply divine, I'd be glad to give you her address."

"Have you seen the excellent sixties serving cart?" Oppenheimer asked.

"Dear Oppenheimer, really, the sixties? You can't be serious about the sixties!"

"I find them quite stylish. By the way, there's a fantastic commode there for you, very ornate, Louis XV, really fine stuff. It has a reserve price of five thousand marks. A steal!"

The apartment was completely stuffed. Two beautiful commodes stood in the hallway; over them hung Dörbeck's Berliner Redensarten.[46]

In the first room were the vitrines, which had interior lighting for the Roman glassware. Next to it was the study: Renaissance, with a large Ruisdael over the desk. Next door, the Chippendale living room with blue velvet, the grand piano, a music stand. Then the salon with small French wardrobes and mighty vases just like those Paul I of Russia had made for Potsdam. There were piles of junk in the dining room: a large, smooth silver fruit basket by a Danish silversmith. The cocktail cabinet, a set of cordial glasses. A small silver candy bowl. A tea set from Meissen, silver, old Berliner and Sèvres breakfast plate sets, glasses with Baccarat etchings, colorful wine goblets—it was all there. Twenty-four silver finger bowls, one hundred and eighty-five grams apiece. Eighteen silver coffee cups, one hundred and seventy grams apiece. Twenty-four silver mocha cups, seventy grams apiece. Eleven plates, five hundred grams apiece. Twenty-four detachable silver fish-bone bowls, eighty grams apiece. A set of silver for thirty-six people with lobster and oyster forks, silver tea and coffee sets, biscuit jars, fruit bowls with matching plates, endless quantities of lead crystal trimmed with silver, endless tins, endless vases. A bronze inkwell, a green marble desk set, a silver smoking table, a silver cigar box, a brown marble ashtray topped with a golden deer, a gray marble ashtray on which a golden dancer perched, a bronze smoking set with individual ashtrays in green onyx and rose quartz. Souvenirs from Italy: majolica plates from Florence, bronze lamps from Pompeii, bronze statues standing stark naked on a red marble base, a farmer with a sickle, a blacksmith, a worker. In the middle stood Goethe, thirty-two volumes bound fully in leather. On the wall was a cupboard with stuffed birds shot by the man of the house himself: an eagle from the Caucasus, strange creatures from North Africa, eiders from a trip to the northern countries, a large variety of southern English seagulls. On the walls, antlers: deer antlers, elk antlers, and a boar's head.

Gustav Frechheim had been an elegant gentleman, a skillful hunter, yacht owner, collector of Roman glassware, and a music lover, a violinist who had given large sums to the philharmonic orchestra in fairer days.

"Look at this enchanting little box," said the countess. "And there are a few very nice embroideries. I'll bid on them tomorrow."

"Just look at this dreadful dining room from 1900 and these silly bronzes, it's too funny for words. There's nothing decent here," said Margot. "Perhaps the runners."

The women even crept into the attic. Margot nearly died of laughter. There stood the suitcases, covered with hotel etiquettes. Negresco, Nice. Daniela, Venice. Suvretta, St. Moritz.

Levy the broker addressed the women: "Have you seen the Tabriz yet, Mrs. Weissmann? A wonderful piece, and you could still use a carpet. I could secure it for you at a very modest price. Perhaps the countess needs something as well?"

"I'll take a look," said Margot. "How high do you think it'll go?"

"Well, about three hundred, Mrs. Weissmann."

"My limit's two hundred."

"That won't be possible, let's say two-fifty. It would be perfect for your winter garden. Hasn't Mrs. Weissmann always been pleased with my services?"

Margot had to admit that this was true. She knew the agent. She had acquired a few beautiful pieces through him. She told him to proceed. The agent took notes. He knew the Tabriz well. He was brokering it for the fourth time in ten years. Mrs. Kohler had sold it in the inflation. It had made its way over to Lola di Vandey in the Grunewald. Once the actress liquidated her household, it came to Frechheim. Now Margot would have it. The countess placed a bid on the baroque wardrobe.

The auction began at ten o'clock in the morning on the following day. The old servants stood together. Emma, the factotum, a cleaning woman who had helped out, Frechheim's old manservant. The friends of the house were there. The auctioneers. And strangers. Elegant women. A fashion show. Only beautiful women. A Burne-Jones apparition, white-blonde in pale green, was speaking to a dark-haired woman in gray miniver. Everything was quickly cleared out. Fat men blew smoke into the air. One man with a long white beard and a Tyrolean hat smelled of onion; another of alcohol. The paintings were auctioned off. No one wanted the Aubusson. Five to six meters high. Who could still use an Aubusson these days? Later came the antique glassware, the commodes, the vases, the silver, the shabby velour, all somewhat more expensive than in stores. But everyone had been gripped by auction fever. The auction went from eleven till eight o'clock. A gray cloud of dust covered everything.

"Lot number 212, canopy bed, Shantung silk. Opening bid? Thirty marks! Who'll give me more? . . . Forty marks, do I hear forty-one? . . . Forty-one, forty-two, forty-five, fifty, fifty-five, sixty, do I hear sixty-one? Sixty-one, do I hear sixty-two? . . . Sixty-two, do I hear sixty-three?"

The gavel struck. "Who's the winner?" "Wittstock." "Wittstock! Number 213, grand piano, Bechstein, concert. Opening bid?... Fifty marks! Do I hear sixty?... Sixty marks, do I hear seventy? Seventy, eighty, one hundred, one-fifty, one-eighty, two hundred, two-fifty, three hundred, three-ten, three-fifteen, three-twenty-five, do I hear three-thirty?... Three-fifty, do I hear three-sixty?... Three-seventy, three-seventy-five, do I hear three-eighty?..." The gavel struck. "Who's the winner?" "Greifenhagen." "Greifenhagen!"

This continued the entire day. Strange men in shabby suits loitered in the hallways, scattered ash on the good chairs, smoked pipes, sported beards and old coats. A large hole was burned into the pale green upholstery of a small white Empire chair with a golden fruit bowl on the backrest. The curtains were already being ripped from the windows. The packers, the movers, and the giants were already carrying out the heavier pieces with moving straps, dragging them off to furniture vans. The sausage man was doing brisk business with his harness tray. He put it on the Louis XV commode in the music room. Even a paper plate was good enough for that. It didn't have to be porcelain from Meissen.

And then everything was gone.

39

All that's left is Minerva's hand and a plaster rose

IT WAS May 1931. Gohlisch, who had meanwhile found a job in
Magdeburg, came back to Berlin on a visit. He bumped into Oberndorffer.

"Do you want to come with me?" asked Oberndorffer. "I'm in a
rush. I have to go to the court on Grunerstrasse, Otto Mitte's hearing
is today."

"Oh really, Otto Mitte's broke now?"

"He went broke partially because of his construction projects.
When you build, the actual building doesn't matter. The financing
is everything. Here's the financing."

They hurried along.

The long rectangular room in Grunerstrasse was filled with people.
The presiding judge sat at the front.

A deputy read out the amounts at issue. Was there anyone in
Berlin who hadn't been affected? The banks had lost their money.
Karlweiss hadn't received his fee. The carpenters hadn't been paid.
Neither old Duchow, nor Schüttke, who'd snatched the contract from
Feinschmidt & Rohhals, nor Staberow had been paid fully for their
contributions. Käsebier had paid ten thousand marks. Scharnagl had
never received the five thousand he had been promised for the construction fence, that wonderful construction fence on Kurfürstendamm.
Even Kaliski was still owed one thousand. Not to mention the salaries! The hearing went quite peacefully. Now and again, someone
would turn the door handle and quietly slip away. The deputy read
in a monotone, "200,000 marks to the Berliner Bank, debt acknowledged by the trustee. 71 marks to Oberndorffer, debt disputed by the

trustee; 150,000 marks to Karlweiss, disputed; 1,553 marks to Duchow, acknowledged; 78 marks to Feinschmidt, acknowledged; 11,444 marks to Schüttke, disputed; 2,500 marks to Scharnagl, disputed; 10,000 marks to Georg Käsebier, disputed; 1,000 marks to Dr. Reinhold Kaliski, disputed; 10,000 marks to Muschler, bankrupt, acknowledged; 2,945 marks to Staberow, disputed; 2,467 marks to Oberndorffer, disputed; 3,000 marks to Matukat, acknowledged; 2,400 marks to Schulz, acknowledged, 300 marks to Miss Fleissig, acknowledged; 1,500 marks to Dipfinger, acknowledged."

The voice of the deputy grew weary. For one hour, he read: disputed; disputed; disputed.

"If we stay here any longer, I'll fall asleep," said Gohlisch. "Shall we go?"

"Yes, let's."

"Disputed, disputed, disputed," said Gohlisch. "Once it was 'Käsebier, the real rubber doll, something for the kids so they'll laugh and won't cry, you can squeeze it to your chest, put it in your bath. Käsebier, the real rubber doll,' debt disputed, debt disputed, debt disputed."

"Have you heard that the *Berliner Rundschau* is being torn down?"

"No, really? Whatever happened to Frächter, anyway?"

"He left the *Rundschau* quite some time ago. Waldschmidt made him an associate, and apparently he's working out quite well."

"What do you know. The world is changing."

"But the demolition is still one of Frächter's projects."

They went to Kommandantenstrasse. The sidewalk had been blocked off. As Gohlisch and Oberndorffer stood there and looked up, Minerva flew down and shattered. A hand and a piece of the historical tablets crumbled on the street. Gohlisch bent down and picked up Minerva's hand and a plaster rose. "I'll have a paperweight for my desk made from this. A memory of Miermann. Our pleasant sojourn in Aranjuez has ceded to the glorious summer by this sun of York.[47] Heil and Sieg."

"What about the fat one?"

"There's none to be had anymore. Farewell, Oberndorffer."

He walked away with Minerva's hand in one pocket and the rose in the other.

40
Finale

ARE YOU familiar with Cottbus, a small mill town in Lusatia?

Four buyers from Berlin, who didn't know where to go that evening, went to a pub with a cabaret. They sat down, ordered beers, and discussed the news.

"Why are *you* talking about struggling along? You have no clue! If you want to know what a bad line of work looks like, try briefcases."

Four young girls wearing rather skimpy dresses were dancing. Once they had finished, they looked around to see whether someone might invite them to dinner.

But the buyers were saying to each other, "What can I say! Topas was canned without notice. He said he'll sue."

"What an awful company."

"Do you think Zwiebelfisch and Kämer, a firm with a working capital of three million, needs to behave decently?"

Then a singer came on stage.

"One beer," a buyer shouted. The singer sang a song about hard times.

"Who's that?" the buyer asked the waiter. "He does his stuff pretty well."

"His name's Käsebier, I think, but I can't say for sure. I'd have to ask the boss," the waiter said.

"Ah, leave it, it's not that important to me. D'you know that even R. Rockstroh and Co.'s facing the brink?"

NOTES

1   Carl Spitzweg (1808–1885) was a German painter famous for his genre paintings of often provincial, humorous character types.

2   A reference to Friedrich Schiller's play *Fiesco* (1893). Gohlisch is referring to the stern republican, Verrina, who tries to emancipate sixteenth-century Genoa from the rule of the nobility.

3   Wolff's Telegraphisches Bureau (1849–1934), one of the first European press agencies.

4   Andreas Schlüter (1659–1714) was a sculptor and architect who shaped Berlin's cityscape in his lifetime, working on the Berlin City Palace and old arsenal. Later in life, Schlüter fell into disfavor with his patron, Frederick I, and left for the court of Peter the Great in 1713.

5   A quote from Friedrich Schiller's poem "The German Muse," written in 1800. The poem, which laments the lack of patronage that the German arts received under the enlightened despotism of Frederick the Great, is misquoted by Tergit, who changes the word "defenceless" to "inglorious."

6   A quote from Theodor Fontane's poem "An meinem Fünfundsiebzigsten" (On My Seventy-Fifth Birthday), in which Fontane writes about his birthday celebrations—the guests for his party turn out not to be the German aristocrats he has written about for years, but his many Jewish readers instead. Some critics have taken the poem as proof of Fontane's anti-Semitism, but it also illustrates the importance of German Jews in nineteenth-century German culture.

7   Citation from Heinrich Heine's poem "Nachtgedanken" (1844). Tired of the strict German censors and of being subject to anti-Semitism, Heine chose to settle in France after the July Revolution of 1830. "Nachtgedanken" portrays the poet as he longingly thinks of Germany by night from his home in Paris. This citation is taken, in slightly modified form, from *The Complete Poems of Heinrich Heine,* trans. Hal Draper (Frankfurt a.M.: Suhrkamp, 1987), p. 408.

8   This refers to the geographical meeting-point of the Russian, Austro-Hungarian, and German Empires during the partition of Poland (1871–1918). The League of the Three Emperors, as this alliance among empires was known, was an important cornerstone of Otto von Bismarck's foreign policy for the new German nation, since it safeguarded the country against Russian and

Austro-Hungarian aggression. The alliance lapsed in 1887, but the spot remained a popular tourist destination until World War I, with the German government even erecting a Bismarck tower there in 1907.

9 Paragraph 218 of the penal code of the Weimar Republic criminalized abortion and decreed that any woman who had undergone or assisted in an abortion could be imprisoned for up to five years or sent to a work house. The law was liberalized in 1926–1927, when a reform permitted abortion for medical reasons.

10 An 1888 novel by Theodor Fontane about a love affair between young Lene Nimptsch and the baron Botho von Rienäcker, set near the Zoological Gardens in west Berlin.

11 Heinrich Heine, "Pomare," in *The Complete Poems of Heinrich Heine,* trans. Hal Draper (Cambridge, MA: Suhrkamp/Insel Publishers Boston, 1982), p. 579.

12 The Aboag was a bus run by the Allgemeine Berliner Omnibus AG (General Berlin Omnibus Inc.).

13 Harry Liedtke was a popular silent film actor in Weimar who frequently worked with director Ernst Lubitsch and who starred opposite Marlene Dietrich in the 1928 film *I Kiss Your Hand, Madame.* Adolphe Menjou was a dapper American actor famous for his suave, debonair demeanor. In 1934 *The New York Times* referred to him as a "perennial member of the world's ten best-dressed men."

14 Claire Waldoff, born as Clara Wortmann (1884–1957), was a cabaret singer famous for her cross-dressed stage persona and bawdy songs in Berlin dialect. Waldoff was a significant presence in Berlin's emerging lesbian nightlife scene, and attained national fame in the 1920s. Her career dimmed significantly after the Nazis came to power.

15 The infamous German expression of the time was *"Stempeln gehen,"* which literally means "going stamping"—an expression that referred to the bureaucratic procedure for collecting unemployment money.

16 The Romanisches Café was a gathering place for Berlin's artists and literati located at Breitscheidplatz. The so-called swimmer's section was a side room with only twenty tables, at which successful artists sat, while the greater mass of aspiring intellectuals sat in the "non-swimmer's section," the main room with about seventy tables.

17 Two news agencies, Wolffs Telegraphisches Büro and Telegraphen-Union.

18 Schwannecke was a small, exclusive locale in which the most successful artists of the time dined. In a 1928 article, Erich Kästner wrote, "There is no clearer means of following the growth of an artist, journalist, or writer in Berlin, than hearing the words: 'He's not going to the Romanisches anymore, he's mostly at Schwannecke these days.'"

19 A popular expression that criticizes the bureaucratic willingness of Germans to kowtow to power and bully the weak. Tergit may also be referring to Carl

Zuckmayer's satirical 1931 play *Der Hauptmann von Köpenick* (The Captain of Köpenick), which explicitly links the well-known expression to bicycling.

20   Refers to Miguel Primo de la Rivera, Prime Minister of Spain from 1923 to 1930, and Aristide Briand, Prime Minister of France for eleven terms between 1911 and 1929.

21   A quote from Friedrich Schiller's 1801 play, *The Maid of Orleans*.

22   Heinrich Zille (1858–1929) was a German illustrator famous for his humorous caricatures of the Berlin proletariat. His most recognizable subjects were prostitutes, beggars, and laborers. A "Zillefigur," or "Zille figure" (as Tergit writes), refers to someone "of the people," perhaps poor and grotesque in appearance.

23   The Berolina was a statue of a woman with a crown of oak leaves and a chain-mail vest that personified the spirit of Berlin. She was designed by the sculptors Emil Hundrieser and Michel Lock, and stood on Alexanderplatz from 1895 to 1927.

24   At this time, it was common for previous renters to demand a moving fee in exchange for vacating the apartment.

25   Adolf Glassbrenner (1810–1876) and David Kalisch (1820–1872) were humorists who founded the satirical magazines *Freie Blätter* and *Kladderadatsch* after the March Revolution of 1848.

26   A semisweet German white wine whose name means "Milk of our Dear Lady" because it was originally made from the vineyards of the Church of Our Lady in Worms.

27   The Kaufhaus Gerson, established in 1849, was Berlin's first department store. Hermann Gerson was an early adoptee of live modeling, and had attractive female employees model the latest fashions for his clients.

28   Haus Vaterland was once the largest entertainment establishment in the world. Situated on Potsdamer Platz, it had cafés, movie theaters, and themed restaurants with room for a combined seven thousand people.

29   Karlweiss is referring to the Ringbahn, a railway line that runs a circular route around Berlin's city center and served to demarcate the inner zone of the city from the outer, suburban neighborhoods.

30   "Dank vom Hause Österreichs," a quote from Schiller's play *Wallenstein's Death*, in which Colonel Buttler, an officer of low birth, sarcastically thanks the imperial Austrian court for thwarting his ambitions to become a nobleman.

31   Richard Tauber was a well-known Austrian tenor who recorded over seven hundred records on the Odeon Record label, starting in 1919.

32   Michael Kazmierczak was a member of the Communist Party of Germany involved in putting down the right-wing Kapp Putsch of 1920, which was backed by General Erich Ludendorff, a towering nationalist figure and war hero of the Weimar Republic.

33   *Leihhaus* means "pawnshop."

34 A tuft of Alpine goat hair traditionally worn as a hat decoration in Austria and Bavaria.

35 The Neue Welt was a concert venue and beer garden established in Berlin's Neukölln neighborhood in 1867, and was expanded into an amusement park in 1910.

36 *Sonnenspektrum* refers to a fragment of a play written in 1893 by the dramatist Franz Wedekind, which depicts an idyllic brothel.

37 Miss Kohler is referring to a cornerstone of Expressionist drama, *Der Sohn* (1914), by dramatist Walter Hasenclever. The play begins as a father-son conflict, but becomes a highly charged social critique in which the son rebels and brings about his father's death.

38 Hans Blüher (1888–1955) was a member of the popular turn-of-the-century German youth movement known as the Wandervogel, or "wandering birds." The Wandervogel were groups of young men who went on hikes together, held Romantic ideas about nature and man, and rejected bourgeois values. Blüher wrote several important histories of the Wandervogel, including a rather scandalous volume detailing the homoeroticism within the movement.

39 A reference to Henrik Ibsen's 1892 drama, *The Master Builder*, in which the protagonist, Halvard Solness, makes empty promises to young Hilda Wangel in order to seduce her.

40 Max, Leo, and Willi Sklarek were brothers who ran a textile and clothing business that furnished clerks and other city officials in Berlin with work clothing. In 1929, it was discovered that they had perpetrated fraud through fake delivery bills and invoices, cheating city government of 2 million marks. This affair turned into a major corruption scandal and brought about the resignation of Berlin's longtime mayor Gustav Böss, while other officials were tried on corruption charges.

41 The Stahlhelme, or "Steel Helmets," were a conservative, far-right paramilitary organization founded in 1918. They strongly opposed the Weimar Republic's parliamentary democracy and integrated with the Nazi party in 1933.

42 The Krantz affair refers to a suicide pact that two young men, Paul Krantz and Günter Schelling, forged with one another in 1927. Only Schelling carried out his end of the pact, killing his friend Hans Stephan before shooting himself; Krantz did not commit suicide, but was charged with unlawful possession of weapons. The case brought about vigorous debates on German youth in the wake of World War I.

43 Fritz Haarmann was a serial killer who picked up young men off the street of Hanover and allegedly killed them by biting through their Adam's apple, later dismembering and dumping the bodies in the Leine River. He was said to have killed at least 24 men before he was caught by the police in 1924.

44 A quote from Hugo von Hofmannsthal's fragmentary 1892 play, *Der Tod des Tizians* (The Death of Titian), which thematizes the divide between life and

art, society and artist. This translation is taken from Michael Hamburger, *Hofmannsthal: Three Essays* (Princeton: Princeton University Press, 1972), 38.

45 Max Kruse (1854–1942) was a sculptor and member of the Berlin Secession. Erich Krüger (1897–1978) was a Berlin painter well known for his realist landscapes, nature scenes, and still lifes.

46 Franz Burchard Dörbeck (1799–1835) was a Berlin-based illustrator and caricaturist who became well known for depicting humorous scenes of life in Berlin, notably in series such as Berliner Redensarten (Berliner Sayings).

47 Gohlisch combines quotations from Schiller's *Don Carlos* and Shakespeare's *Richard III* to provide an oblique political commentary on times to come; the quiet moments that Don Carlos has enjoyed as the Spanish Prince cede to an era of intrigues, plots, and backstabbing that the Duke of Gloucester initiates in *Richard III* in order to accede to the throne of England.

THE PASSENGER
ULRICH ALEXANDER BOSCHWITZ

LEARNING TO TALK TO PLANTS
MARTA ORRIOLS

AT NIGHT ALL BLOOD IS BLACK
DAVID DIOP

SPARK
NAOKI MATAYOSHI

TALES OF TRANSYLVANIA
MIKLOS BÁNFFY

ISLAND
SIRI RANVA HJELM JACOBSEN

CARMILLA
SHERIAN LE FANU

ARTURO'S ISLAND
ELSA MORANTE

ONE PART WOMAN
PERUMAL MURUGAN

WILL
JEROEN OLYSLAEGERS

TEMPTATION
JÁNOS SZÉKELY

BIRD COTTAGE
EVA MEIJER

WHEN WE CEASE TO UNDERSTAND THE WORLD
BENJAMIN LABUTUT

THE COLLECTED STORIES OF STEFAN ZWEIG
STEFAN ZWEIG